THE HOLLOW BEAST

THE HOLLOW BEAST

Christophe Bernard

Translated from the French
by Lazer Lederhendler

BIBLIOASIS
Windsor, Ontario

FIRST EDITION
1 3 5 7 9 10 8 6 4 2

Library and Archives Canada Cataloguing in Publication Title: The hollow beast / Christophe Bernard ; translated from the French by Lazer Lederhendler. Other titles: Bête creuse. English
Names: Bernard, Christophe, 1982- author. | Lederhendler, Lazer, translator.
Series: Biblioasis international translation series ; no. 46.
Description: Series statement: Biblioasis international translation series ; no. 46
Translation of: La bête creuse.
Identifiers: Canadiana (print) 20220469695 | Canadiana (ebook) 20220469725
ISBN 9781771965552 (softcover) | ISBN 9781771965569 (EPUB)
Subjects: LCGFT: Novels.
Classification: LCC PS8603.E699 B4813 2023 | DDC C843/.6—dc23

Edited by Stephen Henighan
Copyedited by John Sweet
Typeset by Vanessa Stauffer
Cover designed by Jason Arias

Published with the generous assistance of the Canada Council for the Arts, which last year invested $153 million to bring the arts to Canadians throughout the country, and the financial support of the Government of Canada. Biblioasis also acknowledges the support of the Ontario Arts Council (OAC), an agency of the Government of Ontario, which last year funded 1,709 individual artists and 1,078 organizations in 204 communities across Ontario, for a total of $52.1 million, and the contribution of the Government of Ontario through the Ontario Book Publishing Tax Credit and Ontario Creates.

PRINTED AND BOUND IN CANADA

To my friends

PROLOGUE

IT WASN'T A GOOD IDEA FOR MONTI BOUGE TO JUST up and declare war on the postal service. The municipal service back then was Victor Bradley, and the municipality, well, it didn't amount to much—not yet. A string of buildings stretched out along the coast between the sea and the forest spilling down from a mountain teeming with game. Saint-Lancelot-de-la-Frayère they called it. Hardwood, conifers, and telegraph poles strode down the slope like legs descending into a bay speckled with as many dories as there were men living in the town. This was the Baie des Chaleurs in the reign of Wilfrid Laurier, when the only government the locals heeded were the migrating geese and the capelins that in late June, early July, rolled stupidly onto the shore. From a bird's-eye view you could see the network of hunting trails running out of the woods and into the few cleared pastures, where they turned into dirt roads and pathways that cracked the landscape between scattered wood-frame structures. In the crook of the arm of the sea, a tiny postal procession made its way to the hotel. It was the aforementioned Victor Bradley. He had just finished his very first mail run. Uttering many a tarnation and many a bloody hell, the brand new mailman led his horse by the bridle, a fine official horse provided by the town and with hardly any mileage on it.

Bradley steps inside and over to the bar with a long drum-roll expression on his face, convinced those are high-rank stripes on the Post Office Department uniform that envelopes his ego.

"There ain't no service here … Barman!"

But it happens that the barkeep that afternoon has skirts and clogs on. And bulges in their sweater. It's the widow Guité, former midwife, now proprietor of the hotel. She wrings out her rag with formidable strength, unconcerned by the less than savoury water dripping all over her floor. She sizes Bradley up at once.

"Well then, Mrs Barman, it appears," the mailman says.

He raps the counter with his remaining fingers as he settles in, his mismatched eyes scanning the crowd of exactly three to pick out the chump he's going to mouth off to all night about being the inventor of the postage stamp. He looks as though he expects to be congratulated. But, with two or three pencils stuck in her chignon, Mrs Guité just keeps on whistling and working away with her rag. The gentleman from New Brunswick, seemingly made of bread, had on his face a candy-box expression peculiar to him alone. He'd come down from his room, all tangled up in his orders and brochures, to mix with people and to work. *Me, me!* he seems to implore from the way he doffs his hat. Bradley doesn't even return the greeting. Nor does he say thanks when his coaster is set down before him and his sherry placed upon it. Sherry. That's what Bradley drinks. Sugar—can't get enough of it. He's the sort of fellow who's at home wherever he goes. *But not here,* Monti thinks as he pokes his head out from under the counter, his arm deep inside the grease trap, where he is extricating something that squeals.

How old is he at this point, Monti? Eighteen, twenty? The age, at any rate, when you still secretly shave the skin between the unsightly tufts of your beard to help it grow nice and thick all over. Leaving his arm inside the trap, as though he enjoys wallowing in grease, he momentarily eyes the mailman, not much older than him, seated at the bar. When Mrs Guité asks Bradley to stop drumming his fingers everywhere, he gives her an impertinent shrug.

"Hey, I know ya," Monti says with his still-green voice.

And that's all it takes for war to be declared.

Anyway. Fact is, everyone knew Bradley. Even if you didn't know him, you knew him all the same. How so? Because of that time in Paspébiac. A man running for the provincial legislature, a crackpot by the name of Poitras, who wasn't from Paspébiac himself—not the best way to start—was holding forth at the crescendo of a campaign speech infused with just the right amount of infantilization yet lacking the slight flirtatiousness needed to grab the attention, however fleeting, of the legion of weirdos seated before him—an assortment of Ti-Claudes and Roger Johnsons, Sylvain "Nuche" Duchesncaus and Deslarosbils—the whole lot of them laughing in advance at the inevitable scandals to come rather than listening to the sophist acting like a minister up there on his cardboard rostrum, dishing out cartloads of pie in the sky. Yes, because of that time in Paspébiac, when the candidate Poitras dared to say—a word of caution here: you must never spout such drivel in front of a crowd of Paspyjacks, as folks from that town were called, dozens of them squirming in chairs not even screwed down, when they've got ants in their pants like on that day—when the future MP Poitras dared to say he loved Gaspésie so much he would *marry* her, my fellow citizens, and . . . On hearing this, Bradley, who craved mincemeat but rarely minced his words, couldn't contain himself. He uncoiled from his chair like a six-foot-five spring to retort in the nightmarish patois of his community, a hilarious gibberish imported from Jersey that the Paspyjacks reel off in a moist staccato, sucking in their cheeks and pouting their lips. Bradley, with his father, his grandfather, and all his uncles at his side, stood up in the middle of the assembly and shouted to the politician:

"Y' been screwin' her for so long, ya really do needs to marry her!"

All hell broke loose. The henceforth proverbial rejoinder knocked the wind right out of the aspiring legislator. His conquest of Gaspésie, not exactly Napoleonic to begin with, had just gone down the tubes. Bradley, meanwhile, became famous overnight, because in those days in Gaspésie it didn't take long for a retort of that nature to travel all around the peninsula. Times have changed.

He didn't make just friends, though, this Bradley guy. Nope. Not everyone found his wisecrack very wise, not by a long shot. You see, Poitras was chummy with a few string-pullers, a sort of unreliable co-op that tried to get organized among the cod fishers in the area. We're talking greasy-carpet-chested, liver-reeking sailors who peppered their jargon with *chiac*. What they wanted, these lads, was to put in power the local politician with the best image, to have the fishing patrols in their pocket, control the quotas, scare off the competition. They didn't read books, but they could count, and it had cost them big bucks to get Poitras where he was. After all, it wasn't the razzle-dazzle speeches the would-be legislator ad libbed throughout these parts that brought in the money to fund his campaign.

Then one day Bradley tripped over a surprise package on his porch. He opened the parcel and thrust his hand into the sawdust. It took a moment after the metal snapped for the pain to kick in. Two fingers sliced clean off like a couple of carrots in a rusty old bear trap. You had to be slow-witted not to start prospecting the real estate in the neighbouring counties. Luckily for his eight remaining fingers, the town of Saint-Lancelot-de-la-Frayère was looking for a new mailman. The last one, Barriot, had just washed up on the strand with the capelins, bloated, his translucid skin marbled with bluish veins.

But those are just details.

Actually, it all started when Monti lost his first life at the Gaspé diocese junior hockey tournament, where the parishes most devoted to sports and perennial grudges faced off. This happened eons ago. For the only time in the history of the event disgracefully organized year in year out by a few volunteer priests who coached in their cassocks, the Saint-Lancelot-de-la-Frayère team, with Monti as goaltender, had reached the finals. The team's name was the Grisous—the firedamps—and, as was true of every edition of the tournament since its distant beginnings, the Crolions of Paspébiac would make short work of their rivals. Because, you see, people in Paspébiac are generally very fine folk, but they aren't put together the same as others. It's not just that they move fast and are made of rubber. Nah. Over there, when you get pummelled by all your ten brothers at once, you roll around on the ground laughing and asking for more because that's exactly what you thrive on—beatings. If someone insists you can't walk on water but you yourself have decided you can, then you can walk on water. Sooo, you stand up, you walk to the far end of the jetty without stopping, you fall down on the shingles even before you've touched the water, you get back up, you come back to the marina bar and sit down with your knees all bloody, and you say: "I told ya so."

But if the Crolions that year still ruled over every lagoon in creation that might serve as an amateur skating rink, it wasn't because they lacked a sense of self-preservation or ate cod three times a day. It was thanks to Billy Joe Pictou. No use looking for that pagan's baptism certificate. He was one hundred percent Mi'kmaq, and his family went about its business, the white community's taboos notwithstanding. His brothers hired themselves out at the sawmill, his mother did housework. The father didn't work. The father had a passion for Labatt beer. A fatal passion. For those and other reasons, in the towns where life led the Pictous, there was always some slur-monger who called Billy Joe a wolf-child, simpletons who threw him cigarettes to tame him. To which Billy Joe had the dignity not to react.

"It ain't a wolf he's crossed with but a mollusc."

Okay, granted, there was something visibly inert about the young Pictou, at least something that might give that impression. He had hit puberty before his schoolmates, and his was a deluxe model. Seen just on the outside, he exuded more sebum than poetry. But even though, at the peak of this enormous adolescence, his nervous system seemed to be running in first gear, there was a whole lot going on inside him. Bursts of awareness were constantly popping between his ears. His pupils signalled depths of the sort that few people dared to plumb.

"You can't hurt him, ain't got any nerves," the older kids in school would say.

To prove their point, they flung hard-packed snowballs in his face.

"You maybe little bit neglected by Big Manitou?"

This time, also as a matter of dignity, Billy Joe reacted. Things were bad at home, he'd gone out to kill some time and ended up at the edge of a backyard skating rink, hands stuffed in his pockets, watching glumly as French Canadians in leather skates pushed a tin can around with sticks you can't find in the woods. He leaped onto the ice and flattened the guy who'd shouted the insult.

That was how hockey became a revelation for Billy Joe, a way to give free rein to what another fellow had called, just once, his inner horde. And he, by the same token, was a revelation for hockey: he certainly wasn't the best skater, but his slapshot was enough to pulverize your children's shins, which, for a team, was priceless. The Indian had found something he could pin his pride on. The following season, he was able to send a puck flying from the coast to Miscou island, provided it didn't cut down a seagull before it got there. Even so, he still had no friends, kept everything bottled up, never shared anything with his peers—mere striplings compared with him—except some fabulous strings of victories. So many truths expired within him. He was rocked beyond belief by massive shifts of fate that had nowhere to go. Something just had to get out sometimes. And it got out through sports.

If there hadn't been some astute coaches keeping an eye on them, the crafty Crolions would have tried to whet Pictou's appetite throughout the tournament by holding a Grisous sweater dipped in broth under his nose. Just to keep him a bit on edge, more responsive. Because, after all, Billy Joe did act his age, and for long stretches of time while he waited on the bench adolescence took over, big time. His eyes went blank as he slipped back into flatness and forgot about the score. So the Crolions couldn't give him too much ice time during a game—just enough to make Swiss cheese out of a star defenceman or paint a new not-quite-regulation red line on the ice with the remains of some smartass twinkle-toed winger.

The game was winding down when Monti, lost in his thoughts and Our Fathers in front of his net, saw the other team's coach use practically all his strength to yank his monster's briefs up into his butt crack. Monti thought it would be the signal for Pictou, that he would leap onto the ice, go, get moving, have one for lunch! Nope, no way. It was much worse than that. The Indian, taking his time, sauntered over to the little door. Monti had a prolonged moment of anxiety down in his small intestine. Too bad, he thought, his hunting plans would have to wait till the next life. Because once Billy Joe was on the ice, it was hold on to your hats, boys. His feet swollen in over-tight skates, but with the laces falling nicely—how peculiar—in pretty little puffed bows, he charged toward the Grisous' net, a bowling ball, not so much skating as running on his blades. Deboned children went flying in his wake. Monti— whose name was Monti for a reason: *mon petit, mon p'tit, mon ti, Monti,* that was how the other orphans had come up with his nickname—really didn't take up much room inside his jockeys right then. Truth is, he could have stepped away from the net and left his goalie equipment perfectly motionless, that's how lost he suddenly felt in his huge armour, which had grown brittle during the match from the forty-six shots on goal.

Forty-four saves. By some miracle, Sicotte had evened the score two-two at the end of the third period, amen. The overtime period promised to be a fight to the death, because the Crolions certainly had no intention of losing, and neither did Monti. He hadn't played all through the tournament like a wolverine reclaiming its cubs just to see the trophy go back to be defiled for another twelve months in Paspébiac, no siree. Obviously, he was afraid of the Crolions' bruiser. Even the puck was afraid of Pictou, who had just crossed the blueline probably muttering *shin, shin, shin*. Except that Monti had a plan. *Ha ha, come on, skate!* he said to himself, eyes half-closed, making the goalposts ring with his stick while he looked for a weak point in his opponent, whose bulk increasingly eclipsed the sun with every stride.

Billy Joe was coming to put an end to this foolishness.

The jugular, Monti was thinking, *some sort of Adam's apple, a piece of Achilles heel, something to work with.* He had resolved to deal a fatal blow. Skate, skate, skate, sk ... Close-up of the young Pictou, galvanized, his wholly elastic hockey stick raised high to shoot. The shot rang out as far as the mountains. The watchful deer in the woods swivelled their ears around all at the same time. A National League slapshot. The puck sliced through the air. Its oblong shadow slid over the pocked ice at a hundred miles an hour. Monti thought, *over my dead body*. Repeating to himself, as in his orphanage days, that you go to heaven when you die, his balls tucked up inside him, he stayed rooted in front of the net without flinching. Yes, his pad would go poof as it disintegrated in a small cloud of stuffing, yes, his leg would go crack the very next instant. But before collapsing, he would have to disregard the pain and stay upright until Pictou—who, unless physics is a hoax, could never stop at this speed—was close enough for Monti to roar and chop off his head with the blade of his goalie stick.

Things didn't go as planned. Not only did Pictou not have a neck, but Monti didn't get the chance to roar for very long either. There were no helmets or cages or visors in those days, so, grabbing his chance in a rare moment of grace, the Grisous' last hope made the stop by catching the puck in mid-air between his teeth—that was how he'd later describe it. And in that same pole-vault movement, Monti struck Pictou across the face with his hockey stick. He nearly dislocated his elbow. The Indian carried him along to the back of the net, where they crashed, knotted together. While Monti's teeth stayed miraculously intact, Pictou's spilled onto the rink sounding like a rainstick.

The referee's sweet whistle echoed for a long time in the curve of the bay.

When he regained consciousness, his head halfway into the net, the puck halfway into his mouth, the net buried in a non-Euclidean heap of runts in the process of killing each other, Monti glimpsed his coach, tomato-red, screaming two inches away from the assistant referee's face, a linesman with different-coloured eyes and jujubes on his breath, who said that was that, he was not going to reverse his decision.

"The goal is good," Bradley said, the black-and-white stripes of his sweater puffed out at chest level. "As sure as that's my dog tied up over there, the goal is good."

Trouble is, his dog actually was tied up there. Which proved absolutely zilch, the flea-ridden mutt.

All this had happened a dozen years before Bradley popped up in front of Monti at Mrs Guité's hotel. The Crolions had won. The tooth fairy filled up her tin. As for Billy Joe Pictou, he sailed bloody-mouthed and gap-toothed straight up in the air with each roughly synchronized heave of his teammates' twenty-six arms. Monti bore him no grudge, their eyes had spoken in the second and a half of their tête-à-tête. But lying spread-eagled on the ice, shifting his jaw from left to right to dislodge the embedded puck, he promised himself, not any-time soon because he'd just given pretty much his all, that he would one day take his revenge on that Paspyjack.

I

DIRECTION EAST

I

A LIGHTNING BOLT STRAIGHT OUT OF A MAD SCIEN-
tist film ripped through the cumulonimbi. The curtain of rain
lit up with twenty billion diodes. The sky came close to caving
in. François wriggled on his chair as he straightened his tie and
face mask. This did nothing to relieve the headache that had
begun to seep into every nook and cranny of his intellect. He
rubbed his temples to stop the emergency room from going
double. The people there were already in pretty bad shape, their
features like putty after twelve hours of waiting. No need to
see them in duplicate. They ranged from a school psychologist
who had been bitten by a student suspected of having rabies to
a gourmand whose stomach X-rays would soon disclose some
amusing things. Others suffered from hair-aches or sprained
belly buttons. François, wearing his faithful tweed suit with
dandruff-speckled shoulder pads, didn't allow himself to look
anywhere but straight ahead. He was too afraid to discover
that the beast had followed him there. But when a troll with an
egg-shaped skull bedecked with blood plonked himself down
in the seat opposite his, it became hard not to squint.

"Hello," François said politely.

The troll wore a dripping mascot costume. He stared so hard
at François that it twisted his face. François averted his eyes.

He shouldn't have. There it was, the furtive moiré of the beast, underneath the chair of a tyke with crayons jammed inside his nose. François, smiling stiffly behind his face mask, turned back toward the troll. Guess what, chicken butt—forget it. An icy bead of sweat had left a distinctly coloured stripe on his forehead. The troll's costume reminded him that the Canadiens were playing against the Boston Bruins that night.

"François Bouge?" a nurse said, yawning over the thunder.

Enough time had gone by for his seat to take on sentimental value. But the separation went well. *Goodbye, you big meany,* François was thinking.

"I'm listening," the doctor lied.

He was an intern and he pounded away on his computer while casting François looks of despair. François, however, was incapable of lying. Ever. The elastics on his mask made his ears stick out. He wanted to tell the doctor the truth, the whole truth, but his case suddenly seemed less urgent at the sight of nurses rushing down the corridor, the security guard in tow struggling to keep up, and paramedics flanking an up-tilted stretcher—code red, code red. His doctor looked like he had other fish to fry. And also like he'd fished around in a live toaster with a fork.

"Sir, I ... May I call you Sir? Needless to say, it depends on the relevant norms, but I wonder if it's customary to use the title of doctor with an intern."

"Get to the point," the doctor said.

That's not exactly what he said, but it pretty much amounted to what he meant. All at once François was hounded by doubt. Yes, his migraine was pushing up into his sinuses like sausage meat, but that didn't justify his being there; he'd been in this condition for six months. And he had no idea how to tackle the problem; he couldn't even begin to untangle the jumble of yarn his reality had become. But there was no question of him lying—none. Not after he'd ruined his life in the name of truth. Nor was he about to blurt out that he had a fantastical creature hot on his heels, right there, behind the pleated curtain.

"That would skew the diagnosis," he replied.

What am I doing here? He should have noted some points on an index card. He himself had trouble following the blue streak of gibberish he directed at the doctor, who was harder and harder to get through to and just wanted to know where it hurt. Something about a sorcerer in the Yukon who was the reason the eponymous drink was, well, eponymous, and somewhere in there was the patient's grandfather, who apparently had been afflicted with a hereditary condition.

"Psychiatric," the doctor concluded.

He turned off the flashlight that had just burned a hole in each of François's retinas. His white smock disappeared down the corridor. Alone, François sat on the edge of the examination table and waited. His mask pushed into his mouth when he breathed. He was all at sea, not knowing whom to turn to now for help.

Enter a fairy godmother wearing a pareu that danced in her wake, a hint of New Age in her gestures. *I'm here to be hospitalized,* François was thinking, *not to have my chakras opened.* Judging from the psychiatrist's tone, he wondered if he hadn't unintentionally spoken out loud. The sight of her constantly scribbling in her notepad during the interview tired him out. The mere idea of writing made his head spin, and he loosened his shirt collar in response to an inchoate thirst.

But he would not give in and found some relief in cup after cup of water. The paper cones were neatly stacked one inside the other in the dispenser. The upshot of the consultation was that, no, François didn't have the impression the secret service was spying on him. And no, he wasn't the reincarnation of the Messiah. And no, his neighbours didn't attack him psychically in order to make him gay.

"I get the feeling you are hiding something from me, Mr Bouge, and so long as that's the case, there's nothing I can do for you. In the meantime, here are a few brochures you can read to see if—"

"I'm quite familiar with every one of these institutions."

François pulled a pen out of his inside pocket. He had stopped listening and straight away started correcting the typos in the brochures. The fairy godmother apparently was not very impressed.

"I'm not sure this is the right place for you," she said. "You don't seem symptomatic."

"I'm the victim of a curse."

The psychiatrist froze. Except for the baubles in her earlobes. And the tulle of her blouse. This might have been François's chance to talk about the beast that was watching him. All he needed to do was draw back the curtain. The shrink, convinced that he was hallucinating, would give him a pink pill at least. He would have to explain yet again that this was no hallucination. It would get complicated to the point that just thinking about it wore him out. And, anyway, the whole business was all tangled up inside him. He was no longer able to unravel it. He was at a loss. Then he pictured himself resuming his dissertation and his lectures next term. Standing in front of his class, a zombie with a tumescent thyroid showering sparks due to the electroshocks. He needed to drink something right away. He and the psychiatrist were not off to a good start. Another cup. A large air bubble floated up in the tank.

"A curse, Mr Bouge? I don't have a prescription for that."

Mr Bouge felt the cunning beast slip between his legs to hide under the examination table. He would have done better to consult Dr Dugas in La Frayère. Assuming Patapon hadn't eventually managed to drive Dugas insane.

"No, Doctor, you really don't understand. It's impossible for me…"

The shrink flew out the window in a trail of magic powder. François stuck out his tongue, which was dry and coated with a white paste. *A near beer, that's all, cross my heart.* He tore off his mask and crossed the empty waiting room, folding, unfolding, and again folding his medical insurance card until it snapped in two, then four. Then eight. Near the glass door on which the gauzy lights of Rue Sherbrooke were stretched in every direction by streaks of rain, he showered the little pieces of plastic into a garbage bin straight out of the space program. The magic eye of the automatic doors never detected François's presence on the first try; for it to open, he had to do a dance step probably a little too ahead of its time.

John Coape Sherbrooke, he thought as he went out. There was trash spiralling in the twisting gusts of wind in the square. *Governor of North America for the English Crown, if I'm not mistaken.* He had been in denial for years, but it was clear now that only in Gaspésie would he find the missing pieces of the puzzle. He could vanish into the picture that would finally take shape there. Freed at last. A lightning bolt hurled in his direction drove him back inside. The stroboscope flashed for a while among the shadowgraph trees in the park across the way.

François chucked the rest of his ID cards into the trash can as he passed it again. Seeing that the only security guard around was busy hammering away at a soft drink vending machine, François stole his way along the corridors and into the heart of the building. He had an urge to shout that Parc La Fontaine was named after Louis-Hippolyte, famous for being the first politician to address the Senate in French after the Act of Union in 1840. Muttering bitterly, with damp locks of hair clinging to his cheeks, François tore a bouquet of rhodo-dendrons out of the hands of the ghost-to-be going the other way in a wheelchair.

In the elevator, the janitor sporting a pair of headphones eyed François. To let the man know that he was there to visit someone, François jiggled the bouquet under the janitor's nose until all the petals were gone, along with the joy it was going to bring. The janitor lip-synched using the mop handle as a mic. The elevator car shook. The beast's fangs were chew-ing on the steel cable, and François panicked a little. Up they went. He hit a bunch of buttons at the same time. Up and up they went. The door slid open and the janitor moonwalked out.

"Goodbye," he yelled.

The elevator took off toward outer space again. Ten seconds later it was François's turn to exit. Having no idea which floor he was on, he walked along a row of windows that seemed to have melted in the rain, speeding up when two surgeons came around the corner behind him with their somewhat annoying scalpels and the fourteen years they'd spent learning to use them. Lightning flashed again among the cauliflower clouds. It made his headache ring like nobody's business. He realized he was higher than he'd thought when, against the burst of light, he saw the rough, rotting roofs of the Centre-Sud district crowded with crackling antennae. When the squeaking shadow of a cart full of soiled sheets appeared at the far end of the corridor, François stepped—not broke, it wasn't locked—into a patient's room.

It was as dark as a bear's ass. He groped his way to the nearest bed, checking with his hands to see if there were feet under the sheets. He must have wandered into the amputee unit. There were none—feet, that is. Never in his life would he have shared a bed with a legless guy. He followed his nose, guided by a smell of fermentation, playing blind man's bluff, to the next bed. After a tango with the wheeled stand he'd just bumped into, he felt his way up to the IV bag hooked onto it and then to what must have been a respirator on the pillow. There was a face under the mask. Tubes everywhere. François had shaken off the beast under cover of darkness. The old man in the bed appeared to be in no mood to argue. If he was counting sheep, they were surely distorted when, as a precaution, François once or twice pressed the IV drip button. Patapon was fond of this opiate-laced juice too. Gramps and François lay side by side. François took the whole blanket.

He awoke with a jagged spasm. He fell out of the bed even before remembering that he was lying in it. He bounced back up on his shoes, and his whole being shot up into his noggin. *Lord, oh Lord,* he groaned, blind as a mole in the darkness. Befuddled, he tried to slide the radiator to one side, to find a way out through the wall, panting, in hopes of eluding his tormentors. Soft at first, then slimy, the beast brushed against his ankle, jingling like a bell. When he swung around, François noticed a crack of light at the bottom of the opposite wall, as though this was where the darkness came unzipped. He could already hear the breeze in the valleys, the chirping birds.

As he jumped over the old man's bed, François got entangled in intravenous tubing, which ended up writhing on the terrazzo floor. He staggered robotically toward the light streaming in under the door. Research ideas came to him as he bent down. He was about to slip his fingers into the crack when someone knocked three times, almost melodiously, on the other side.

"Mr Langlois?" the nurse whispered into the doorway. "I've come to … What the …?"

The woman was so terrified she had tendered her resignation even before François shoved her aside bellowing, "She-wolf of the ss!" Scratching himself everywhere, in a fit of hiccups and convulsions, François took off. Instantly, the fluorescent lights froze his brain. His throat clicked when he swallowed. The devil take his soul for a shot of Yukon. He had seen in the unleashed light that there was no amputee in the first bed. *There was no one!* Okay, fine, he realized where he was. It wasn't a concentration camp, nothing like that, but even so, he sensed danger as he slipped into the elevator at the other end of the corridor. In the background, the nurse crawled on all fours to get out of the way before the floor-cleaning Zamboni turned the corner in three, two, one.

On the ground floor, yet another member of the hospital staff was in shock. Huddled in a corner, her uniform splattered with multicoloured stains, the triage supervisor was hypnotized by the clapping of elevator doors jammed open by an empty cafeteria tray. A round of applause—nice mess! The hallway walls were smeared, clumps of food littered the floor. The tray hadn't been empty a minute ago. Nor was the woman's uniform brown, green, purple. She'd been coming back from the cafeteria with her dinner, her cellphone, when the elevator stopped. Then it appeared, that thing there. A lunar creature with a pair of hundred-watt bulbs for eyes. It had quite simply trampled her. The tray had gone flying. Brown chicken juice, little green peas, purple Jell-O everywhere. With each step the freak's limbs came loose and then snapped into place again as he barrelled toward the emergency exit. He rammed right into the automatic door. He backed up, doing a jig, and the door opened onto a cyclone of dead leaves and cigarette butts. A lightning bolt supercharged the night. The tatters of an umbrella fluttered among the tree branches, its mutilated ribs reminiscent of a tragedian's fingers. The rain absorbed François as if he belonged to it.

2

FAR FROM THE OVERLIT ENTRANCES OF BUILDINGS
and pawnshops, beyond the reach of cameras whenever possible, Poupette was foraging on Rue Ontario. He quickened his pace under the street lamps. Their halos steamed in the swirling rain. His crusty hands abruptly let go of the garbage bag they were gutting. Nobody out in a storm like this. Poupette sniffed, hunching his shoulders against the rain. The air snaked out through the holes in his cartilage. Then he straightened up and disappeared, dissolving into a display window full of skeletons, vampire faces, and anthropomorphic pumpkins. His bottles rolled onto the sidewalk. The dregs of beer joined the rivulets flowing to the gutter.

"Shit, shit, shit."

Someone was trotting toward him. Ordinarily, Poupette would have skedaddled by reflex, but his reflexes in that department had been deactivated long ago. Instead, he pulled up his hood and ducked into a bus shelter. His teeth jiggled in his gums. He pretended to be quietly waiting for the 125, which actually didn't run at that hour. He couldn't make out the clumsy silhouette tumbling down the slope of Rue Plessis, a shadow necktie whirling in the downpour. Poupette prayed it wasn't Le Roy.

The lucidity that came from going without gave him a clear picture of his dealer's medieval collection methods—a little too clear for a good night's sleep. Le Roy didn't have the patience to listen to your stories. "You have to pay up," he would say, blindfolding you himself. After that, he'd step away to avoid getting splashed. What's more, Poupette figured, Le Roy's debt collector probably didn't call ahead before showing up at your place to teach you, say, the laws of the animal kingdom. A sexy guitar riff full of harmonic crescendos from his eighties glam metal compilations could bring tears to his eyes, but he did not love his neighbour. Nor did his rumoured indulgence in cucumber face masks and the occasional lasering of upper-body hair make him any less likely to tear yours apart—your upper body, that is.

But hold on now. Poupette peered through the bus shelter entrance to get a better look at the guy coming toward him. *Isn't that* ... He needed money, badly. And if this matchstick man was who he thought he was, maybe he'd be able to pay off his debt and score a hit faster than he would recycling bottles for nickels and dimes. The pedestrian flashed between the notches of a lightning bolt.

"You must be kidding!" Poupette squealed as though he'd swallowed a kazoo. "Françoué! Françoué!"

He almost jumped for joy, his shoulder blades protruding like wing stumps under the fake coat of mail he had on. A chorus of howling dogs and boozers rose up far and wide over the glug-glug-glugs. In his Converse sneakers and tight jeans tucked into his socks, Poupette started to cut a few aerobic moves on the sidewalk. François, swivelling his hips to sidestep an oncoming fire hydrant, said "Hello" like an automaton. He swung around to make sure the hospital wasn't following him.

Standing in a moonbeam that had punctured the clouds, Poupette shouted, "Frankie! Jeez, I can't believe my eyes!"

His prayers had worked better than usual. François owed him sixty bucks. And a lock. Near the top of a utility pole studded with staples, a transformer sizzled and sputtered above a closed dépanneur. Poupette struck a pose that gave the impression he existed in not exactly a two-dimensional world but one where there was just north and east. François had other things on his mind, but he nevertheless stepped up to the glass wall of the bus shelter and cupped his hands goggle-style around his eyes.

"I can't see you," he said tentatively. "Who are you?"

Dominique Boisvert, a.k.a. Poupette. Five-eleven, one hundred ten pounds. Age thirty-one, indeterminate gender. Residing in the Hochelaga-Maisonneuve district, in a slum where, if you ever had the misfortune of getting lost, you might be able to survive on the bottles of Ensure dug up from mountains of still-warm trash. No job—anything but that. And so many distinguishing features that it didn't matter anymore.

"It's me, Françoué! It's Dominique!"

"Zounds."

After this, to say the least, lukewarm reunion—warm on one side, cool on the other—the duo moved off, reeling in the rain with the electric wires overhead swaying in their sheaths. The conversation was one-sided; François was too preoccupied.

"Well, say something," Poupette protested. "What's the matter? Ordinarily you'd be harping on about Rue Plessis being named after Joseph-Octave Plessis, the first cardinal of Gatineau, or whatever!"

"Archbishop of Quebec City, Poupette, Quebec City. If I've told you once, I've told you a hundred times."

It was obvious that François owed him money, because sometimes when they bumped into each other Poupette didn't even recognize him. Poupette would straight away try to inveigle him with his found bicycle shtick, offering it to him for a twenty and a couple of cigs. He forgot that the François he loved had an aversion to cigarettes.

The diffracted beams of emergency lights ejected sudden sharp-edged glints from the runoff along the sidewalks. François tried to remember if Plessis had been archbishop of Quebec City or Gatineau. *Where was that cardinal?* Poupette had planted a seed of doubt in his mind.

"Would you have a bit of spare change?" Poupette, acting purely on reflex, asked a businessman stealing out of a sauna.

This was the only reflex he had left. François had not broken his stride to wait for him.

"I've got pocketfuls," the businessman replied.

He stepped into the chemical-blue glow of a Mercedes, which sped off toward Westmount. Poupette, all grimaces and jingling pennies, struggled to keep pace with François. The two of them blended into the increasingly amphibian sheen of the storefronts. François's ragged gait smoothed out as they ventured farther into the inner-city areas. Not that he was walking any straighter, nope. Rather, the buildings around him grew more crooked. They had crossed Avenue De Lorimier. Lightning bolts froze in the sky, then crashed down here and there in large white chunks on the concrete structures. François didn't object to being followed, because when Poupette was around, the usually unrelenting beast left him alone. He—Poupette—kept up a non-stop free-jazz flow of blather.

"Yeah, so that's how it is, Franky boy, if you had my dough, that would suit me fine. Eh, buddy, it's good to see ya, cripes... And, anyways, where've you been hiding, you didn't come to the happy hour on Thursday."

When they turned around and faced each other, Poupette's breath nearly burned François's olfactory hairs. By association, François thought it was a lucky thing the Indigenous Peoples had remedies for the settlers' scurvy, otherwise present-day Montreal would have the same population as Johan-Beetz Bay on the North Shore. He also wondered if Étienne-Jean Pictou was still alive. It might be useful to interview him.

"Phew, sorry, I just belched yesterday's fries . . . Jeez, man, my breath reeks to high heaven, haha! Come to think of it, when are you going to ... Hey, isn't that Le Roy over there at the service station? Quick, quick. And you can forget about my lock, just gimme twenty-five bucks instead."

Poupette might just as well have been speaking Swahili. All François could hear was the word *halitosis* reverberating in his skull, where his thirst-hardened uvula was clanging away as if inside a cracked bell. Near the Frontenac metro station, his drenched jacket clinging to his body, he trod on a particularly squishy Kleenex.

"Solids—I can't digest them anymore," Poupette continued. "What'll you dress up as for Halloween? Me, I dunno, I was thinking of renting some fur and horns, and besides, we were looking for you, we were. It's been, what, three days, I'm not sure anymore. What's that got to do with anything, is what I said to Momo, then Tibi, but now, when they—"

"You wouldn't by any chance have something to drink?" François said, his eyes directed down the street.

"Now, listen, Le Roy, I realize it's not your problem, but me..."

It wasn't clear if the sky was hung with clouds or nuclear mushrooms. With no warning Poupette grabbed François by the collar. He sniffed at him this way and that.

"What did you just say there, eh, forgetful? What did you say? Come on, say it again."

Poupette was hunting for traces of hooch.

"I was just saying—" François began.

But Poupette, his hair looking like linguine, pinned François crosswise against some bicycles. His yellow eyes rolled every which way in their sockets. François could have frightened him. He knew the key words. Poupette waved a nicotine-stained finger in front of his green, orange, red, green-again face tinged by the traffic light at the corner.

"Oh, you ungrateful bum!"

"Forget it," François sighed.

His spine had wrapped itself around a U-lock.

"And would you be so kind as to let go of me, please. Otherwise you'll damage my last decent suit."

François belonged to that species on the verge of extinction that still dressed to the nines for a medical appointment. He had been raised that way, it was part of his mentality. Poupette twisted François's psychotronic necktie around his wrist. His face was dripping wet, but this didn't even bother him.

"You son of a bitch. Shut up and listen to me. Just listen— okay? Is that what you've been up to for ten days? Admit it, you little prick, you went off to drink? Do you think of us sometimes? I'm done, do you hear me, done, you little prick, with coming to get you in—"

A bolt hooked onto the lightning rod of a nearby office building, and Poupette went completely limp. He closed his hand as if to catch something invisible three inches in front of François's face, allowing him to break free.

"You must compose yourself, Dominique. Come now, I drank nary a drop. I was working on my research."

"Well, that's even worse!" Poupette said indignantly.

Resigned, he lost his balance. Then he began to tug at a ten-speed on the off chance it might be unlocked.

"Ah, just drop it, you and your obsessions. Do whatever you like, but give me my dough before someone finds you all stiff in your chair."

"You need to rein back your outbursts," François said, redoing the knot in his necktie in order to unstrangle himself.

"What was that he came out with, Graton, the other time? 'Carrying in his shirt pocket a perpetual eviction notice.'"

"Yes, no one else could say such a thing."

"Because that's what's going to happen to you."

They reached an intersection where the rain rode the wind horizontally. Poupette started bugging François more aggressively again. All he wanted at this point was to be paid back.

"Now stop, I already gave you back your money."

"Say what—you gave it back to me? You did not give it back to me, you nut, you slipped a lottery ticket under my door."

François would never have stepped through the doorway of Poupette's place without spelunking gear.

"Yes, I told you it would be the winning number. You just had to take my word for it."

"I did take your word for it, but that's neither here nor there. I can't find it."

François's theory was that his friend had unconsciously managed to make the ticket disappear, knowing full well the money would destroy him the very day of the draw.

"I'm expecting more incomings soon," he continued. "An advance, royalties."

"I don't give a rat's ass about your homecomings, I have needs right this minute."

"I'll have you know that I, for one, find rats quite interesting from a historical perspective," François said, shivering.

They began to scuffle but stayed on course nevertheless. Poupette tried to turn the pockets of his friend's sports coat—which was looking less and less decent in the rain—inside out.

"Gimme my dough."

"Why don't you go to Mile End or the Plateau," François said when Poupette pushed him. "Go leech off the well-to-do. Show them your pictures folded twenty-seven ways."

"Pay your debts!"

Poupette was clutching François's trousers. He was being dragged over the asphalt and was in danger of being spread like a pat of margarine. François dragged him all the way to the corner of Avenue Bennett. Poupette climbed up his debtor's back, grasping his shoulders. His tendons jutted out. He brought his now half-painted lips closer to François's neck. The instant François felt the hickey, his elbow struck out automatically.

"My, oh, my!"

At first François thought Poupette was dead, but he got back up holding in his lips a cigarette butt he'd fished out of a puddle the rain had churned up, rimmed with candy-pink foam. If you killed a Poupette, another one would come walking out of the Lafleur restaurant at the corner of De Lorimier, still another out of the washroom at the UQAM, and a third from under the stairs at the end of Rue Saint-Christophe.

"Please forgive me, I don't know what came over me."

Poupette stepped away a few paces. He mumbled his social insurance number in order to hold on to his humanity. What a humiliation. The more François asked to be forgiven, the more Poupette hissed his hostility, making broad, mysterious gestures. The rain falling between them muddled him, and his hissing soon degenerated into a sort of halting yodel. A blade materialized in his hand. He waved it gracefully under François's nose. Behind a window with construction-paper witches taped to it, a sleeper yelled for them to drop dead. It was raining buckets. There they were, thrashing around, trying to extricate themselves from a wrestling hold that hadn't gone as planned. Poupette botched a technical move, allowing François to twist like a contortionist and slip between his legs. He made a mad dash down a fogbound alley toward his basement apartment. He had Poupette's knife, a nail clipper, jammed between two ribs.

3

JEAN DE BUADE DE FRONTENAC, FRANÇOIS EXPLAINED
to Poupette as he recalled the Kleenex.

They wept in each other's arms to make up. Shedding tears
of joy, Poupette laughed tenderly, one hand on his companion's cheek. Then, with one swift tug, he removed the knife
from François's side. "You've got until tomorrow, or you're
a dead man," he'd said. They walked down the three steps to
François's place. Ambiguity and bias were seeping into his
historical knowledge. Poupette had made him doubt. Some
tough flowers had taken over the cracks in the cement.

"Two grammatical particles!" François marvelled, fixated
on *Louis* de Buade de Frontenac. "In spite of that mongrel
name, he was governor of the colony under Louis XIV. Or
was it Louis XV? I'm not sure anymore."

He turned toward Poupette to see his response. He
was responsible for Poupette's education. But, surprise,
Poupette was gone. Too bad for him. François opened the
door, which was never locked. But the door wouldn't open.
Because it was locked. He stood there holding his nose and
grumbling, his eyes brimming with water. He plunged his
hand into the letter box and with a look of disgust immediately pulled it out. He had touched something warm,

pasty, squishy down there. And again this year no grant from FQRSC or SSHRC.

He climbed back up the three stairs to sea level and slalomed through the whatnots left lying about by his neighbours' children. White bread eaters. A former future player for the Montreal Canadiens. A sequined darling. An Ovid of the neighbourhood mythologies. He went around the building by way of the colourless courtyard. The same hateful raccoon, velvet feet and burglar's mask, had once again littered the ground with rubbish. François stopped. With his foot he pushed against a ground-level window, one of the few his apartment had. It too—locked. He looked to his right, to his left. Then he leaned down and picked up a very dapper-looking garden gnome abandoned next to a planter of by now inedible basil and rosemary.

"Don't you touch that!" Poupette screamed.

He popped up out of nowhere like a jack-in-the-box.

"Ah, there you are!"

"Seriously, Françoué."

"You're looking well. Been away on vacation?"

Poupette dropped his appalled expression in favour of his worried look, motioning with a sideways glance to somewhere over there as he silently mouthed the name of Le Roy.

"As I was saying," François resumed, "Frontenac. Bold antagonist of Heathens and the Anglish, who—and not just because he wore the appropriate wig—fought bravely for his people, his king, and boatloads of fur acquired in exchange for a shard of broken mirror."

"You really know your history."

Without losing its smile, the garden gnome sailed noisily through the glass.

"Goodbye," François said to his pupil.

He vanished into the shadows of his home.

"Françoué!" Poupette exclaimed under his breath.

The fact he was not invited didn't stop him from crouching at the window, convinced that he'd seen the gnome dart behind the exposed box of a wall plug hanging on its wires.

"Honey," François called out after regaining his balance on the spongy floor of his kitchenette. "I'm home."

The echo of his voice faded into a wounded snicker. He switched on the UFO-shaped ceiling light. He watched with some interest as the silverfish scuttled away on the warped surface of what had once been linoleum. An endless theremin note vibrated in his head. Acting on a quirk inherited from his mother, he straightened a laminated picture, a gift from his students to thank him for never coming to class and for giving them good grades. That was shortly before his dismissal, which he preferred to describe as dropping out by degrees. Nothing to drink in the apartment. The telephone was sprawled on the floor amid clumps of dust; he replaced the receiver in its cradle.

His back pressed flat against a wall, François ventured a glance at his desk. A piece of furniture thrown together out of beer crates and chipboard and thrust into a wavy corner of the living room where the lighting withered away. He didn't want to. *I don't want to.*

The desk sagged under the weight of a manuscript, a compact pile of irregularly white sheets.

As François stepped closer, his urge to get drunk was such that he had to stop himself from running outside to gorge on the fruit of his service tree. *Prospecting for Gold and Rural*

Development: A Case Study was written on the title page, a title that had not changed since he'd submitted his dissertation proposal somewhere in the distant past. Below, the subtitle began with *The Village of Saint-Lancelot-de-la-Frayère under the Influence of Honoré Bouge* and ran on like that over half a page, constantly growing longer as, with the passing years, François lost the thread of his discoveries and speculations. Never, since arriving in Montreal for his undergraduate studies, had he gone back to La Frayère. But now the time had come. He hadn't seen anyone from back home again, either, except for his cousin Steeve, who was actually his second cousin. There were people François had to see. The lopsided chair pulled itself up for him to sit down at his desk. In fact, François hadn't left Montreal since receiving his bachelor's degree. His whole workspace, with his pencils and his sharpener, beckoned him to come sit by the papers and contemplate the superfluity of living.

Now my suitcase, he thought, once he had mechanically stuffed the manuscript into the briefcase he used when he was teaching. For François, Gaspésie amounted to more than the cross at Gaspé and Forillon National Park. It—Gaspésie— was more complicated for him than for others. His fingers clenched around the poorly oiled handle of his wonky closet. The door opened amid a swarm of spores onto a Poupette reeking of the abyss and folded in three by a fit of coughing.

"What the … "

Poupette thrust the suitcase into François's arms. A sort of oversized lunchbox that François began to cram with his effects.

"You wouldn't have seen Thierry Vignola in there?" he asked, pointing to the closet.

"I could use something to munch on," Poupette replied. "D'you have some Ensure? I've started to self-digest."

Don't eat that, Poupette. Don't eat yourself.

"Good lord, Dominique. At times I get the feeling that I have invented you. Help yourself in the refrigerator."

The telephone line, by the way, had been disconnected for months. François, one time, had called a museum in Dawson City, passing himself off as a Dexter. He gratuitously made the receptionist feel guilty because George Mercer Dawson, a geologist from Prince Edward Island and LL.D. (McGill University), in a surge of megalomania, had shown great originality in naming the city after himself; he told her to wait a minute while he went to look for the file with the required concession number. The receptionist grew tired of waiting. She put the call on speakerphone. Then she forgot about it and went on vacation without hanging up. Three days later, François found himself with a case of pneumonia and the kind of phone bill you never get over.

"Get a move on, eh," Poupette shouted. "The night is young, but there's about a million places to go to before I go home."

He rubbed his little round belly in front of the fridge. François, meanwhile, was spinning all over the place like a top. Collecting his gear from under the futon, in the laundry hamper, and chucking it into his suitcase.

"You know what happens when I get caught out by the dawn," he thought he heard Poupette say in the other room.

François kept going back to the closet only to remember each time that there was nothing there for him. Intrigued, Poupette sniffed the leftover grocery store sushi, wondering why a human being would inflict such scraps on himself.

"You'll see," he screamed at François.

Then, not as loudly, he added:

"I'm gonna finish it for you, that goddamn book of yours."

François finally laid hold of his six-month AA chip. His personal amulet. Full of new pep, he flipped it into the air with his thumb and caught it in the pocket over his heart.

"I believe there's been a misunderstanding, dear Dominique," he answered from his bedroom, the second most depressing bedroom in the world. "I won't be accompanying you to your apartment."

He pulled too hard on his bureau drawer. It nearly went flying into the wall. *Calm down, amulet,* François thought. He emptied his wastepaper basket onto his wine-stained sheets. He would be needing some capital for his trip.

"How come?" Poupette said.

The knife with which he'd tried to kill François he now dipped into jars of condiments. He was making himself a sandwich. It was either that or sodium bicarbonate. Or sushi. He therefore had opted for beef slices with turquoise-coloured streaks, topped by his favourite vegetable, ketchup, on a chunk of mouldy baguette cut lengthwise. And some Swiss cheese. He cut around all the holes in the cheese. Someone had once told him never to eat the holes.

"C'mon over to my place, kiddo. Move in for a spell."

So, thought François. Arms spread wide, rocking from side to side in front of his bed, as if ready to grab something fast-moving. He grabbed the scissors. Then he joyfully tore up the two-week-old edition of the *Journal de Montréal.* Right away, he set about marvellously cutting out pieces of paper the size of banknotes. A nice heap later, he pulled an envelope from the stationery on his bed. He inserted his cut-outs and sealed everything with a lick. Except that, because he had no saliva, he used his glue stick. After that he uncapped a felt pen. He wrote *$5000* on the envelope. *But what am I going to do with all this money?* he wondered, contentedly hefting his life savings.

"Thank you for such a warm invitation," he mumbled, chewing on the envelope.

He tugged his suitcase into the corridor. His briefcase banged against the wall.

"Ah, why don't you come," Poupette said, standing in the doorway on the far side of the room with a full mouth. "You could set yourself up in—"

The envelope dropped on the floor.

"I'm leaving tonight for a journey that I must undertake alone. My historiographic work has reached its limits and I must engage in some fieldwork."

"What's that money, eh?"

Panting inside the bathroom where he had barricaded himself, François leaned his back against the door. He had his briefcase, but the suitcase had stayed in the corridor. The door shook on its frame. Then the tremors in the hinges and the hook latch petered out. The scratching and pounding on the other side grew more sporadic. Poupette, short on anger management strategies, cursed for a few minutes. François heard him slide down against the door. He—Poupette, that is—began to lisp fawning phrases, sweet nothings punctuated by sniffing and whining about hunger. The glass saucer shielding the naked bathroom lightbulb was full of dead flies. Hiking up his shirt in front of the sparse patches of silver backing in the mirror, François examined the wound left by the knife. It felt as if his gallbladder oozed when he pressed down on it. *I am not a doctor.* That's how he decided not to worry. He wasn't sure how they had settled their accounts, but either way he was the one holding the clown-flavoured sandwich with a bite missing. Through the door panels, he could hear the gurgle of Poupette's stomach.

Everything happened very fast. His briefcase held aloft, François, energized by the amulet, gave the door an astonishing kick. Poupette, stretched out like a siren, instantly began to flap his tail when the sandwich, pitched underhand like a softball, sailed to the far end of the corridor. Now, this François here—he didn't wait for permission to scram. *As far away as possible from the 514 area.* Once outside, drawing on what he'd learned from the shows he watched as a kid with his brother and Patapon before he began to have suspicions about the people inside the TV, he jammed the back of a patio chair under the door handle, leaving Poupette to his frenzied feast.

4

THE PARKING LOT ON RUE BERCY, NO POUPETTE IN
sight. It was still pouring rain. *Pouring a drink,* said someone
in François's consciousness. He hobbled along the streets, one
hundred pounds dripping wet in his suit. Above the asphalt,
his hems floated on the wind. The beast, snout gone completely bald, fur plastered against its flanks, had found his
trail again. François had glimpsed it under an awning out
of the corner of his eye. The rain streamed down the wrist
holding his briefcase, which was heavier than it appeared. *I
need a quarter,* he thought, and he thought, too, of Patapon,
whom he was eager to see again, of his mother, of the smell of
varech, and of jellyfish burns on the bay. His father he would
think about later, because meanwhile he had, what, seven
hundred kilometres to go? With a briefcase holding a one-
and-a-quarter-ton manuscript and the troublesome feeling of
having played Tetris forty-eight hours in a row. Gaspésie, on
foot, was very far away. The bus? François mistrusted it. Too
many eyes. Too many ears.

And to think that in Laval the weather was fine. The sub-
urban firmament was cloudless over the above-ground swimming pools and the back-to-front baseball caps. François
swam westward on Rue Ontario. He went by a karaoke bar.

The shower had turned into a downpour and drained the Centre-Sud of its night owls.

The establishment was overflowing with debauchery and performances to be regretted the next day. To see if he knew anyone, François inventoried from the entranceway the chops vociferating all around the counter amid a mishmash of stretched-out, taut, sweaty arms. The octopus behind the bar covered all the angles, serving two-for-ones that would hammer as many folks as possible. "I have five thousand dollars," François said out loud over the crystalline clash of change against the chrome surface. The fleeting, foamy wipe of a dishcloth. There was a special on bombers. Shooters, unlimited. The twenty-sixer of Yukon stood out from the row of bottles behind the bar. François rocked from one foot to the other, convincing himself that he might step inside just to get some small change. But it was enough for him to touch the amulet in his pocket, his AA chip, and he was off ambling through the city again while a woman being feted made a complete fool of herself belching out her favourite Gerry Boulet hit.

Poupette was still imprisoned in the apartment. His sandwich was squeezing enzymes out of his stomach that he hadn't produced in a long time. He was seeing things. Went around corners holding his knife out with both hands. Escaping wouldn't have been that complicated, but Poupette had a hang-up. He would rather have vamoosed down the toilet drainpipes than through one of the windows. They were a little high, anyway. Actually, what he would have liked most of all was for one of Le Roy's thugs to come get him. Le Roy wanted to finish him off with a bat, but, you know, Poupette didn't think like Mr or Mrs Average. So he'd spent the past twenty minutes punching his dealer's pager number into a telephone that had been disconnected for longer than he'd been sober in his adult life.

Eyes glued to the sidewalk as he searched for coins, François veered down Rue Logan. Two super-cops accosted him. The fellows asked him if he'd seen someone suspicious and potentially dangerous go by. One of them pointed to the hospital with his nightstick. The storm kept pounding away. It never would have occurred to François to utter falsehoods in the face of the law. "It was I!" he exclaimed with disarming sincerity. The police burst out laughing. Shoving him aside, they returned to their cruiser for some manly mumbling on their two-way radio. The beast loomed up in the glare of the headlights, coppery, greening, perched on a mast whose flag had been carried off by the wind. Once, François had gone to see them, the police. He spoke to them about the murder, about Dexter. He drew a diagram to show them the correlations between what had happened in the North and the present situation. They locked him up for the night.

He turned onto Maisonneuve.

Sieur de Maisonneuve, he recited to himself. *Christian name Paul, de Chomedy. Bangs cut short, ermine collar, discovered Montreal. A zealot's brow atop a sourpuss mug. Rather mediocre, the man was, in his management of the colony and therefore harshly confined to ten minutes in the Secondary IV history course.*

Yes, the plot against Monti, all that, the magic spells, the poisoned gifts—still, François was a lucky man. Perennially pooped, on the brink, dingleberried, but he needed a quarter and he found his quarter. In the warmth of an ATM booth. It smelled of urinal cakes and Ringo. Ringo was snoring, curled up in a corner, his name written on his coat with a marker. It smelled, more exactly, like the morgue. Ringo surely wasn't a pretty sight when the moon was full, he wore liquor store bags for boots. François skirted around him on tiptoes to scan the premises, mucking up the briskly mopped tiles with his galoshes. Ringo's upper body faced frontward, his lower body away. He had a runny nose and a killer cough. Because, stretched out on his delivery boxes, under a blanket with a life of its own, Ringo had the flu. One of those viruses that you blast with your shotgun out behind the shed. The quarter was waiting there on the floor next to him. It must have rolled out of his Styrofoam cup, on which a young child had drawn a family, smiling flowers, a dog whose four legs were lined up in a row. Behind François, his shadow darkened the ATM filled with tightly stacked wads under its armour plate. The background noise was the radio dissecting the three-nothing rout of the Canadiens at the hands of the red-hot Boston Bruins. All François had to do was lean down and, thanking his ancestors, scoop up the serendipitous quarter. The trouble was the quarter lay in a gob the oyster-coloured membrane of which shaded toward smegma white more striated in the protoplasm. Briny bubbles were clumped together in the mucus around a, say, granular filament. Chlamydia looks like that. *I'd sooner kiss Poupette,* François told himself. But Ringo let out a snort, and *God Save the Queen.* Kneading the amulet in his pocket, more Françoué than ever, François reached out his hand.

Lying on her couch in flip-flops and curlers, Louisette Potvin woke with a start in front of what looked for all the world like a porn flick, whereas three seconds earlier it had been *Legends of the Fall.* She had just heard, rising up from the ATM below her one-bedroom apartment, a scream like nothing she'd ever known.

François took shelter in a phone booth. He kept his contaminated hand in a brown paper bag, which he held as far as possible from his body. The rain dripped onto the shapeless mush of the phone book through a twisted joint between two vandalized sheets of Plexiglas. He put down his briefcase and, with his free hand, wrapped the phone receiver in his tie. He rummaged in his pocket with his bagged hand and slipped not the quarter but his AA chip into the pay phone slot. The clouds crushed together a little harder in the atmospheric kaleidoscope. The chip did not pop out; François trembled as he searched for his sponsor's name in the directory. The page was missing. This time he inserted the quarter and dialed the phone number of a taxi he somehow knew by heart. It rang, he felt himself falling, an answering machine came on. The telephone gobbled up his coin with a dull clink.

When he went out, intending to smash the phone with a sewer grate, François noticed a flesh-coloured Volvo stopped at the red light, a station wagon half-shrouded in the swirls of its exhaust fumes. The taxi's dome light pushed the night aside.

"Hello, sir," he said, rapping on the window.

Usually the doors would lock, the tires would crunch from left to right, and the driver would hit the gas pedal while in neutral. But not now. The window rolled down. Smoke curled out through the opening.

"Tell me, would you be so kind as to take me outside the city in exchange for a substantial compensation?"

Standing in the rain, François flourished the envelope marked *$5000*. A lightning bolt lent the paper an acid-purple hue. The car had no licence plate. François didn't notice. In the taxi's dark interior, a cigarette glowed red.

"Didn't understand a word you said," a voice inside growled as if bathed in formalin. "But I was expecting you, big guy. Get in."

II

THE PRANKSTER

5

NOT LONG AFTER HE WAS INSTALLED, VICTOR BRADLEY, groggy round the edges, showed up again one morning at the Guité woman's hotel. As it happened, she was testing a snake decoy she'd designed and was fine-tuning it with a penknife.

"I think it works," the innkeeper had said to Monti just before the mailman came in.

She had just seen him going past a window in the early autumn grey.

Monti always arrived right on time. He was already well into his workday. He was perched up high, about to re-varnish some beams he'd just finished stripping. The moment he saw the tip of Bradley's hat in the doorway, his horse grazing in the background, Monti wagged his head as if to say *uh-oh,* smiling from ear to ear. His brush dribbled on the rungs of his stepladder.

"Shall I serve yous up some medicine, corporal?" Mrs Guité asked.

Bradley snapped his suspenders and sat down on his stool as if straddling a cattle fence.

"He's no corporal, Madame Guité," said the NB peddler, also seated at the counter with a plate of charcuterie he was busy slicing into thin rounds. "He's the mailman, surely you must remember!"

He adjusted his fob watch, his picot-edged table napkin. Because he knew he was right. He was about to leave; his merchandise trunk sat on the floor beside him. His season was over, with not much commission to show for it.

"Well, well, kind sir, then I must be mistaken," Mrs Guité answered as she served Bradley his sock juice. "I s'pose it's on account of the uniform."

The mailman, his cheek stamped with blanket creases, his shock of ginger hair combed with a fork, confined himself to disdainfully slurping his coffee. He scanned the premises. Monti, delighted by the scene, kept trying to catch Mrs Guité's attention until he was certain she was watching him. He fluffed up his hair like Bradley's, went goggle-eyed like him, put on the same grumpy expression, then, sorting imaginary envelopes, pretended to lick his finger, except that it was one the mailman no longer had. Mrs Guité hid behind her cup, her shoulders twitching away. But Bradley was oblivious. He swivelled his upper body from left to right to see who else was there.

"I'll have some sugar," he said, but in such a way that what he very nearly got instead was salt, or arsenic.

He poured a spoonful into his cup. Another. Yet another. A fourth. Surely he would stop at some point. But he didn't, the spoon oddly positioned in his mutilated hand.

"Whose foal is that?" Dr Maturin asked.

Maturin re-buckled his belt as he stepped out of the latrine with his reading material, *Le Vivier,* the local newspaper.

A few still-stiff necks sitting at the tables craned toward the window to see if there really was a horse there. The coffee drinkers exchanged glances. Nodded their heads by way of confirmation. There was indeed a horse. The leaves on the branches were starting to go orange. Now, Maturin, he wasn't exactly a doctor, which was probably the reason Bradley didn't deem him worthy of an explanation. He kept his back turned away from his mount, which patiently kept its four shoes planted with aplomb in the teeth of the wind.

"Lovely creature," Maturin gushed.

Nothing more needed to be said for the other customers— because they knew—to appear momentarily to be sitting on sea urchins. The front page of *Le Vivier,* a month old and bearing a sort of hysterical exclamation point, showed the largest squash ever recorded in the county. Between the columns was a photo of mean-faced Pancras Canon alongside his vegetable in a wheelbarrow.

For the New Brunswick peddler, it was truly a wonderful place, Gaspésie. What hospitality! What common sense! Such fine folks! He was sure of being right in this regard. Fun-loving and all that. And kin to the Acadians, cousins. Watching them, he felt a blend of admiration and displeasure. He had no wish to pack up his paraphernalia. He would have liked to settle down one day in Saint-Lancelot-de-la-Frayère, start a family, get established. *No matter,* he thought. *We'll come back to do business in the area.* With the possible exception of the aforementioned Canons. Never again would he set foot in the house of those sadists. The mere thought of henceforward lodging at Mrs Guité's on a regular basis drove him into a dreamy melancholy. A little older than him, but widowed. She would have made a heck of a good match for him, Mrs Guité. He definitely didn't want to spend his sunset years under his sister's roof. Bradley, smug as ever though still but a mailman, turned toward him to disturb his musings and explain how things worked in New Brunswick, Acadia, and such places. Monti cut him off, blurting out that he'd take them all.

"All of what?"

All of what, of what . . . The muttering spread through the clientele. By virtue of being made to shut his trap, Bradley's face sank into his head.

"All your books that you've got there," Monti said, excitedly pointing a trembling finger at the peddler's trunk. "Your big almanacs, I'll buy them all."

"Oh, that. They aren't almanacs, it's an encyclopedia! Eight volumes bound in chamois leather, guillotined with a saw."

The sum of human knowledge, the brochure promised. Which weighed as much as a steer and two sheep.

"To get me through the winter," Monti said.

Seeing the NBer grunt with joy and lick the tips of his greasy fingers before shaking the rascal's hand, Bradley became even more riled up. Especially given what he had just witnessed. Mrs Guité had asked Monti to take a bottle down from the top shelf, describing the picture on the label rather than saying its name. *He'll use it to light his stove, that encyclopedia,* Bradley told himself. Then, for no reason, he glared randomly at a lad sitting farther away, Yves Allard's boy Langis, and it was always somehow unpleasant and disjointing when Bradley eyed you. Because one eye was blue, the other brown. The colour spectrum dissolved. You saw rainbows.

The NBer got up from his stool. All aglow in his lard, he shook Monti's paw once again, this time covering their clasped hands with his free one. Then he sniffed his palm. It smelled of paint stripper, but he certainly wasn't about to make a fuss. Brimming with love, he shouted:

"A round of beer for everyone! It's on me!"

He instantly regretted it—his cheeks shone like freshly baked buns—having quickly totted up his share of the sale. The guys clinked their glasses and everyone was happy. 7:30 a.m.

"I'm going to take this up to your room right away," the peddler told Monti, making it sound like a marriage proposal.

Because that was the arrangement. Monti kept a room in Mrs Guité's place in exchange for doing odd jobs. He had a pallet upstairs in a four-by-six cubbyhole with a chamber pot in one corner and a crucifix on the wall. Undecided as yet about what he wanted to do with his life, he sometimes bedded down there.

The municipality of Saint-Lancelot-de-la-Frayère, however, knew what it wanted to do with his land. No one was aware of any ancestors of his in the vicinity, nor of any descendants. Monti never opened up about this, any more than he did about the spotty education he'd received in the orphanage. After being away for some months, he'd come back from the woods one fine day with his rifle and his game bag, some recipe ideas, and a crumpled piece of paper supposedly proving a certain plot of land, virtually teetering on an overhang in the mountains, was his by rights, every square foot of it bristling with resinous trees and owls, overflowing with debris and bramble, and so deep in the woods that to get out it was better to go to the far end and then all the way back around.

In any case, the Town persisted in wanting to buy back the patch and rezone it in order to run the aqueduct right through the middle. The bend in the river Frai (as in "small fry," hence the town's name) was such that you had no other choice. But there was something truly exasperating about the negotiations.

Monti would sell. Monti wouldn't sell. Sell. Not sell. Mayor Pleau dreamed of having the bailiff distrain upon Monti and lock him up if he squawked. Nah, come on, this wasn't Pleau's way of doing things, he wasn't that much of a tyrant. Meanwhile, Monti, whose sole desire was to live as he pleased, stubbornly hung on to his property. To go hunting, he said. Back then, hunting still meant getting drunk in the woods for a week to shoot, butcher, and feed on game. Not to go off to the woods, like they do today, *after* a two-week binge to fill your own cavities with a blunderbuss in a cabin with neither door nor window.

"No, no," Monti told the peddler.

It was too early for the stuff, so he drained his untouched mug of beer in the sink. Mrs Guité cast a distracted look in Langis's direction to see what could possibly be the cause of the stammering state of shock he was in. Was he hallucinating, or had he just glimpsed the postal horse through the window blowing its forelock away from its eyes? Bradley, showing signs of stiffness, added two more heaping spoonfuls of sugar to his coffee.

"Not to your room?" the NBer asked Monti. "That's fine by me, I can wrap it right here."

The Paspyjack loaded another spoonful.

"Have the mailman deliver it to my house instead," Monti said.

A bar stool jumped. Bradley's still-uncracked ankle boots were dusted with sparkling sugar.

They would be cracked by sundown, those boots. The Paspyjack wasn't especially conscientious; Monti remembered that about him from the hockey games. He recalled that Bradley seemed to have a hard time blowing the whistle when the Crolions played dirty along the boards. Bradley half-assed everything and after a few days on the job he had pretty much already worked it out in his noodle that it ought to take no more than four hours to do his run, four and a half at most. If you added the time he whiled away in every dive and watering hole along the way, you could be sure his mail delivery amounted to eight hours for the taxpayer.

But the encyclopedia episode chastened him. It was a cool day and he stopped toward noon to feast on *ragoût de pattes* and country bread in a roadside establishment and toast his tootsies hard by the hearth. He even had his bread soup brought to him. He drank unhurriedly and, since this relaxing hole in the wall was to his liking, decided to leave his place setting where it was by way of reserving his seat. He would deliver Monti's parcel in no time, he promised himself, and immediately come back to bask by the fire and loosen up while concluding his exposition on various aspects of phlogiston for the benefit of the publican, who confessed he was as deaf as a post.

Bradley was unaware that in Monti's vocabulary "my house in the woods" stood for a cabin lost somewhere at the top of the steepest path, a two-hour trek just to get there. At first he convinced himself he enjoyed it. In the ever-cooler air, he pretended to admire the flaming foliage. But the woods in the mountains could close in on you if you lacked the grey matter to find the old portage trails. And your horse could never make it through—no way.

With his lips shading to purple, his wrists red, pine needles in his pockets and cuffs, and in his cap and the crack of his ass, with the encyclopedias constantly falling off his cart, which kept snagging on the rampant vegetation, the mailman eventually reached the cabin. The air was fragrant with snow.

Shaking in his waterlogged socks, having necessarily forded the Frai river, Bradley pounded on the door as though he wanted to break it down.

Now who in the world could that be? Monti wondered. He'd completely forgotten about the encyclopedias. Ordering them had been nothing more than a joke. He wiped away the spit he'd just left on the decoy Mrs Guité had ended up giving him. Buff naked underneath a pair of overalls too big in the seat, he scratched his balls and opened the door.

"My, my," he said in surprise, his mood softened by a flask of brandy. "We've got company!"

Bradley, totally bushed, unloaded the parcel. There was snot hanging from his nose hairs. His stomach was so needy that he bit into the heady aroma wafting through the half-open door. Must have been game simmering. And it was warm inside. The do-it-yourself wood stove was pumping it out back there.

"Y' didn't take your nag along?" Monti said, seeing nothing but Bradley's cart behind him. "I'd of invited it for supper!"

Late that night the mailman hobbled down a road blurred by drizzle and fatigue toward the tavern where he'd left his glass and conversation at lunchtime. He grumbled as he went, intending at least to quench his thirst till he couldn't see straight anymore. The angels wept on hearing him. Because, wouldn't you know it, the place was closed. As he waited for cock crow, there was nothing for it but to press his face against the window and watch his sherry evaporate in the still-inviting glow of the embers inside.

6

THAT RASCAL MONTI HAD FOUND THE TRICK HE'D played on the mailman to his liking. He wanted to do it again. Which is why he showed up right after the spring tides at Mr and Mrs Berthelot's general store wearing an earflap cap and a frock coat, ready for another round.

"So, here he is, how's the boy?" Mr Berthelot inquired.

He stopped sorting the canned goods in the storeroom.

"Not bad, not bad," Monti replied, blowing on his knuckles. "A bit nippy this morning, eh?"

On the floor in a corner was a field mouse under an upside-down pickle jar. Mr Berthelot slowly wiped his hands on his apron and flashed his usual good-natured smile, which always gave you the impression it was your turn to speak.

"Tell me," Monti asked him obliquely, "Joséphine—has she already made her delivery here today?"

"Oh, yes," Berthelot said, his hands surely dry by now. "I guess you missed her by a quarter hour or so. Do you fancy her, you skirt-chaser, you?"

They put up their dukes as if about to start boxing. Berthelot burst out laughing unaffectedly. He gave Monti a friendly slap on the back. Monti gave the grocer his sincere regards, then he lowered his head and passed underneath the wobbly staircase on his way to the lean-to that served as a mail drop-off.

"Well now, been a while since we clapped eyes on this one," Mrs Berthelot said, leaning on her bent broom. "Been holed up in your lair?"

She always concealed her corpulence more or less unobtrusively under the same flowered dress, the same oversized cardigan. Monti sniffed the air. The drop-off smelled of Bradley.

"I wanted to know," he blurted without preamble.

He knew very well that with the Berthelot woman you could dispense with the rigmarole.

"About the mail—how's it work?"

"What's that you say?"

She had more moustache than her mate, Mrs Berthelot did. She was the embodiment of kind-heartedness.

"Well, I mean, I gives y' this, my parcel, and then what? It can't be such a snap."

"Got a little money? You'll be needin' to buy a stamp. After that the lady'll take care of it."

Frowning, Monti tapped his badly patched frock coat. It sent out puffs of dust. He somewhat nervously turned the pockets of his hand-me-downs, his threadbare pants, inside out, looking for a penny here, a penny there, amid bread crusts, toenail clippings, braided lanyard.

"Looks about right," the Berthelot woman reassured him without even looking. "Gimme your envelope."

She licked the glue on the back of a tiny stamp pinched gingerly between her sausage-like fingers.

"No, no," Monti said. "It's not an envelope. Outside I've got two sacks of gravel I want brought to my place."

"Well, in that case, it'll cost yous more."

"Hey, I dunno, you said I was gonna hafta buy a stamp."

"Cripes, for a shipment like that I dare say it'll take a foot-by-a-foot-and-a-half-size stamp. Ain't sure you're inclined to see that big a portrait of the King of England. I can put it on your bill, if y' like, otherwise … "

She wiggled her behind, her palms pressed together at the top of her broomstick. She added:

"I mights have a job for yous."

They both cast a glance at Mr Bethelot to see what he was up to in the aisles. The lady's throat sounded to him like turtledoves.

"Let's hear it."

Later that afternoon, Monti came up from the cellar by a staircase as hair-raising as the one behind the hotel counter. The burlap sack on his shoulder was crawling with vermin. He blew black snot out of his nose and, disentangling himself from the spiderwebs he was covered in, hoisted his haul over the shelves so Mrs Berthelot, on the far side, could see what he'd brought up in the way of field mice. The gentle matron signalled that it was hunky-dory, be seein' ya. She cancelled his parcel and let him choose a pastry on his way out from among those Joséphine concocted each week for various outlets.

Alas, two days later, Monti had returned to his cabin but still had not received a visit from his mailman. That was Wednesday. Leaves fell without let-up from the flaming trees. On Friday he brought his rocking chair out on the porch and went in again to uncork a bottle of dandelion wine. He came back wearing a large knitted scarf around his neck, prepared to wait out part of the morning drinking and smoking. The forest crackled on all sides. *Now, what can I do with those field mice?* he wondered as he eyed the burlap bag—he'd promised himself to put it to good use—nested in the crotch of an elm tree. In the end he decided the mailman had better not come after all. The irreparable would be committed, Monti was convinced of this as he went back inside. When he stepped out again, he sat down with his rifle in his lap. He rocked for a long time, rocked to the point of carving grooves in the floor of the porch.

"That mailman of yours is inept," he fumed later on in Mayor Pleau's office, the latter a tad ruffled by this outburst. "Tar and feathers! Give 'm the boot!"

The day would come when Monti would get preferential treatment at City Hall, but until further notice he was to go through the main entrance like everyone else. On hearing the ruckus in the corridor, the mayor, seated at his desk with his elbows resting on it and the letter opener nearby in case things got out of hand, had had ample time to think about what he would say. He stood up from his chair and straightened his clothes. He snorted. Monti was about to eat the incriminating delivery slip from his unfilled order. Sporting a herringbone suit and gripping a pipe between his teeth, Pleau strutted for a minute under the oil-painted gazes of his predecessors.

"Listen," he said.

He closed his fist around his pipe bowl.

"Bradley ain't all wrong. From here to your land we're inside town limits. Beyond your land till the last bend in the Frai river—that's part of town too. But your land, well, your land just ain't part of town. No sir. By the way, your shirt's inside out. 'Cause you ain't willing to sell that land of yours to the town. It appears you don't care two hoots whether or not the

men and women of La Frayère have clean water and drink
their fill. Us folks, we ain't looking to skin you, Monti. But it's
the bylaw. And common sense too. It'd be absurd, wouldn't it,
for the municipal mailman to be obliged to deliver the mail
outside the municipality. So do like the Indians, bucko—they
never get mail, eh—and go collect yours at the Berthelots'
place."

Monti turned up the visor of his earflap cap. He slipped his
hands under his armpits, which were sprouting alfalfa. Rocking on the heels of his fishing boots, he said:

"Ya, well, youse can be sure that come next elections you
won't be getting my vote."

The silence that descended on the room was brutal. The
mayor cleaned one of his molars with his tongue. It had just
dawned on Monti too. There were little coughs of uneasiness,
the shuffle of old shoes on the wooden floor.

"You realize—" Pleau said.

"Enough said, please. I know."

"You realize that even if you don't vote for me, you won't
be any more entitled to vote for someone else if you ain't registered in Saint-Lancelot-de-la-Frayère?"

The door slammed so hard behind Monti that a groundswell lifted the carpet all the way to the incumbent mayor's
phlegmatic shoes.

"That's right," the politician muttered. "Shove off, you blasted scallywag."

Monti must have had acute hearing as he instantly stormed
back into the office and charged in a huff over to the armchair
behind the desk, where he sat down with his best administra-
tive expression and a finger in his nose.

"You've got some nerve, you! Get out of my seat before I tan your hide!"

On the front page of its very next edition, typeset as always to give you the impression of being shouted at, *Le Vivier* announced that we were finally going to get our aqueduct. The work would have to wait at least until the ground thawed, but Monti had sold. By the way, if you were in *Le Vivier,* you had a fifty-fifty chance of being on the front page. It was a two-sided sheet.

As he was going to file the deed of sale he'd just validated, the notary Langevin saw a field mouse skitter across the town hall corridor for the third time that week. Then he pointed out to the bailiff, first, that Monti had gotten his witness to sign for him and, second, a clause had been scribbled at the bottom of a page stipulating that he ceded his land on one condition. Now, your average wharfside layabout could not have broken down the technical details, but as far as the townsfolk were concerned, the surveyor's new map annexed the residence of Honoré Bouge a.k.a. Monti to the municipal territory.

"Cheeky little wretch."

In sum, Monti maintained the right to live in his cabin even if it was thereafter located on public property. The sale didn't make him rich, but no matter: he'd still be able to live off the fruits of the transaction for a spell, and it was clearly his turn to pay the lads a round of drinks. This was before he'd found his gold, back when the townspeople's hardships didn't make them less generous with their joviality. Back before money, whether you had any or not, stank up every last skivvy in Saint-Lancelot-de-la-Frayère; after that, even the plebeians began to rot inside.

Once he'd cashed his due, Monti raced to the general store with the intention of buying the heaviest, most cumbersome items they had in stock. Had weight itself been on sale—hang the expense!—he'd have taken two. He eventually did buy something, which he once again had posted to his place in the woods. There were scads and scads of stamps on the parcel. When Bradley unavailingly circled around to find a hold so he could lift it, he felt the mosaic of George V staring at him like the eye of a giant fly.

Meanwhile, Monti had run some errands. He borrowed tools from friends who were butchers or carpenters, and from the blacksmith. He then hired Maturin's mule. The pseudo-doctor gave the animal's rump a good slap and licked his lips as if telling the renter to enjoy the ride. Although the beast of burden walked with its legs splayed, Monti made his way back to his cabin with the whole load intact and his dough hidden in the lining of his frock coat. He still didn't understand what banks were good for. At a spot where the slope became quite steep, he took a swig of rotgut. Then another. And as he screwed the lid back on the Mason jar, he knelt down on the trail to examine the indecipherable tracks, scattered across the first snow like glass jewellery in the sunlight, of a mysterious beast.

Bradley could not conceive of going back to live in Paspébiac. He had no desire to end up on the shelves of the fish shop, canned in brine alongside the cod. The complaints against him were piling up. If he didn't deliver, he'd be deprived of his livelihood. But on the day of the second heavy parcel, you'd have thought his old referee's whistle was stuck somewhere in his plumbing. He wheezed audibly on the mountain. Lungs full of razor blades, he didn't even have enough breath to rattle off complaints as he climbed toward the cabin in the cold he'd refused to dress for. His arms had grown a good yard longer from hauling the cart, which sagged under the massive parcel. Faced with this load, his plug had never lifted so much as a hoof.

On a ledge, a plump-cheeked squirrel was weighing the possibility of reaching a certain spruce branch on the far side of the gap when a hand reduced to three fingers suddenly clutched the tree's roots. Bradley succeeded in hoisting his carcass up to a flat patch of snow and, huffing and puffing, dragged his cart up behind him. *Made it.* Brushing down his uniform, he turned toward Monti's cabin to give a holler. He was seized by a sort of existential tetanus and his fist, including his phantom fingers, clenched inside his mitten.

The cabin was gone.

The holler came out instead as a fluty moan. There was nothing left but some sawdust, a few twisted nails, and the tracks of hooves that could only belong to a satyr. Bradley surely must have strayed from his usual route, confounded by the surrounding whiteness, but his pride was such that rather than admit his error, he preferred to concede the point to his adversary; later, in the public houses, he would report that Monti had dismantled his cabin and moved it elsewhere.

On the evening of the first snowstorm worthy of the name, a merry congregation gathered at Mrs Guité's hotel, in the court-yard, on the staircase, everywhere, on the balconies, the roof, and stretched their tongues out like skis to taste the snowflakes. The young people of Saint-Lancelot-de-la-Frayère had come to get their fill of malt after an epic snowball fight in the streets now muddled with footprints. Inside, perched on a barrel amid

the dead bodies and overturned demijohns, was a nearly phos-
phorescent fiddler accompanied by a washtub-bassist and a
concertina player. The trio could have gotten a crowd of quad-
riplegics to tap dance; Monti, feeling overheated on the quaking
floor, went out with a crew of carousers to cool off and smoke.
He interrupted the tale he was inventing as he went along and
lit another cig, shielding the flame from the inshore wind. He
tossed the match into a snow-covered spittoon on the gallery.

"So then," Sicotte asked him, "what'd you do after you took
the shack apart?"

Not as soused as the other revellers, Monti told them he'd
lodged his complaint *before* moving his cabin, so that the parcel would never arrive, and then ...

"You little lecher," Skelling lisped, dropping his glass between
his moccasins. "I get the feeling you're smitten, am I right?"

"I..." said Monti.

He'd lost the thread of his inventions.

"I ... No ... I ..."

In the face of his disconcerted audience he plucked the flask
from Sicotte's listless grasp and drained it in sombre silence.
He then removed his hunting cap and was attempting to
smooth his locks when Joséphine Bujold, a girl of wondrous
beauty under her ear warmers, approached the group. She
was accompanied by a few girlfriends, not as perfect in Monti's opinion but not unattractive either, especially when they
dolled themselves up.

Joséphine, though, was in another league. Piano lessons, acts
of charity. Yet she wasn't the least bit snobbish for all that, and
Monti hovered around her without declaring himself. They
had first met at the bedside of Old Man Guité, who was dying

of a failing pancreas. The young lady brought him words of consolation on behalf of her father, the official town doctor, and Monti certain items that were out of bounds for the dying.

Earlier that night, Joséphine had had to slip out of her father's house on the sly. It wasn't long before she and Monti began to make eyes at each other. The maidens, for their part, were eager to learn what had happened with the mailman. The turn of events had given rise to much tongue-wagging. And none of them would've balked at taking Mrs Guité's protege as her beau, just long enough to go off on a binge and squander the still-juicy bundle the sale of his property had yielded. That news, too, had gotten out.

"Afore we're old, dull, and ugly," one of the girls said.

"Married!" Sicotte exclaimed.

Returning to the teeming warmth, the young folks made merry. The boys wooed the fair sex for a while. But not Monti—he was paralyzed. Joséphine acted the self-sufficient woman, her coat collar raised to hide that all she wanted was for him to ask her to dance. She gabbed with acquaintances, relaxed, outgoing, free of the mannerisms that girls of her standing often displayed, equally at home discussing the *poètes maudits* or bareback horse riding. Sicotte had launched into a rigadoon in the arms of Coraline. Joséphine lowered her head to suck a cautious draft from her brimming beer glass, her braids shimmering in the music; she simultaneously turned her eyes up to Monti, who, off in the clouds somewhere, struggled to recall how to use the formal *vous*. Skelling nudged him in the ribs while artful Flavienne joined him inside his peacoat.

"Smarten up, there! You oughtn't leave the doctor's daughter in limbo like that."

Monti was going to say something, anything, to Joséphine. He was going to tell her that one time at dusk he'd cleaved a bat in mid-flight with his axe while chopping wood at Langis's place. But he waited too long. Just when he swung around to pay court to her, that other joker Bradley popped up. A hand's width away from his face. His favourite Paspyjack, in a rough wool vest and cowboy boots, with his goatee and his little yellow pencil. A mouth organ player had joined the band. The horsehair in the fiddler's bow was snapping. Knees were flying on the bewitched dance floor, propelled to shoulder height by the reels and hee-haws. Flavienne and Coraline pouted, as did other lasses in the hotel. There was no denying Bradley cut a fine figure—tall, hirsute—but he'd already developed a reputation as a womanizer, and every little lady in town knew he was a boor. Before Monti could even ask him what he wanted, the mailman proffered a greasy form along with his stunted yellow pencil, so chewed up you felt dirty just holding it.

"I forgot to get your signature for the encyclopedias I delivered to you on October 18 of this year," Bradley said.

The green shadow of a raptor glided over the snowbound stubble of a nearby field. Monti darkened. Joséphine felt protective. As for Bradley, he brightened up. Bradley who, needless to say, didn't exactly produce Shakespearean verse when he sat on the crapper. He couldn't read much more than an address. Joséphine was about to put him in his place when Monti took the little yellow pencil. If he struggled, the snare would tighten. He took the post office form. Everyone around him had shut up. Then, as the damsels and Joe Blows looked on, he signed at the bottom of the page with a nice *X*. The little pencil broke.

7

WHEN WINTER ARRIVED, MOST OF THE SEASONAL
workers packed up their chattels, and by February the casks
at Mrs Guité's place weren't draining very quickly, though a
few toque-topped elbow-benders were still there to stop the
beer from going to waste.

The hotel-keeper, lugging in each hand a brimful bucket of
water from her leaking roof, was trying to push the door with
her foot when it suddenly swung open unaided. Mrs Guité
barely managed to steady herself against the doorpost and not
plunge forever into the annihilating mass of winter fog that
shrouded the porch. She lowered her eyes and saw nothing in
particular. It would become a story she trotted out for years
to come on the rare occasions when she was in her cups. Back
behind her counter now, her eyes blank, she sank all at once
into the slough of despond. Out at sea, fish were frozen on
the icy waves. Mrs Guité called out to Monti in a glassy voice.
Perched on a bar stool, befuddled by idleness, Monti fitted
his head back onto his neck like a cup-and-ball.

"What's the matter, boss? You look down in the dumps."

"Come over here, son, I need to talk to you."

"There's no need," Monti said on his way upstairs to get his
belongings. "I understand."

Not that Mrs Guité wanted to get rid of him, on the contrary. But there wasn't any work. Monti could still come for the occasional free meal, he knew that. He would always be welcome to a cuddle whenever he was in the neighbourhood. Mrs Guité was a mother to these lads. After her husband's funeral a For Sale sign had gone up for a while in front of the establishment. The hotel business had not been part of her plans; she'd intended instead to use the proceeds to consolidate her midwifery practice. And, my, what a horde of kids she'd delivered in Saint-Lancelot-de-la-Frayère. Elsewhere, too. Going off at any hour of the day or night to help the women on the Indian reserves whenever there were complications. She and Old Man Guité had never reproduced. Who knows, maybe a mechanical problem. In any case, it was no secret the hotel was Old Man Guité's baby. As for Madeleine—that was her name—well, she had ten thousand of them. And much of the pleasure she derived from life was seeing them grow up. But the day Bariot, the mailman before Bradley, washed up drowned on the pebble beach, she removed the For Sale sign from the front of the hotel. She took some solace from the notion that he'd died from bingeing on capelin. She went inside and cleaned up the bar, straightened out her accounts, exterminated the flour mites in the cabinets, changed the bedsheets. She'd delivered Bariot, and his drowning had dealt her a heavy blow. She sensed it was time to stop bringing little ones into the world and start taking care of those she'd already delivered, protect them from themselves unbeknownst to them. So they wouldn't feel watched. Because the men of La Frayère—not the women—lived in two worlds. One world where they had their mothers, grandmothers, sisters, aunts, nieces, wives. Like anyone else. And another where they were alone among themselves, a situation liable to get out of hand; this was the world Mrs Guité vowed to guide, not police, with a firm yet benevolent hand. It was a tad different with Monti, though she hadn't witnessed his birth any more than other folks had. He sometimes joked that he'd been spat out by a scallop. Mrs Guité had taken him under her wing just as she had so many others—he deserved a break. You see, he was a hard-working son of a gun, Monti was, not afraid to get dirty, and the hotel had thrived during his time there. He'd go far, but Mrs Guité believed she wouldn't be doing him a favour by keeping him all to herself. And, to be frank, for Monti too, the time had come to move on. Ever since the night of the broken little pencil, nothing gave him any satisfaction. That a sputtering postie should stoop to such baseness had shaken him up.

"And a sherry drinker to boot!" he thundered, hopping mad.

Although he'd have done better to go for a bleeding at Maturin's place, he headed off to his cabin. Hunting—now *that* was something he enjoyed. He went hunting every few days or so in hopes it would lead to more than just killing animals. As he chewed his grilled porcupine or cleaned his rifle barrel with a large pipe cleaner, he wished that everybody would go hunting all at the same time, that everybody would disappear together in the mountains, to see what really transpired in the woods. It wasn't very clear to him yet, but his thoughts often returned to that idea.

Hunting aside, one evening the mailman himself indirectly handed Monti a good plan for a punishment and, as it were, the relevant instructions. Sitting in his undershirt, Monti leafed through one of the few volumes of his encyclopedia to have been spared by moisture. Laundry dripped on a make-shift clothesline among muskrat hides ready to be tanned, if only it would stop snowing someday. Even completely alone in the forest he felt ashamed to have to toil so much over the lines he was perusing. Still, he appreciated the variety of topics covered. Suspended from a beam, his oil lamp swung on its hook. Over the past months, Monti had applied himself to reading. Whenever he was stumped by a rudiment of the French language, he pulled out from under his pallet—acting as if someone were spying on him—a primer with a cracked spine. Joséphine occasionally substituted for her mother at school and had let him take the reader home because he'd corded her wood and was a nice guy. Monti, though having no illusions, recalled every word she'd said to him that day. Among other things, she'd explained that his freedom was enviable and he ought to be proud; mulling over all this, his heart had soared as he left the school with his primer, its spine as yet uncracked. Except that, no matter how liberal Dr Bujold may have been, in Saint-Lancelot-de-la-Frayère, as anywhere else, the have-nots didn't mix with the haves.

Monti tucked his reader back between two wall planks. He helped himself to another shot of caribou from a preserves can he'd opened with a screwdriver he really ought to have returned to the blacksmith. He took a moment to silently appreciate the workings of the eavestrough he'd installed with all those tools. Then he dived back into the encyclopedia. The lamp's metal framework threw a carousel of shadows on walls pounded by the weather. His curiosity was piqued on seeing a list of equipment pencilled in by an anonymous hand in the margin beside a map of the Klondike. *The Yukon—is that in*

Canada? he wondered. The gold rush had been over for fifteen years, but Monti wouldn't have known that. There it was before his eyes, printed in a book. And books didn't tell lies. Now the snow fell in golden flakes. Gusts of wind whipped up dazzling streaks. *The big hunt could wait.* From that point on, Monti thought about nothing except prospecting. He was still thirsty, but didn't know for what. As if what he wanted didn't exist. He kept sipping caribou from his can as he read on, not even taking care, amid the welter of his emotions, to not cut himself on the metal barbs.

The caribou kicked in all at once. Monti dropped back on his pallet as though felled by an uppercut. He didn't fall asleep so much as faint, bleeding at the corner of his lips. The rifle he'd been planning to clean lay across his thighs. The skin on one side of his face grew blighted with shadows that spread as the wick of the lamp burned down. His dreams took the shape of a shimmering beast made entirely of malleable night. Of a shimmering moose made entirely of night. In his dreams he wandered braying through a nearby forest that gave way to obscure landscapes of rocks Monti no longer recognized.

The rifle shot woke him up such that he might never sleep again. There was a simultaneous clang and a dent appeared in the jerry-built chimney pipe. Monti must have fired in the depths of sleep. That morning, he saw that gold would one day allow him to tell Daddy Bujold he could keep his dowry, his daughter was all Monti would take from him.

Once his shakes had stopped, he got up in his sagging long johns looking like a newborn calf. He put his rain boots on the wrong feet because he hadn't waited to rinse his gizzard with coffee, which he'd brewed so strong he might as well have bashed himself in the teeth with the coffee pot instead. He shat a rock into a pail and went out into the great haze of evaporation, beneath ice-covered branches shedding drops, each filled with a tiny sun. After sun-up the weather turned pretty fine, and Monti went first thing to check the traps he'd laid along rarely trodden trails. Just in case, through some rent in reality, he'd snared the weird creature of his dreams, whose tracks he was to keep on seeing everywhere.

8

OVER THE PAST MONTHS, BRADLEY TOO HAD META-
morphosed. It happened right in the middle of Lent. He was
crossing town all cruddy in his poorly mended trousers. A
half moon stained his shirt, open at the collar despite the
freezing temperature. His bridled horse dragged its feet, and
any pedestrians or busybodies in front of the shops revitalized
by the generally milder March weather were subjected to the
Paspyjack's contumely.

"Looks like the Dubuc woman didn't go easy on him," folks
said.

The Dubuc woman was Marie Dubuc of Rang Saint-Onge.
A backcountry shrew, a harpy that certain forked tongues had
rechristened the Virgin, though several such tongues couldn't
deny without sinning that they'd already licked the salt off her
epidermis. Even the priest in his confessional was no longer
shocked to hear that another Saint-Lancelot-de-la-Frayère
youth who'd come of age had sought underneath the Dubuc
woman's togs validation of the fables about cabbage-patch
babies and storks. No different from anyone else, the mailman
needed warmth and he'd found himself shacked up with her.
Once you'd gained a reputation for fickleness, it wasn't long
before you were shunned by every respectable wench in the

village. "You missed your turn, big fella," they said, which explained why all that winter Bradley and the Dubuc woman had studied anatomy on a sticky-sheeted cot in an attic on Rang Saint-Onge.

"Will you get a move on!" Bradley barked at his horse in the middle of the road on that Lent morning.

The shutters in an upstairs window snapped shut. A few seconds later the shutters in the next room slammed shut and locked. Then the downstairs shutters. Mothers thrust their arms out of doors, and where toddlers had played a moment before, nothing remained but toys suspended in mid-air. Curtains were drawn in the dormer windows. Eyes were pressed against judas holes.

"What's the matter that you should be gawking at me so?" the mailman asked Flavienne and Coraline in an all-at-once-honeyed voice.

Alarmed by the commotion, Joséphine's companions were just leaving the dressmaker's, where they sometimes went to caress the cloth. Bradley blew them damp kisses while he tethered his horse in front of the general store, drawing the reins so tight the bit distorted its face. He had a ring of dried molasses around his mouth, but it wasn't until he began to worry at his zipper with his truncated fingers that the girls took shelter behind their shopping bags. With a flick of the wrist, the mailman released from a bursting tuft the fearsome grey pecker he was endowed with. He pressed a fist against his hip and flexed his knees. One, two, three, and voilà: a bit of smut in sputtering yellow cursive on the crackling quartz-like snow. Flavienne, unable to resist, chanced a peek through the loop of her bag. Strange all the same that she would end her days in the Saint-Michel-Archange asylum.

"Mr and Mrs Berthelot," the mailman said, muddying the general store's floor.

It started with a square-nose shovel. Bradley grasped it without first cleaning his hands after so grossly handling the unmentionable part of his person; when he saw it was for delivery to Monti—the shovel, that is—he swallowed his pride and silently wagered that Bouge, the big oaf, would unwittingly dig his own grave with it. Except there was more involved than just pride. Things had gotten complicated. Bradley had received a dressing-down and, with his job at stake, he was treading carefully of late. Mayor Pleau, annoyed to the point of summoning the mailman to his office, had decided enough was enough. He'd asked Bradley to explain why folks were lining up for the purpose of lodging complaints against his highness.

"Seems to me it ain't all that hard to mail a letter."

So thought the mayor. What vexed him most was that Bradley would not leave off prevaricating. Even so, the Paspyjack left the town hall wondering how he might keep drinking at the level he aspired to while shirking his duties less.

He therefore bowed without fussing to the requirement of delivering a square-nose shovel to Monti Bouge. *It's nothing,* he repeated to himself. After finishing his rounds that day, exhausted by his constitutional, he ended up tipsy pretty fast for a jack with his constitution. The shot glasses of plum liqueur knocked back at the hotel had weighed his ankles down with iron balls. Slouched over the bar, he waited for the chance to give that illiterate a lesson. Because when the mailman had knock-knocked on Monti's door earlier that afternoon, the guy was nowhere to be seen. And if Monti wasn't lurking in the woods, he was wont to while away the hours at Mrs Guité's place—not in a hundred years would he have held anything whatsoever against her. But there was neither hide nor hair of him that evening, and no one in the place was apprised of his peregrinations. Bradley blew his pay at the bar cooking up some dirty trick to take revenge. It all came to nothing when he ran out of coin, grandly mopping his face as double vision heightened his appalling sense of detachment from the material world.

Next, shipped straight from the mill, came a raw tarpaulin made of puncture-proof canvas, rolled and awkwardly bound up with a rope that was a plague of splinters. Bradley loaded up and climbed the mountain to Monti's place to say hello. The tarp kept catching the wind, and the wind didn't let up. Over the following days, amid the *turluttes* and twisters blowing down from the mountain, the mail depot got cluttered up with two axes, a spare handle, ointments, turpentine, a first-aid kit, crampons, a grappling hook, a harness, a mountain-climbing belt, ice axes, a halter, a length of chain, and a deck of cards. And some mousetraps. And other stuff too. Bradley had smoke coming out of his ears, not to mention his calves.

"Where are you, where are you, smarty-pants?" he hummed hoarsely, forever on the lookout at the Guité woman's hotel.

Using his cigarette smoke as a blind, he stayed glued to his bar stool to make sure the scamp wouldn't budge him from there again. But could never flush out his prey. Three times he'd ascended the steep path capped with the cabin stained blue-green by lichen in that forest of dry brooms and meagre game.

Monti had disappeared, yet he persisted in his machinations, ordering a tent, cast iron skillets, towels, a sealskin parka, fishing line, a compass, leather satchels, a can opener, a block of resin, a pocket atlas, a whetstone, talcum powder, and a thing-amajig that everyone named differently. Meanwhile, Pleau got wind of more rumours about crooked dealings ascribed to Bradley. They were trifles but, then, word of mouth ... The mayor took it badly and, in his words, "didn't give a good goddamn," as any scandal was necessarily exaggerated because people in Gaspésie do exaggerate. Bradley had to deliver. If the city dismissed him—and this hadn't changed—he risked finding himself in Paspébiac, filleted and gobbled up by sailors belching on the steps of the marina between swigs of brew. You would have to be a liar like Bradly to say that he turned somersaults on the narrow mountain path.

One evening, his nerves as taut as harpsichord strings, he started walking faster than his shoes to catch up with Monti, who was headed toward a kind of will-o'-the-wisp above the spot where the beach usually lay. With beads of sweat on his lip, Bradley finally nabbed his persecutor and flattened him against a craft that had appeared out of the dark. The boat rocked, and Bradley was disoriented because he had water up to his hams, but even more because of the meek expression of the joe standing before him, stammering an apology for not being Monti. He showed Bradley he was just coiling a rope that had been left pell-mell at the bottom of the boat. The Paspyjack returned home, lay down in his bed, blew out his candle end, and shut his peepers. He opened them again, indisposed by the Dubuc woman's snoring. Up among the joists supporting the attic he saw the selfsame will-o'-the-wisp as the one he'd seen earlier on the shore.

After that it was a coffee pot and grinder, a clay teapot, woollen blankets, a roll of wire, a pulley, a cradle, a chuck, forks and knives and spoons, a snuffbox along with a pipe and a buckskin tobacco pouch, wooden buckets and tin buckets, a bundle of shoelaces, a phial of quicksilver.

In the spring, the surveyor in charge of drawing the preliminary boundaries, Mr Lionel, and his apprentice, Gouin's youngest, came upon the good mailman near the Frai river. They were in the woods to measure the differences in ground level along the aqueduct's route.

"Quicksilver! *Quicksilver!*" Bradley said, quivering as he scraped his foot on a stump after trampling down a swallow's nest.

His collarbones began to clatter as he jerked out of sight in last year's tall grass, strewing in his wake the jolts of his murky laughter.

The next shipment contained three pairs of scissors (including a defective one), sifters, a hat beyond ugly, a French dictionary, a French grammar, an English-French dictionary, hemorrhoid lotion, Vicks, boot liners, a horsehair brush, a bitbrace, enough wick to reach from Saint-Lancelot-de-la-Frayère to Dalhousie, a telescope, a rifle where the mug of the guy shouldering it was reflected, stretched, and distorted, six pairs of sheepskin mittens, five yards of mosquito netting, five hundred pounds of candles, fifteen pounds of nails, the same amount of tallow, a hammer, a checkers set, and an entire expedition outfit. Bradley's horse said no. It went completely stiff and stayed that way even when its enraged master spurred it bloody. What's more, Monti took the trouble of returning the defective scissors.

Spent, unable to unbend in his bath, Bradley was having the calluses under his feet filed down by the Dubuc woman.

"Can you scrub farther to the right? There, there, that's it."

"He'll grind yous down if this keeps up."

There was dust in the air from all the Virgin's filing.

"I'll give him a wallop that he'll feel for a century."

"Can't wait to see that."

"You won't wait for nothing, I warrant you."

"Or maybe it's just that he's better than yous."

Such heart-to-heart chats didn't help the mailman bide his time. Buck naked in his tub of brownish, turbid water, he made his gonads promise that should they one day engender little Bradleys, this offspring would nurse a hatred steeped in scorn and malice for the name of Bouge, or better still…

His logorrhea was smothered by the rumble of the avalanche: two hundred pounds of bacon, four hundred of flour, ninety-five of preserves, fifty of cornmeal, thirty-five of rice, and more, always more. Bradley obsessively returned to the store, in case the cavalry was on its way.

Eyeing him over the top of her ledger, the Berthelot woman fretted about his fits and the long white blotches where his body was completely numb. With the recent rise in sales she'd bought herself a new dress exactly like the old one. The next time Bradley showed up, he had to endure the thousand and one pieces of advice the shopkeeper spouted. She'd climbed the walls when she saw him. He'd taken a tumble in the nettles and sharp-edged ice.

It had become a matter of honour. He'd hardly swallowed the last bitter pill when he wobbled away again with twenty-four pounds of coffee, a sack of tea, twenty-five pounds of pickled fish, a gargantuan amount of canned soup and onions, and casks of sugar totalling about a hundred pounds. He hauled his shipment on his toboggan when he should have used his cart. The snow was gone, but his joints were chapped to such a degree that a sudden frost made them pop like overripe berries. If he ever collared him, the killjoy, Bradley was going to peel him with a paring knife till nothing remained but the oyster pieces, and … Fifty pounds of oatmeal, potatoes, wagonloads of legumes, twenty-five boxes of salted butter, a hundred pounds of beans, lardons, four dozen tins of condensed milk, fifteen pounds of salt, one of pepper, eight of baking powder, two of soda, half a pound of mustard, thirty-six pounds of yeast, and five cakes of soap, which seemed rather little. And, oh yes, two hundred and forty matchboxes too. The mailman, lost in the night after straying from his familiar shortcuts, struck one. The bit of mind he had left was consumed in the green crackle of the pilfered flame.

9

BRADLEY DRAGGED HIMSELF KNOCK-KNEED TOWARD the hotel. Through the window, the customers saw him coming. The inside of his chest must have been eroded, judging from the groans it was letting out. The ginger curls on his brow had lost their fire. Under his chin, at the end of his long, craggy throat, hung a turkey wattle. True to form, the Paspyjack tied his horse to an old harrow abandoned in the bushes without leaving enough slack for the animal to drink from the nearby puddles. Everyone smoking outside had witnessed this before returning to their beers inside. Horse, rope, harrow. No sleight of hand there. The mailman kicked open the door as if entering a saloon. His lanky silhouette stood out against the sunlight in the doorway. No one said a word as he pounded the floorboards with his heels. But then, this wasn't unusual; sometimes whole evenings passed without a word being spoken.

"A drink!" Bradley mooed, unabashedly shoving aside our national NBer, the same one as always, back from his province, this time not on business but on vacation.

Mrs Guité raised her chin to ask the mailman what he was drinking.

"Sherry," said the black hole in the red beard.

There was none left, dammit. Monti, fork in hand, was drinking the last glass to wash down his glimmering plateful of clams. It was enough for Guité to say she'd have some more delivered by mail to make the whole crowd crack up. Since he wasn't as put out as Bradley by their being in the same place together, Monti felt he was in a position to act magnanimously.

"Serve him some cider, ma'am. Put it on my bill."

Mrs Guité served Bradley the last of the cider, full of pulp and pits and debris, then opened the trap door and went down to the cellar to poke around her reserves. The NBer, meanwhile, tucked his wallet back in his coat pocket, deprived by Monti of the pleasure of picking up the tab. Crestfallen, he donned his bowler and turned around to take aim before lowering his prodigious rump on the stool. He was still toying with his waxed-tipped moustache when Skelling entered the hotel, his cheeks daubed with soot. Just then Mrs Guité emerged from the cellar with an armload of small jugs, and she cautioned him so no one would tumble headlong through the open trap door. Skelling sat down, nudging the mailman, and said:

"It's cider tonight, is it, Bradley m'boy? That's pathetic."

And he started pulling burrs out of the fringes on the Postal Department uniform. The Paspyjack grumbled, as mulish as ever, and his fangs showed as he swivelled his eyes toward Monti. Sipping his little concoction, he searched for a barb to hurl at him. Monti calmly poured the rest of his sherry into the sink while Skelling made a gesture like he was unscrewing his temple to signal his puzzlement at Monti's generosity toward the mailman.

"It's because y'hafta see him drink to distinguish his puss from his anus," Monti explained.

More bursts of laughter in the room.

"Talk about a waste of apples," Skelling added, and ordered himself a cider too.

The Paspyjack spit wide of the spittoon. Already well into his second glass, he was champing at the bit. Three ciders later, nothing bothered him. Monti was getting thrashed at cribbage by Langis and couldn't hear over the racket what Bradley was blathering on about, but he seemed to be inflicting some cock-and-bull story on the available victims. He spread his arms as wide as possible, and when the lads shook their heads to contradict him, he puffed up his cheeks and said yes, yes; then he pretended to reel in a big one, shielding his eyes with his hand as if scanning the horizon. His listeners stood up one by one and went off to other tables to suckle. Not the NBer, obviously—he was gobbling away. He found Bradley's fabulations altogether amusing. He occasionally gripped the edge of the bar and rocked his bulk on the stool to buttonhole a passing patron and convince them to come listen or to warn them the trap door was still open behind him.

Now, it needs to be understood that in Gaspésie, from Les Méchins to Miguasha, from Tracadièche to Manche-d'Épée, people lay it on thick. In those parts, there's no point *swearing* you once sliced a bat in half while splitting wood. You just have to *say* it. Folks will believe you. They *want* it to be true. Because if it's true, it's more interesting.

So when Honoré Bouge, a.k.a. Monti, commanded Victor Bradley of Paspébiac, in front of witnesses, to stop telling lies, there was a moment of dumbfoundedness. When it came to slander, this was beyond brazen. The NBer howled as he covered his eye, where a bit of peel ejected from the mailman's teeth had lodged. Bradley had roared something before pouncing on Monti. The NBer rocked on his stool and disappeared. Mrs Guité intervened and applied her sobering-up hold on the Paspyjack. He struggled unavailingly. His blue eye turned brown and vice versa.

"It ain't lies!" he sputtered. "It's as true as my horse is tied up outside."

Looking as philosophical as can be, Monti stepped behind the counter. He bent down and reappeared with a cutting board and a cleaver flashing great silver beams. Groans rose up from the cellar. Monti took his time. He sedulously aligned the sparkling blade with the edge of the board and placed a barely touched twenty-sixer close by.

"I'll betcha your horse on it," he said to Bradley, whom Mrs Guité had perched back on his stool.

When they chatted about the outcome later on, many who were at the hotel would realize they'd all of them had a feeling of déjà vu.

"What's the bet?"

Monti was going on a journey and walking wasn't part of the plan. Back then, going on a journey still meant putting on your Sunday best for the New Year's party at your cousins' or packing your bag for a pleasure trip on the far side of the pond. Not standing in front of the locomotive's headlight for a one-way ride, your ticket punched by God the Father in person.

"I'll bet your horse it ain't outside," Monti said, upping the ante, and straightened the cleaver blade by a few millimetres. "Meaning if your horse ain't outside, it's mine."

Next day at dawn. A salmon-coloured sky. Seagulls soaring over the sea. Feeling like his aching head was wrapped in a turban of thick bandages and poultice, the NBer lugged his suitcases from his room to the roundabout with the well in the middle in front of the building. He stopped, without speaking, to settle his bill and make sheep eyes at Mrs Guité. He checked his watch and saluted the hotel-keeper with a polite yet troubled nod. The NBer was going off to recommence his business beneath skies more . . . not very different, in the end, from these. The wagon waited alongside a stack of lobster cages. The donkeys pawed the ground. Once his baggage was loaded, he momentarily considered how to avoid killing himself and then hoisted himself up on the seat next to Sicotte, whose lap was muffled up in a sneezy blanket. A drowsy flick of the riding crop and the wagon pulled out. *Heave-ho and away we go.* They were headed to the train station in the neighbouring town.

"There's partridge these days," Sicotte said, eager to break a silence he found awkward.

Pfft, so long he don't toss his cookies, he thought, looking at his passenger. He didn't do much to urge his jennies up the hillock that seemed insignificant but soon became the Appalachians. He began chuckling to himself along the way, surrounded by plumes of smoke rising from the houses below, because seeing the NBer sitting on the edge of the seat, immobile and clutching his duffle bag, brought to mind that time in primary school when he'd had something hidden in his pants under his desk, and as he was inattentive, the teacher had chosen him to come solve the problem on the blackboard. But he came back to the present when he spotted down below, at the far end of his thirty-foot-long shadow, the mailman towing his cart.

"What's got into him, making deliveries so early in the morning? And on foot?"

"Well," the NBer began.

At which Sicotte, making fun, pretended to jump, as though surprised to see it talked. Their gazes collided, sending out a spark of sympathy.

"It's on account of the youngster," the peddler continued. "The kid who used to work at the hotel."

"Monti?"

"Yeh, Monti, that's it."

"Trotted out that puck story, I'll wager?"

"Oh, I'm all through with wagering. What puck story?"

Sicotte told him about the famous save Monti had pulled off back then, using his teeth to block the slapshot of an Indian as big as a logger in the final of a tournament against the Paspébiac Crolions. Sicotte emphasized, by the way, that he was the one who'd scored the tying goal that had sent them into overtime. He also described how it took two men, not boys, but men, to pull the puck out of Monti's face. Both his cheeks were bulging. The coach yanked his head on one side, while on the other Labillois's father—Labillois played defence for the Grisous—tugged at the sliver of puck sticking out of his kisser. After finally extracting the thing, they duly noted the bite mark.

"Criminy!" the NBer said. "So you won?"

"Nope. The referee gave the Crolions the goal anyway. And guess who refereed the game?"

Sicotte pointed his thumb back over his shoulder toward Bradley in the distance, at an acute angle with the road.

"My, my, you don't say."

"Wasn't even a matter of favouritism, in my view. Just a passing whim, that's all."

"Either way, what happened yesterday makes more sense to me now."

In an ashtray voice jolted by the bumps, the NBer recounted the episode as he remembered it from the night before.

"So your mailman accepted the wager," he said toward the end of the ride, out of breath just from talking. "He was going to bet his horse, sure. And, hey, I know an animal like that is worth something, if only for the hair. Anyway, Mr Bradley naturally asked what he had to gain from the venture. Monti raised two fingers. Meaning—and right then I didn't think it very bright of him—meaning he was staking two of his fingers, the same two that Mr Bradley's missing. The mailman, he's . . . he's full of spite, that man is. He just went batshit. To the point he didn't hear the clippity-clop sounding on the upstairs floor. The room got serious as heck when Mrs Guité, white as a sheet, stepped away from the cutting board, the twenty-sixer, and the slaughterhouse implement. She waved her hands in protest, as if to exempt herself from the butchering job in the event Mr Bradley won. We'd all of us seen him at it when he'd tethered his horse to the harrow at the far end of the yard. Your mailman chugged his drink, then chugged mine too, then he shamelessly stood up to test the blade. Slice a finger clean off, one of those cleavers! But he had no qualms, that one. He went to push open the door so everyone could see his horse. Except, I don't need to tell you, the door to Mrs Guité's hotel opens *inward*. It was hilarious. Mr Bradley eventually sorted it out, but when the door swung open, he stopped short. Gobsmacked, I tell you. Us folks, we were itching to see what the wonder was. He was standing in the way. Jesus Mary Joseph, I wasn't liquored up, after all . . . Well, all right, I was pretty well-oiled, and I hurt myself yesterday. When it's not my sister bashing me, I do it myself. I guess I miss her, but I'll say this. I'm not the sort to spin theories in life. I sell junk for a living. I'm no kook. I swear to you, what I saw yesterday was still giving me the shits this morning. Search me as to how it managed to climb up there, the unicorn, but after Bradley realized his horse wasn't outside anymore, Monti whistled and the clip-clop on the ceiling ceased. I saw it. Saw it with my own eyes. The horse's muzzle appeared at the top of the stairs and it came down on the landing as casual as you please. Light-footed, my man, and all hoity-toity. As though singing a song, I tell you. Had to be some sort of power lifted the roof, by gum! That's when, as you can imagine, Mr Bradley started screaming. Out of primal terror, I warrant you. It was heart-rending."

The wagon trundled out of a vault of bud-laden branches and began its descent toward a vale spotted here and there with patches of stubble and rectangles awaiting the plow. The vehicle rolled up to a station that was indistinguishable from the other buildings. The two fellows, having craned skyward on the lookout for crows and omens, had cricked necks lying in store for them.

"If you say so," Sicotte finally said, "well, sir, then it must be true."

III

THE FIRST NIGHT

10

KILL 'EM ALL HAD BEEN PLAYING EVER SINCE THEY'D arrived, and the inside of Laganière's uncle's sound system was agleam with death. The gent must have signed the kind of cheque that could feed the average Gaspésie family for three months for the speakers alone. He'd had them made in some obscure shop in Abitibi-Témiscamingue by a semi-autistic artisan who crafted just a few pairs a year but was the subject of esoteric articles in specialized magazines from the depths of Scandinavia. Laganière's uncle wasn't even a huge aficionado of sound, electroacoustics, high-fidelity, and such. On the contrary. What Laganière's uncle loved was silence. He loved hunting. Only, when he bought something, it had to be the best, the biggest, the most expensive. He was like that about anything, be it his heat pump or his potato peeler. It had to gleam. That's how he liked it. And he had the wherewithal. Voluntary simplicity? Not so much. A baby boomer is what Laganière's uncle was, with desires and RRSPs. Paid his taxes. Voted Conservative federally, Liberal provincially. The wires connecting the speakers to his space-shuttle contraption were worth six hundred bucks, and—make no mistake—the gent took good care of his system. He was a maniac. So much so that he played nothing but flute music, Pavarotti, or Gregorian chants on "his radio," as he called it. At most, the soft rock station, but never without sticking Blu Tack on the screws to dampen the vibrations. Laganière knew it. It was absolutely forbidden to turn the volume up past one. The volume was at four.

"Guys, the stereo, I'm serious, my uncle's gonna rip my head off!"

With his beige polo shirt twisted around his fist, Laganière was running all over the place—from the undesirables in the kitchen to the living room—under the shifty gaze of the stuffed moose head hanging above the armchair. Under the even shiftier gaze of Marteau, dressed up as a bride, whom he'd just addressed. No response.

"Your father would be proud, again ..."

Laganière was not on top of the situation, not even close. It was like patching a hole in a hose only to see the water frothing out of another hole further along.

"Steeve. Come here, Steeve, we need to talk. Don't you think you've had enough to drink?"

Steeve was sitting in the vibrating armchair.

The problem was that Laganière's uncle's cottage was to the other cottages in that neck of Gaspésie what his sound system was to prototypes of the gramophone. The gent had invested a good part of his retirement savings in it, not to mention his libido. Even the cabinet handles were milled. The place just oozed luxury, and the nephew scurried around doing his best to keep the havoc at bay so his savings account wouldn't be sucked completely dry when his uncle sued him. If he didn't rip his head off first.

"At least pick up after yourselves ..."

With the armchair in massage mode, Steeve looked at him

as if to say *shove it*. Laganière spit on a dishrag and started to scrub beer rings from the mahogany. It was back—that funny odour, tickling his nostrils again. He swung around. Nothing behind him but his shadow weirdly bent in a corner crowded with the hunting weapons. *Where's that smell coming from, for God's sake?* He sniffed his armpits, then a mocking whistle slipped away in a blind spot on the edge of his poor vision.

"Where'd that Montreal dude go to?"

The odour faded, and Marteau in the kitchen answered with an unpromising laugh. The guy from Montreal was the culprit, it had to be him. *Search me,* Laganière thought. He turned around again, and his shadow stretched across the floor all the way to the boots by the front door.

"Can we turn the volume down? Please?"

His head would look nice too, mounted on a wooden plaque on the wall next to Bullwinkle. And another thing: How had the boys found out the cottage was available? Lorraine must have told Cynthia, who had told Yannick. That would explain the mystery. Lorraine was unaware that he was planning to take her to the cottage for the evening, but she knew his uncle had gone to Florida.

And the weasel was nowhere to be found.

"I'll turn down the stereo," Steeve answered.

Steeve Allard, with two *e*'s. Emanating from the vibrating armchair, his words sounded like a failing droid. He was Yannick and François's second cousin on his mother Mireille's side, Mireille, the daughter of Lucie Bouge, Henri's sister, who— Mireille, that is, not Henri—had married Raymond Allard, the grandson of Langis Allard, who'd known Monti, but eventually divorced—Mireille, that is, not Langis—a few years

later and married one of the Cousineaus' grandsons, Marc
Guité, whose great-aunt had operated the hotel for many years
before it was taken over by the Guérettes, and whose grandmother, when she'd started out, had directed the library that
Joséphine Bouge, Monti's wife, Henri's mother, and François
and Yannick's grandmother, had founded some fifty years earlier, and which Laganière, the very same, now devoted himself
to properly managing. Ah, the outlying regions! When Steeve
was a teenager, he'd migrated to the Montreal metropolitan
area. After his stepfather's hydroplane accident, his mother
had used her share of the inheritance to move back to Gaspésie,
where she merrily rolled her *r*'s. So Steeve was visiting his mum
and his friends, the locals. From a strictly scientific point of
view Steeve was a prime specimen of oaf. You could see his
crack when he bent over, he was apt to turn purple, and his
hair was cropped on top and cropped even closer on the sides.

"If you insist," he added.

He reached for the amplifier with the ginger root that, judging from its ingrown toenail, was his big toe, and turned the
volume not down but up. Concerto for chainsaws. The bass
boomed so loud a framed photo hanging above the sound system came loose and broke the tone arm. Seeing this from the
kitchen, Marteau spat a mouthful of beer onto the silverware.

"That's not funny!" Laganière exclaimed, but was immediately drowned out by one of Metallica's best whammy bar
passages.

The frame held a picture of his uncle's retirement dinner.
Flanked by his colleagues, the gent was using what looked
like a scimitar to uncork the champagne, his eyes red not just
from the flash.

"It's worth a lot…"

Marteau answered something, but it got lost in the mish-mash of decibels. The Sound of Music. La-la, la-la.

"What did you say?"

Laganière had trouble reading his lips. Marteau clearly hadn't just quoted Ringuet. Steeve bellowed with simple-minded joy, proving that high school stardom doesn't guarantee you'll turn out all right. He cranked the armchair vibrator all the way up.

"Hey, bard, go write us an ode."

No response. Laganière didn't even bother answering anymore when the guys called him bard. *They'll get fed up before I do,* he thought, as stubborn as ever.

Outside, it was raining so hard the walls were about to knock on the door so they could come inside and warm up. There were fourteen clocks and dials spread around the cottage; time passed, but not any faster even so.

"What's he up to, your friend from Montreal?" Laganière finally asked, unaware that he was spilling all the dirt he'd just collected in the dustpan.

Again, no response. He knew very well the guy from Montreal was playing hide-and-seek. He hadn't gone out; his shoes were by the front door.

"Ah, he can stay in his hole for all I care."

"That reminds me," Steeve said.

He told Marteau what had happened earlier when they were out hunting. He'd handed the Montreal dude a Glock. The guy went nuts. He started holding his gun a little slantwise, like a gangster, touching his nose with his tongue as he looked around for something to shoot at. Off to the side, Laganière was crying in the rain. Marteau, in front of the oven, relished what he was hearing.

Steeve said, "I think you were doing much better teamed up with Yannick. The guy's moose calls nearly lured two or three scrawny calves away from their pasture."

"Fellas, it's gonna be salty," Marteau promised.

While he was salting his broth, the top of the totem-shaped salt cellar had come unscrewed.

Although the underbrush wasn't teeming with wildlife the way it used to, the four hunters had killed enough rabbits to eat the next day without having to go out in the storm. That's what Marteau was cooking for them, rabbit stew, but without the help of a recipe. He in turn described what had taken place in the woods, once they'd split up. Steeve, Laganière, and the Montreal dude went off in one direction, and he and Yannick in another. Yannick wanted to test his slug. He was in luck: a rabbit was frisking about ahead of them in the lush grass. A slug is a ball of raw metal the size of a Lady apple that you load into your twelve-gauge where the cartridge goes. The rabbit's four legs kept running over the meadow and the fords, except there was no rabbit on them anymore.

"Speaking of Yannick," Laganière said, somewhat shocked by the anecdote, but hey, you had to take it with a grain of salt. "Is he ever coming back? He can't have been hunting all this time, what with the crappy weather. Because if I could give him a piece of my mind, I'd tell him this just won't do."

The others ignored him. He toyed with his wedding band, rotating it on his ring finger with his thumb. Steeve stood up and stroked Marteau's hips through the wedding gown in passing. With "The Four Horsemen" playing, he went to lie down in the master bedroom. Laganière peered outside. Was that Yannick down there? He wasn't wearing the right glasses and it was dark, but what the ... In the worst surge of rain yet, the window looked like an Impressionist painting. After a minute the scene came into focus. It wasn't Yannick but a vaguely humanoid bush behind the row of driveway reflectors his uncle had installed so you wouldn't hit the snowmobile shelter backing up.

The same unbreathable odour returned to Laganière's nostrils. He faked a pivot to the right and then lunged to his left.

"There you are."

It was the Montreal dude. He had something hidden behind his back. Fumes of dibutyl phthalate spread out in front of his smart-alecky face.

"What did you just spray me with?" Laganière shouted. "Show me!"

The two of them clutched at each other's jackets. Yee-haw! They pulled each other's hair and scratched each other as Marteau looked on in fascination.

Steeve had arrived with this character on the morning bus. Word was the Montreal dude had strutted into the Orléans Express terminus full of big-city swagger and let loose a couple of cock-a-doodle-doos before two or three of La Frayère's patriarchs. "He wouldn't last long at the far end of the Tapps's road at Saint-Maurice-de-l'Échouerie," old Marcel had reportedly said from behind his cold one. The terminus was in the snack bar managed by Patapon's mother. Upping the ante, Fernand's son Gabou had apparently replied, "His face is in the dictionary beside the word *dickhead*." Joking aside, the Montreal dude may have measured three foot six, but he exuded a two-hundred-fifty-pound aura. He tried to, anyway, with his loose-fitting duds. He and Steeve didn't know each other that well, but they were co-workers at the roads department. Steeve said he hadn't even invited him. The Montreal dude had followed him onto the bus. Ten hours later he alighted when Steeve did. Laganière found this fishy. He was no Survenant, no Outlander, this one. The guy hadn't turned up in Gaspésie, with no baggage and barely a coat on, to go back to the land.

The Montreal dude twisted himself free of the hold that Laganière was going to apply, a time-worn version of Mrs Guité's legendary sobering-up hold. Actually, it was old Marcel who'd shown it to him. *Is he on air tonight?* Laganière never got the chance to pick up a copy of the new CBSU listings. The Montreal dude whipped out a can of hairspray and spritzed him in the teeth. It tasted the same as it smelled.

"Give me that before you melt your own cornea!"

The Montreal dude played leapfrog with the furniture and zigzagged through the chairs, making torturous scraping noises as he shifted them about. It didn't take long for Laganière's legs to give out in his hiked-up corduroys. Lorraine had put them in the dryer yet again and they'd shrunk. He mopped his forehead as if wearing the wrist bands he usually used for badminton. The Montreal dude taunted him from across the room with the jerk-off hand signal. The wind whistled between his ears. Laganière got even by calling him a scatophile and savoured the twofold satisfaction of insulting the other party with a word he doesn't understand.

"Hey, bard, go write us an ode," the Montreal dude countered.

Laganière didn't retaliate, but, at the risk of popping an aneurysm, he truly wished the weasel would burst out of nowhere and leave this midget with one less ear. Nothing bound him to the others here. Yet when Laganière asked himself what his own bond was with Steeve, Yannick, and Marteau, he found nothing, except that they were all *Gaspésiens*. And they had all known Thierry Vignola. Which had just occurred to him because he'd noticed Marteau's tattoo. A faded pennant marked *1986*, the year Vignola had disappeared.

"This isn't your place," Laganière said. "It's my uncle's cottage."

Besides, the Montreal dude was the one who'd let the weasel in. "It's boiling in here," he'd decided earlier as he was getting out of the whirlpool bath, reeking of brown water, his manhood wrapped in a towel bearing the lord of the manor's monogram. Then he opened the patio door, with the rain pouring down and the temperature outside at four degrees Celsius. The weasel darted into the warmth, an entrance they all found entertaining.

"Your uncle's in Florida!" Steeve yelled from the master bedroom, where he was luxuriating in satin while contemplating his angst in the ceiling mirror.

It was like this: That morning, the three rapscallions, with the Montreal dude at their heels, had hit on the idea of requisitioning the cottage to celebrate Yannick's impending fatherhood. They'd found out that Laganière's uncle had recently migrated to his pastel condo in the Fort Lauderdale area and they'd decided the cottage would make for a pretty fine hunting camp. Anyway, being down south, the gent surely couldn't give a damn. Wrong. He did indeed give a damn. Before leaving, he'd made a tour of the property with his nephew, who was charged with watering the cacti, checking the thermostat, and all the other little maintenance tasks he obsessed about three thousand four hundred kilometres away. "The smoke and carbon monoxide detectors don't work, I've got to rewire the whole thing." None of it was rocket science, but Laganière was still warned—more sternly than necessary— not to use either the bath or the shower on account of some plumbing problems. "There's a ton of shit got into the wells." In the end, his uncle, looking grim, had entrusted him with the key, tugging on his end before letting go. After which he scribbled, without exhaling, the code for the alarm system on a Post-it. Then he exhaled, for a very long time, and said, "Come over, you and Lorraine, and enjoy the home theatre." The gent opened the door to the master bedroom. On each pillow of the satin-covered bed lay a lollipop.

11

"NICE WEATHER TONIGHT," THE DRIVER SAID TO François over his shoulder.

"Yes, very nice."

Behind the wheel of his cab, the driver improvised, freely reinterpreting the highway code in the traffic near the Jacques Cartier Bridge. The surrounding buildings liquefied in the storm. *Very nice, huh,* he thought, waiting at a red light. The Volvo stood askew across two lanes among the cars on Rue Notre-Dame. A screwdriver rolled around at François's feet in the back.

"Watch the road, there," François said in a curve, thrown sideways by the centrifugal force.

A few minutes earlier the driver had cut across the median strip. He'd wanted to follow a girl in a Volkswagen before heading to the South Shore. François hadn't quite recovered yet. He felt as if he were experiencing a never-ending accident. The driver had asked him thirty-five times if he'd seen the girl. "Look at that girl," he kept saying. François had seen nothing but black spots and, in the distance, surrounded by a soothing light, granddad Monti waiting for him alongside grandma Joséphine. But one good thing about his cabbie's disastrous driving was that he was less fixated on the meter.

On getting into the cab, he'd asked the driver to stop when it reached five thousand. He would get out then, wherever they happened to be.

I'm certain Patapon would be delighted to come get me if necessary, he thought.

I can tell him anything, the driver thought. *They've put me on a case with a zombie.*

"Oops, looks like I'm in the wrong place."

The taxi cut across all the lanes at once amid a jarring chorus of horns. François couldn't recall whether Cartier had made landfall aboard the *Émérillon* or the *Santa María,* but he did remember why it had been years since he'd climbed into a car. He'd talked to himself for five minutes while trying to buckle his seat belt. Except that it was already buckled. His corrupted hand was still in quarantine inside the brown paper bag. Some dipstick was yelling next to the window from inside its motorcycle helmet. The driver waved little bye-byes at it. He lit a ciggie and between puffs spoke a line from a western to the rear-view mirror. *We'll really put him to the test,* he thought as he studied his passenger.

"Hey, François?"

"Yes?"

"Nothing. I forgot what I wanted to say."

Seems to me I'd find it odd if someone knew my name without my telling him. The thunder was sounding bass notes over the bridge. The sky merged with the river, the two connected in every direction by long dotted lines of water. François, his eyes shut so tight they were edged with cracks, held on to the ceiling handle. He pictured soft things: kittens, bathrobes. *I can get him to say anything at all,* the driver thought. *This is going to be too easy.* They were fast approaching the Sorel / Québec exit. So pretty, all those lights.

"*Vade retro!*" the driver screamed at the rear-view mirror. He cut in front of six buses to not miss the ramp.

"I beg your pardon?" François asked with a start.

He'd opened his eyes again. The brown paper bag on his hand was crumpled. If it hadn't been squeezed between a hockey equipment bag and his hip, his briefcase would have slid across the seat.

"Nothing, nothing," the driver said. "Just checking something. And please don't tear that handle off."

He took an interminable drag on his cigarette. Still looking at himself in the mirror, he said something in English, flawless English, but with a different tone of voice. He'd let his jaw muscles go slack so that his chops swung from left to right. As far as François could tell, the guy was acting a film scene, as if about to fight in a duel.

"Have you seen that film? I nailed it, don't you think?"

They were on the highway now. The last echoing peals of thunder died away. Occasionally the two-way radio crackled with bits of information, the unenthusiastic relay of a code or dispatch. The driver showed no interest. He switched the radio off. François had spent the last little while facing the rear window, watching civilization recede as they barrelled toward the ends of the earth, straight for Leviathan's maw, which devoured cars straying too far from Montreal. Just thinking about the next lightning bolt filled his bodily cavities with an aftertaste of cinders. The oversized portrait of a girl advertising a telephone package deal or something swept past them on an Econoline.

"Whoa," the driver said, "I think I know her."

Lighting another cigarette, he heard François moaning in the back.

"What's up? Is she your girlfriend?"

The red numbers on the taximeter rolled on in their relentless inflationary march. *I don't see why we're going to all this trouble,* the driver thought. *I could've taken him to the overpass in La Frayère two days ago and told him to wait underneath while Danny roused his troops.* The engine roared under the square-shaped hood, soon to be radically dented. *Wrecking a car for nothing. Hmmm, I guess it's all part of the plan.*

"Do you have a girlfriend?" he asked François.

In the oncoming headlights the night exploded into polygonal suns. Looking again in the rear-view mirror, a small cardboard fir tree dangling below it, the driver noticed François was examining the taxi permit posted near the headrest.

"I'd just come back from vacation," he said.

He turned his eyes toward François with what he believed was the same expression as the Black man in the photo. He stretched toward the glove compartment but then changed his mind. *Too soon.* He cracked a few yoga jokes as he straightened up.

"Oh, I know what I wanted to say back there. Seems there's a curve in Sorel that sees a fatal crash every day on average."

"I know," François replied, wondering what was inside the glove compartment.

He says he knows, the driver thought. And, right then, he really had to keep from laughing. *A crash every day.* Yeah, a little over the top that was, but hey, the guy's a bore. *Maybe it's about time the city put up a sign.* The guy's an incredible bore. If the driver was going to spend ten hours in the car with him, he'd have to entertain himself. His foot grew heavier. For François, the highway wasn't an improvement. He had the dizzying impression of not moving while the scenery streamed past at rates that varied with the depth of field. The cardboard fir tree danced on its string.

"No," François said.

"No what?"

He'd sensed the driver was going to say something. He'd taken a chance and answered before it was said. The driver shrugged, curious to see what sort of hideous hand his passenger might be hiding in that brown paper bag. He took a drag like James Dean. The next like Humphrey Bogart.

"Are you a music fan?" he later asked, looking around for something.

"My father is."

François was having trouble digesting his dinner of fingernails chewed to the cuticles. The thirst had returned to play in his pharynx. The needles rising from it multiplied in time with the taximeter.

"Does he like Yukon too?"

"We receive a bottle at home each week."

Okay, that was dirty, the driver thought. *The guy's pitiful.* He was having a bit too much fun at his expense. After that, conversation gradually flowed more easily between them. François learned the driver had dual citizenship because part of his family was from the States, a country the cabby admired. The driver learned nothing new about François. He'd already been apprised of everything he needed to know. His fifty-something paunch rocked contentedly to the purr of the engine and the roll of the highway, like warm gelatine.

Near Drummondville, the chat again lost its to-and-fro. The driver was still looking around for something, in the door, on the dashboard, in the ashtray. But not in the glove compartment. *Now where did I put that iPod?* he thought. They were going down a long banana-shaped hill. François hadn't said a word since his authority as a history scholar, which he'd asserted to settle their dispute over the origin of poutine, had been rejected. The oncoming cars seemed to be travelling up the incline on a chairlift. To patch things up between them, the driver, smoking three cigarettes at once, did his neurotic Woody Allen–style New York Jew imitation. *Okay, we'll have to work on it some more,* he thought when he saw François's total lack of response. On the downhill side, he hunched over the wheel and was even more liberal with the gas.

"Thirsty?" he said.

"Very thirsty," François said with a grimace.

Then not another word. François said nothing despite the car's interior depressurizing in little spurts. Everything needed to get him talking later on, the driver told himself, was in the glove compartment. The Volvo sped down Highway 20 for a while. François saw two screws by his feet, next to a Phillips screwdriver. The windshield wipers had better not come off. A cigarette drooped as it burned down between the driver's black-ringed fingers, his hand on the fake-fur cover of the steering wheel. His Gothic rings clashed with his sweatpants and the sweater bearing a wolf's face. *I guess I should let Gramps know we're on our way,* he thought. He switched the two-way radio back on. The airwaves immediately began to crackle.

"Toussaint?" said a woman who must have just inhaled helium from a tank. "Toussaint, are you there? It's Chantal, at the dispatch office."

Chantal at the central wanted to know where Toussaint was, because Tony had a flat tire, Marco had been mugged again in the north end of the island, and she sure wasn't going to be the one to pick up the Bolshie-sounding nutcase in the Atwater area who'd called for a cab seven times in the last twenty minutes.

"Chantal, you knockout," the driver began. "You'd never guess."

He turned toward François, who sat shrouded in second-hand smoke and his brown suit. "Take notes," he mouthed.

"Toussaint?" Chantal asked. "Toussaint, is that you?"

"Yes, yes, it's me, Chantal. It's Toussaint. Listen, I can't go pick up your Communist. I'm on my way to..."

François let himself drift in the rain while the driver led Chantal on. He had a waking nightmare in which the sky bristled with broken faucets he had to repair under his father's and Yannick's judgmental gazes. Through the window, the buildings along the highway rose and fell like pistons with every bump. Rousing himself, he ran his hand over the hockey bag taking up most of the seat. He wanted to see if something was moving inside, but it appeared to contain just sports gear. *I've shaken it off,* he thought. He again pictured his intangible beast. Then he withdrew his hand from the brown paper bag, which he kept open and within reach in case he felt nauseous. With the driver busy chatting up the dispatcher, François ventured to touch him with his sick hand, saying, "Tag." Cured, he opened his briefcase and pulled out a Canada exercise book.

"...Promise, you and me, Chantal, my love."

"You're not Toussaint," Chantal said.

François snapped the briefcase shut.

"I told you. Toussaint asked me to do him a favour for a couple of hours. So, I'll pick you up Monday, okay? Where do you live?"

When he saw the notebook and François nibbling on his pencil's eraser, the driver motioned to him to hurry up and write everything down.

"If Toussaint doesn't contact me in the next five minutes," Chantal said, "I'm calling the police. You got that?"

"Okay, see you Monday. I'll take you somewhere special, you'll see."

François wasn't paying much attention. He scribbled in his notebook, fairly certain a piece of his palate had come loose, that's how thirsty he was. There was also the question of the maximum amount the meter could display. The driver kept on with Chantal but in a more openly lewd vein, almost making love to the two-way radio before finally signing off.

"Attaboy," he said. "That Chantal, if I would have my druthers, I would—"

"If I *had*," François said.

Or maybe that piece of palate was the eraser. There was none left on the end of his pencil.

"Sorry," he added.

After a few kilometres, the driver turned on the two-way radio again and dialed in a frequency where the silence was distorted.

"Hello, is there anyone there?" he said into the microphone. "It's Rock."

"Rock," a disembodied voice repeated on the receiver.

Shades of Papa's red telephone, François thought with a shiver.

"Or Toussaint," the driver said, glancing at his passenger. "Toussaint, my surname. We're getting close to Quebec City."

The glow of the street lamps slid leaflike over the taxi's wet steel. François, abandoned by the muses, held his pencil aloft.

"An easy run," the driver continued. "We'll be on time. Danny's already there, with the brother."

The radio silence must have lasted a minute. *Hmm, the plan sure is complicated for nothing,* Rock thought.

"I'm waiting," the voice said.

François detected an American accent. Rock switched the radio off again.

"That was my grandfather," he said.

His stifled laughter turned into a grunt. The asphalt ahead of the car seemed to boil in the untiring rain.

"Mine is dead," François said.

"Oh, mine too," the driver said.

The water in their wake peeled off the wheels like shark fins. François saw nothing in the guy's machinations but his eight bits of intelligence and his emoticon appearance. Sitting up under his seat belt, he was about to cite a Transportation Department statistic, but the driver was quicker than him.

"I wanted to point out, about Chantal."

"Yes, yes."

"There's no magic involved."

"All right."

Rock slowed down. The water curled in lazier arcs alongside the car. The truck that had been behind them for a while gradually closed the gap.

"Magic, that's another matter. Seduction, at some point, you've either got it or you don't."

"You wouldn't have something to drink?" François asked.

The swath of mist on the window his head was leaning against expanded with every puff of breath.

"That's all I wanted to say," Rock concluded.

The truck caught up with them at the top of a gradient. An acidic light flooded the cab's interior and was instantly diffracted into fourteen thousand fragments as the trucker moved into the passing lane. His load of logs bounced furiously in the trailer. Rock gave the steering wheel an insane Hollywood-style twist and cut in front of the truck at the last moment before it passed them. His paunch swayed. The Volvo fishtailed. The car tacked on the groundswell that the truck, its horn blasting away, had churned up as it yielded in the nick of time. The windshield wipers sliced the wave into julienne strips. François's pharynx was now carpeted with needles right up to his back teeth. Something hard rolled around in the glove compartment. The lines on the road snaked along with the swerving car. *Pothole,* Rock thought as they approached a hollow in the pavement. Gravity gave way when they hit it. Weightlessness overtook the car's interior. Cardboard fir tree, briefcase, hockey bag, screws, screwdriver, Canada exercise book, leftover ethnic food and related menu, everything floated around.

A gunshot, wild geese taking off, and François came to. Rock was drumming on the steering wheel and dashboard. The lights of Quebec City receded behind them. François saw them madly whirling and flowing in the passenger-side mirror. The mirror hung at the end of the cable connecting it to the car. As François licked the condensation on the window, a licence plate slid out from under the seat and struck the sole of his shoe. He bent over to pick it up and handed it to Rock. On the plate were the words *Je me souviens.*

"Do you know," the driver began, "the one about the shit-house supervisor and the—"

"Yes," François answered.

He made a Jedi gesture in the rear-view mirror to discourage Rock from speaking to him. He wished to refocus on himself, on his energy centres. The Jedi move didn't work.

"And the one about the big-mouth frog that—"

"I've heard it," François whined. "I've heard them all."

12

BACK AT LAGANIÈRE'S UNCLE'S COTTAGE, THE SITUA-
tion was not getting any better. The stench of hairspray, Laganière, the Montreal dude, Marteau and his stew, Metallica—
everything had continued along the same lines for an hour
or two. The beer came home to roost, making the boys lump-
ier. While François rode down Highway 20, they punished
anyone who yawned. The stew quietly burned amid overall
indifference. The Montreal dude must have been on the verge
of finding himself unbearable too. *Someone get a lasso and tie
him up,* thought Steeve. *A fine case of hyperactivity,* thought
Laganière. *Kill 'Em All* started replaying for the umpteenth
time. Not as loud as before. The transistors must have melted. If Lorraine were there, things never would have gone this
far. And to think that Laganière had prepared a personalized
adventure. He was a prisoner of the backwoods in the middle
of the night. A doomsday downpour threatened to carry off
the cottage. He was kilometres away from so much as a cell
signal and had the tragicomic feeling of being a guinea pig in a
behavioural experiment. Yet he refused to indulge in self-pity;
instead, he picked up the wrappers, tortilla crumbs, dirty socks,
shreds of tobacco torn off cigarette ends, backgammon pieces,
tampons, empty cans—yes, tampons—empty bottles, soaking

towels, rabbit entrails, all the heterogeneous waste, whether organic or manufactured, adorning the premises.

"Are you ovulating, or what?" Marteau asked him.

"'Are you ovulating, or what?'" Laganière mimicked.

Marteau chatted as he sliced his larded beef on the stainless steel counter. From time to time he popped a raw cube down his throat. He had on Laganière's aunt's wedding gown. The outmoded symbol of a soporific union. The boys had found it in a closet, along with the rat poison.

"Jeez, Martin, that's not funny, eh, my aunt Sylvaine's gown."

Marteau was on cooking duty. That's why he was the bride. With his zits and his tattoos. That was the first rule they'd laid down in the cottage shortly after discovering the gown. Already flying high, Marteau stopped slicing the meat, and time stopped too. Then he wiped his hands on the muslin train and opened a lukewarm beer.

"It was her mother's wedding dress, and now you're ..."

Laganière was down on one knee.

"Anyone know what time it is?" the Montreal dude asked again.

To put this in context, if Laganière's uncle didn't see the time for even a moment, his head started spinning, he stopped having fun, the seconds he had left to live began to come out of his ears, and he invariably wiped his brow and made a note on his virtual assistant to schedule an appointment with his notary. To further complicate matters, the fellow was unable to wear a watch, he just couldn't, because the tick-tick-tick reverberated over his whole being. Hence the panoptical arrangement of fourteen dials and clocks throughout the cottage, including the pretty-hard-to-miss grandfather clock in the living room.

The Montreal dude constantly wanted to know what time it was. *Rock and Yannick's brother should arrive tomorrow morning,* he told himself as he harked back to the conversation he'd had with Dexter at the library via MSN. Just as Laganière was about to ask him if they should get out the clepsydra, Marteau tugged at a broiler pan in the cabinet over the oven, and the grater, the sieve, the pots and ramekins, and the entire paraphernalia crashed down around him. The food processor blade plunged into the hardwood floor like a *shuriken.*

"Hare Krishna," Marteau said.

What he meant was hallelujah. His face lit up. His scrofulous face. He must have been dreaming—this was too beautiful. Hidden right there behind the cookware. His taste buds leaned out toward the shelf like sunflowers toward the sun. Bottles of just about every sort of liquor and liqueur said hi to him in that cabinet. Liqueur and more. The wines tucked away there! Okay, Marteau was no sommelier. All the same, he knew more about wine than he did about lepidopterology.

"What have you just dug up for us there?" Steeve said.

He dropped his beer on the bedside sheepskin rug and teleported himself to the kitchen with a lollipop in his mouth.

The music stopped dead.

Holding their bottles, Steeve and Marteau looked at each other. They looked at Laganière. Laganière had just found the remote control in the drawer where you put everything you didn't know where to put. The hunting rifles were propped up against the woodbox. Steeve buried his agricultural laugh inside his overripe flesh. He put down his bottles and leaped away from the counter and from the rest of the alcohol, doing entrechats.

"Would you like a shot?" Marteau asked Laganière.

He had just uncorked a vintage bourbon bottled the year the bard's cousin Viviane was born. Steeve suddenly saw Laganière reaching for one of the guns. He picked up a twelve-gauge and pointed it in their direction.

"Maybe you ought to put that bottle back," Steeve said to Marteau.

The bride rubbed his bachelor palms together in anticipation of the liquor tasting he was about to dive into. Steeve smoothed out the back of Marteau's dress a bit. The barrel swayed a little as Laganière strained against the weight of the shotgun. Steeve's only hope was that he would dislocate his shoulder blade if he tried to shoot.

"Put the bottles back where they were," Laganière said to Marteau.

"Hey, don't be such a party pooper," Marteau answered, and set the bourbon down on the counter so he could take out the glasses.

"You want to see who does the pooping," Laganière replied, "just say 'I do.'"

The floor creaked under his feet.

"We invite you to come hunting with us," Steeve said, "and you, you..."

Now, *invite* was a big word. They'd shown up at the place at noon, not a soul in sight. Laganière was devoutly performing his professional duties. Being a librarian was his dream job. He was passionate about the history of La Frayère, and the library was the best place to delve into it. That's where the archives were, and he always needed to check on a few points in the stories old Marcel told him. He and the old man had developed their relationship on the basis of their shared interest in history. Anyway, Laganière had just finished sorting his books. He was clipping his fingernails to put off phoning Mrs Turcotte, because whenever you called Mrs Turcotte to tell her the books she'd reserved had arrived, she found a way of stretching the call out for twenty-five minutes to blather on about her rheumatism or her cat who'd puked on her magazines again. He was thinking about Lorraine and their night of adventure. She had never seen the cottage. *You're going to flip out,* he said to himself. He hadn't even let her know he was taking her there; it was a surprise. Lorraine was unaware that he had the keys or that his uncle had entrusted him with taking care of the property. All that was left for him to do after work was to pick her up at the Perraults' store after he'd gone home to feed the budgies.

He was stamping newspapers and munching on raw veggies when the Jeep zoomed into the library parking lot almost on two wheels and stopped next to his car. *Isn't that Yannick Bouge's Jeep?* Laganière wondered. Quite a coincidence; he'd just been thinking about Marcel. Marcel was a childhood friend of Henri, Yannick's father. He'd practically been brought up in the Bouge household. He was an eccentric who had known everyone and was considered an authority when it came to genealogy, the history of buildings, and the escapades of bygone days. Things most folks in La Frayère had forgotten but that had made the town what it was now. Occasionally Laganière would go see him to listen and chat.

As the Jeep's occupants closed the doors behind them, Laganière thought Yannick or his workers must be using their break time to come have a dump in a cultural setting. He removed his far-sighted glasses in favour of his near-sighted glasses. *Well, well.* A visitor from Montreal. Steeve Allard, last seen three hundred years ago. Another fellow with him, not very big. This other fellow tried to climb out through the sunroof, but someone must have grabbed him by the ankle, because he suddenly disappeared again. Laganière couldn't place him. Not a local boy. *A kobold,* he thought. *Or a hobbit.* In the end, the fellow got out through the passenger door like regular folks.

Come to think of it, Laganière had to go see Marcel again, and not just to pick up the program schedule. At some point they'd all be gone, the men and women born in the old Saint-Lancelot-de-la-Frayère days. While his visitors made their way up the wheelchair ramp, Laganière, holding his rubber stamp, licked a finger, the better to turn the page of *Le Vivier*. A pair of puffed-out torsos appeared in the doorway. Laganière's finger went dry.

"What's up."

"Bonjour."

Sucking on a mint intended to mask his hydroponic breath, Steeve walked in and rested his farmer-tanned forearms on the counter but then folded them back against his chest when he realized his old X-acto knife scars were plainly visible. The hobbit, meanwhile, scurried over to the public Pentium uttering exclamations meant for someone else and opened a chat session on MSN. They were both dressed in hunting gear and... Correction. Steeve was in hunting gear. The other fellow had one leg of his very low-slung camouflage pants stuffed inside his sock. *Hip-hop hobbit,* Laganière was thinking.

"Nadine's number, I guess you've got that in your files?" Steeve asked.

Nadine Chabot, his old high school girlfriend. She occasionally popped in to borrow VHS movies for her kids. She'd dropped by earlier that day for a renewal, on her way to a job interview. Back in the day, Steeve had been served with a court injunction to the effect that he had to stay away from her. There'd been incidents of harassment. He wasn't the only one of their generation who'd engaged in serious delinquency after Thierry Vignola's disappearance. Vignola had been that gang's main man. Steeve's family at least had had the good sense to relocate him.

"It's nice to see you, too," Laganière replied.

He quickly logged off the user database on his Commodore 64. The library's budget had allowed for just one Pentium. The hunters began to poke about in the aisles and stacks, giggling and talking to each other like we are right now. Laganière cleared his throat and rapped on the counter with his Bic. *Can you believe this!* He pointedly cast his eyes at the Silence sign. Steeve went to sneak around in section 121K. Philosophy. He picked out a seven-hundred-page hardcover tome before going to check out the crapper. Now it was the hobbit's turn to step up to the counter.

"You don't work Tuesdays?"

Wouldn't you know it. The hobbit had a Montreal accent so thick you could cut it with a knife. Shiny red eyes too, and not because he'd just been to the swimming pool.

"For your information, I *am* working. If you have any other pertinent questions, there's a booklet over there on the stand that you can—"

"A totally ivory-tower job, yessir."

There it is, Laganière thought. The sort of Montreal dude for whom work means standing around between two traffic cones in a safety vest pretending not to be paid for doing nothing until 5 p.m. Through the window, while they talked,

Laganière could see Martin "Marteau" Pelchat approaching, a cigarillo stuck between his teeth. He was a mechanic at the Pagé garage across the street; his boss had the responsibility of reintegrating him into society.

"Someone wrote 'Fight the cake' over the urinal," Steeve was thrilled to announce when he returned from the washroom.

"What time is it?"

The telephone rang. Laganière answered. Hell and damnation, it was Mrs Turcotte. It took him ten minutes to convince her she hadn't dialed the parish newsletter want ads but the Joséphine-Bujold-Bouge Municipal Library, where the books she had reserved happened to be waiting for her. Here, Laganière missed a golden opportunity to shut up, because gramma rambled on for another ten minutes trying to recall why she'd reserved those books, eventually drifting to the matter of her rhubarb preserves and... He hung up on her.

"No. That's going too far!"

Laganière rushed after Steeve, who was riding the returns cart, propelling it with one foot like a scooter, and guess what he saw next: the Montreal dude, lounging in the children's area all nicely decorated for Halloween. He was leafing through an edition of *Allô Police* on the education-coloured plastic side table. As Laganière wound up to sling a shoe at him from the far end of the room, the service bell at the counter went off. Marteau, already juiced in his oil-stained overalls, was pressing down on it. And smoking indoors.

Laganière would have none of it. He was going to swat the cigarillo out of his mouth and then jump on it with both feet. But it was three against one. Steeve and Marteau dragged him by a leg and an arm while the Montreal dude jabbed him in the ribs. He managed to reach the telephone all the same. He threatened to call the cops, but when he picked up the receiver, Mrs Turcotte was still on the line repeating, "Hello? Hello?" That's when he surrendered; for a second his lust for life gave way to spiritual exhaustion. When Steeve brought the philosophical tome crashing down on his pumpkin, Laganière didn't even have the reflex to dodge it. The scuffle petered out. Everyone kept their shirts on. They plopped Laganière down in his office chair with a damp compress on his forehead. The pumpkin, specs all askew, looked about three weeks past Halloween. Laganière saw little noumena fluttering on high.

"Yannick's going to have a kid," Marteau said.

Arms folded, chin tucked in, Steeve nodded yes for a long time. The telephone started ringing again.

"Yay for Yannick," Laganière said.

A Bradley baby, he was thinking, except that some truths are better kept to oneself. The telephone rang for the third time. Marteau lit a cigarillo using a lighter with a nude girl on it.

"We're going to celebrate in the woods," he added.

Laganière stared at each of them in turn. Yannick was leaning on his horn in the parking lot, and the telephone rang for the seventh time.

"Need some reading material?" Laganière said.

His ticker was pounding underneath his shirt. He realized he couldn't win. His shirt was ironed to perfection. His only defence mechanism was sarcasm. The phone rang. His shirt was ironed to the point of looking like plaster. He stretched his hand out toward Steeve as if to take his library card, knowing full well that Steeve had no intention of borrowing *Critique of Pure Reason* so he could knock himself out with it too.

"You're coming along—it's not negotiable."

Kantism wasn't happening in the town of La Frayère. Eleven rings. Twelve. Thir—

"I'm *working*," Laganière replied, while unabashedly throwing the Montreal dude the dirtiest look he could manage.

"Pure goldbricking."

The Montreal dude had a South Shore accent—Brossard, to be exact. The answering machine kicked in, and was Mrs Turcotte ever confused.

"And how about finding Nadine's number?" Steeve said, remembering.

It was an old-model voice mail machine, and you could hear Mrs Turcotte venting her rage, unaware that she was leaving a message. Laganière took a sip of herbal tea from his Thermos bottle and began to type on his keyboard as though they'd all moved on to something else. *I'm not going anywhere.* Actually, he was randomly forgiving fines throughout the library system, a step before sabotaging the whole thing. Letting the smoke stream out of his nostrils, Marteau laid a balaclava and a pair of handcuffs on the counter.

"Okay, where are we going?" Laganière asked as the Montreal dude ripped the wire out of the telephone outlet.

Library users' privacy comes first. As Steeve leaned over the counter to look at the screen, Laganière dragged the hard disk icon to the trash; the Commodore nearly imploded. He obediently let his three aggressors pull the hood over his head with the eyeholes in the back, slip on the handcuffs, and take him out to the rumbling, mud-caked Jeep. He didn't put up a fight but stayed stiff as a fence post in their arms. Futzed around inside the balaclava. Yannick opened the car door from the inside.

The Jeep was the opposite of a police cruiser; the doors opened only from the inside. The lads started to scuffle over who was going to sit in front. "You're it!" and "Eeny meeny miny moe" drowned each other out. Things were getting pretty rough for Laganière. The hood rustled in his ears. Behind the steering wheel, Yannick let fly a string of führer-like barks, and in the end it was Laganière himself who spent the ride in the passenger seat.

"Aren't you happy to come hunting with us?" Yannick asked him.

Kill 'Em All was already playing on the Jeep's sound system.

"Couldn't be happier."

"Cut the lousy attitude, I'm gonna be a dad!"

Break out the bubbly and the noisemakers. *Shit,* Laganière thought, *a pinata while we're at it.* His hood, or maybe his breath, stank. The three in the back were packed in like sardines. With their country-boy physiques, Steeve and Marteau were more comfortable than the Montreal dude, half-smothered between them. Over the chatter you could hear the rattle of the ammunition boxes. Old Marcel was the one who'd pointed out to Laganière that Yannick had mismatched eyes like Bradley the mailman. "Henri never saw the point of a paternity test," he'd said at the hotel, his Molson close at hand. Given Bradley's reputation back then, it was hard to believe Liette Bouge could have cuckolded Henri like that. The Jeep, full of jostling and rollicking, rolled on. Laganière wondered if his kidnappers weren't speaking the *langue d'oïl.*

From the occasional bits he could make sense of, he gathered that Yannick was telling them about a new hobby he'd recently taken up: provoking the pooch his folks had just adopted. Croquette they called him. The nuisance. A pesky yapper breed, a sort of Rottweiler mounted on a shrew's frame, which had revived the part of Liette that had died after the boys left home. During his long hauls, Henri would drive his truck with the mutt proudly perched on his knees. Even Laganière couldn't suppress a snort of laughter when Yannick swore Croquette was a direct descendant of Caillotte. He said that for the first three weeks of the romance between his parents and the dog, he was so disgusted to see them go into raptures over this useless clump of fur that he furtively cruised past their house in his Jeep every day, and whenever he noticed his folks were out—for a bridge party, to the pier, on one of his father's vague errands, whatever—he would slip inside, undetectably scoop a handful of candies out of the jar, and lure Croquette with a piece of *sucre à la crème,* his staple food. When the dog was close enough, he would grab him by the extra fold of skin on his neck and crucify him on the rug, pinning him on his back for twenty minutes. As of day two, Croquette glared at him, head tilted to one side, eyes bulging, a predator growling impotently, baring an inch and a half of pink-and-black gums. For three weeks, Yannick stole inside to torment the animal with increasing cruelty until the dog wanted to kill him; he hated him more than the mailman, more than the dogs on TV that set him stomping in front of the screen with howls of indignation. The problem was Croquette loved *sucre à la crème* more than he hated Yannick. Then, one fine day, the perfect chance came his way. Liette phoned Cynthia. She had prepared a pile of unneeded baby stuff, but she wanted them to come see if it was worth saving.

"Naw," Yannick said to Cynthia. "Don't bother with that, honeybun, I'll swing by my parents' place and collect it on my way back from work."

Cynthia was a good girl. She was capable, had a way with people. She could have done something with her life, at least gotten her CEGEP degree, if she hadn't ended up under Yannick's thumb. He was a lot older than her, jealous and possessive to boot. His running joke was that he'd won her at pool.

"Well, then, I guess I'll just stay home and do nothing," she said.

Yannick, hiding his excitement, had hardly alighted from his Jeep and gone up the walk to his parents' porch when the yip-yips in the living room suddenly stopped. Croquette dropped his silicone chicken fetish and scuttled between his master's legs, a tad more aggressive than usual, barking a bark akin to an auditory rash. Henri wondered what had gotten into his pet and scissored his legs around his chest, which was just as well because the dog was going for his tormentor's jugular. Yannick, always the actor, pretended to shit himself at the sight of those tiny teeth. He scattered a whole pile of leaves as he stepped back toward the wheelbarrow. He picked up a rake in case he had to defend himself. His father stood in the doorway with a look that said *you must be kidding*. Yannick looked back as if to say *nope*. Then Liette, forever lagging behind, rushed outside with eighteen bags of baby paraphernalia and a string of apologies even though she had no idea what was happening. She'd been upstairs just a moment earlier, folding laundry in François's room, which they'd turned into a nursery. She too was much younger than her husband. Tongues had wagged at the time. Over all the yammering, a very flustered Henri tried to get Croquette to shut up; the dog, spinning around like some infernal turbine, was about to spit blood from yapping so hard. Henri Bouge wasn't exactly a paragon of patience and, unable to assert his authority, he crossed the line beyond which it would take three days for him to cool down. His foot shot out on its own. He gave the mutt a kick worthy of a forty-five-yard field goal and propelled Croquette and his whining load of psychosis against the side of the garage. Liette screamed: "You, you old crust! If I ever see you strike that dog again, I'm stickin' you in the retirement home, you'll see that you're . . ." The fight was on. Gloating over the wantonness of his prank, Yannick simply climbed back into his car and told his mother to go back inside and put away the baby stuff. Before screeching away, he rolled down the window to let his parents know they needed to put that parasite to sleep if they wanted to see their grandson grow up. With their François already off the radar, that really hurt Liette.

The bullfrogs sprang out of the Jeep's way. They'd been driving on a dirt road for about ten kilometres when the rain started pouring down. As though a suspended lake had come loose.

"Hey, Yannick, is that the right time there, on the screen?"

Yannick ignored the Montreal dude, just as he'd ignored him earlier when he'd insisted they slow down beneath the overpass at the intersection with Rang Saint-Onge on the northern edge of the town. He'd wanted to take a good look at the structure, to see how much clearance there was. Now he was constantly checking his cell against the company's, which Yannick kept in his Jeep. The wheels toiled through the gushing water. The gear in the trunk—guns, pickaxes, construction helmets, everything—bumped together foolishly. They went down the Sainte-Cluque hill at a slight angle, skidding a little, Laganière could tell, despite not seeing anything inside his hood. The crate of twenty-four bottles chimed at his feet. Then the chiming stopped. His ears popped. The Sainte-Cluque hill was the only place in the area steep enough to make your eardrums applaud like that. *Oh, come on,* he thought. The Montreal dude was pestering Steeve and Marteau—and it seemed to bother the hell out of them—for the best shortcut to return on foot to the overpass now fading into the distance.

"It's a three-hour walk," Steeve said.

"Six hours in your case," Yannick said.

"Cut across the Canons' field and you're there," Marteau said.

The lads found that one pretty rich. Laganière crossed his legs, uncrossed them, crossed them again. His sciatic nerve had gone numb. Branches swished against the car like paintbrushes. *I think what I'm going to do, I . . .* The Jeep stopped and a commotion erupted. Yannick left his keys in the ignition. Laganière heard the bottles being popped open. He heard the *whoopees* and *wahoos* rippling out amid the pouring rain, the dripping birches, the hydrographic fractals.

"D'ya know where we are?" Yannick asked him over the deluge.

They'd pulled Laganière out of the car. Now he was curled up on the ground with a pointed rock for a pillow and a samara for a blanket.

"On a beach in Acapulco," he answered.

A laggard mosquito buzzed inside his balaclava.

"Gimme the alarm code," Yannick said.

His defeat a foregone conclusion, Laganière gave it to him, but paused for a century after each number. Seconds later, framed in the gaping cottage door, Steeve was bent in half, his face swollen and purple. He was paralyzed with laughter beside the kitchen table, which was laid with two cast iron beer mugs, a pewter candlestick, some very imaginative dice, several lead figurines, and a pile of Dungeons & Dragons books. Also a Pyrex bowl, for the nachos.

"What's this here, Laganière?" Steeve said.

"Are ya some sort of bard?" Marteau asked.

Laganière stood in the corner, all contrite.

"I prepared an adventure for Lorraine. Don't you touch that!"

At the far end of the table, the Montreal dude had picked up a character sheet inserted in the *Players' Handbook*. Marteau, out of habit, turned on the range hood to smoke. Not an industrial-grade hood, but pretty close.

"Who's this Gwinyedling...?"

The guys laughed. The Montreal dude held the character sheet under the light. Gwendolyn of Artemis, eleventh-level elf wizard.

"That's Lorraine's character, and don't touch it, otherwise—"

"And this, what's this?"

"A four-sided die, obviously."

The character sheet soared across the kitchen. It hadn't yet been sucked up by the range hood and already the Montreal dude had opened the bag of tortilla chips and was stuffing his face.

All this happened yesterday, so to speak.

At present, with Steeve and Marteau frozen in front of him, Laganière replayed the kidnapping in his head three or four times. Each time, he imagined in ever greater detail what he might have said, what he should have said, what might have happened if he hadn't given up karate after getting his yellow belt at the age of eight. His left hand tightened around the shotgun barrel. Steeve anxiously wagged his head a little to signal *no, no* when he saw the Montreal dude sneaking up behind the bard with his spray can.

"The fun's over, boys," said Laganière.

His right hand tightened around the trigger. Right then the patio door slid open, the sound of the downpour surging before it slid shut again.

"He's here!" the Montreal dude said, giving Laganière a shot of hairspray even as he lost interest in him.

Laganière swung around in a half Lutz, but the Montreal dude had already hidden somewhere out of reach. Laganière found himself face to face with Yannick. Holding a flashlight in his mouth, Yannick propped his Remington up in a corner along with his twig-camouflaged game bag. Steam rose from his shoulders. There were a couple of beers in the pockets of his soaking wet jacket, which he wore over a beige-and-brown plaid shirt. He lifted the twelve-gauge out of Laganière's hands. Laganière didn't resist.

"Well now, Yannick, I . . . Give me back my rifle, please. I'm in no mood for you to—"

"Mix me a light drink, boys," Yannick said. "Let's ease into it."

The music started up again. Steeve washed some snifters while Marteau became engrossed in the illuminations on a liquor label.

"Now, Yannick," Laganière said, "I'm going to ask you all to leave. My uncle will rip my head off if he finds so much as an eyelash in the sink."

Once he'd approached within a hair's breadth of Laganière's cap, Yannick let loose his stag bellow from hell. The entire cottage was engulfed behind his tonsils. Laganière backed into the plundered gun rack with a faint *ah*. The three other Cro-Magnon men were tearing their clothes off, laughing. *I just shot myself in the foot*, Laganière thought as he plunked himself down on the couch. The Montreal dude laughed louder and longer than everyone else.

"Laganière . . ." Steeve finally coughed out with an ugly sneer. "It's a good thing Lorraine got out your brown pants this morning."

Laganière didn't respond. His valves were knocking. With every car that drove by her window, Lorraine's features were probably swelling up a little more with exasperation and an urge to kill. Yannick, without removing his Docs, sat down next to the librarian. He momentarily closed his brown eye, his blue eye.

"Oof! Fried is what I am. If you see me running, you all better run too. It'll mean somethin' evil's running after me."

The Montreal dude, a case of twenty-four open beside him, pitched him a beer three feet too high. Yannick didn't even try to catch it, and it touched down in Aunt Sylvaine's cactus collection. He took off his Bouge & Fils cap, which was padded in the front and netted in the back. He put it back on sideways and, looking at Steeve, who was leafing through the *Monster Manual*, pointed at the Montreal dude with his chin.

"Is that stew ready yet?" Yannick asked.

He stood up. His combat pants had wetted the couch cushions.

"It's coming," Marteau, mixed up in his pots, giggled. "Didya bag us some ruffed louse?"

A pair of partridges, their tongues lolling out, appeared on the silver service platter. Marteau had meant to say *grouse*. He knocked back a swig of seventy-dollar bourbon. Got caught up in a very serious stare-down with the range hood. Actually, the air quality was deteriorating. The smell was a combination of gnu and something burning. Metallica played non-stop, bottles popped open one after another and, once empty, rolled onto the linoleum and the carpets. Outside, the nighttime clouds went from bad to worse and broke up beyond the branches. The Montreal dude, always holding a bigger glass than the others, had started boasting that in a few days he'd be richer than all of them put together and all their relatives too and everyone they knew, that he couldn't tell them why, and also that he'd have any woman he wanted. He kept on repeating to Laganière that, if he liked, he could pay for the damages. It would be a snap for him. Laganière didn't even bother to turn away anymore to avoid the spurts of hairspray.

"What time did Perrault say he'd show up?" Yannick asked Marteau.

He found things were getting sluggish. Marteau answered with a three-minute shrug. On hearing the name Perrault, Laganière had abruptly stopped humming "Tico, Tico."

"What?" he said. "Romain Perrault is not going to set foot here—forget it!"

Lorraine worked for his parents, but Laganière couldn't stand him. Not even weaned yet and already riding around in a nearly new Civic. There was no way Romain could pay for it by selling parsley and white sugar.

"You're going to pack your bags and your—"

"Christ, there it is! There it is!"

The weasel zigzagged its way through their legs and across the kitchen before disappearing. Bedlam ensued. Everyone went hunting for the animal. Steeve let out a scream fit to split open his skull.

"Behind the fridge!"

Laganière saw the whole thing coming before it came. A blast from the twelve-gauge hit the fridge just as Metallica's lead singer brayed, "Seek and destroy." The fridge shot back a volley of hard and soft debris. The Freon leaked out onto the woodwork. Laganière crawled behind the ottoman with a traumatized bleat. Steeve looked for Marteau amid the chaos. Marteau calmly continued to douse his increasingly experimental stew with alcohol. Yannick could hear nothing now but the ringing in his ears. Laganière searched desperately for the balaclava to hide his head in. Next to the woodbox, the Montreal dude's beautiful big baby eyes glowed triumphantly. The shotgun smoked in his hands. A spray of wires spluttered and sparked. The sparks swirled in the air. The rain had stopped. It was snowing. The snowflakes were about the size of chicks.

13

WHILE LAGANIÈRE TRIED TO REPAIR THE FRIDGE, François was cooling his forehead against the car window with his eyes on the hiccuping flow of the highway guardrail. The rain hadn't yet changed to snow in the part of Quebec the taxi was cutting through. He was afraid the smoke permeating the car's interior would seep into the knife wound left by Poupette. He would have liked to stuff Poupette in his suitcase. He couldn't make a fist anymore.

"Rock," the same mournful voice as before repeated on the two-way radio.

François pricked up his ears. The same Yankee accent. It gave him gooseflesh under his jacket, and not because the tweed was still damp. His father, when he and Yannick were kids, would refer to a red telephone if they disobeyed his many rules or did something that ended badly. It was in a way Henri's version of the bogeyman. Whenever he scolded them, he said the red telephone would ring. One day Yannick countered that he was going to answer the phone and tell the party at the other end to buzz off, and his father said he had done that himself once and it hadn't gone well. At night he would imitate the voice to frighten them or keep them in line, and now, François thought, he was hearing that very same voice.

"Yes," Rock answered as if on autopilot.

"I need a puppet name."

"It won't be long. Give me another couple of hours."

The driver put back the mic, his skin radioactive green in the glow of the dials. The amount showing on the meter kept climbing.

"I'm not the designated event organizer," Rock said.

Even though he'd gone into vacation mode after passing Lévis, he found it was a very long ride and it was getting him down. He watched François in the rear-view mirror. François was looking for the first aid kit so he could drink the peroxide. In spite of the plan playing out without him being apprised of all its particulars, Rock had an urge to pull over on the gravel shoulder, haul his passenger out by the collar, give him a couple of slaps on the mug, sit him back in his seat after loosening his tie, then drive on and let the good times roll.

"You've got family in Gaspésie?" he asked.

He cackled inwardly at this. François somewhat regained his composure. He cleared what was left of his throat.

"None whatsoever."

Why don't you ask him if the Bouges are cursed while you're at it? Rock thought.

"Friends?"

"On occasion."

Grandpa was right. We'll have to get him drunk to loosen his tongue. A detour on the highway took them to a road still under construction, a treacherous stretch of mud studded with rocks. The whole bucket of bolts rattled while Rock summarized a B-movie he'd seen recently with a plot quite similar to their unfolding situation. Sitting crosswise in the back seat,

François fluttered his eyelashes and fanned himself with an ethnic restaurant menu left lying around. He was in the desert, sand in every direction, camels, hookah vapours, arabesques. The car was skidding, but the driver still managed to splash a couple of hitchhikers on the brink of cannibalism as he drove by. The boy and girl receded into the distance, shaking their blunt, blurry fists. Rock was amused because they were hippies. Then, on that straight road with no junctions or level crossings or anything, up out of nowhere popped a traffic light.

"Mind if I have another smoke?" the driver asked François, coaxing one out of the pack into his upturned hand. "Want one?"

The light turned red and he stopped with lots of attitude. The glove compartment clicked open of its own accord. The magic potion fell out, chiming like a triangle, and the twenty-six-ounce bottle of Yukon rolled onto the passenger seat. Voices started jabbering in Arabic inside François's head.

"You know," he said uninhibitedly.

It's as simple as that, Rock thought. Unlike the way it had sounded on Rue Ontario, François's voice was gritty, riddled with holes. *Lost his tongue before, now he's going to spit it out.*

"My grandfather," François said, "played a major role in the history of that company. Yukon, that is."

"Mine too."

Oh, am I ever mean, Rock thought. To the east, the river gently widened into the macrocosm. It wasn't half-bad, that sci-fi movie he'd described earlier; it gave him some ideas. François couldn't see very much through the curtain of smoke except the hazy glimmer of the meter, but he must have hit the four-figure mark at, what, La Pocatière? *François de la Combe Pocatière,* he thought.

"Some name," he said.

"Hey, is my iPod back there?" Rock asked. "Underneath my hockey bag, maybe?"

The bottle barely fit in one of the cupholders on the console. Rock hadn't opened it. A premium edition, no less, aged in oak barrels. The light glanced off it as though it had been Photoshopped. The picture of perfection. François had no idea what an iPod was. His Adam's apple bobbed up and down involuntarily. He was thirsty.

"You may not believe this," he said, leaning forward between the two front seats, "but our family receives a bottle of that beverage once a week. One bottle a week since the brand was created."

"Since the days of Victor Bradley, if I'm not mistaken."

"Ah, you know Victor Bradley? He left us shortly after I was born. Lyme disease. Otherwise, he probably would still be among us."

"Have you seen *The Shining?*"

François gradually worked his way into the passenger seat, leaving his briefcase in the back beside the hockey bag. Although he was not naturally loquacious, except on the subject of his *research,* he knew that a bottle is something shared by "buddies." The driver spent a good quarter of an hour in the role of Jack Nicholson playing Jack Torrance. Some twenty minutes of conversation went by with François telling stories. The time when Mayor Fortin had carted Monti all over the town in a wheelbarrow. That other time, when the bishop, in his dazzling purple cassock, was in the church with Onésime Canon, who was having a fit and screaming for them to lock the doors so they could catch that bug.

"Sooo, you're some sort of genius, eh," Rock said at one point. "All you need is a three-cornered hat and a puffy shirt. Have you ever considered trading pelts in Old Quebec?"

They passed a town, no idea which, didn't see any signs. Rock offered François a cigarette, which François broke under the guise of a cough. The rain burst like pale buboes on the asphalt and everywhere they looked: on the misty quilts of the roofs, on the flooded patchwork of the fields stitched together with foaming fence posts. François spoke more to the bottle of Yukon than to its owner. *The guy's loosened up,* Rock thought. *And he's a trip and a half after all.* A few times, without overdoing it, he asked his passenger about his friends in Gaspésie. But François wasn't too far gone yet and expertly dodged the question. Rock lit another cig, took a drag, parked it in the ashtray.

"We're gonna nickname you the Marquis of Fidget," he said near Kamouraska.

He began to tell François about the time he unwittingly wound up at the Fêtes de la Nouvelle-France, with a conquest who turned out to be bipolar, and, boy, he couldn't get over how funny they dressed in Quebec City.

François recalled his mother's sartorial whims, and when the driver asked him if she was beautiful, François let him go on for a while. Rock jumped at the chance to instruct him in the art of the pickup. *What a Neanderthal!* thought François. When he finally partook of the liquor, it ran down his neck and inside his sleeves. Even so, he swallowed methodically. With each gulp the pointers on the dashboard dials spun around wildly. The blinking multicoloured lights were accompanied by electronic chirps. The driver told François to take notes as he presented him with a series of movie quotes, from

Jules et Jim to *Die Hard*—depending on the girl—that could serve as overtures. With the bottle between his legs and his head haunted by shows or commercials he'd seen long ago and would rather never have committed to memory, François managed to change the subject to hockey. It was all he watched on TV and there was hockey gear on the seat. They quickly realized their views on the makeup of the Canadiens' first line were irreconcilable. But what irked the driver most was François's use of the word *disc*.

"It's a puck, dammit, a *puck*."

Predictably, the objection prompted François to recount the Paspébiac Crolions' goal that Bradley the mailman had allowed against his grandfather, who had just about turned a somersault and stopped the most devastating slapshot in the history of Gaspésie with his teeth. He swore it had taken five burly men to get Monti to spit out the hockey puck. Four to hold each of his limbs and a fifth to drop his full weight, knees first, directly onto Monti's rib cage. Rock laughed and said no thanks, not on the job, each time François proffered the bottle.

"I gather you play hockey yourself," François said, turning toward the bag in the back.

"Nope, not at all."

Hockey puck was the compromise they'd arrived at. *Too bad, anyway, that what needs to happen has to happen,* Rock thought. Forgetting that he'd put his cigarette in the ashtray, he lit another one. François found he was a dead ringer for Mario Bros, minus the moustache. The humus along the salt marshes was being churned into relish by the colliding bulrush stalks. François showered his stomach with a long braid of shimmering liquor. He told about the time when two old geezers of La Frayère, Péo and Captain Labrie—as much of a captain as Captain Marvel—had gone to small claims court after Péo's dog Caillotte—a genuine genetic anomaly—had bitten Captain Labrie. They'd made peace long before they finally got a hearing, and in the end it was the two of them who put Judge Blais on trial. Péo was down on all fours mimicking his dog while the magistrate kept banging his little magistrate's gavel as Captain Labrie accused him in front of the whole town of poaching moose, collecting unpaid tickets, and tumbling so-and-so, such-and-such, and what's-her-name behind his lawfully wedded's back. Lost in his reminiscences, François had a thought for old Marcel and wondered if he still hosted that show on BSUC. Rock slapped his thigh.

"This story of yours, Marquis old friend," he managed to get out, "is it all true?"

It was a thorny question that made François knit his brow.

"All Gaspésiens are liars," he said.

"Everyone?"

"That's the Epimenides paradox. Since I'm a Gaspésien, the statement cancels itself out, because if I'm lying, I ... Oh, just forget it."

The highway ravelled out its rolls of asphalt in beams slashed constantly by the rain. The bottle of Yukon bore the words *The taste of gold*. François had confused himself with his paradox business, but his headache, at least, was gone. He drank some more. Rock lit his cigarettes on his still-burning stubs. He gave his passenger a detailed synopsis of a TV series he had in mind, not quite based on a paradox like that but the plot of which contained equally confusing distortions of reality. One of the episodes included a fishing scene, which made a dispute unavoidable. The driver had never once seen a flounder or for that matter eaten any fish apart from the frozen sticks he bought in bulk at the supermarket.

"No way," he said. "Flounders aren't that big, not even close."

François argued as a matter of form. It would have taken a syringe to get anything into Rock's head. What's more, the man had a problem with exaggeration. He was not going to like Gaspésie. Measurements are woolly down there.

"Listen, Mr . . . Mr who?"

"Dexter. But call me Rock."

"Dexter—what a coincidence. That's the name of one of Yukon's two originators, whose product I'm currently imbibing."

"You don't say."

"Listen, Mr Rock. We're not talking minnows here. Whether you believe me or not, I assure you that Marc Guité caught a flounder this big in the middle of the Baie des Chaleurs."

He did, admittedly, open his arms very wide.

"I'll stake my honour that it isn't so," Rock said. "We'll check on Yahoo if we get the chance to stop before your buddy drops out of the blue onto the car."

"Check where?"

"Yahoo."

"What's that? And which friend are you talking about?"

Rock was in stitches. To the point that François didn't know what to do with himself. So he began to laugh too, but it was a metallic, regulated laugh that seemed to come from behind his shoulder blades.

"What did I say? Let me point out as well that Marc Guité, my cousin Mireille's second husband, used an age-old technique to—"

Bucketfuls of storm crashed down on the windshield. The driver jabbed a noogie into his passenger's thigh.

"I need to catch my breath, Marquis old friend . . . You'd have me believe that you were an adjunct professor in I dunno which crazy college, lecturing like you did earlier on the screw-ups of Prohibition in Montreal's red-light district or the log drives in the eighteen hundreds, but you don't know what Yahoo is?"

François mumbled profanities as he massaged his charley horse. A patchy Velcro beard had silently sprouted up to his eyeballs. Electricity filled the air and permeated the sky, waiting for a channel of lightning.

"Well, I'll be damned," Rock said.

IV

CAME THE BEAST

14

AND TO THINK THAT NOT THREE SECONDS AGO, WHEN
he felt a slight dryness in his throat, Monti had had to control
himself so as not to throw his cards and tobacco pipe into
the air. He had to stop himself from lapping up a puddle of
rotgut on the table, where, flipped on its back and wiggling
its legs, a potato beetle lay drowning. *How long does it take,*
he thought, *to get used to not licking up someone else's mess
for a top-up?* He then ordered—with a smile because he was
enjoying himself—another pint of ale from the Pole, raising
his hand behind the pile of cash redolent of the lush life he'd
been amassing since the night before.

At poker.

All right, the pile of cash wasn't all that impressive either,
what with the tabs of cans and cork stoppers for chips. Still,
for a hobo from Saint-Lancelot-de-la-Frayère . . .

Monti made a toast to the other players, three Yankees.

"To your health!"

His cuckoo cowboys, he called them. They, meanwhile,
were almost down to their last pennies and nursing their
drinks more and more. What's worse, this Gaspésien with
ants in his pants had only learned the rules of poker the night
before. Now, with his moustache of suds and his jackalope

face, he'd well-nigh cleaned the Yankees out. Even harder to swallow was that, while he easily had the means to be generous, he wouldn't so much as buy a round for the table.

"Yeah, so, y'know," he said, and, it being his turn to shuffle for what would likely be the last hand, laid hold of the deck.

This is the story of Honoré Bouge, alias Monti, during a period riddled with blanks—later nicely filled in through the research of his grandson François Bouge—when, to make his fortune, he adventured to a place he believed was somewhere between Baffin Island and Alaska but found nothing save ordinary rocks and dried rabbit shit. Monti was convinced he'd arrived at the Klondike. With a margin of error of four thousand kilometres, give or take. He'd travelled for weeks. Only, after he left Quebec, he couldn't understand a word that was said to him. So when he got to the first camps someplace east of Timmins, about three hundred kilometres from Sudbury, he took a chance and *decided* that he'd arrived. In any case, it was just as well he stopped before the land dropped away. This, then, is the story of the most revealing, the most incomprehensible night of his gold rush, the story of the most decisive night of his life. From the way he would tell it later on, you knew his entire destiny depended on that round of poker. He never shared much else about his journey aside from that.

The game took place in a shack with a dented roof that a Pole had turned into a bar. The roof and four walls had been erected among a collection of huts where Monti sometimes went to eat, not realizing it was at the expense of the company that owned everything. He came there to socialize every two weeks or so, when he felt inclined to trek for a whole day from the spot in the middle of nowhere that he'd claimed for himself because of its

reasonable likeness to the description of the Yukon in his encyclopedia. He was unaware that these men had been hired by the
management of the Hollinger mine. "Who is this Noah fellow?"
he was always asking. He thought they were guys like him, come
to try their luck, but he found them foolish to be prospecting
so close to each other. Once the booze had broken down the
language barriers, he explained to his one-night friends that
he'd soon be pushing on to Dawson City. The lads cracked up.
Well, how about that? Monti wondered, and laughed along with
them. He set out again at dawn, crossed the Porcupine, and
secluded himself on the far side of a burned-out forest.

Thanks to the nearby prospectors' quarters, the Pole got rich
attending to their thirst after their day of pickaxing and panning.
He served them solvent that you had to be fairly alcoholic to
pay for. The night of the poker game, Monti showed up in the
grip of a prodigious thirst. Had the Pope arrived to bum a few
drops off him, Monti would have pulled his cassock up over
his head and shoved him down the hill. He latched on to the
three Americans and they quickly grasped that he understood
only every tenth word they said. One of them was a genuine
veteran of the 1897 gold rush called Dexter, who, after realizing
that the Frog believed this was the Yukon, derived a twisted
pleasure from getting Monti to spout nonsense. When Monti
used the back of a coupon to draw the bizarre tracks—belonging to no identifiable creature—that kept appearing around his
bivouac, the threesome, certain that a dick like this could easily
be relieved of his coin, hit on the idea of a poker game. It was
friendly at first, not very high stakes. The Yanks clinked their
glasses amid swarms of geometer moths. Despite their guffaws,
Monti had soon won enough to keep him in drinks. Always a

step ahead of everyone, he was well aware the others took him for a dunce. Which is why he didn't buy them a Scotch after he'd bluffed them with a non-existent flush. And so it went until he'd cleaned out all three of them. Not that he was very quick with numbers, but he had a great knack for making misleading faces.

"Come on, Henry, shuffle," one of the bad guys said.

Monti, dubbed Henry by the threesome so they wouldn't break their jaws on Honoré, shuffled the deck. Cut the deck. Arched the deck into an accordion by riffling the cards in his vault-shaped hands, which the others watched voraciously. At this point in the evening, the Americans asked for nothing better than to catch an ace up a sleeve, a trick behind the smoke. At times in such situations, fights broke out here among the not-so-sharp-shooters. Not often, but sometimes.

It was a tense moment. You should have seen their faces. Trouble was that Monti, too starry-eyed to sense the danger, would laugh whenever things got too serious. In short order, his companions asked him what he found so funny, while Monti, still shuffling the cards, tried not to piss his long johns. His bladder felt like a water balloon perched on the pine stump he was sitting on. The atmosphere was not one where you stood up when you felt like it and went out to relieve yourself with your eyes scanning the constellations. You held it in. You had to *play*. Monti cut the deck one last time and tapped his pipe on a leather patch that he'd sewn on his pants.

"Don't look at your cards right away, Tomato," he said as he dealt the first card to an Anglo version of Louis Cyr.

The card slid across the table and stopped deader than dead when a paddle of a paw slammed down on it.

"You," grumbled the aforesaid Tomato.

This was followed by a string of threats, in English, during which the heavyweight stood such that his torso overshadowed Monti completely. From behind his stills, the Pole watched the goings-on, his source of entertainment. People called him the Pole, but no one knew if he actually came from Poland. He ate starchy foods and used an extraterrestrial language to communicate.

"Try and call me Tomato again," the big boy growled, gathering up his tiny cards as he eyeballed Monti, who may have appeared puny in comparison but had his toes curled up inside his woollen socks to keep himself from exploding with laughter.

The big boy was none other than Donald W. Bead, raised on a farm somewhere near Warren in Washington County, Vermont. The Tomato moniker had something to do with his blood circulation, and he didn't like it. Before coming here, Donald had been the champion of a clandestine boxing circuit on which bruisers like him slugged it out in barns for the amusement of the betters. Let's just say it was better to have him on your side. French Canadians often crossed to Vermont from Quebec, so he'd heard enough of their patter to get the drift of Monti's Frenglish and his jibes. When he sat down again, he sent a chug of beer arcing into the back of his throat. Wiping his lips on the back of his sleeve, he peered at the dregs in the feverish rays of a lamp engulfed in that vast territory. There were particles swirling at the bottom of his glass. He gave his brother sitting beside him a knowing look, gauging his reaction.

"Don't take offence, there, my potted herb," Monti said by way of apology.

That was another thing he'd learned from an encyclopedia: a tomato is a herbaceous plant. He was now so crapulous that he had to hold on to the edge of the table to keep his body from flying away with the cards he continued to deal out. The table amounted to a softwood log sawn in half lengthwise that the Pole had joined with no frills or fuss. He'd even left the bark on. A few shaggy branches protruded here and there. For a week after a night at the table, you'd still find resin and needles in your clothes. But it was good wood, including the legs, and another card soared across it to the next player.

A milky hand slipped out of a shirt sleeve adorned with a cufflink. A pickpocket's hand, it scuttled spider-like over the table toward the card. The card rose up on nimble fingers. At the other end of the arm was Charles K. Bead, the eldest Bead brother. Donald was the baby. Looking very New England, dressed to the nines in this miners' shack in Timmins, Ontario, Charles appeared more gentleman farmer than his kid brother. But his elegance wasn't to be trusted either. There were other areas where he was lacking in grace. For Charles Bead was a highwayman, wanted in a dozen states and proud of it. Proud, too, of the bullet-punctured marshal's badge he sported on his jacket. Hence compelled to come to Canada with his brother. He was here to be forgotten. Specializing in debauchery, he planned in the meantime to garner the capital needed to open a distillery. He'd already discussed it with Donald, and Donald had mentioned it to William. Fully attuned to the game, he ran his thumb and ring finger over the strings of his bolo tie. The glass he lifted to his stern lips was no bigger than a thimble and contained a nectar of nitroglycerin.

"No cheating," he said in English, and then withdrew far behind his cigarette holder.

Monti never doubted for a moment that his partners would

gladly have hanged him right next to the shack. By now he was worth less in their eyes than a thieving rogue. They'd have strung him up with his own ceinture fléchée, provided he had one. His tongue was already swollen, due to the alcohol. And his rough-hewn jaw. *Happy days are here again,* he thought, because, in his experience, people didn't kill each other. In Saint-Lancelot-de-la-Frayère, evil was when your sister was also your mother. The last card to be dealt was snagged on the fly by two fingers belonging to the fourth player.

This was William Dexter, from the western US. He squinted against the smoke of an unsmokable cigarette stuck in the thirty-two-canine-filled, off-centre hole between his cheeks. Another miscreant, he too would be short on credibility when he finally came before Saint Peter. *Keep an eye on this one,* Monti told himself, having got wind like everyone else of his reputation. Some raconteurs in the camp had dubbed Dexter "the Warlock." Monti wasn't sure he'd quite understood. But a few weeks earlier, on another binge night, when he'd ended up in the river with a few other guys, shooting at empties lined up on the rocks, a veteran of the gold-prospecting circuit—he hailed from Saskatchewan—also a Klondike alumnus of 1897, told him a story. Monti had almost been his death that time, because whenever the Gaspésian shattered a bottle with an impeccable rifle shot, he would holler "Noah!" like a madman in the night. The Saskatchewanian, or whatever, described how a scoundrel named Mojo Bayou had been caught dipping into another man's vein at the Au Lapin River near Dawson City. Straight away a group of mounted vigilantes was formed to hunt him down, Dexter and the Saskatchewanian among them. They eventually cornered him. Bayou, sweating buckets, backed into the river up to his navel. He hid his nugget behind his back, whimpering at the sight of the riders on the shore drawing their guns. All eyes were on him. Dexter's gaze was the fiercest of all. Then—and this is the part Monti found hard to fathom—Dexter began to chant something, and Mojo Bayou's hand, the story went, *separated* from the wrist behind his back, no blood or anything, and sank into the churning river, the murmuring algae. Monti, well, he in turn had recounted the time he was chopping wood at Langis Allard's place and split a bat in half on a stump. After that, rumours about Dexter proliferated among the miners. The lads told other stories by firelight. Cartwheels breaking in the middle of an argument, hair puked up after the vomiter had pilfered the last piece of bread in the dining hall, the foreman's milk gone sour between two gulps after he'd chewed someone out. No one knew exactly where Dexter came from or where he was headed. No one knew why he never washed. He travelled with a French woman; she seemed to be his mistress and wasn't trusted any more than he was. Spoke to dead tree trunks. The two of them made deals with people who would come to their senses the next day when they realized there was nothing in it for them. The guy from Saskatchewan said Dexter hadn't aged a bit since the Klondike. Monti didn't understand. This was the Klondike right now, wasn't it? Then the Saskatchewanian added that Dexter's looks hadn't improved either.

"No cheating," Dexter said to Monti.

His grimy fingers drummed the air above the blond-wood grip of his revolver. No one dared look at their hand. The Yankees could still recoup their cash, but it was now or never. The Pole slapped himself, once, twice. He thought he'd seen a dark mass, a shadow, hovering over Donald. The players, too grim to wonder what ailed him, didn't turn around. It was Donald, first, who tilted his head back and lifted a corner of his cards.

"Go ahead, Tomato," Dexter said.

The stumps started flying in every direction, seams came apart—yikes!—bruises appeared, the shack reeled for a minute.

"No one calls me Tomato!" the giant bellowed.

He flattened the offender—it sounded like ground steak—and pinned him on his stump. Dishevelled, Dexter blew cigarette smoke in his face.

"Okay, *Donald.*"

The cards, the chips, nothing had moved. They were all breathing hoarsely but said nothing. The Pole served a round of sedatives, plus a shot of hooch for Donald.

Monti fanned his five cards out like a peacock's tail. His eyes, sly and steeped in piss, peered over the top. Then they opened wider than wide. He quickly put the cards back face down on the table. His eyes had spirals instead of pupils, and he rubbed them with his fists, wondering if he'd cheated involuntarily. *Now hold on, you.* However poor his knowledge of strategy, arithmetic, and the rules of the game was, he didn't need to be a genius to recognize that something marvellous had just occurred. With his mask crumbling and half his body spilling out through his gills, he snapped up his cards again and, yup. *If that don't beat all.* Clubs. Ten, jack, queen, king, ace. Royal flush. Right off the bat.

"I uh, uh, b-buh ..." he stammered, struggling to regain his command of French despite having spent much of his voyage studying dictionaries and grammars and such. *And, while we're on the subject, how come the word* français *has an* s *even in the singular? I mean,* françai, *you know, like* rivière *or* village, *right?*

By now, the first prospectors who'd struck gold in this area must already have returned home, Monti figured, with bagfuls of nuggets, unprocessed, as misshapen as newborns. The warm months were on their way. The news would spread. They'd surely come flocking to this area. From all over the continent. There'd be no end of traffic on the river. The din of it would ring throughout the Chilkoot Pass, which had disappointed him. Monti felt the encyclopedists had overstated the difficulty, but he, of course, had taken the most negotiable slopes on that route of renown. The camp would expand. As would the economy. Monti recalled how, never looking back, he'd crossed the Matapédia valley, the whole country, to get here. He hadn't found his vein, but today, with this prodigious hand, he'd struck it rich. This here was the future served up whole. No more piggy-bank finances. He smelled the musky scent of the ambiguous beast close by. He sensed the gold throbbing under his soles, under the earth's crust. Gold unfolding spasmodically, stretching like marshmallow into the hairline cracks in the rock and flowing in every direction like quivering capillaries of light. Time to haul ass. Prospect his share. With tonight's winnings, jeez, he'd have the means to get better organized. Maybe even hire men. It's in the bag. He would mine enough to fill the cellar of his house, whose construction, for the benefit of Joséphine and their children, he was already detailing in his daydream.

He came back to earth, landing on his stump, all awry in his clothes. A drop of piss seeped into his pants. Technically, he couldn't lose. With the cards he was holding, Monti could not lose. It was in the bag, but he still wanted to teach these three utter morons, these representatives of the master race, that they'd once too often made a sub-citizen of Lower Canada feel that his natural posture was with his arm elbow-deep up a cow's arse. *I'm not Dr Maturin, after all.*

Too carried away to realize there hadn't been a peep out of anyone, he cut the Yankees a mean glance. The place was dead calm. But the ambient taciturnity wasn't to be trusted. In reality, the boys were spilling out of their drawers. Okay, that's an image meaning the moon was oblong. Which is another image meaning things were tense, the boys were tense. Motionless behind their cards, their minds light years away. Monti had gotten a grip again. *I'm drunk as a skunk,* he said to himself. He was no more loquacious than the others, but even so, the last time he'd had this much fun was back home in the Canons' mud pen, at the greased pig contest.

No one had anything left to bet. The cash flows had all drained into the pot that Monti had wangled. Still, given his good mood, our Gaspésien was open to discussion. Donald chugged the rest of his beer. Tossed the mug. The Pole ordinarily would have said, "Hey." But the Pole had vanished. Donald Bead, not changing his cards either, declared in that muted voice of his—he surely had mooring ropes for vocal chords—that he bet a herd of . . . Monti didn't quite know what. He hadn't had enough time to turn the dial to "English." Probably sheep, cattle, French Canadians. Donald, in sum, was staking agricultural property. The shack's counter, the stills—it all disappeared. Part of the floor, too.

Monti shivered with excitement, already picturing himself as a cowboy. With an artistic flourish, Charles Bead whipped out a beautiful, dazzling flask. It contained a velvety liquor that he'd distilled himself in advance of commercial production.

"Yukon would be a good name for it," Dexter suggested.

This fuelled the conversation for a while. There were no barrels, no other tables left in the shack. Everything was disappearing. The refreshments were all gone. Charles, too, kept the cards he'd been dealt, hiding them from view. As Monti reached for the flask, knocking over the empty glasses, the bandit brought out various documents, a patent, a pen, an inkwell. In short, the winner of the jackpot would never again be thirsty.

With his face muscles abnormally defined, as if he'd just been gelded, Dexter, for his part, kept them waiting. It's true he was just about cleaned out. He didn't cave in, didn't change his hand, and presently fished out of his gear the deed to a concession that a Canadian government official had casually signed over to him fifteen years earlier at the Klondike. *Looky looky,* Monti thought. Dexter spread it out on the table. He spent a long time smoothing out the creases. There was nothing left in the shack except the table, the seats, the cards, and the pot. Dexter pulled out a wee yellow pencil. Monti nearly shouted, "Watch out," not so much because the point was sharp enough for a game of darts as on account of an unpleasant memory. In order not to die altogether wiped out, Dexter, pressing down hard, drew on the deed a map of the lot that went with it, indicating the areas where he hadn't panned much before his departure. The wee pencil's lead was left thoroughly blunted.

Monti told himself he could maybe relocate to that lot in the next few days.

Then Dexter unholstered his revolver, whose massive weight was enough to skew his hips. The barrel took eight minutes to fully emerge from the leather. *With a piece of machinery like that,* thought Monti, *you don't need magic tricks*. When Dexter laid the weapon on the table, they each felt the clonk resounding in their teeth.

"All here have wagered plenty," he said. "But should a dispute arise, heed the Lord's warning, the verdict shall be rendered by this here gun."

"Sold," said the poker game.

North of a certain latitude, where the cute red-hatted centaurs known as Mounties grew scarce, the laws had to be entirely overhauled.

"May I?" said Monti, one hand on the sorcerer's thigh, the other stretched out to stroke the revolver's grip.

Dexter cleared his throat. He pulled his thigh away, somewhat embarrassed by his bad timing. He'd neglected to wait for Monti to make his move before issuing his decree. Once again, Monti hadn't grasped the gist of what had been said. But a shooter of that calibre lying out in the open, more hair-trigger than Jesse James inside a bank—that was a universal language. Monti toyed with the chips, a half smile on his face. The six eyes around the table followed the to-and-fro of his fingers.

"Well, then, I'm folding," he said as they lifted their butts off the stumps, dazed and red-faced.

The four of them finally dropped back down on their seats, red-faced and dizzy. Around them, all was dark, vanished into the void. Donald was going to explode if he didn't stop drawing in air without exhaling.

"On second thought!" Monti bellowed.

He was going to play. But on *one* condition.

"How's that?" said Donald.

"Which one?" said Charles.

He was adding *his* proviso. Even without a six-shooter to ratify it.

"Otherwise what?" said Dexter.

"Otherwise, g'bye," said Monti.

More howls and squawks and fists on the table. Monti, arms folded, decided he had no wish to watch them sulk and got up to leave.

"Sit down, Henry, sit down," Charles said, pulling him back down by the lapel of his frock coat, which he dusted off with the politest little taps.

Bending over, Monti let out a furtive fart. A sizzler. And seeing the Yanks turn green like that without venturing a complaint, not even the slightest phew, delighted him no end. He was still a child at heart.

"Me, no less than you fellahs," he said with a show of bluster, "I could've lost my shirt. More than once. I been milking yous since last night. And there may've been a double or nothin' in there besides, I can't recall. Sooo, y' vote for my motion, or else . . . or else . . . There ain't no or else. Y' vote for my motion, period. What I require, my little cowboy clowns, is your unanimous consent to cancel the *equality principle,* so to speak. Which is to say. If ever our hands was to come out equal right here tonight in this jurisprudence, well sir, by virtue of the herein aforesaid stipulation, the winner is me, y' got that?"

Technically, there was no way for him to lose. Royal straight flush, you can't lose. Unanimous, stipulation, jurisprudence. Monti sure had read the dictionary. His clause—that was just to piss off the Yankees. However, his tirade did lose some of its punch when he had to repeat the whole thing in his non-English English. Cocky as he was, he could have earned a bullet between the eyes right quick. But, hey, *that's just how Gaspésiens are.*

They all agreed. Monti and the three Yanks, having no other choice, played that closing round.

The outcome may at first have looked pure, mathematically pure, but it was too much of a shock to be pretty. As soon as they showed their hands, the kitty was instantly bereft of any value. Well, not quite instantly. The players, each and every one, took a minute to register the combinational aberration that had just ripped the game from its moorings and axioms. A gaping hole had opened into which certain trivialities of life, like the pleasures of ownership, had been sucked. The four poker partners were now standing, discombobulated, in a reality with little still holding it together. *This isn't possible,* Monti thought.

Each of them had been dealt a royal straight flush.

Monti in clubs. Dexter in spades. Charles in diamonds. Donald in hearts. The chances were one in six-hundred-forty-nine-thousand-seven-hundred-and-forty-to-the-fourth-power.

Beat that.

The upshot has always remained moot. Yet one thing was sure: it was wrong to measure the phenomenal thirst that overwhelmed Monti against the yardstick of a gizzard that, like his, had spent the winter cloistered in the infinite forest. The equality principle being applicable, the first right he exercised in his new, more affluent life was to lovingly chug the virginal flask of potion he'd just purloined from Charles Bead. So succulent was the taste he told himself that never again would he crave another water, not even to gargle. Which is why he chucked the empty flask and flew at Charles to get more of his product. But the alcohol had seriously befuddled him, so the polychromatic streak trailing behind him as he leaped distracted him. Taking advantage of this, Dexter pushed Monti, who went glancing off the table and kinking all over. Limp as he was, he spun around and landed on his feet, as surprised by his caper as the others. He shook in his boots like a bowl of noodles. He wanted to open the door. Except there was no more door. No more shack either. The table levitated in the cosmos. The Yankees' brown faces hovered there as well, the word *revenge* branded on their brows. Right then, Monti's eyes joined together in the same socket and fixed themselves on the beast he was forever bothering everyone about, which had just materialized before him. The animal's morphology transformed beneath its rainbow fur. But the Yankees stayed blind to the apparition. Things were stalling, they thought. Monti pounced on the revolver still lying on the table with the kitty, the empty glasses, the upturned cards. The table began to dance again in the chaos. Everything floated up in a jumble: the stubs, the glasses, the empties, the cards, the bark, the cash, and Monti, aiming cock-eyed. He fired. The blast died away and everything settled back down. The smoke streamed over his fist. They all stood there stunned. Then the villains roused themselves. They let the full weight of their bodies drop onto his in a perfect rugby pileup. The northern wolves howled from peak to peak while the salvoes rippled over the huts and tents in a salute to the gunshot. The Yankees eventually managed to disentangle their arms and legs, got up, dusted themselves off, and put their hats back on, only to realize Monti was gone. He was chasing after his beast through the charred trees, with no intention anymore of harming it. The near-total amount of his winnings jingled inside his sweater, which he'd folded into a marsupial pouch.

V

BAD LUCK

15

ARE YOU GREENING, MARTEAU?

The sun wasn't yet about to rise over Laganière's uncle's cottage and already they'd lost Marteau. Sitting at the table with the others, he had the consistency of a hologram. Ever since his earlier Armageddon, he was in communion with plants, his complexion chlorophyll green. His friends looked for a way to prop him up and keep him upright, but they soon gave up. The guy was severely sloshed. Bottles of every size and colour were passed around, guzzled down, knocked over, sent rolling, righted again, staining the table littered with forty-six thousand shreds of cardboard and tobacco and scrapings amid the various parts of the infrared scope Yannick was installing on the barrel of his Remington. The cottage was full of jabber, mouths were loud, pasty, foul. Outside, in the cold, the eaves had grown crooked icicle teeth. The long, tired ash of a contraband cigarette lengthened Marteau's green lips. Steeve waved his hand in front of his face. Marteau mumbled algebra formulas into his beard of foam and slim dress.

"And to think that as a tyke he wanted to be an astronaut," Steeve said.

"He was such a dynamic young man," Yannick added.

Marteau's father proudly sported a Céline Dion T-shirt he'd bought at the Forum during her Incognito tour, but he remained a model citizen in town all the same. Without him there'd be no Operation Red Nose at holiday time or free breakfast milk in our schools. Kids with calcium deficiencies would snap like pretzels on the dodgeball field. It's depressing all the same, because when you keep the porch light on all night to make sure your Block Parent sign can be seen from the street, the last thing you deserve is to have Marteau sharing your DNA.

"Married the wrong person."

Marteau's tattoos showed through his dress, which was soaked with sundry liquids. The logo of the speed metal group that he'd tried to play bass in. His kanji. He couldn't recall what it meant anymore.

"Hey, someone, what time is it?"

I need to find an excuse to get them out of here, the Montreal dude was thinking. He hadn't quite managed to assert his leadership. *Worst-case scenario, I'll torch the place a few hours before Rock arrives.* The excess kilopascals of steam under the lid of the pot billowed toward the range hood like small thermal sheep. The stew gave off a complex aroma. Scraps of vegetables, scraps of the fridge, and glass rustled under the soles marking time beneath the table. The guys stood up, sat back down, changed places, and sedulously imbibed. Despite being told eight hundred times to let it simmer, the Montreal dude constantly got up to stir the stew in its broth of blood. *The sort of kitchen boy you send to run errands,* Yannick thought. The Montrealer objected that it was cooking into a solid block. It didn't matter, the others told him, we're not fussy.

"Want another smoke, darling?"

The wedding dress cascaded down to the foot of the chair, with Marteau on the verge of evaporating inside it. On his lips, the cigarette dangled precariously. The Montreal dude, his face three-quarters hidden behind his sheriff's glasses, finally stopped acting important with his cellphone. Everyone knew there was no signal at the cottage. He slipped a du Maurier into the bride's nostril as she swung a vaporous arm up to swat him away. To no avail. The boys were clumped together.

"Watch out, he's as mean as a crolion," Steeve whispered.

Vermouth, Yukon, beer, and tequila. It's called an Armageddon. That's what had put Marteau in that state. Oh, and milk. Floating in his glass was a miniature plastic sword thrust into nothing. Marteau had made a toast, all labials, and no one had caught to what. Then he'd drained his glass and they had lost him.

"What's a crolion?" the Montreal dude asked, perched on the edge of his chair.

Yannick saw, reflected in the sheriff's glasses, Laganière sitting catatonic on a footrest behind him. The can of hairspray stood guard on the counter in the shadow of a cake dome.

"Oh, that."

Marteau's cigarette ash crumbled in the draft from the fan. All the chairs around the table flew back or toppled over or both, and the guys stood at attention, backs flat against the walls. There was Marteau, knees bent, willowy in his gown, clutching the edge of the table, his every ligament stretched tight by dry heaves, belching from the depths of his spine. Nothing came up; he didn't puke. In short order everyone sat back down. They sat Marteau back down too, his arms crumpled together, one hand sticking out at the end of his limp wrist. Framed against the window, his mug was a pastiche of psychedelic posters from the sixties, with his lime-coloured complexion backgrounded by the confetti of snow.

"So, a crolion—animal, vegetable, or mineral?"

The Montreal dude wanted to feel included. Rock's instructions were more and more fuzzy, and he told himself he really ought to ease up on the booze.

"Dude," Yannick said, "stop moving around like a DJ, I'm trying to screw on my scope."

The motion sensor light in the Tempo shelter was triggered by some tiny creature's presence on the storm-pixelated grounds, and the ray falling through the window onto the floor outlined the trap door to a non-existent basement. Yannick gave Marteau the glass of Yukon that Steeve had just poured for him.

"I can't drink that," he said, setting up five shooters of different liquors instead.

Arrayed atop a cabinet were earthen jars full of macaroni, Mason jars filled with agates from the Magdalen Islands and periwinkle shells, decorative plates, a salamander-shaped guiro brought back from some banana republic. The Laganières didn't often go south. Ha! They must have amassed enough Aeroplan points to buy Air Canada outright. Marteau groaned. His head slowly tilted back. The gullets around the table swallowed intermittently in sloppy dissonance.

"Yo, what is a crolion?" the Montreal dude asked.

"Wasn't it Marcel who came up with that in your father's garage?" Steeve asked.

"Rings a bell," Yannick said.

"Ask the bard," Marteau mumbled almost inaudibly, and everyone applauded. They were proud of him.

The conversation went off on a tangent. The boys made fun of BSUC, of Marcel, who hadn't entirely left behind his hippie years and clung to the past with his show, the forgotten truths that he propounded on air, his progressive rock playlist—Gentle Giant, Magma, Procol Harum, Maneige—on vinyl or not at all.

"Forget Pink Floyd—too commercial for him."

"He'd come to the house when I was a kid," Yannick said, "to listen to his records with my old man."

Otherwise, Marcel didn't get out much anymore. He generally stayed holed up in his lair on Range No. 4, with his tie-dye headband and his Indian necklaces. Occasionally, though, he'd come in for a beer at the Guités' hotel, now owned by the Guérettes. Sometimes Laganière joined him and also ordered a beer, a root beer.

"Tell us what a crolion is, Laganière."

Still, old Marcel wasn't so after-effected as to believe he was immortal, and over the last few years, in preparation for his departure, he'd crammed a hefty chapter of La Frayère's collective memory into Laganière's noggin. That, and Alys Robi's complete discography, explained why it was so swollen—his noggin, that is. The boys made fun, but not without a degree of respect. It's intimidating to discuss local mythology in the company of someone like him.

"Ya, well, I guess the librarian has also morphed into a flower," Steeve said.

His back square to the footrest, Laganière peered at a newly formed crack in the stucco. Everything in him hardened even more whenever he heard someone say BSUC instead of CBSU.

"Nah, I don't think so," said Yannick.

The fact was, everything inside Laganière was dead. Which wasn't quite the case for Marteau, who was deeply interiorizing the most minute stimuli.

"Day after tomorrow, I'll buy you fifteen more of those fridges," the Montreal dude promised.

Steeve was already writing Laganière a cheque for the damages, which he'd torn out of his uncle's chequebook. *Fuck it, I'm thirsty,* the Montreal dude thought as he poured himself another Yukon. Wearing his sheriff's glasses, he felt invincible. He mentioned his deal with the distiller, but no one listened; they were talking about turning on the radio to laugh it up even more. But Yannick didn't want to cut short the endurance race the Metallica album had become. Then Steeve took the plunge:

"One time, a Mi'kmaq, an Acadian, and a Paspyjack were having a drink on the porch of the marina."

Laganière rapidly blinked his eyes.

"All right, what's he gonna dish up now?" Yannick said.

He set the nut on the scope and tightened it on the receiver of his rifle until his tendons turned white.

"What was that last one you said?" the Montreal dude asked.

"A Paspyjack, but that's not important for the story."

Yannick shouldered his Remington to test the red dot on the bowling trophies.

"The three guys," Steeve continued between two gulps, "are arguing about which is the most dangerous animal in Gaspésie. The Mi'kmaq claims it's the bear, because a bear, if you get close to its cubs, it becomes incensed, and you'd better not—"

"Tsk-tsk-tsk," went Laganière, at the same time realizing, to his horror, that he'd been tapping his foot to their music for a while.

"The Aca . . . The Acadian says nah. The most treacherous animal in these parts is the moose."

The moose head mounted on the wall remained stoic, but it sure was listening closely even so. Go ahead, Steeve old buddy:

"The Acadian tells about the time his Ski-Doo was butted by a set of antlers in the ZEC, the controlled zone near Podunk, when—"

"That's not how the story goes," Laganière cut in like a guillotine.

It cast a chill over the room.

"Look, Laganière," said Steeve. He was rattled and started fidgeting with a matchbox. "I'm the one telling this joke. If you know it too, good for you, you can just . . . you can just . . . Why dontcha . . ."

The Montreal dude didn't feel the chill. He was in a sweat. Fanning himself with a life insurance brochure he'd found lying around in a wicker basket, he didn't quite see what the matter was with Steeve, who was now on the verge of hyperventilating. The matchbox was getting a rough ride.

"Go on, Steeve," Yannick said.

Match, n.: A short, thin piece of wood, cardboard, etc. tipped with a composition that can be ignited by friction.

"So, the Paspyjack. The Paspyjack," Steeve resumed, with a fresh burst of Steeve. "The Paspyjack, he's categorical. He says: You're wide of the mark! The most intrepid, most repugnant, most fearsome creature on the whole Gaspé Peninsula, from Mitis county to l'Anse-aux-Gascons, before it merged with Port-Daniel, is the crolion."

Incensed, treacherous, intrepid—Steeve did have a vocabulary. You could tell there was some Monti in those chromosomes.

"The what?" the Montreal dude asked.

"The crolion," Steeve repeated, banging his fist on the table.

"Anyway," Laganière said.

It was enough for him to say the word for a generalized itch to go around the table. The Montreal dude consulted his watch. Felt nothing. Except that he had no watch, and it was the prospect of just such a case that had prompted Laganière's uncle to send for a life insurance brochure.

"So, a crolion—what's that?"

"You are seriously Montreal, you are," Yannick said.

At this, the guys cracked up. Because, for them, a Montrealer would always be a tourist with a spray-on tan who won't swim in anything that isn't chlorinated because he hallucinates jellyfish all over the place, a tourist in sandals, capri pants, a sweater knotted around his neck, who claims to have some bogus allergy when you serve him a fabulous crustacean fresh out of the water, still steaming in its shell, with its Martian antennae and that sort of gastric magma that you're supposed to nonchalantly spread on a soda biscuit and eat without flinching, if you have that kind of fortitude. But then there were also varieties like the Montreal dude.

"That's what the Acadian and the Mi'kmaq want to know too. A crolion—what's that? 'A crolion,' says the Paspyjack, 'it's got a *crocodile*'s head at one end and a *lion*'s at the other.' When he says this . . . the porch of the marina goes quiet. 'So if I've got this straight,' the Acadian finally says, 'a crolion doesn't have an asshole?'"

"You're not telling it right," Laganière said.

Here, without thinking, without malice, out of *pain,* really, in a contraction, a *spasm,* Steeve scraped a match across the matchbox's thin strip of sandpaper with his thumb and flicked it at the bard.

"To which the Paspyjack replies..."

The flaming match described its phosphorous arc, illuminating along the way the can of hairspray standing on the counter with its Inflammable symbol.

"...'And *that's* what makes it so mean.'"

Spontaneous combustion, Yannick thought, too far gone to link cause and effect, as the hair on the back of his neck flared up and he saw reflected in the Montreal dude's glasses, not Laganière, but a human torch, as he would later hyperbolize, a pyrotechnical puppet bounding toward the cactuses, contorted, arms stretched out in front, a Bengal light at every nerve end.

16

BEYOND THE CHAIN-LINK FENCES, THE RAIN PELTED
down on rows of rusted bundles of wire and forty-five-gallon
drums full of toxic materials. Guarded by a bulldozer bereft
of its animality, a company's detritus was strewn around the
Volvo as far as the forest.

"Which reminds me," the driver said to François, "you mentioned a while ago your friend in Gaspésie, Michel."

François combed his greasy hair to one side with his very
long, impossible pianist's fingers.

"Michel? I don't know any Michel. Perhaps you mean
Kevin?"

Even though François, like everyone else, had called him
Patapon all through his youth, Kevin was the only friend he
had in Gaspésie. *You didn't mention anyone to me, you damn
fool,* Rock thought. He waited for François to knock back a
few more slugs of Yukon.

"Yes, that's it," he said. "Kevin Radisson."

"Plourde," François replied. "Kevin Plourde."

Bingo, Rock thought. *It's in the bag.* François didn't mind
the storm anymore. He was in a video game. Lives unlimited.
He'd been rehydrating for several hours now, but the bottle
still seemed full. Yet the alcohol had ennobled his temples.

The bridge of his nose, more prominent than ever, lent him the profile of a centurion. His sideburns were more and more luxuriantly embossed. *He can hold his liquor,* the driver inwardly observed. The same thick radio silence began once again to spiral with the smoke inside the car when he turned on the two-way radio.

"Kevin Plourde," he said, without emotion or anything.

"I'm casting the spell," answered the red telephone voice. Rock instantly switched off the two-way.

The lightning thrust its trident into the river and the thunder rippled into the distance. The driver favoured François with his most winning smile. He wiggled fingers bedecked with cathedral-size rings like someone working a marionette. The Volvo was in a race with the thunder, which rolled over the landscape toward some primordial milestone. François lapped up his Yukon like a hummingbird. He talked about Patapon, his inseparable boyhood companion, as he put it. They'd lost sight of each other, but the last he'd heard, Patapon was ill, gravely ill. François had learned this when, in a moment of mutual discomfort, he'd bumped into his cousin Steeve—or his second cousin, he wasn't quite sure—in Montreal. Patapon apparently alternated between fits of insanity and periods of depression during which he pissed in bottles so he wouldn't have to get out of bed. François's erratic licks at the Yukon were a far cry from his earlier, frankly piggish, swigs.

"We were bosom friends," he said, wiping his mouth with his tie. "He was always inviting me to his house, where we devoted entire afternoons to inventing highly elaborate games, or we were happy just building secret hideaways on my parents' property. We were untouchable in those hideaways. His mother loved me like a son, and he in turn adopted my parents, whom he considered a second family, which he joined at the slightest opportunity so that our astounding adventures would not be interrupted."

"What a nice story," Rock said. "Did you get married in the end?"

"I'm eager to see him very soon. Would you happen to have a pencil? I seem to have misplaced mine."

With his Canada exercise book in his lap, François gave himself a pat-down and searched through all his pockets.

"Here," said Rock.

Out of force of habit, he handed François a cigarette.

"I really mustn't let this idea slip away," François said as he took it.

For a good thirty seconds he tried to write with the cigarette. Eventually, he realized his pencil was floating upright in the bottle of Yukon. Once he'd retrieved the instrument, the lead screeched on the notebook like fingernails on a blackboard. Amid the rain a hard mass struck the hood.

"A hailstone," François noted, having raised his head.

"It'll come down harder than that in a minute, I'll guarantee it," Rock said.

He hoped Danny was following instructions. *The fellow, after all, wasn't too hard to buy off.* Then he told himself it didn't matter whether or not Danny followed the instructions; either way, whatever was supposed to happen would happen. *William Dexter moves in mysterious ways.*

All at once the troposphere crumbled. Distracted by doomsday hailstones long ruminated at more nitrogenous heights, François, having committed his idea to paper, gave

Rock his pencil back. The driver put the pencil in the ashtray. Ping-Pong balls bounced on the roadway and car. A craving for microwaved popcorn, always on offer at his parents' house, welled up in François. Rock lifted his plumber's ass off his seat and leaned his face closer to the windshield so he could concentrate better.

"You were sitting on this," François said.

"Is that right?" the driver said. He took the iPod his passenger held out to him, its cord wrapped around it, and placed it in the cupholder.

Thrown off guard by the question, François peered at the driver, fearing this was an acid test. *Is that right?* he repeated to himself. The iPod's shiny cleanliness was inversely proportional to that of anything he'd ever owned.

"What is it?"

"An iPod."

François reasoned that it must be a new kind of remote control. He downed a more voluptuous mouthful to keep from wondering remote control of what. Every farmer in the vicinity must have been standing at the window in his nightcap alongside his large family while his wife prayed on her knees in a corner. Then the hail stopped. The bottle was a millimetre less full.

"You see, we say *baleine*," Rock said a little later with his Montreal accent (*ba'leyn*).

"That's what I said, *baleine*," François replied with his Gaspésien accent (*ba'len*).

It was already quite a bit colder downriver than in Montreal. The conversation between the driver and his passenger was now peppered with, respectively, talk-show radio opinions and facts worthy of quiz show champions. Cacouna, L'Isle-Verte, Saint-Éloi-Station. The signs shimmering in the storm had been washed of any trace of bird droppings. The two men talked taxes. Talked lockouts. Talked 9/11, and here François went seriously berserk. *You want a conspiracy, I'll show you a conspiracy,* the driver thought. He pulled a Stars and Stripes bandana out of nowhere and wrapped it around his skull. He called his second homeland "the Eagle" whenever he referred to it. Their discussion went from the Olympic Stadium to reasonable accommodation, inevitably circling back to Claude Julien's choices as head coach of the Montreal Canadiens, at which point Rock wore himself out trying to make François understand the impact of productions like *Slap Shot* and *Lance et compte* on his personal growth.

"Films, I've seen them all."

"Not my aunt Charline's colonoscopy," François said.

"You know what I mean."

Outside, the rain dragged on, took on a chrome sheen. The iPod monopolized François's vision. The white rectangle intrigued him, with its white wheel, its grey screen, its elegant empty spaces. He would have liked his life to be as seamless and smooth. Yet at the same time the total absence of buttons disturbed him. He continued to drink like a pro.

"Is she good-looking, your aunt Charline?" Rock asked.

He'd decided it was time to give François his second pickup lesson. He started in again about Chantal at the central. At the sight of François writing away, he raised his voice and paused more often to allow him to keep up.

"Because it's not just a matter of charm, you have to think on another level. On another level, Marquis, my boy. A meta-level.

Make a note. Write it down. I'm saying this for your sake. You can't show up as some average heterosexual guy. Picking up the Kleenexes lying around, burning incense, that's okay, but arrange the lighting just so, buddy, fine-tune your cocktails. Atmosphere needs to be managed, gauged, tamed—make it work for you. Forget your Saturday corn dogs, your two litres of soda pop, your chicken wings. Start with a salad, something fusion, throw in some mango, a couple of scallops, nice and lemony. Take any sort of salad dressing and pour it into a pretty bottle with a spout. Tell her it's a recipe you learned on a sailing trip. No feeling sorry, no second thoughts—stick to your game plan. Ta-da, a triple chocolate mousse for dessert, something light. You haven't eaten yet, you're just showing her. Or a fourteen-dollar macrobiotic fruit juice. Buy a few bottles and open every one so she thinks you drink it all the time. You untie your apron and tell her about your travels while you mix her a more adult drink without her even realizing. First thing you know, the girl says she isn't hungry and licks the celery salt on the rim of her Bloody Mary. Then you shift into high gear. You trot out a compliment. 'You sure look swell in that sweater,' you say, taking the glass out of her hand."

Change just a couple of words, François said to himself, and it was his father Henri talking about his company. But he was only half listening anyway. He wrote in his notebook with broad, off-centre gestures, scarcely paying attention to the blue lines. The weather wasn't improving; pretty soon, people would be going down the streets in canoes.

"Are you noting everything down?" Rock asked.

Don't mention your book to him, don't mention your book, François thought.

"No, I'm writing a book," he said.

"A *book?*" Rock replied with undisguised revulsion. "Why not a film script? Who reads books? Besides, what sort of book?"

"I'm writing a masterpiece."

"A masterpiece about what?"

"A masterpiece about my family."

Monti in hell signalled to the Pole to serve everyone another round. The woods streamed by the window like the scratched celluloid of an archive film.

"He doesn't know what Yahoo is," the driver repeated after the chit-chat petered out.

His cigarette bobbed between his lips. He placed the iPod on his thigh. The iPod was drowsing.

"What is that?" François couldn't help asking again.

"Say what?"

"That. What is it?"

François pointed at what he and only he would have called a digital Walkman.

"Oh, this," Rock said. "Well, you press down and the car blows up."

17

IN THE TOWN OF LA FRAYÈRE, ON THE NIGHT THE stars aligned above François's taxi and Laganière's uncle's cottage, beyond a flaking bronze statue of Mayor Fortin, with its verdigris, its scatological graffiti, and a finger that would have pointed commandingly toward the horizon had it not been snapped off by some joker one Saint-Jean-Baptiste evening, at the very end of the street where years ago Monti Bouge had had a house built that had always stayed in the family but wouldn't much longer, where the wood grew denser, wilder again, and full of wasps' nests, where the asphalt gave way to gravel, a pale-brown trailer with a dark-brown roof mouldered away. Bunches of unpaid bills and rubber cheques spilled from the mailbox like flowers from a flower box. At the far end of a corridor with faded, tacky, discount decorations, in an L-shaped room, the world's most depressing room, with a cheesy smell and posters of wrestlers in spandex underpants, on a sagging mattress sans box spring or headboard or anything, a fellow named Kevin Plourde, but called Patapon by everyone in La Frayère, languidly stretched himself awake. He put no premium on decor. A sombrero hanging on a derailed sliding closet door, ramen leftovers, a fake crystal dragon on a piece of Formica furniture, an ancient TV, the nurse-of-the-

month calendar from five years ago. An unobservable presence had just shaken Patapon, not too roughly, and he luxu-
riated there for ten minutes, a patch of drool on his naked
pillow, with the delicious feeling of being refreshed after a
night's sleep, a sleep populated by those pleasantly indigestible
dreams that occasionally make your day. *You have to wake up,
Kevin.* There was a voice in his dreams, the voice that had just
said that in another language, a mournful, falsely mellow voice.
It told him he had to get up, to get moving. All pain had
melted away. His problems were meaningless now, it wasn't
his fault anymore, he wasn't in control anymore, wasn't
responsible anymore for the shitty life he'd sunk into. Patapon
turned over to go back to sleep—what a sensation of well-
being—to enjoy his liberation for a little while longer. *Don't
go back to sleep!* the voice said more loudly. And as if tugged
by a thread, his arm jerked into the air. Followed by his other
arm. Then his leg, which flopped back onto the bed. All at
once, Patapon felt an uncharacteristic, incredible urge to
move. The mattress creaked as he propped himself up on his
elbows, a silly grin pasted on his face. He groped around on
the nightstand crammed with pill bottles for the clock that
as a rule he preferred not to see or hear. With the blind still
down in his bedroom, he thought it was afternoon, the time
he usually surfaced for his three hours per day of waking life.
A peek through the grimy slats of the blind confirmed what
the clock said: it was still nighttime. *Not even close to sunrise.*
He was overwhelmed with enthusiasm, given everything the
night had to offer. It had been a long time since Patapon—
henceforth to be referred to as Plourde, for the sake of dignity—since Plourde, then, had seen that hour of the day, owing

in part to the dull and deadening pills, which, in their labelled bottles, suddenly seemed to him like multicoloured, fun-shaped candies. Just handling them made Patapon, henceforth to be referred to as Plourde—for real this time—smile, kneeling in his bed now like a kid sleeping over at a friend's. His dream catcher, hanging on a single thumbtack behind him, was laden with feathers and magic. Patapon's—Plourde's!—mother was ultra-superstitious. She'd bought the dream catcher on a reserve, from the shaman, she said, to drive away the cunning spirits that dwelt in her son. It hadn't worked. Plourde slept so much in a week, the dream catcher must have been saturated. Actually, Plourde felt like calling his mother. Monique, her name was. He felt like calling her, while she was busy in the next room, to thank her, to say he appreciated her. Except that the voice told him not to call, they were going to surprise her. Kevin, an invisible hand clamped over his mouth, chuckled with pleasure at the thought. Even though he loathed whatever Dr Dugas prescribed to protect him from himself, right then there was something beguiling about his pills. *You don't need that,* whispered the voice, which tickled inside his head whenever it spoke. He wanted those pills, he wanted Dr Dugas to be proud of him, but just as he tipped a whole cocktail of them into his open hand, he was checked by a resistance come out of nowhere, as if, once again, someone had yanked a string attached to his arm. He was cured, anyway, and they looked so pretty, the pills he'd just spilled on the floor, that he opened all his bottles and emptied them in every direction. *Okay, that's enough,* the voice said. *Come on, let's go.* Kevin felt cured. It was over, the depression that had engulfed him since his late adolescence, an illness with more socio-cultural causes than the Tourism Department was willing to admit to. Kevin bounced from his mattress directly into his sneakers. Life was a breeze. He had the impression someone else had jumped for him. He turned on his TV. *Still diddling around? Come on, I said.* Plourde had never found the strength to reconnect the cable after his TV was moved a few years earlier. Captivated by the static, the snow, the fizz inside the box, he placed his hand on the screen. Then he rushed over to the mirror to look at himself. There'd been a transfiguration. Instead of the chubby fellow with hair on his shoulders, there was a healthy-looking hunk, a really cute guy with killer dance moves. For a while he had fun making his bed, getting a thrill out of seeing a corner of his fitted sheet slip off the mattress when he pulled on another corner. *This way, this way,* the voice said. Plourde felt as though someone had just slipped eight new batteries into a small compartment in the back of his neck. He was done lazing around, vegetating, acting like a jerk with his mother and everyone else. He wanted to go pick berries in the mountains, join an origami club, ride a unicycle on a wire. Anything to not have to gaze at his damned dropped ceiling, with its moth pupae and its greenish ring stains. *Step on it, Kevin!* the voice urged. He knew what time it was and that the rest of the planet might not be in sync with him yet, but it hardly mattered. He had to get going. He wasn't quite sure where, though, there were too many options all of a sudden and scraping the leftover glue from an old Sega sticker off his mirror became a high priority. But the invisible hand touched the small of his back, his hip, and turned him away; his preparations began in overdrive. His head was buzzing with plans. He'd register for adult education and finish high school in no time. After that he'd go to Henri Bouge's place nearby, with a spray of flowers for Liette, and beg him for a job. *Now, don't overdo it,* the voice said, and without understanding that presence, Plourde felt it coursing through his every fibre. Then he'd call Welfare, the Health and Safety Board, Gérald at the convenience store, and promise them he'd get a grip on his life again, that something inside him had already gotten a handle on him; he'd detail his plan to them and what they meant to him. He'd bring back hope to La Frayère, find Thierry Vignola, glue his pieces back together if necessary. The news that he was going to get a grip on his life again would be enough to make Dr Dugas take notice, Plourde being the dark trophy in the doctor's semi-glorious career, the same Plourde who had just interrupted his preparations to shadowbox a couple of tae kwon do moves while providing his own sound effects. *All right, feel better now? Hurry up.* Had Dr Dugas seen him this way, he would have sent Plourde for observation in a padded room, confined him, put him under sedation, with no laces or sharp objects. Because right then his serotonin levels were seriously out of whack. Patapon cartoonishly stepped out of his room, which he hadn't left in days. Okay, rewind: *Plourde* cartoonishly stepped out of his room, which he hadn't left in a while. He walked away from that sour space, which, despite a host of negative associations, now seemed safe and uterine, walked away with a blend of bliss and nostalgia. *You're going to a nicer place,* the voice said, very hoarsely, and, as it were, cleared its throat. Magnificent in his old no-name, no-laces sneakers, Plourde held in his arms a bulging duffle bag. The plan wasn't clear. He'd jammed the dream catcher in his bag but left the pills on the floor. He'd also combed his hair with a half-melted comb that he'd retrieved from the electric heater. For ten years he hadn't combed his hair, but now he'd combed it till it was block-shaped like a Playmobil figurine's. *You handsome devil.* He moved down the corridor. A newborn child. Everything fascinated him, and not because the trailer where he kept hibernating at his mother's expense was all that fascinating. The place had macramé lampshades. The electrical appliances sometimes shut off on their own because of the bats in the walls. Patapon skipped—and, for now, let's just drop the Plourde—till the end of the corridor, where, up to that night, he would walk to the crapper like someone going to the electric chair. That's why he'd taken to doing his business in a pot in a corner of his bedroom. Through the window, the Bouges' house, looking a bit smug on its hill, overlooked the bungalows that had proliferated right up to their property line. The thrum of the furnace resounded inside him. Patapon entered the bathroom and instantly froze in front of the cabinet. He leaned, enraptured, on the algae-ridden sink and was captivated by the faucet. It leaked a non-stop thread of chalky water, but he couldn't care less. He slowly lowered his hand toward a random toothbrush and the tube of Colgate. The toothpaste spurted out, a mother-of-pearl wonder, and spread unaided over his brush. *No cavities, beautiful teeth,* the voice said. Patapon had never experienced anything so powerful. He had to kneel down. He cooed as he brushed his teeth. In the next room, his mother pricked up her ears. She wondered what in hell she was hearing. She never heard a peep out of her son except when he belched or bawled her out, saying everything was her fault. She reached out a clammy hand to light her bedside lamp. A tad worried as to what her boy was up to, she made as if to go see. Patapon's one-night stepfather grumbled as he looked for his cigarettes.

"Shush, Ovila," she went. "Stop that. Listen, listen."

The stepfather was a dead ringer for Ovila Pronovost on TV, but a foot shorter. Monique had brought him home from the snack bar where she worked the last shift. *Am I nuts,* she thought, *or is Patapon banging around in the kitchen?* Even his mother called Kevin by his nickname, but, regardless, Kevin was indeed arranging the cans on the shelves, the notes on the message board, and the knick-knacks along more symmetrical lines. *The thing is, we're in a bit of a hurry,* the voice told him, climbing four octaves in the process. A craving for harmonious shapes, complete groups, immaculate surfaces. Kevin wore yellow dishwashing gloves. If his limbs hadn't nudged him in a different direction, he'd have gone back to the bathroom with his tool box to teach himself plumbing. Instead, he began to wrap the leftover hash and pineapple ham sitting on the stove in aluminum foil, and that is when he tumbled irremediably into joyfulness. The fridge light sweeping across the foil was like the inside of a photocopier. A rush of burning joy plowed through his abdomen. *Yippee!* the voice scoffed. An epiphany. To the point where Kevin, his duffle bag slung over his shoulder, grabbed the vacuum cleaner in the closet. *It may come in handy,* he thought on his own, but thinking on his own—he wasn't too thrilled about that.

18

LAGANIÈRE WAS GOING TO HAVE TO ACCEPT IT. HE was not soaking in amniotic fluid. First off, it smelled of low tide. Secondly, he had a faucet embedded in his neck. He wasn't in his mommy's belly, he was in a bathtub. "Don't use either the bath or the shower!" his uncle had told him somewhere in his endless list of proscriptions and threats. Dirty brown well-water was what he was soaking in, fully dressed and curled up like an ampersand. He couldn't quite recall his dream but, ouch! A swarm had replaced his head and it was chock full of pain. His eyeballs felt like wet sponges being squeezed very hard behind his eyelids, which were sealed, cemented, impossible to open. Yet there was no way to go back to sleep, to black out again, what with the phantasmagoric commotion in the kitchen rife with echolalia. It reverberated along the pipes to where he was. He lay wallowing in this putrid tepidness, a jungle of toucans and palm trees animated by the sway of the shower curtain, his mind running on empty, drifting for a long time until, for no particular reason, he hit on the thought that, to his shame, he'd never learned to use a jig saw.

Maybe his eyelids had just fallen off—he didn't know. At any rate, his eyes were open now. His pupils contracted. *No, no, it can't be true.* It was hanging from the ceiling. Upside down on the ceiling. Glossy and tense. Laganière wanted to shut his eyes, but his eyelids were gone. The weasel overhead studied him with the tiny pair of blood-red marbles that were its eyes. The walls closed in and retreated at the same time. In a panic, Laganière reacted unthinkingly. He *pulled back* his roasted leg, taut skin and all. Not to mention his pants, which had fused with his burn. The weasel made old phone-line modem noises as it analyzed his torment.

In spite of his adrenalin overdose, climbing out of the whirlpool bathtub was an agonizing ordeal. *Join up, they said.* He stayed on the floor, the stormy floor, until he knew he wasn't dead. The polystyrene ceiling tiles, pierced by twenty expert claws, began to groan. *Not dead, not dead,* Laganière thought. His feet were like flippers on the jazzy ceramic floor. He felt as though his head were inside a pot that someone was beating with a stick. The weasel is the smallest carnivore. The contents of the medicine cabinet—tubes, pill bottles, bandages, creams, syringes, Viagra, eternal youth potions—went flying. Laganière couldn't find the Aspirin and was going to rub himself down with Mercurochrome instead, erratically glancing over his shoulder. The weasel was approaching at sixteen images per second. The bathroom went around and around and around, and at the fourth go-round Laganière snatched a passing cyan kimono off its hook. Then he went out, slamming the door so hard you'd have thought he'd just shut in a velociraptor.

A slice of prosciutto came away from his burn when he undressed in the corridor. At least the wound was mostly confined to his leg, although there were more benign patches here and there, red blotches, loads of pinpricks. His contaminated clothes plopped down in a puddle of well-water bacteria. Laganière dragged himself toward the kitchen, one knee turned inward, his caramelized knee, which clung to his aunt's desperately sexy kimono. The floor rocked. Laganière's aunt used Bounce. The vestibules in his ears were on the spin cycle. Two feet stuck out horizontally at the end of the corridor. Three threads stuck out from the tips of the woollen socks. *You're a disgrace to the Roman army.* They were yakking it up in the kitchen. A lot of wah-wah in the voices. The corridor undulated like a snake. The shadows of the guys around the table appeared on the wallpaper, mafioso shadows, with long, sharp-edged chins. *What the hell is this?* Laganière had not just stepped on a wad of cretons, but at first glance ...

"Pull up a chair," said Perrault, recently arrived.

"Greetings, Romain," Laganière stammered. "Hello, gang."

The cigarettes were burning out of control. The table bristled with bottles: beer, bourbon, rum, and other, less common products. The guys were pretty glad to see him. Yannick and Steeve, and Perrault, who'd come to finalize a deal. Perrault, quite a bit younger than the others, had a Pierrot face and wolfhound hairs on his sweater. A twirling bowl full of stew with a fork thrust into it came to a stop in front of Laganière.

"Put some butter on that," Perrault said, pointing to the burn.

Laganière draped the panel of his kimono back over his leg. While Steeve gave him a massage in order to be forgiven, Yannick showed him his frizzy hair. The fireball had played havoc with his mullet.

"Eat, eat, eat," they chanted in unison.

Residue fluttered around a halogen bulb near the flattened

collection of cacti. Outside, an honest-to-goodness snowstorm was in the offing. Somebody had assembled a model with the lead Dungeons & Dragons figurines, all neatly arrayed in bold, disturbing poses. Laganière began to make cooking suggestions, in case Marteau someday made another stew.

"Hey, you, watch your manners."

"Don't talk with your mouth full."

As they looked on admiringly, he chewed and chewed his forkful of lipids with tears in his eyes.

"Anyway, I'm sorry," Steeve said. "I didn't wanna burn you, I wanted... I don't know what I wanted."

"What happened to Martin?" Laganière asked.

His food rolled around in his mouth. Marteau lay snoring on the floor among the empties with his feet in the corridor. The strap of his wedding gown hung sensually on the shoulder marred by his kanji. The kanji signified "samurai."

"He threw up," Perrault said.

Ah. So that explained the cretons in the corridor. And over there between the chairs, and there, in the living room, on the table amid the bottles, everywhere. It also explained the new layer of smell.

"Whatshisname from Montreal made him smoke about thirty cigarettes at once," Yannick said.

Hence the plate full of butts among the hardened remnants of stew. Yannick pointed his Remington toward the Montreal dude deep in REM sleep on the massage chair vibrating at maximum speed.

"Pretty classy," Steeve said.

"Marteau choked so hard it brought him back to us. He didn't do much talking, eh, but he hung out with us awhile."

Yannick pinched the bridge of his nose. Steeve rubbed his temples. Laganière was glad not to be the only one with a headache. The wind outside engulfed the cottage, and if not for the accumulated snow pinning it down on all sides, the building would probably have left the ground.

"And after that?" he asked as he wiped his plastic smile with a paper towel so he could spit out his morsel of stew undetected.

"He got thirsty again."

Laganière took a silent oath to go vegan, effective immediately.

"He mixed himself another Armageddon."

"Freehand. He kept adding ingredients and kicking out to keep us back. "

"First thing we knew, he was puking his guts out in the sink."

"You missed it."

"Us guys, we laughed."

"And that hurt his feelings."

"He called us Hippocratic."

"Go figure."

Ten to one Marteau meant *hypocrites*.

"He grabbed a big handful of biodiversity in the sink."

"His vomit."

"Pitched it at us. It hit the fan."

"It was all over the place."

"It's still all over the place."

"What about him?" Laganière asked.

They all recoiled when he pointed his fork toward the Montreal dude blurred by the vibrations. The sight left an afterimage on your retina.

"Oh, him."

"He's just fine where he is."

"To Laganière!" Yannick blurted.

He raised his glass. The liquor surged out of it like the tentacle of a lurking monster.

"Cheers!"

"Yes! To Laganière!"

Laganière—it drove him up a wall. There must have been three hundred and eighteen Laganières in the Bas-Saint-Laurent–Gaspésie phone book alone. His name was Joël.

"Wait, wait, our bard's got nothing to drink."

"Our bard" drove him up a wall even more.

"What's your pleasure?"

The bottle of vintage bourbon couldn't be found anywhere. So Steeve went for the whisky. Not a drop left. He went for the vodka. Not a drop of that left either. Or rum, or crème de menthe, or almost anything. Laganière wanted a glass of water and a couple of Aspirins. He stretched out his hand toward the pill bottle in front of Romain—the label had been torn off—but Steeve pushed it beyond his reach.

"Believe me, you don't want these pills."

The guys snickered, and Perrault insisted they give him some too. Laganière, whose perceptive powers had been, let's say, misplaced, thought he'd heard the word *Alcide*. He didn't understand. A neighbour named Alcide lived about twenty kilometres north of his place. A lone bottle shone brightly among its tired and flaccid peers. Yukon. A glass appeared in front of Laganière. Then liquor appeared in his glass.

"You know very well I don't drink."

Laganière would beat himself up armed with the Chic-Chocs. *You're not going to soften these guys' hearts.* He brought his ring to his lips and looked down at his drink. The circle of Yukon in his glass made him feel that he was about to dive into a bottomless well. He pushed the alcohol away, as in *No*.

"Drink up," said the Remington.

"No, but it's good. It's special. It tastes a little like . . ."

The rim of the glass tasted salty.

"Wait, I'll have another taste. 'The taste of gold.' Nicely put."

A respite. Perrault put the mandolin, which he'd gotten out of his Civic to anaesthetize them, back in its case. They'd all realized the extent to which Metallica had finally gotten on their nerves. Perrault gave Yannick another couple of pills, but he didn't know where to put them. Perrault forgot the Aspirin bottle on the table as he tidied up his fanny pack, out of which a portable scale peeked along with some blue freezer bags meant for breast milk. He told them how his probation was going. Because, despite his Boy Scout manners, you always had to watch your back with Perrault. Sometimes that's what comes from getting a nursery rhyme with every spoonful of Pablum. A vulture. Born in a cocoon, this mama's boy was. Swathed in love and hope. Just before the first referendum. Even so, what followed in quick succession was the school psychologist, the Youth Protection Department, juvenile court. A few detention centres later, there he was again, prowling around that night with the dregs of La Frayère, long past his curfew.

They were all standing in the kitchen now, everybody on the radar. Laganière was pestering Yannick for a detailed account of the time Monti stopped the puck with his teeth and was choking while four fellows had to use a giant pair of pliers to pull it out of his throat. He wanted to know if

Yannick had ever seen that puck. Marcel had told him it was still somewhere in the Bouges' house, and so long as he had Yannick's attention, Laganière kept on talking, but Yannick didn't answer and turned toward Perrault as if to say there was no bite-marked puck anywhere, no phantom Indian on their porch in the middle of the night, and especially no gold in the mountains, that to his mind it was all a cock-and-bull story, one he'd heard his father trot out in a thousand versions his whole life. He wanted nothing to do with it anymore.

"You'll never guess who called me earlier, before I drove up to Saint-Jules," Perrault said.

Someone's going to have to write a doctoral dissertation one day explaining why evening get-togethers in Quebec always end up with people standing in the kitchen.

"Who?"

"Patapon."

"Seriously? He hasn't finished falling apart yet?"

"What did he want?"

"He was all out of breath. Said he forgives me."

"Are you heading back to Saint-Jules soon?"

"Nah, I've wrapped up my business. I won't be hanging out there very much for a while to come."

"I…"

Steeve was going to say something. It got away from him. On account of Alcide. He tried to remember, but he was starting to get confused and the only thing he could recall was the phone number of an old commercial for English courses.

"I forgot what I was going to say."

Two five four, six o, one one. Twice. Then this occurred to him.

"Hey, Yannick, that reminds me, I didn't tell you this, I bumped into your brother in Montreal a couple of months ago."

Yannick, well, his hit of acid was kicking in too. He felt ready for some enchantment. Wherever he held out his hand, matter was deformed.

"Not doin' well, your brother," Steeve said.

At the mention of François, Laganière wondered why they'd never hung out together. And he remembered that when François was young, he'd always been Patapon's lapdog, while Laganière himself had been Patapon's number one punching bag. *Before his big heartbreak,* he thought. In a little while Yannick would be enough of a magician to pull a live rabbit out of the stew pot. His acid was offering him new possibilities by the minute.

"Hey, Yannick?"

"Ya, what?"

Perrault asked him when they were due, if Cynthia's pregnancy was going all right, was it a boy, was it a girl, all those dumb questions.

"A boy."

"What about her job?"

"Cynthia's the store manager now. The job comes with maternity leave, and can we change the subject?"

Cynthia, she had a smile like a xylophone when you quickly run the mallet over the bars. At your service. *I'll never understand how she ended up with this psychopath,* thought Laganière. It was Cynthia who'd sold him his shoes, the ones by the front door. She'd sold forty other pairs of those same shoes that week.

"That sucks. I won't be there to help you move," Steeve said.

"You're moving away from Chemin Restigouche?" Perrault asked Yannick.

"With the baby coming, we're going to need a bigger place. Plus Cynthia's stressed out 'cause of the biker downstairs."

"Whereabouts are you moving to?"

The Montreal dude's head was nodding in the armchair. It wouldn't take much for it to come loose and go rolling under the buffet. The little hand on the fourteen dials and clocks was approaching four.

"We're moving into my folks' place," Yannick said.

"No," Laganière said.

Yannick shot him a blue-and-brown look through his murky glass. Laganière put his search for Aspirin on pause, his arm halfway into the cabinet.

"Let's just say my father's handing it down to us in advance."

"No, it can't be true."

Laganière couldn't believe it. He stayed stock-still. His burn oozed and throbbed beneath his kimono. Perrault was counting money with the look of a little boy. The others bantered and laughed more and more for no reason, leaving the librarian alone with his thoughts, his Yukon, his disappointment. Laganière was disappointed because there had already been talk about one day converting Monti's house into an interpretive centre. It was unlikely that François would ever come back to Gaspésie for good, but if he did, all would not be lost, and maybe he'd fight for Monti's inheritance. Still, François was the youngest. To make things worse, Yannick didn't have the resources, any more than François did, to keep the house standing for very long. Cars, tools, myths, girlfriends—the man destroyed everything he touched. The saddest thing, though, for Laganière wasn't that a historic house was bound for ruin but that Victor Bradley, even if it had taken him nearly a hundred years, would ultimately have gotten the better of his dear enemy. The mailman's bastard son was taking possession of all that was left of Monti's empire, only to raze it to the ground.

19

MOVING LIKE A TORERO, PATAPON UNHOOKED HIS faithful Perfecto from the coat rack and with the help of invisible hands, which had lost patience, pulled it on so hard the sleeves just about tore off. He was alarmed by the number of wrappers in his pockets—what a mass of junk he'd eaten in his life. But he sorted them out. In spite of the voice's grumpy orders, he returned to the kitchen and burned them in the sink. His solar plexus glowed red as it was vascularized by the flame. Patapon felt capable of walking through a cement wall, of galloping away to build a shopping mall where he would organize telethons. Speaking of going out. He went out. *About time,* said the voice. Ah, the aroma of seaweed in the air, of the land, the lowing of heifers. La Frayère appeared a tad more bucolic in Patapon's derangement than it did in reality. He very nearly died of euphoria when he saw O'KEEFE written on the decrepit rug on his equally decrepit porch. It was sublime, but not as much as the faded pinwheel planted in the grass. A triumph over evil. It literally brought a tear to his eye. He delighted in the heavy snow, the kind that pinches your face. *Now, go down the three stairs, please.* Patapon whipped out his keys. He twirled them on his finger like a revolver and pocketed them again, giving his Festiva a wink.

Wow, my Festiva, ain't she a beaut, he thought, confusedly, over the other voice ordering him to get a move on. *We haven't got all night.* Dazzling under the snow, his Festiva. Patapon hadn't taken it for a spin on the dunes for, what, easily four-five years. *Burn some fuel,* he thought. *I'm the one who does the thinking here,* the other voice cruelly countered. Plourde was batshit crazy. It made his eyeballs sparkle. He went up and down the few steps of his porch several times with a sensation in his gut of free fall and bounce, like when you bungee, until the voice got fed up. *That's enough!* it screamed, hoarser than hoarse. Once his bag and vacuum cleaner were in the trunk, Patapon sat down behind the wheel. He buckled up. Adjusted his mirrors, his seat, whatever could be adjusted in the Festiva. He inserted the key in the ignition. Where he was headed he didn't really know. *Me, I know,* the voice said, betraying something deep, something raw. Whatever had been subdued in it was drying up. Not many places you could go in this hole at this time of night. Far away—that's where Patapon would go, and in a car to boot. He was going on a journey. *Like.* A long, long journey. *Very long.* Say, to Peawanuck, Ontario. The dashboard lit up when he turned the key. And immediately went dark, completely fried. *Okay.* Plourde, his exuberance intact, climbed out of the tight space. He opened the hood. The hamster underneath was lifeless in its running wheel. No more Festiva. No sweat. For a minute he tried to find the best angle to lift the car and hoist it onto his back. He absolutely wanted to take it to Peawanuck. But the invisible hands gave his Perfecto a tug, making him dance in mid-air. He managed all the same to grab his vacuum cleaner, leaving his duffle bag behind in the trunk, and set out on foot toward the Bouges' place. His gait was on the fritz, with his feet and hands going off in all directions. As he walked through the streets, where the snowplow was already at work, up welled a slew of heavily enhanced childhood memories of the days when La Frayère was still worthy of a mention, at least in the shape of a black dot on the maps distributed at the Tourism Bureau kiosks, before the place practically reverted to the Duplessis era and became the backwater it was now, plagued by unemployment, drug addiction, and the exodus toward service hubs, because, well, there's more to Gaspésie than the Historic Site of the Battle of the Restigouche and Percé Rock. Plourde saw himself again as a happy kid, before the illness surged up from his cereal bowl one morning and promptly sucked him dry of vitality. He may have intended to drop by Henri Bouge's place, but he'd actually just walked right past it. Monti's house receded behind him a little more with each step. Plourde saw himself in his over-tight T-shirt, one day when his mother once again had forced him to play with François. Whereas all he'd wanted was to hang around with Yannick and his friends, his girlfriends in particular. *Good ol' Yannick, I really ought to put together a card to congratulate him,* he thought through the dense static of his mind. His mother had heard the news at the hair salon. He couldn't really imagine Yannick as a father, but Patapon made it a point of honour to be there if ever he needed support. *You must know,* the voice said, *how to get to the overpass, eh?* There was a hint of uncertainty in the question. Patapon marked time, unsure which way to go. That time with the over-tight T-shirt, his mother had called Liette, François and Yannick's mother, to ask if François wanted to come to their house to play, saying she'd stick the two little guys in front of the TV. The trick was that the Bouges would have to take Kevin back for supper afterwards because his mother was working the night shift at the snack bar. François rang the doorbell at the Plourdes', carrying a library bag bursting with books in case Patapon wanted to read with him. Patapon didn't even turn away from the TV when François came in. François didn't want to sit down beside him. "I don't like television," he told Monique, Patapon's mother. And he began to follow her around the house while she was trying to get ready. Monique eventually managed to park him on the living room couch, luring him with orangeade and a bowlful of cheese puffs, which Plourde immediately pulled toward him and proceeded to gobble down one after the other with metronomic regularity. Everything was fine. They silently vegetated in front of a wrestling match and after that in front of the badly dubbed American soap operas to which Plourde had become addicted at an early age. Suddenly François started laughing. A horrible hyena laugh. At first in brief jags, and then continuously. Yet there wasn't anything especially funny about a three-time divorcee realizing his brother wasn't his brother because he himself had been adopted by a woman whom his father had impregnated while leading a double life for fifty years after learning that his wife was sleeping with his father. Patapon, his fingers sticky with artificial cheese, turned toward François to suggest he go read one of his books in another room. But seeing him laugh like that, and during a commercial besides, pissing blood from the nose, Patapon was scared almost to death.

Holding François's hand, Monique led him across her lawn and then the neighbours', all the way home to the Bouges'. Patapon watched them through the living room window with a cheese puff in his mouth. At no time had he let go of the bowl.

For heaven's sake, Liette thought as she accompanied Mrs Plourde down the walkway, with no end of apologies after Monique had explained what had happened. François disappeared into the house with a tissue in his nostril. Kevin, despite his pleas, would come join them in a couple of hours. "Not a problem," Liette told Monique. She fished in a plastic container full of water for pieces of celery that she was going to stuff with Cheez Whiz, like Henri did. Meanwhile, François, now wearing his footed pyjamas, asked permission to make himself a nest of quilts in the basement. "Of course, sweetie." She went downstairs soon after to bring him a snack, thinking how she would have liked for her husband, always busy and not around much recently, to see this. Bundled up in his blankets, with his coloured crayons scattered around him, François was as engrossed as a lizard in the latest edition of Larousse, which his father had demanded that he and Yannick get him for Father's Day. The pages of the dictionary rustled. They were shiny and nice-smelling. Liette went back upstairs to scour a stain that had kept her on edge for a week and to call a friend for a report on her session with the clairvoyant. Presently, Henri returned from the hardware store with Yannick, who was sulking as he stepped out of the van to unload studs for the gazebo under construction. Because it was always the same story with Henri. He treated you like an adult, saying he didn't need any help running his errand, nope, he needed *your* help. Except that, instead of the half-hour he'd said it would take, you spent the afternoon listening to men haggle over prices in a garage, acting pretty rustic, to be sure, and getting very much stewed. Anyway, chit-chat, yadda yadda yadda on the phone. Liette, all cigarettes and filter coffee, flashed her blotto but chipper spouse a smile as he crossed the kitchen without removing his workboots. Liette motioned to him to go down to the basement and spy on François for a second. Fine, because he happened to need his measuring tape, which was on the workbench downstairs.

"... So I said, honey, why go up to New Carlisle for that? It's in their catalogue. Edgwige ordered two of 'em for me and ... Sorry, hold on a minute. The kettle's whistlin', I'm gonna turn off the burner."

There wasn't any water on the boil. *You're way off beam, girl,* Liette thought. The element wasn't even switched on. And yet. A crescendo rose up from the basement. A crescendo rose up, that is, from her husband in the basement.

Instead of going over to the Bouges', Patapon would've preferred that his mother unfreeze the meatballs so he could cook himself some burgers in the microwave. But she was too broke until Thursday, and they'd have to get themselves invited anywhere they could for a few days and manage that way. At least, anywhere but the Bouges' place. First of all, Patapon couldn't name the better part of what was on his plate. All right, corn, that was something he could identify. But he'd never eaten any that wasn't canned. Second of all, he had no clue what had gone on in that family between François's hemorrhaging laugh and the present moment, but no one spoke or looked at anyone. There was just Liette emitting little chirps of astonishment with every mouthful. Although. No one looked at anyone? Not quite true. Yannick, balancing on the back legs of his chair, chewed as slowly as possible while glaring at Patapon with his mismatched eyes.

"Is it to your taste, Kevin?" Liette asked.

Patapon held his breath as he brought a forkful of he-didn't-know-what closer to his barely open mouth.

"Oh yes," he said.

He ventured a suicidal glance in Henri's direction. Actually, it was only because he was afraid to be killed that he forced himself to eat the stuff. The man's red nose protruded from his greying facial hair, and he looked pissed off. He was wider across than the table.

"His name's Patapon," Yannick said.

Henri took a slow sip from his glass of beer, which he'd salted.

"In this here house, it's Kevin," Liette said.

"But his name is Patapon," François mumbled. His mashed potatoes resembled a Japanese garden.

"Hey, not a peep out of you," Henri said.

This was nothing like the scream he'd let out earlier on the basement stairs. That scream could have cleaned out a pair of two-packs-a-day tubercular lungs. Whereas he'd just spoken as calm as could be. Every syllable carved out with a knife. Patapon focused on his plate, on handling his cutlery. Mashed potatoes, he knew what that was. Still, there had to be zero lumps for him to like it. He hoped nobody would say anything else. So Henri wouldn't lose his temper again.

"So shaddup, eh, Françoué," Yannick said.

He used his spoon to catapult a chunk of meat at his brother. François's footed pyjamas were spattered all over. Patapon's skeleton rearranged itself in his chair.

"Hey, express yourself properly," Henri told Yannick.

"You really ought to shut up, François."

François pretended to be asleep. His face hovered over his

plate. Patapon started eating with the same zeal he'd displayed over the bowl of cheese puffs.

"Are you staying overnight, Kevin?" Liette asked him.

The tears welled up in the youngster's eyes. He couldn't summon up the courage to answer. He'd heard the man screaming from his house. It had begun as a high-pitched whine and quickly, exponentially, gained in volume. Yes, Henri loved his children, but a line had been crossed. He wasn't very good at managing disappointment, and when he'd found François scribbling in his Father's Day present, something inside him snapped. François was on the receiving end of a first-class earful. And even when the storm had passed, nothing was over, because the worst part was to have everyone sitting around the table and eating in a semblance of normality.

"I said, not a peep out of you," Henri repeated to François.

"You just told him that," Liette said.

"Yannick, tomorrow you're going to help me. We're going—"

"I helped you all day. Why don't you ask François sometimes?"

François might have grown two inches taller had he not heard Henri's response.

"He's a child!" Liette protested. "Could you pass me the sauce, Kevin?"

"Patapon!" Yannick said.

"He's not a child," Henri said. "He's eight years of fatherhood with nothing to show for it."

François, his head resting on his shoulder, pretended to snore. His father pounded the table, nearly ejecting him out of his buttoned-up pyjamas.

"You're going to help me tomorrow, Yannick," Henri said again.

"We know," Liette said.

"We're going to pour the gazebo's foundation."

Patapon was crying. Liette gave Henri a flick of her napkin. "Don't cry, buddy," she said to her guest. "You'll stay here tonight with us, okay? We'll spend a nice evening together."

She ruffled his hair. *I'm having a ball,* Yannick thought. Then he drained his father's beer.

"I ... I can't," Patapon began to say. "My mother wants me to—"

"I'll talk to your mother," Henri said decisively. "It's okay. You'll sleep over."

Patapon bowed his head to hide his sobs. Liette, so beautiful, still so young—he loved her more than a body could admit. But she had just served him another helping of everything, while Henri explained to Yannick yet again what to expect the next day. He took pains to peck away at François's self-esteem.

"That's enough," Liette cut in. "Get a grip. All because of a *dictionary,* for Chrissake. We're not going to disown him besides."

Henri was on his feet when she said that. Unable to find his beer, he'd stood up to pour himself a Yukon. The mailman had delivered the bottle that afternoon.

"The gazebo, I wanted to build it for him. For François. Under the weeping willow. I pictured us spending special moments together. Father and son. Leafing through my brand new Larousse. A gift from my boys, goddammit. We'd have cultivated the flair for languages that the Bouge family has in abundance."

"He drew a couple of lines in it, eh, it's not as if—"

"It's fit for the dump!" the man bellowed.

Patapon, gasping for breath, turned toward Liette, his arms spread wide, fingers clawing the air.

"Why doncha pour yourself a glass of milk for once," Liette said.

She stood up herself and snatched the glass of Yukon out of her hubby's hand.

"Kevin, you'll sleep here," Henri said, and took another glass out of the cabinet.

Liette stepped on the pedal of the trash can and dropped the first glass into it still half-full. Henri handed her the second glass too, and Yannick, along with everyone else, ducked for cover. The father, even as he poured himself a third, would never own up to his sickness. "I'm a bon vivant!" he would declare, more eloquent for having imbibed, and you couldn't expect his doctor to say otherwise—he drank just as much. Yet pleasure never prevented Henri from working, far from it. Without having finished high school, and with a knack for business, he'd made good financially. He was the only one of his siblings able to cover the high cost of maintaining the family house, which he'd bought from his father after Monti was forced to borrow against it in his later years. Given his love of the French language, Henri was also the only one who could talk literature with their mother. Yet no one was jealous of his success, even so. He could be munificent and obliging. What's more, he always tried to stay fit, especially following his parents' death, because he wanted to keep up with the two sons he'd had late in life with a woman fifteen years his junior. At the time, Liette Nault had felt pressed into adulthood. She moved in with Henri. She'd known Henri Bouge since she was yay high. He'd bought her a soft ice cream one summer.

"What's the rush?" Pierre Nault had objected. "You're only young once, ya know." He was right, her father was. Liette's close friends and relations believed it had broken her to get married so young, and to someone who was at a different stage in life. After the ceremony, when the parade of honking cars drove down the boulevard, a couple of young bucks were humbled, leaning on their motorbikes in the bowling alley parking lot, in front of the ice cream parlour, or roller skating on the boardwalk along the shore. Their reflections glided by on the side of Henri's Lincoln Continental. His hand hung proudly against the door. He was taking the most flamboyant part of the town toward the sunset, trailing a string of cans on his rear bumper. The other fellows might have felt less bitter if they'd known that Liette already had a bad seed sprouting in her belly. Actually, it's not clear whether Henri was aware, whether he'd married her first and foremost out of a sense of responsibility. Even Marcel, his best man, never knew if Henri knew.

20

"I JUST WISH TO SEE," FRANÇOIS SAID AS HE WORKED the radio dial, "if we're already getting a signal from CBSU."

"CBSU?" Rock asked. The driver poked around for leftovers in the ethnic food containers.

"It's La Frayère's community radio station."

The term *community* was an overstatement. The station's audience might just as well have been the animals. The studio was located quite a way from the town, on a wooded mountainside, because CBSU originally broadcast from a transmission tower at the top of the mountain. François wasn't familiar with the details. He scanned the stations, twisting his arm so as to avoid any contact with the still switched-off iPod.

"I can put on some music," Rock said.

"Shh, shh," François went, straining his ear.

Through the interference, he'd just heard a few barely audible notes from a synthesizer. The same measure seemed to be repeated in a loop.

"CBSU, eh," Rock said, shoving the stump of an imperial roll down his gullet.

There were two-minute silences during CBSU's news bulletins; sometimes you heard pages being turned, toilets being flushed, other staff members talking behind the newscaster. That was why François called it BSUC.

"Want some?"

The driver proffered some oily noodles mixed with clotted sauce. François pictured the restaurant delivery man slapping hands with Rock whenever he came to his house with an order. Give Rock a kiwi and a spoon, he wouldn't know what to do with them. And when the delivery man went away, you could be sure he was headed for the corner video club with Rock's overdue films. *I hope this won't be your last meal,* the driver thought as François rolled down the window and simultaneously grabbed the container. The road sign it slammed into reverberated like a gong.

"What're you ... My supper!"

Off-centre in the windshield, Saint-Simon began to emerge from the downpour. A vacation slide melting in the projector. François, increasingly garrulous, wished he could climb out into the storm through the sunroof, except there was no sunroof, so he stayed in his seat sucking on his Yukon. On the radio, the looping keyboard grew more and more distinct as they neared the transmitter.

"Wait, let me get this straight," Rock said in reference to an earlier conversation. "Your grandfather went to the Klondike..."

François had cleared many a tavern table with that tale. It was always the same refrain, the same soliloquies. To the point where he'd alienated his circle of friends. A fellow gets tired, and his chums would bolt without bothering to finish their beers, even during *Hockey Night.* Momo, Armand, Graton, Tibi, all the familiar faces. It had gotten so that no matter what you talked about to François—say, your plantar wart and the unsuspected delights of a liquid nitrogen treatment— he invariably found a connection to bring the conversation back to his grandfather's saga. The connection was at times very flimsy. At first the guys stuck around because François would order a bottle of Yukon for the table on the pretext of showing them the hidden clues on the label. Then he'd pour himself a glass, acting as if he didn't have a drinking problem, and his friends would replace it with a Pepsi. But after a few months of this François never missed a chance to produce a jumble of maps, facsimiles of registered prospecting claims, archives he'd pull out of his briefcase and flatten but which proved nothing except that paper turns brown over the years; his friends got fed up with having to chip in each time to pay for the bottle when the evening was over. François was sure of it: Monti had done something to somebody somewhere. He had a theory as to the offence at the root of the curse. High on Pepsi, he'd start to ramble on about how the Bouges' decline, all of La Frayère's decline, was a story of revenge for the mur- der of someone it was best not to name offhand like that in a respectable Centre-Sud tavern. The guys told him the curse was more likely to be dispelled in an AA meeting than with a book that had been stalled for the last ten years. It was Tibi, one of the stalwarts of that circle, who finally told him that if he was so determined to keep on digging in the North, he should chuck his pencil, find a shovel with a six-thousand- kilometre-long handle, and stop busting their balls. Everyone stood up, offering bogus excuses, put on their coats, and went home. Poupette was the only one who stayed. He followed François outside. He sat him down on a hot air vent in the street and said: "Y' know, Françoué . . . your grandfather, he really only went to northern *Ontario*, eh."

"If you say so," François replied.

"Okay, so tell me this," Rock said. "The gold rush, what year was that?"

"Eighteen ninety-five."

Rock dipped into his pack again. He must have taken a hundred and twenty cigarettes out of it. The world was reflected in the jolts of the broken wing mirror bouncing against the side of the car.

"Something like that, eh. And you, how old are you?"

"How old do you think I am?"

"You know, looking at you, I really couldn't say. Somewhere between twenty and sixty."

"Right on the mark," François laughed, giving the driver a friendly nudge. "Show a little tact, now."

"'Cause I'm twenty years older than your brother."

"I never told you I had a brother."

François spun his head around toward the driver. *Oops,* Rock thought. *I just hit a nerve.*

"Seems to me you mentioned him a while back."

"Absolutely not."

"You're just too soused to remember."

"Now listen, I am not drunk."

François whistled the national anthem. The alcohol throbbed in his muscles, that was all. The scaling of the high notes wasn't exactly glorious, but there was no mistaking Calixa Lavallée's sublime melody.

"Okay, fine, I'm twenty years older than your brother if you have a brother. And *my* grandfather went to the Klondike.

Which means that your grandfather couldn't have been much more than a child at the time."

At this point, the only thing the driver wanted was for François to become aware of the trap that was closing in on him. Rock, out of empathy, wanted him to understand where their ride would end. *But there's a module missing in his brain,* he thought. François answered that it should be "if you *had* a brother."

"So, tell me, Yannick and you, are you close?" Rock asked later.

Wrists held fast on the vibrating rail. "Let him go, Yannick, the train's coming." A band of little pale-faced rascals slowly retreats in the tall grass.

"Neither close nor alike in any way," François said.

He drowned his memory in a swig that, given the late hour, did double duty as breakfast.

"We do not spend time together," he went on. "We do not love each other. And, besides, how do you know his name is Yannick?"

"Well, I love you."

A light lit up on the dashboard. *What on earth could this mean?* François checked in the owner's manual but found no explanation. Accompanied by this sign, they crossed Rimouski. Otherwise, nothing worth saying about Rimouski. The antenna on the side of the hood searched in every direction. When they reached Sainte-Luce-sur-Mer, François held forth on the *Empress of Ireland*. He'd insisted on taking the road along the river.

"Ten thousand drowned in a ballroom filled with salt water," he said. "Just imagine, the guests floating amid shards of porcelain and boutonniere roses."

"I really love you, Marquis old friend."

François didn't know how to take these declarations. He looked at the driver, aghast.

"I..."

The rest of his reply sounded like Klingon. *He who mutters tells no lies,* he thought. Through the window, the strand along the river blended together with the heavy gouache of the landscape. François was definitely starting to smell like compost. The cardboard fir tree was no match anymore.

"You don't get it," Rock said. "I like you, understand? I don't know any brainy people like you. You talk to me and the neurons start popping in my head. Man, I watch you writing and I tell myself... Me, I wanted to make films, not waste my life as a flunkey for a bunch of bootleggers..."

"Mr Rock?"

"... constantly mixed up in funny business involving pussy and black magic. Yes, what?"

"How is it that you know I have a brother named Yannick?"

No one noticed when it stopped raining. The moon disengaged itself from the clouds in retreat. But almost immediately after the taxi had officially entered Gaspésie, scarcely three minutes past Sainte-Flavie, the clouds began to swell again and soon took on the texture of Plasticine. Then they let go and the azure sky was fraught with snow.

"*La famiglia,*" Rock answered, with a gesture picked up from *The Godfather*.

Squinting against the thread of smoke unravelling from his cigarette, he listened to François read him the text on the back of the Yukon bottle. However, the reader's enthusiasm was dampened when the driver explained that it wasn't a magic spell but a shoddy software's poor translation.

"Then you must be unaware of William Dexter's reputation," François said.

"I'm more aware of it than you think," Rock replied. "Hey, can you reach back into my bag and get me my hockey shoulder pads?"

Unbuckling his seat belt, François complied and dropped back into his seat, mesmerized as he tried to discern even the vaguest shape through the snowflakes immolating themselves in the headlights.

"How is it that you know my brother's name?" he said, not yet entirely back to earth.

"Would you hand me my elbow pads and shin guards?"

Which François did, giving Rock an unquestioning look.

"It's for when I bail out in a little while," Rock said.

"Do give me an answer, gadzooks."

After that the mood went flat. The driver chewed the inside of his cheeks, still in disbelief and somehow peeved that his passenger had used the word *gadzooks*. He plugged the iPod into the auxiliary outlet. François exploded. And collected himself almost intact when he saw nothing had happened. The driver now doubted that Danny was capable of carrying out the plan he'd detailed for him over the internet. *I mean, have you seen this guy?!* But he knew that one way or another the plan would ultimately set the proper wheels in motion. It was always like that. They would just have to find a way afterwards of getting across the line, though he didn't need to worry about that right then. The same six synthesizer notes kept on playing over BSUC's airwaves.

"How did you come to know," François asked for the fourth time, "my brother's name?"

Oh, how the snow has snowed! he thought, remembering the Nelligan poem. The closer they got to La Frayère, the stronger his Gaspé accent became—it was psychological. Rock tried once more to convince him his memory was slipping, that although he didn't realize it, he was more hammered than a nail.

"You've been talking about Yannick since Montreal!"

François wasn't buying any of it, but he gave up. They'd be arriving pretty soon anyway, another hour and a half or so. He was captivated by the storm over the greater metropolitan area of Amqui. *What are the throes of life?* They shut their traps for an hour or two. François's off-white face resembled a melting latex mask. Later, with a dickey of sour drool on his shirt, he spoke about what the peninsula represented for him, making various references to the things he was going to accomplish there.

"Hand me my sweater, in the bag."

François did so and spoke of his love for Gaspésie, the dreams he had for it, while Rock pulled on his San Jose Sharks sweater. What he ought to fall in love with, the driver told him, was a woman, and he had a few pointers.

"Thanks, there's no need," François said over the noise of the snowplow in the other lane.

"You go see the girl. You buy her, say, a cosmopolitan. You let her talk about herself, her tai chi courses, whatever she likes. You confide in her too, you play the vulnerable card, but as soon as she starts to mention her ex, you place a quarter on the counter and you say: 'Call your father, babe, tell him you're not coming home tonight.' Would you grab my helmet in the back, please? Last thing, I promise."

221

François fitted the helmet onto the driver's head so he wouldn't have to let go of the steering wheel. François also snapped on the chin guard and adjusted the cage. It was a Spalding helmet.

"Because, you see, Marquis old friend, all those books, or whatever, they'll drive you insane. So go and fling that brief-case off the end of the pier. Live what's left of your life, man. Get out there. Fight. Have kids. To my mind, Gaspésie, as you say, has left you with a massive heartache. And at some point your heart will split open all the way to your noggin."

The ride was coming to an end. The maw of the grille was less voracious in the final kilometres as the Volvo entered the vortex of dusky light forcing its way between clouds that swelled as if from within. The night was like a solid substance. Rock drove with his face over the steering wheel. His helmet nearly touched the windshield. You could barely see the front edge of the hood. François felt the Volvo slow down. On his own initiative he held out the hockey gloves to Rock, now suited up from head to foot. To keep driving on the 132 became impossible. The cab couldn't make any headway. Too much snow on the road. The plow hadn't yet cleared the stretch in front of them. And you wouldn't have wanted to surf on the sea, off to their right, either. Rock stopped the Volvo before it got stuck. *I'm willing to bet this is part of the plan,* he thought. François looked at the storm the way he'd have looked at his parents copulating.

"I believe," he said, "we had better go back and take our chanc-es on Route Sainte-Cluque. Then by way of Rang Saint-Onge."

Rock gave the steering wheel a twist and turned the cab around. The hockey gloves didn't make this any easier. The car slid backwards a little, before the tires bit into the ice. *It always has to get complicated.* François was surprised at not being more emotional as they approached his hometown. Had he left La Frayère the day before for a short trip to Carleton and back, his biochemical response would not have been much different. They turned inland on a freshly cleared road and drove on for about ten minutes. Rock switched the car radio to auxiliary and turned on the iPod just when, at the intersection of Route Sainte-Cluque and Rang Saint-Onge, the overpass, grey against a grey background, loomed up ahead. *The fall of man,* he thought as he made out the silhouette straddling the guardrail.

ONCE THE WALL OF HIS STOMACH WAS THOROUGHLY
lined with rabbit stew, Laganière was amazed at the amount
of hard liquor he was able to ingest, since he'd always deferred
to his Lorraine's opinion that her Joël, with his build, well, a
capful of cooking wine and you'd find him lying spread-eagle
on the nearest flat surface. Right now, though, Lorraine, the
wedding ceremony, the cards with the guests' names so they'd
know where to sit at the dinner afterwards, cards he was supposed to have picked up at the print shop yesterday, all that
was light years away from his current preoccupation with his
role as storyteller. Hooded in the shawl his aunt kept on the
back of the armchair, he held the three who were still awake
in suspense with a pregnant pause. He'd almost concluded
his account of Thierry Vignola's disappearance, in which he'd
merely changed the names, ages, setting, and texture. Steeve
stood off to the side listening, behind Perrault, who'd been
about to leave for two hours. Scanning his audience with a
look of defiance, Laganière knocked back another shot of
Yukon. His silence persisted till it verged on the unbearable.

In high school, Thierry Vignola had been thick with Yannick and Steeve, but Laganière had also fraternized with him,
in some extracurricular club, because Vignola, despite his solid

core of delinquency, was the kind of guy everyone liked, flitting from one bunch to the next and involved in all sorts of things. Laganière simply renamed him Julien in his narrative, and then had Yannick hanging on his every word.

Vignola, what's more, had a brilliant future in store. The summer when he vanished into thin air one weekend, he'd set his sights on college, a serious relationship, a lower intake of soft drugs. The others who'd gone camping with him—including Marteau, actually—spent a good part of the night searching for him in the woods, but one thing was certain: at that age, when you've just gone through that sort of event, what you really don't need is to be lectured for not having alerted the authorities sooner. The statements they gave were patchy, to say the least. The rescue team never found anything but some clothes and personal items scattered through the woods, which gave rise to all manner of speculation.

For his grand finale Laganière lit a flashlight and held it under his chin. The three trippers were dangerously impressed. The electric impulses shot through their neocortices, like rafting whitewater, only worse.

"And that year," Laganière said, the contours of his features heightened by the stark beam, "one of the Létourneau sisters was at Rivière aux Émeraudes in her tent, when she heard an adolescent's voice nearby, Julien Drolet's voice. Screaming like a banshee, he blamed her and everyone else in the village because they hadn't found him, hadn't helped him, hadn't ever thanked him for sacrificing himself for them."

In response to the grotesque caricature that he saw in Laganière, Steeve had backed away toward the master bedroom as the story was being told. At least it had a parental atmosphere and a TV. The spooky stories that Yannick and Perrault had told before Laganière started in, stories about pentagrams written in lamb's blood in abandoned train stations, beds that begin to shake for no reason, or Ouija sessions after which a model son murders his parents with an axe, those stories seemed like silly jokes compared with Laganière's tale. It was an outlet for the librarian's sadistic side. He wanted to wring their guts, because of the cottage, and especially because of Monti's house. He wanted to make them relive something primal.

"Meanwhile, the other Létourneau sister and her friend Colin still hadn't managed after a couple of hours to find their way out of a cave they'd tumbled into. As they searched around using a lighter, their feet snagged on a slashed-up K-Way. I saw with my own eyes the notebook that was in the jacket pocket. It's in our archives at the library. Julien must have jotted down his thoughts in his final moments. He told his girlfriend he loved her. He also tried to describe, to the extent you can describe the indescribable, the bloodthirsty creature he was hiding from. He said that he'd stepped out of his tent for a piss, and when he saw it near his friends, he dashed haphazardly into the forest, far away from their campsite. The notes stop at the beginning of the next sentence, 'I …' Nothing else. The whole page was splattered with blood."

Laganière laid it on thick, of course. But Thierry Vignola's disappearance in fact had terrified the entire community of La Frayère. Had he run away, committed suicide, had an accident? Or been murdered? No one knew. Everyone had their own theory, which often gave rise to vivid displays of guilt, paranoia, and collective psychosis. For a long time, Vignola's headshot remained a fixture on milk cartons and the post office bulletin board. The xenophobes had a field day with it—it's the Indians, those frigging Indians—and the crypto-zoologists even more so. This went on for over fifteen years, the conjectures and the stories that scared little children, like the one Laganière was about to conclude.

"Next time, I'll tell you what a hunter from Coin-du-Banc once told old Marcel and which old Marcel later passed on to me. The story of an unknown beast, vaguely humanoid, that he'd managed to shoot near Rivière aux Émeraudes. Three shots with a twenty-two, but the animal got away. The bullets jingled inside it like small change in a piggybank. I don't know about you, but I think that may be what we heard outside before…And so ends the story of the Rivière aux Émeraudes disappearance."

"Okay, okay," said Steeve.

In his desire to organize the next activity himself, he clapped his hands and kept repeating, "Okay." The lights in the kitchen and the living room were turned on. The curtains were drawn shut against the barbed wire of brambles at the jagged edge of the sullen, snowy woods, where earlier the guys had indeed thought they'd heard bells tinkling in the storm.

They each got busy doing something else after that. Steeve, his eyebrows moving like flippers in a pinball machine, swept the floor, taking care, out of respect mixed with incomprehension, to go around Marteau's body, still stretched out in the same spot on the floor. Marteau was still afflicted with the same bouts of apnea, the same mucus. A spray of flowers taken from vases of dried ones stuck out from between his hands, which had been joined together over his stomach. The

Montreal dude was . . . the Montreal dude, restive and loud
even in his sleep. Perrault was on his knees in the corridor
testing the floor's springiness in preparation for his stretching and physical stage-work exercises. Laganière, meanwhile,
found himself alone with his high-grade headache, which
had returned despite the alcohol's analgesic effect. His burn
caused him excruciating pain, not to mention the scrapes on
his fingers, which he'd inflicted on himself earlier trying to
fold back beer caps like Yannick. And Yannick, driven by some
unresolved personal issue, had furtively slipped out to follow
the trail of Vignola's ghost.

When he reappeared out of the howling wind and raging
snow, the small hands of the cottage's fourteen clocks and dials
touched six. Upside down on the table, a "cradboard" box, as
Laganière's uncle would say, was bumping its way unaided
through the crowd of bottles. The Gaspésiens had decided to
punish the Montreal dude for being so antsy, for his soldier's
medallion, his trite questions, his nasal questions you didn't
have time to answer because he was already eight questions
further along. They wanted to punish him because he was
from Montreal and smug about it, and things didn't work
that way in the outlying regions. Because he dressed like he
was in a music video, whereas their standard style was beige
and the right size. They wanted . . . they *had* to punish him
for behaving shabbily toward their bard. For showing him a
lack of respect. For making Marteau smoke until he was sick.
For shooting at the fridge with a twelve-gauge. Which wasn't
covered in the extended warranty, eh. He had to pay. If Yannick had shot at the fridge, they all would have said, "You're
too much, Yannick, my man," but the Montreal dude, nope,

he'd transgressed too many unwritten taboos. The scene on the TV in the master bedroom was a lynching in black and white. A throng of peasants was quartering some poor wretch to a player piano ragtime tune.

Characters like Monti, Laganière thought, *are where this town draws its very lifeblood.* He found the business about the house too depressing. Eyes bugged out, foreheads beaded with yellowish sweat, Steeve and Yannick plotted under the kitchen range hood. The light bulb's acid glow enveloped their confab. They were psyching each other up. Marteau on the floor clutched at their pant legs so they would tow him into consciousness. The cradboard box shifted on the table.

"We'll play the weasel trick on him."

That's what was stirring under the box. Yannick had caught it when he came back from his time alone. The weasel was right there in front of them.

"Is everyone clear about the plan?" Yannick asked.

"Ten-four."

"Give us a recap anyway."

"You, Steeve, when I say go, you raise a corner of the box. As soon as the weasel comes out, I trap it in this bag full of bags here. Perrault, you stand ready with your golf club, and you send the rodent off to Pluto if I miss my—"

"Fore!"

"Ow! Fucking jackass!"

It happened very fast. The weasel was writhing inside the bag. Whereas Steeve had just been walloped in the breadbasket with a seven-iron. And that's exactly what was mystifying about Perrault. He was wearing his Mona Lisa smile. You never knew for certain if he behaved like a jerk intentionally, so you excused him when you shouldn't have. Steeve grimaced as he lifted his sweater away from a bruise shaped like Minnesota. *Still,* Laganière thought in his bubble, *the Montis and company are also to blame if you're not a man in this town unless you can down a twelve-pack and not slur your words.* The Montreal dude was still sleeping, but things were about to turn nasty for him. Perrault went out to the recycling bin and brought back a length of PVC piping a good four inches in diameter. Yannick doused his cigarette. He held the bag at arm's length while the weasel thrashed about inside. It was spitting with hatred.

"What time is it?" he taunted. "Eh? What time is it? Eh, eh?"

The Montreal dude moaned, "Jennifffer," as Steeve unbuttoned his trousers. They pulled up his sweater and the tacky tank top underneath. The glutton had smoked as much as everyone else, in spite of the Nicorette patches all over his torso. The Gaspésiens slipped one end of the pipe inside his pants. They traded silent glances. At the outer edge of the universe, the Big Bang kept on expanding, clearing a path in the void. *I wonder if François knows about the house,* Laganière thought. He was taking no part in any of this. He was still looking for Aspirin in places where he'd already searched twice. Now Yannick inserted the other end of the pipe in the bag, where, almost at once, all movement stopped.

An invisible scratching ran along the pipe. The weasel went berserk in the Montreal dude's boxers. In no time he was dancing the *kozachok* in the middle of the living room. Even Yannick withdrew into the background when the mammal thrust its hyper-detailed twitching maw out from the collar of the undershirt.

"Such things just aren't done!" Laganière shouted.

A piece of flesh went flying and dropped into a cocktail glass. The vodka splashed out. At least, that's how the guys would tell it later on, but in fact the glass was empty. Steeve began to giggle nervously when he realized what he'd just done. He looked at Laganière, who was biting with nothing to bite into. He bit his own teeth while the Montreal dude was being ripped apart. Yannick turned toward Perrault to take the golf club out of his hands. Perrault had bolted. You could hear his Civic starting up outside. The tail lights instantly vanished into the powder snow. He clearly had chains on his tires. The Montreal dude continued to flail about for another minute in his bloodstained clothes until the weasel ended up butchering what could pass for a deltoid. *It's time to get going,* he managed to think. *Rock should be arriving soon.* He swivelled around and toppled directly onto his back. The weasel was flattened outright.

"Oops."

And to think that at that very moment Laganière's uncle was living it up in Florida, wearing a lei and doing the bunny hop on the patio of a tiki bar.

An hour later, Yannick and Steeve were cooling down on the couch. They'd gone on a tear, riffing on ideas about the most utterly ludicrous foods and dishes. Béchamel butts. Teeth-encrusted muffins. And other bullshit of that ilk. Banannies, cockanuts. Laganière hadn't been in a laughing mood for a while.

"Stop sulking," Steeve said, hiccupping and wiping away his tears.

"He'll get over it," Yannick said with a slight cramp in his diaphragm, like a balloon full of hot air.

Laganière's headache was more and more worrisome, he felt nauseous, and his field of vision had a curly black edge as he again stood at the window with the curtain pushed back, watching for the Montreal dude's return. Except there was zero visibility, even in the morning light. The ultimate yeti blizzard was blowing outside. The front yard was Nunavut. And Laganière felt responsible. For starters, this was, provisionally, his place. Like it or not, he was the host. Plus, he'd prayed so fervently for the Montreal dude to die an indescribably brutal death that it would almost be his fault if ever.

"Milkballs."

"Fartlafel."

You didn't need to look at your calendar to estimate the life expectancy of a Montreal dude out in the woods at the apex of a Hollywood-grade snowstorm, partially clothed, emotionally challenged, and with nothing but the bottle of liquor hidden in his coat to help him cope, toting a hunting rifle twice his weight and a soldier's medallion.

"Hey, I know him a little," Steeve added, his stomach aching. "He's oversensitive. He'll go snivelling to an owl saying the others don't understand him. Then he'll come back here once he's metabolized his blues into testosterone. I guarantee it."

"Mammary tortes," Yannick blurted.

His body in tatters, the Montreal dude had grabbed a handful of bullets and the most action-packed rifle in the armoury. As well as the vintage bourbon, which they'd looked for all evening. Yannick fumed while Laganière emptied the sodium bicarbonate onto the weasel stamped into the carpet.

"Mammary *tittytortes,*" Steeve managed to enunciate, making Yannick choke with laughter, his mouth gaping soundlessly.

The Montreal dude had pulled on his canvas sneakers and flimsy windbreaker. "I'm going hunting," he'd announced. That was the second-to-last thing he'd said to them, just before calling them hippocrats. *Rock said he'd follow me one way or another,* he'd thought. Aided by the wind, he'd slammed the door so hard that Marteau had jumped to his feet and started washing the dishes. They'd all looked at each other.

"Gone hunting. Gone hunting," Laganière said by the window. "Hmm."

22

PATAPON WAS PROPELLED ONTO A SCREE, EXPELLED from the woods through which he'd taken a shortcut. *We're getting close, hang in there.* He shook the exoskeleton of snow from his Perfecto and reached Rang Saint-Onge after nearly drowning in the ditch. Once on the other side, he did his touchdown dance to celebrate his victory over the forest, but the voice whistled him up. That forest was full of rusted nails and the old half-buried remains of cars. In any case, he'd survived. *Hey, come on now, don't die right away.* He'd given a little kiss of gratitude to each of the orange ribbons marking the trail where he'd left his spoor. With his vacuum cleaner still pinned under his arm, he walked along the shoulder of the road littered with cans and empty cartridges, and then leaped, like in those dreams where you're flying, over a disembowelled coyote. He turned around to pet it and suddenly felt like running, why not. *One, two, one, two.* He was well on his way to making up for all the exercise he'd neglected to do since his high school gym classes, in another life, when he got teased in the locker room for showering in his T-shirt to hide his breasts. An anthracite-coloured Civic careened around the curve. *That's Perrault's car there,* Patapon thought. The voice used his head to think about something else at the same time.

His cheeks followed the path of the airstream. To a certain degree, so did his mass of hair. Perrault was coming back from the inland, where he must have gone to fight with other rednecks. By pardoning him, Patapon had lightened his burden. Nothing would ever again spoil their new friendship. Two minutes had elapsed since the Civic had dissolved back into the storm, yet there he was, still rooted in the mixture of snow and gravel, waving goodbye. *Time's a-wastin'.* Patapon figured he must almost be in Ontario. He'd been running for quite a while. *Go, go,* the voice cheered him on. *The world is your oyster.* And so he started away again toward that grim overpass a little farther down the road, across from a bankrupt summer camp where you sent your kids if you never wanted to see them again. Patapon scooped as many snowflakes as possible out of the air to fill his pockets, thrilled at the thought of observing them later under a microscope. *Now hold on,* he'd have said to himself had a kind of loud background noise not swamped his consciousness. To get to Peawanuck he should have taken the 132. Near the cement plant, his eyes shifted nervously behind his frozen happy-face mask. *Can someone tell me what the hell I'm doing here?* he thought, though unable to hear himself over the voice now multiplied and reverberating loudly in his skull. Clutching his vacuum cleaner, he wanted to slow down. Turn around and take the 132. Only, he was having a devil of a time checking his enthusiasm and had no other choice but to keep walking straight ahead toward the overpass. As if the enthusiasm weren't *his.* It was a free-floating enthusiasm belonging to no one in particular. Untethered somewhere inside him. *What's going on?* His thoughts were once again lost in the vocal farrago. He strode more and more exuberantly toward the shoddy concrete structure of the overpass. His smile, meantime, never faded altogether, in spite of the forgotten sensation—since he hadn't felt anything for a while—of a knot in his stomach that arose in the middle of the gas station parking lot at the town limits of La Frayère. He did not want to go to the overpass. To the point where he slackened all his muscles, but without collapsing as planned. They advanced on their own, his legs, their gait at once soldierly and jaunty. *Hurry up,* the voice urged him. *They're coming. Quick, quick.* The surveillance camera above the pumps caught him walking as if his feet were magnetized by the asphalt in front of him. His hands clutched in vain at anything available along the way. Actually, the moment he began to panic in earnest was when he realized he'd dropped the vacuum machine next to the air compressor. He twisted his trunk around on his pelvis, arms stretched out to retrieve the appliance. His fingertips moved farther away with every step. Yet his feet wouldn't stop and the next thing Patapon knew, he was standing on the overpass. *Welcome back,* the voice said. He'd barely regained consciousness after fainting in a self-propelled body disconnected from its command centre. His body moved closer to the cold, concrete, unprepossessing guardrail. His senses had attained an unbearable degree of sharpness. Patapon saw an Italian Renaissance fresco in one cloud, a model of the human genome in another. The dawn broke wanly over the whole scene. His shadow lengthened behind him on the roadway below, in the harsh headlights of a Volvo hurtling toward the overpass. The driver-side door was wide open. Patapon's shadow stretched to the breaking point. *Okay, bye, I'm outta here,* the voice said. Patapon pitched headlong over the guardrail.

23

THE VOLVO DROVE ALONG THE HEART OF LA FRAYÈRE, and François saw the futuristic apple logo light up on the iPod screen. Two small apples of light shone on his corneas. He turned toward Rock, but there was no one in the driver's seat anymore. With the door open, the vehicle continued on its path, powered by momentum alone, and that's when the windshield shattered. The hood folded into a V, the rear wheels left the ground, and François's last necktie was splattered with little pieces of Patapon. The car plowed into a field of sickly potatoes. The grating of twisted metal gave way to the twitter of titmice and grosbeaks in the snow-muffled branches.

VI

GOLD

24

A FEW MONTHS ON, HIS STETSON OVER HIS FACE, A
loaded pistol under his bolster, Monti awoke tangled up in
his boiled wool blanket, from which he extricated himself by
pedalling like a madman. Genies of ochre dust rose up. He
thrashed his hat against his knee and shook his union suit.
His spade was propped up against a frost-split tree. He rubbed
his beard and out fell twigs and dry clay. *It was nothing but
a nightmare,* he thought. *There aren't any maggots. Nor any
Dexter.* Even so, standing in the middle of his slapdash camp,
with dry spittle at the corners of his mouth and his joints
poorly lubricated, he checked under his blanket. No Dexter.
It'll pass. Just bad dreams.

He then laid out the sum total of his gold, barely scabbled,
emptying his dirt-covered bags on the blanket. If it's gold you
want, well, here it is, and he soon found himself luxuriating
in it again. They laughed, he and his echo. This was the entire
fruit of his labour. And now that he was on his way back to
Gaspésie, he promised himself he'd return there in triumph.
To the sound of fanfares he'd throw presents to the children,
like the rich man he'd become.

Or the man, period. He'd toughened up, Monti had, through
months of digging underground and building his enterprise by

bossing around labourers a sight more experienced than him. He'd struck it rich quite a way from his original spot, a two-week trek from the mining operations that were turning the surrounding area upside down. In a creek seeming to match the spot on the map Dexter had drawn for him on the title deed he'd won at poker that night. Whatever was left of his baby fat had thickened, no doubt about it. Wallowing in his gold, he rolled off his blanket onto the embers of the night before. In the distance, a slab of rock came loose from an overhanging needle. The tops of the three fur hats that had been following him for days disappeared in the undulating bushes.

Using his bare hands, Monti poked the embers in the circle of stones to rekindle the fire. There was something mischievous about the flame in the still-dark dawn. Miles and miles of bleak nature stretched all around, a crudely drawn landscape, yet the crests and gorges and pits carved out by erosion were trimmed with icy lace. *The White Pass must be, what, a half day's hike from here, I'd say.* His horse stirred somewhere. Monti heard branches snapping, pebbles shifting. He thrust his pistol back into its holster. He practised ten minutes a day. He unholstered it. Then holstered it again with a snicker.

One thumb hooked inside his belt, which kept his gut in check, Monti chewed on his coffee. The white steam of his breath was so dense he could have sliced it up with a knife and stored the pieces in a box as a memento. The tracks on the ground were his and the horse's. He said to himself the magic beast would guide him once again when the time came. He thought of Joséphine and recalled another dream he'd had two nights earlier. The women of La Frayère had no faces, no mouths. They all spoke with Dexter's muffled voice. He unscrewed his tobacco tin and placed the quid on his waiting tongue.

With his Stetson slung over his back, he shaved in front of a pocket mirror that had lost much of its silvering. No foam or soap. The impossibly sharp razor blade rasped across the prominent bone of his lower jaw. A proper shave was essential. Monti said to himself he'd have the first sidewalk of Saint-Lancelot-de-la-Frayère built at his expense. Out of oak. From his house to the church. He'd put his neck of the woods on the map. Smooth as hard candy, he stepped back to admire his portrait and trod on his mess tin. The porridge spilled out and the greased toast lay wrong side down in the ashes. He hoisted the heavy bags of gold onto his horse's back.

"Yes," he said to his mount, "you're a magic beast too, you are. More magical than William Dexter, of that I'm certain."

He rubbed his muzzle against the horse's. He put himself right with a dose of hooch, which helped him deny the shakes that afflicted him of late when he wasn't drinking. It wasn't as good as the Yukon, but it would have to do in the meantime. Once he'd stowed away his flask, he finally, after several failed attempts, got into his saddle and tore off before slowing to a trot. The horse's bulk underneath him, its fullness, gave him satisfaction.

The ride to what Monti believed was the White Pass was uneventful. The panorama made up of terraces, rock slides, and crevasses shimmered just from the scarce ripples of vegetation alone. The horse's belly joggled, its legs twisting on the loose stones. Sunbeams splintered by branches mottled its coat with light. Monti plodded along like this, a sitting hen's look on his face, for most of the day. Never realizing he was being followed. Once in a while he would right-angle his flask and pour a good glug or two down the hatch. Under that Stetson, thoughts of investment abounded.

He'd gone perhaps one ten-thousandth of the way. His eyes beset by mosquitoes, he distracted himself as best he could. Taking a swig, he polished some lines of his very own poetry. He was quite liberal with the *O*'s, but it wasn't half bad for a scamp who, the previous spring, could not have conjugated *Simon says*. The sun in the middle of the white sky appeared somehow blunt. At the foot of an escarpment Monti reined in his horse. A buzzard was circling over a watering hole farther along. He promised himself that, once he was in a spending mood, freshly shampooed on avenues with the latest fashions on display, he'd purchase a flashy typewriter just like the one at town hall. Ice skates too, and tailor-made suits. As soon as he got settled in, he'd organize a grand hunting party that would fulfill his wish to make Saint-Lancelot-de-la-Frayère known far and wide. The vision, the form of the event, still eluded him, but that would come. When he got bored, he pulled out some carrots, with which he taught his horse to say "Bradley."

"Pow!" he said, drawing his revolver.

Balls of entwined branches bounced among the slabs of shale sliding in all directions on the plateau. Monti pulled up and, unsheltered from the wind, used his incisors to gnaw at a strip of beef jerky. He chewed and cogitated on penny-ante games with the image of Dexter and the Bead brothers in his head. It made him smile. Penny-ante, well, that was when there was no real money at stake. When the stakes amounted to stunts and trinkets. Penny-ante was for wimps. For fellows like Dexter and the Beads, who didn't drink, at least not anymore.

Because they didn't have enough money to drink their money away. And if you didn't drink, you couldn't join grown-up card games. So you couldn't win any money. To play real card games you had to think big.

"If you don't drink, you can't think big!" Monti shouted.

He wrapped up his meat. Above him, on one of the outcrops that ringed the plateau, a spurred boot was set down. Clouds collided and it began to drizzle. There were four times as many mosquitoes as before. The trail grew faint among the crevices. *"Dondaine la ridaine,"* Monti hummed, but off-key, and he didn't know the rest of the lyrics. Instead, he concentrated on boozing by the light of the lantern swaying on the side of his stallion. Suddenly the horse balked.

"Jumpin' Jehoshaphat! Do you hear ghosts neighing?" he asked it.

He stroked its nose to calm it down. But when you've hardly spoken all day, it's your own voice that sounds ghostly. Maybe they were nearing the Dead Horse trail. When he heard himself, Monti decided he was tuckered out. Ghost horse or not, he stopped. This is where he'd camp and get some rest. There was a clayey escarpment to lean against. A puddle of moonlight silvered the tips of his boots. Out of the darkness came animal snorts, the glimmer of wet nostrils, the gleam of the bit. Monti staggered from one task to the next. The fire that had to be lit. The bags he buried each night. He was fastidious on that score. He wrestled with his tarpaulin and the ropes, repeatedly hiking up his pants. Drunk enough to drive one right through his hand and not feel a thing, he knocked in the stakes. In the absence of a hammer, he went at it with his pistol butt.

Lurking behind a mound of clay that had built up on the slope, Charles Bead watched him without stirring. After a few more slugs, Monti seemed to slip on a banana peel with every step. Bead was sorry Dexter had to miss such a touching show. The sort of unintentional clowning that, when you describe it afterwards, isn't very funny if you didn't see it yourself. Dexter had spent the day gathering special herbs and minerals from which he'd scraped off a powder; he told the Beads he'd follow them at a distance and, with his hood pulled over his skull, then ground up the ingredients he'd collected.

But Charles still drew some consolation from knowing his brother must be witnessing the whole scene from his hiding spot on the other side of the hollow where Monti had chosen to repose. In fact, he discerned a bulky patch moving in the darkness. Something gave way and Donald tumbled into the scrub. Monti scratched his head and talked to himself in the shrunken glow of his lantern.

"Easy now, easy now," he said to a rock that he mistook for his horse.

The fella's dead drunk, Charles thought. *Or Dexter's taken out his grimoire.* Somewhere in the roiled shadows the horse pawed the ground. Charles heard his brother, crouching in the vegetation, himself give way to hilarity at the slapstick scene before him. Monti had just keeled over and flattened his tent. Donald couldn't contain his mirth. Monti heard him and stepped in his direction. But the lantern, hooked onto a branch, failed to light up that corner of the night.

"Kitty kitty," Monti said to the shrubs.

Between his numb fingers Monti rolled a bunch of leathery berries he'd just picked along with half of the bush. Big Bead had lost his gun in a penny-ante game. That was really a shame. It would have been more expedient to just put a spyhole through the man than to have to demolish him barehanded.

"Kss-kss, come over here, little critter."

The berries were about to turn into jam from being crushed between Monti's fingers. His other hand was ready to grab whatever figment he imagined was the cause of that rustling.

"I won't hurt you."

He chucked the berries over his shoulder. Thrilled, already enthralled by what he was about to discover, he struck a match taken from one of the two hundred and forty boxes Bradley the mailman had delivered the previous winter.

"Hello," said Donald in the flare of the match.

Monti's face all at once resembled his liver of twenty years hence. He somersaulted away, gouging out hoops of dust. All for nothing. There was no *rat-a-tat-tat*. No spray of limestone on the rock face. His tumble mostly left him disoriented in the darkness. Donald stood up a few yards away from him. He had couch grass stuck to his back. Tangled up in his trousers, Monti deftly unholstered a handful of air. He'd left his revolver behind in the darkness, next to the tent stakes. Now Charles, steam rising from his hide, sprang in slow motion from behind the escarpment, brandishing a spade in slow motion, the spade he'd glimpsed before the match went out and had grabbed as he passed. Slack-jawed, he let out a low roar and bounded, cricket-style, as if through maple taffy. For a split second the arcing moonlight glanced off the beast's head. *You better not miss me,* Monti thought. His blood spurted in a mist before his eyes and onto the invisible rocks.

"Swell," Charles said.

He flung the spade against the escarpment and smoothed his eyebrows with two wetted fingers. Straddling his victim, he pulled a comb from his boot and parted his hair anew. When Donald arrived, the two bags of gold slung across his shoulders, Charles was prodding at the pulpy, throbbing carbuncle on Monti's unconscious skull with a little stick.

"Now what?"

Passing it back and forth, they drained the bottle, which they'd just purloined from Monti together with his future. It burned like hell to start but soon left a snowy sensation deep in your thorax.

"It's not Yukon, huh?" Charles said.

"Now what?" Donald repeated.

In the light that Monti's dangling lantern cast between them, the brothers looked each other up and down. It was a telepathic exchange. A blast of wind played flute in the fissured rock.

"I guess," Charles said slowly, "we'll meet up with Dexter and divide up the loot."

Donald encircled his brother's biceps with his grip.

"You and me were raised in a kennel. Fed on turnips. Weaned in a trough. You were already strutting around town when Mama started ailing. It was me who ministered to her. I was only a child."

Charles made no attempt to free himself. The wind scattered his face. He'd seen something for sure. His face, white as a sheet.

"Mother would go deaf, dumb, and blind soon as the old man set foot in the house and I even…So then…I don't really know anymore why I'm telling you this. What I'm trying to say is that you…that when you…"

"What you're trying to say," Charles said when his fright had passed, "is to hell with William Dexter. We can just decamp with his share."

"We don't need him, I say."

The wound varnishing Monti's pate crimson glistened in the gloom. At dawn it would add a touch of colour to the Canadian Shield.

"Let's stick to our agreement. We'll go meet William. You'll head east to buy land and equipment. He and I will go west to talk to investors. A deal is a deal. Yukon. Yukon, Donald. Soon we'll all be millionaires."

He gave his brother a hug. He looked melancholy, resigned. Then he dipped into one of the bags and slipped a twisted nugget into Monti's breast pocket.

"A tip for Charon," he said, patting the pocket, and the brothers took off through a breach in the surrounding rocks.

Thirty years later, a Texas oil tycoon, a big shot that the lowliest Dallas shoeshine boy was allowed to call Howie, his given name, signalled to Charles Bead through a dissolute crowd to follow him behind a curtain of pearls. They were in Morocco, in the private parlours of a luxury casino, joylessly squandering obscene amounts of money considering that the shadow of World War II was gradually enveloping the globe. "And Dexter, where was he when this happened?" Howie had asked Charles earlier that week while cruising off Rabat aboard the *Belle Starr*. "A few miles away." Since the start of the cruise Howie had been intent on drawing him out, on tenaciously worming out of him the most reprehensible, the most villainous particulars of his story, the story of Yukon, the distillery through which he and Dexter had made their fortune. A self-made billionaire—of very short stature to boot—has the right to know what he wants to know. "So you and your brother, you went off without Dexter and followed this fellow, Monti, who didn't have a gun or anything?" he'd later asked at the casino in Casablanca. "Correct." The croupier, impeccably attired and apparently lobotomized, sent the roulette spinning again. A cool hundred bucks down the toilet. "I'll never understand why you went back to meet up with Dexter," Howie had said, visibly displeased, as he casually placed his chips. No answer. "Or why you didn't simply bump him off." This was the part where the story became unclear, and Howie, well, it nagged him. He might almost have written a blank cheque to get Charles to come clean. But Charles wouldn't talk about it. Ever. Having bought him his aperitif and then all the whisky, all the *mahia,* all the houris in the world, the Texan drew him aside, far from the gambling tables and the hubbub, behind a curtain of pearls that opened onto a secret boudoir, where he treated him to hashish from the central Rif, purchased in the port of Tangiers. The drapery began to move and merge with the fragrance of incense and harems, while Howie smoked and shared compromising confidences about certain hastily dug graves in a certain desert abutting El Paso—stiff competition. Then he again put the question to Bead, now in free fall deep inside himself. "Why didn't you leave Dexter behind? You had the gold. It's not as if you needed that warlock to start the company! Your brother might not have ended up that way had the two of you stayed together..." Charles abruptly grabbed him by his tuxedo lapels. The smoke pouring out of his mouth streamed back in through his nostrils. He swore to Howie that when he and Donald stood eyeing each other in

Monti's camp, plotting against Dexter after the holdup, he'd seen one, two, three snakes sliding out of his brother's mouth. They swiftly slithered away, leaving faint furrows in the dust like a rake.

25

THE LITTLE BAMBOO RODS OF THE CURTAIN TAPPED against each other again. The Chinese had just stepped away from his Go board and disappeared into the back store cluttered with mobiles, paper lanterns, and kites. Once Monti was certain the second-hand dealer wasn't watching him from behind his monocle, he began browsing and touching everything, his nostrils tickled by the camphor vapours that pervaded the confined half-light. He plunged his calloused hand, on which the frostbite had barely had time to scar, into one of the many baskets sitting at various heights on the motley shelves. The grains poured through his fingers, just as the riverbed on his claim had done through his sieve eight million times. He could find no French word for the sensation this had left him with. He ventured another glance at the smoky counter in the back. The shopkeeper hadn't resurfaced from the chaos. Monti was feeling pretty superior. He thrust his nose into the grains to smell what he realized too late was a dwarf variety of shrimp, dried in the shell and stinking to high heaven.

Recoiling in disgust, he upset a basket chock full of prickly-skinned fruits. The fruits rolled down the aisles pell-mell and sent the fowls squawking in all directions. Monti played the innocent, thinking no one was the wiser. But he straight away turned around and bent over as if to clean up when he saw in a mirror the shopkeeper perched on a stool, watching him. *He only half saw me,* he told himself reassuringly. The monocled merchant appeared unruffled, intrigued, lost in thought. His chimpanzee, sporting a bow tie and a cone-shaped hat, had also witnessed the goings-on and booed the customer from its cage. Monti hurriedly picked up two or three of the mutant fruits and put them in the wrong basket. Clutching the money inside his pocket, he pointed his freshly shaved chin at a broken-down typewriter on a shelf. With all that weight, the shelf had better be properly anchored.

"*Combien?* How much?"

Granted, his *much* sounded like *mush*. After endlessly dragging on his long, slim pipe, chafing its embers, the shopkeeper, his cheeks hollowing with a rustle of papyrus, grasped a jar; in it, revolving in a sort of bile, was a batch of fungi not quite the soft yellow of chanterelles or the smooth eruption of oyster mushrooms or anything like the twisted ideas brought on by boletes. The store was deserted but for him and Monti. And the chimp, now busy delousing itself.

"No, no," Monti said, and mimed typing. "The *chose* there, tap-tap-tap."

The man swivelled his neck, like an owl but worse. His smoke followed his movement and wreathed him about. *I might as well speak Greek for all the difference it would make.* Monti kneaded the handful of coins in his pocket. Having turned his face back in the right direction, the tradesman dipped his pen in an inkwell. He wrote something in a dog-eared notebook, which he then pushed toward Monti, nodding profusely by way of invitation.

"Okay, I taking it," Monti said, convinced by the still-damp figure on the page.

He thumped his forefinger against his chest and lit a cigarette off a candle on its last legs.

The shopkeeper climbed up to take the typewriter down from the shelf. His arms were like wires and the machine must have weighed as much as a ship's anchor. He showed no sign of strain. Monti, meanwhile, used his burning cigarette to threaten the chimpanzee, too comfortable on its perch for his liking. He failed to see the use of a single item in that whole bazaar, aside from the typewriter. *That and the candle.*

"Here," said the Chinese.

The only Asians Monti had ever seen until then were the navvies on the trans-Canada railway. Thinking of which, he nervously patted himself to make sure his train ticket was still in his jacket. The typewriter wasn't exactly tip-top tap-tappy. It wasn't as heavily varnished as the one in the town hall back home. But it would do while he waited to land a job with an outfitter or whatever. *I haven't lost it, I hope,* he thought, anxiously patting himself faster and faster. The ticket was no longer in the pocket where he thought he'd put it. While Monti proceeded to pull his clothes almost to pieces, the shop owner painstakingly wrapped the machine in a partly crushed hat box, putting Monti even more on edge. *Oh, come on, where the blazes did I put it, I ... Phew!* He'd slipped the ticket into his back pocket, as if to give himself a scare. For he never ever put anything in that pocket.

"Well, good evening," he said as he was about to push the door open.

He calculated what was left of his money to make certain

he had enough to get thoroughly pickled the next day on the train in the presence of the ladies.

"Mister! Mister!" the odds-and-ends dealer called out to him. He said "mister," but what Monti heard was *mystère*. Which made him feel something he rarely felt: bemused. He came back to the counter where, alongside the little joker of a chimp in its cruddy wood shavings, the old man, veiled in fumes, held out his pallid hand. Not for Monti to shake, uh-uh. The fingers were curled inward. *To be kissed. A little pat on the privates to go with that,* Monti thought, but without screaming bloody murder either. The screeching monkey, the signs through the smoke. He really didn't know. They didn't have these customs back home. Acting matter-of-fact, he grasped the merchant's hand—a relic, a piece of mummy—and brought his lips closer.

"Your change, mister."

Realizing the Chinese didn't want a kiss but was proffering his change, Monti's reflex was to shake the hand harder. Then, in a blunder that, before he'd been left for dead in the wilderness by thieves, would have made him howl with laughter, he started to scratch at a blemish on the man's hand as if to remove it. The coins clinked dully on the pewter change plate. Monti shoved off, his self-esteem six feet ahead of him and the Remington in his arms trussed up like a cast iron turkey. He walked, leaning back somewhat as a counterbalance. The bell over the shop door rang until the following day.

Toronto, Tkaronto. *Where the trees rise from the water,* Monti thought. You had to go out into the metropolis, among the throng of free electrons, the jets of steam everywhere, the caleche drivers' crops, to grasp just how smoky that second-hand store was. *What was it I said—good evening? It's the middle of the afternoon.* Vendors of all shapes and colours were hawking their goods amid the streetcars charging full on in a metallic corrida. "I'll go back to my room, take a load off, revive myself somewhat," Monti muttered, his head bowed. He turned up a teeming thoroughfare, Queen Street, walking a tightrope through the scraps left behind by vegetable stalls. A rag-clad four-year-old girl was drawing pictures on the paving stones with a pebble while her older brother, as tattered as she, offered services of all sorts. *I'll find myself one like him tomorrow to lug my suitcases,* Monti thought.

He blew the black out of his nose, without a hankie. Soon enough the buildings began to converge overhead toward a vanishing point beyond the stratosphere. The Remington knifed into his biceps and wrists. It weighed as much as all the books that could have been written on it. He set his machine down on some empty crates and leaned against a wrought iron railing, trying to bide his time.

"Do you understand what I'm saying?" a plebeian sitting on the ground asked him.

The man tugged at his sleeve, trying to tell him something. Monti roused himself.

"Qu'est-ce que tu là?" Monti replied, tugging in turn on the plebeian's sleeve.

"Do you speak English?"

"Yes, no, Toronto," said Monti.

He gathered up his parcel, now heavier than before, and continued on his way. At the intersection, the streets, you might say, collided. Out of them poured an unstoppable torrent of people. Monti wasn't quite sure of the route back to his lodgings. It was enough for a flounce to brush by him to make his eyes light up like thousand-watt bulbs. A few minutes later, on Yonge Street, contemplating his reflection in the Eaton's display window, he convinced himself he was a handsome lad. With his trimmed beard and stylish suit, he cut a fine figure. The typewriter lent him the appearance of a war correspondent on leave, or a star reporter. But the foot traffic forced him to budge, and when he turned back to the window, his reflection was no longer superimposed on the store mannequin. Looking back at him was a worm-eaten image, the image of a failure in threadbare togs scrubbed too often on the washboard. On the other side of the glass, an Eaton's employee with a feline moustache and a broomstick up his rectum invited Monti to get away from his storefront. *Goods Satisfactory or Money Refunded,* a notice read. Moving on, his arms numb, Monti wondered about the constant obsession in the capital with giving people their money back.

He may have been unaware that in the city you took back your change and that Toronto wasn't the capital of Canada; on the other hand, he could recognize the Guinness trademark anywhere. Either his hand trembled less and less with every swig of stout or the pub was gradually adjusting to his trembling. His typewriter sat on the stool opposite him; you'd have thought they were having a pint together. The other customers were also imbibing at their tables, between the tables, under the tables. *Your change! To hell with that, your change!* His hand on his liver, Monti pondered this. Whenever he noticed a spot on his Remington, he wiped it away.

When a beefy waiter tossed him the daily menu, Monti, holding his fork like a tool, flipped his frayed necktie over his shoulder and jammed his napkin into his collar. The patron at the next table was eating a bowl of glue topped with laurel leaves for a touch of urbanity. *A pint equals a steak,* Monti told himself. He would drink instead. *For the yeast.*

After his second glass his hands were seventy-five percent steady, so he ordered another for the other twenty-five percent. *Thirty less two for the stable,* he counted, *plus those ten bucks of mine to get from Montreal to the village.* Through the clamour, he observed the well-heeled clients and gave himself a pat on the back, because in Gaspésie they might not wear top hats with a band that matched their morocco bootstraps, but neither did they fuss about every penny. He still hadn't gotten over that business with the second-hand dealer. *Your change, your change.* No one east of Rimouski ever asked for their change back if it was under twenty-five cents. He used the back of his knife to sweep the head of foam off the pint he'd just been served. A financier, whom Monti suspected of wearing a rug, was having a big belly laugh as if everyone in the place had come just to hear him. *Look at him,* Monti thought, *with his bank investments and his rosy cheeks.* He'd have liked to see him stripping the shingles off a roof in the blazing sun with the Canons back home. *Showing off for that other stuffed herring in a crinoline dress.* Outside, the soot-coated gaslights lit up the block. Monti licked the blade of his knife. *Whoa, now. Drink up. You've got to cool off.* Despite the ambient babel and the strident orders, all he could hear was the lemon the financier was squeezing over his oysters. Well, all right, he couldn't hear it, but it was still driving him crazy. He sprang to his feet to pay his bill before he killed someone. *Four bucks for a room in Montreal, plus two for Joséphine's present.* He was pulling coins out from his handful of change one at a time when the slurp of a sucked oyster assaulted his ears. Distracted once again from his budgetary calculations, Monti slammed all his change down on the counter.

"Sir! Sir!" the waiter shouted after him as he elbowed his way toward the exit, a cask of beer in his gizzard and the typewriter under his arm.

For Pete's sake, Monti wondered, *have I gone astray in my peregrinations?* His armpits patched with sweat, he tried to locate the copper-green steeple near his rooming house, or the pint-sized Union Jack in the corner of the flag on the building across the way, or the statue of a hero that could serve as a landmark. He sensed something like black eraser crumbs on his palms. The typewriter was slipping from his hands. And, boy, was the city ever ugly! An unoccupied bench came into view in a square. His energy gave out. Granting himself a respite, Monti sat his bum down and leisurely ogled the many Joséphines going by at different speeds. The band had gone brown on the shapeless hat with which he wiped his face. His thoughts unravelled like a spool of thread down the avenue that stretched from his temple to the jumble of cars and pedestrians. He asked himself if he was closer to his lodgings than to that bar, where he was tempted to return. The shadows of the tall, window-riddled monoliths overlapped on the pavement. He tried not to let the crowd make him dizzy and doubted that these city dwellers could be sure who they were in such a zoo. *You could just as well be that fellow over there, or him or him or him—what difference would it make?* Then, vowing to pack himself inside a crate within the next few weeks and get Bradley to deliver him to Mrs Guité's place, he laughed out loud.

"I wouldn't mind enjoying myself as much as you," said a nice fat citizen wearing gold-rimmed glasses.

He'd popped up on the bench next to Monti. The sitting position pushed his paunch up to his chest. The man stabbed at the headlines in his newspaper as though they were Monti's fault. *Can't a guy regress in peace?* Monti thought. He scooched his behind to the very edge of the bench. But the citizen was already holding forth with broad legislative gestures. His cane, its knob embossed with a crown, was propped against the back of the bench.

"Robert Borden," he said. "Robert Borden. Robert Borden."

The man said other things too, but that was all Monti understood. In any event, he'd quickly stopped listening when it became clear this wasn't the oyster eater from the pub. *Give or take a couple of details.* The citizen's pinky stood up as he unfolded, scanned, smoothed out, and again folded his newspaper, taking pains to make as much noise as possible. Monti hadn't uttered a single word since the man had shown up and had to concentrate so that the slap to the back of the head wouldn't lash out on its own.

He also understood: "Sir Wilfrid Laurier."

But he didn't know who these people were and, while not listening, told himself that when he got back to the village, he might possibly mate his horse with Maturin's mare. *If the good doctor hasn't already knocked her up himself.* Arms folded, legs intertwined, he turned his back to the citizen, but the flow of words would not be checked by such trifles. The man's limbs and neck stretched out toward Monti. Behind his glasses his eyes took on a larval aspect. Monti was better able to grasp what he was saying.

"Establishment. Robert Laird Borden. Frenchies. Laurier."

One out of every hundred and fourteen words on average. He still kept mum, nodding to everything, nodding to the breaking point. But when the man waxed patriotic and touched him, Monti thought, *Hey, hands off!*

"Laurier. Frenchies."

Now the citizen was addressing the nation. His face was so puffed up, the blackheads were about to burst from his pores. With one hand on his heart, he displaced entire populations with the other, redistributed vast quantities of natural resources, whole provinces so as to redraw the map of the land. People strolling in the square gave the park bench a wide berth. Monti was just waiting for this Father of Confederation to climb onto his lap so he could play giddy-up and send him skyward.

"Cheap labour. Establishment. Frogs."

"Can I touch you?" Monti cut in at the magic word.

The citizen nearly had a conniption fit when Monti rubbed his thumbs all over the man's lenses. *Comes a time when you've gone too far beyond the pale.* Cries could be heard in syncopation with Monti's damp steps as he walked off:

"My cane! My cane!"

Monti, already far away, naturally had to ask himself if the citizen was shouting "my cane" or "my change." Farther on, he identified the sign of a wholesaler of whatever you didn't need. *Our grandparents did without.* He held the typewriter against his hip now, with one arm bent like a backwards *C*. His liver had metabolized enough alcohol for the need to make itself felt again. *I spent six bucks for the room, two for the stable boy, so I should still have ... Good day, ma'am, good day, Joséphine, good day.* The arm holding the machine shook from

shoulder to fingertips, while the cane he'd unknowingly confiscated from the Canuck left concentric rings in the puddles.
Ah si mon coeur était grenouille! The rain put him in a merrier
mood even though he was on edge. Hamming it up, he waded
through back-alley puddles and rivulets with a self-imposed
urge to sing a *turlutte*.

There it was, his rooming house. He announced himself
by ringing the doorbell with the knob of the cane, opened
the door with his elbow, and shut it again with his butt. His
boots made the same noise sixteen times to the top of the
thirty-two stairs, accompanied each time by a tap of the cane.
He was about to drop the Remington when he opened the
door on the landing. He closed it behind himself and got
quite an earful.

"Good day, even so," he said to his landlady.

No resemblance to Joséphine. He hadn't said another word,
but already the grouchy dwarf was wagging her head in disapproval under her shawl, which was draped over woollens
the same funereal hue as her heavy serge skirt. *You're due for
a visit to Eaton's, you are.* Now it was the door to his room he
was opening. He closed it behind him. Then he opened and
closed it again so the landlady would be quite certain he'd
closed it. She heard the thud of the typewriter, which Monti
had just dropped onto his pallet. She heard him moan with
relief. Then she heard the key clicking in the lock and the latch
snapping shut. Do not disturb.

Monti soon got up from his pallet. He had the impression
the bone-setter had missed him. It was well past the time for
his medicine. His beard bothered him even though he had no
beard. There was mould creeping up from the floor onto the

GOLD

plaster. Trembling, he laid his effects out on the floor around the typewriter. Cigarette butts with one or two puffs left in them, pieces of wet paper, a camping knife with some unusable tools. And his title deed. On the back, the map of his river was marked with an X at the spot where the multicoloured beast had revealed his deposit to him, the same X as the one with which he'd signed Bradley's form in a previous life, less than a year earlier.

His razor blade scraped across his bare cheeks, which he'd smeared with a dab of dirty soap using an old, completely stiff washcloth for want of foam and a brush. He'd been to the barbershop the day before, but it didn't matter. With the tepid water left over at the bottom of the chamber pot, he shaved his face. Not his beard, his face. The integument. The bar of soap encrusted with particles and tow flew out of his hand whenever he grasped it too tightly. If he was to return to his village dirt poor, at least he wouldn't look lice-ridden. The blade travelled across his tanned hide. He opened his jaws to test their elasticity. One eye half-closed, the other bugged out, he sharpened the razor a little more on his whetstone. He said to himself if he never stopped, the blade would eventually disappear. He shaved another patch of his jaw as smooth as the bone underneath. *Before I left, Gontran Arsenault owed me twenty-five bucks for my muskrat traps.* His sunburned torso, bushier than before, contrasted with his cleanly stripped mug. While William Dexter and the Bead brothers roamed around at his expense, the blade plied along his mandible, removing yet another layer of skin. The water in the chamber pot turned crimson.

Having dried his face, Monti stretched out again on the pallet to relax. His thoughts raced between his ears or were spoken out loud. He rolled over on his stomach, his red chin cupped in his hands, which soon began to tingle. The religious picture on the wall sat in judgment of him. Cotton threads stuck out from his cut. He opened a book by someone named Homer, his dictionary close at hand. It was the only French book in the room. The grouchy dwarf used it to keep the window open. Intent on not disappointing Joséphine any more than he was already bound to disappoint her, Monti saddled himself with some reading. *Never in a hundred years would a girl of her class walk down the aisle with me now.*

"Book I." It took him quite a while to read this far because, even though Monti had taught himself the rudiments of spelling and grammar during his exile, there was still a lack of mortar between the words, nor did he know how a book worked, so there was something touching about the earnestness with which he read every word of text—the title page, the publisher's address, everything. The author, he told himself, would sooner or later get to the point. It began: "O Muse!" *That's Joséphine.* "O Muse! Sing of him, that nimble, many-sided man, rich in wiles and stratagems . . ." *Stratagem.* Noun. Cleverly devised trick or scheme. *I can do this.* "O Muse! Sing of him, that nimble, many-sided man, rich in wiles and stratagems, who, having razed the walls of sacred Troy . . ." *Now, hold on a minute.* "The walls of sacred Troy . . ."

I'll read this later, he told himself, and closed the book. He got up and went to sit at the desk, which, like his landlady, was tiny. He set about counting his money in one-dollar stacks: one, seven . . . *I'll start over.* A buck and a quarter for the room, the pints at the pub, then . . . The mental image of Joséphine once again derailed his calculations, so he returned to Homer.

Don't give up. "O Muse! Sing of him, that nimble, many-sided man, rich in wiles and stratagems, who, having razed the walls of sacred Troy, wandered scores of years, saw many peoples, learned their minds and manners ..."

Homer's book landed in a heap somewhere behind the chamber pot. Monti wasn't in the mood for stories. He stood in the middle of the floor. Inspired by a dockside parade he'd seen the day before near Wellington Place, he wanted room to manipulate the cane he'd filched from the bloke in the square. After several minutes of fooling around with it, he managed a few figures that weren't too bad for a beginner, with twirls and majorette-style juggling. And the more he went at it, the more his confidence grew. His cane split the air, flipped, twisted like a top, while he himself gyrated faster and faster with some fancy footwork. He batted his eyelashes, extended one leg back for the arabesque, and the religious picture on the wall was transfixed by a blade. The blade, planted in the wall, quivered with the sound of a musical saw. Monti looked around. His razor was there on the floor. As was his pocket knife. The blade was longer than that, he noted, and the crown on the knob grew visible as the steel's vibration diminished. It had pierced right through the wall. On the other side, the grouchy dwarf began to rattle off rosaries at the top of her lungs. Monti, as surprised as her, turned away from the pious etching and saw that what he held in his hand was just a wooden sheath. An empty scabbard. The other half—how about that—of a sword cane.

26

"YOU'RE DRAGGING YOUR FEET!" MONTI COMPLAINED to the porter he'd hired.

Or, rather, the whipping boy he'd found in the vicinity of his rooming house. The youngster seemed to be cut from the same cloth as the boy he'd glimpsed the day before. Monti wasn't entirely sure they weren't one and the same.

"*Moé* to have job *pour toé,*" he'd shouted from the window of his room.

By way of an advance, he'd dropped a handful of pennies down on the sidewalk below, promising a couple bucks more when they got to the train station.

"I'm your man," the little guy had said.

At worst I'll have Bradley mail you the rest from back home, Monti had said inwardly. The kid had taken Monti's Gaspé accent to be a sign of mental deficiency.

"Your sister not *avec* yourself?" Monti asked after coming downstairs with his gear to join him.

He understood, of course, that this wasn't quite the same child as yesterday, whose sister decorated the sidewalks with her drawings. But since they all seemed interchangeable to him, these Torontonians young and old alike, he wanted to check.

"I only have brothers," the kid replied.

On arriving in Toronto, Monti had seen a toy like that in a shop. A wooden figure to which you gave a specific personality simply by adding your choice of accessories and distinctive features with the help of magnets.

"Sir, wait!" the youngster called out now as they approached the station. "Sir!"

He must have been no more than thirteen or fourteen years old, and it was only so his mother could put some butter on the potatoes that he let himself be treated like a mule. He struggled with the trunk full of Monti's effects.

"Hurry up!" Monti shouted from the other side of the street, disappearing intermittently behind the passing cars.

He raced toward the station as if it were running away from him. The youngster would surely have lost sight of him in the crush if Monti, unable to tear his eyes away from the building's brickwork arch, hadn't almost fallen on his back when he stepped underneath it.

"Sir ..." the boy puffed as he caught up to his employer.

But Monti was already off again. *Ask the conductor to punch my ticket before I take my seat,* he rehearsed as he hurtled forward. Around him the travellers rushed in every direction. At a quick estimate, all of Saint-Lancelot-de-la-Frayère could have fit into the train station. The air rippled in the heat of the engines, and then, through the ballet of baggage, Monti spotted up ahead the ephemeral zigzagging patch of colour that had been guiding his steps for a while.

"This way! This way!" he cried, turning toward his porter, once again pushed back twenty feet by the throng. "This way!"

Except that it wasn't this way, and Monti wasn't going to calm down until he was ensconced in his seat, enjoying what he considered a well-deserved state of oblivion. The beast's presence in this place unsettled him. The tumult echoed under the domed ceiling, and the pigeons up there were in a flap. Monti charged through the crowd, waving his ticket in full view. The train whistles, the traffic, the all-English signs, the whistles, the English. He swung around obsessively to make sure the kid was still following behind. *I should have hung little bells on the boy's halter.* His trunk stayed more or less afloat amid the human tide ceaselessly closing and interflowing between the porter and him.

"Giddyap!" Monti shouted.

He urged the boy on at a distance with his ticket, losing the beast's trail among the scissoring legs and the steam a locomotive had just expelled through its nostrils.

He inched forward in the queue, his hair a mess, showing his ticket to people nearby. He moved his lips, muttering. As he came closer, he stared at the train conductor more and more intently, into the depths of his soul. The conductor responded with a friendly quip. But Monti didn't laugh. Never in his life had he not laughed like that. The conductor's attempt to punch his ticket was all it took for Monti to shove him into the crowd. The shock wave raised skirts and reproaches. Monti held his palms up in a gesture of innocence. To reassure everyone, he hummed a lullaby of his own making.

Once he'd taken his seat, feeling about as comfortable as he'd have been in a sheet metal folder, he tried to doze off. He counted sheep in hopes of catching one by the tail and getting pulled along, hippety-hop, to the cattle car, where he might get some sleep in the hay with his horse and the rest of the crèche. But sleep eluded him. Monti had no more circulation in his feet. He stood up and, mimicking the gait of the rail employee ahead of him, he went exploring.

A short while later he made his way back to his seat, holding on to the headrests or the heads resting on them. He finally fell asleep, his noggin propped against his neighbour's shoulder. His arm formed a jug handle attached to his side, the outside of his wrist pressed against his hip. A jolt of the axles and there he was, asleep, with his buttocks gone slack and his shoulder blade about to protrude from his back. Another jolt and he was sleeping with his arms tightly folded, his mouth gaping toward the ceiling. Something stirred, climbed up his pants, which were twisted around his shanks, paler than the rest of him, and a shiny muzzle peeked out from under his... Around him, people had their chins on their chests and springs instead of necks. Monti rubbed his eyes and stretched. Had a gargle. Capped his flask again. Smiled like an asylum runaway at the snooty rich dame seated nearby, reeking of perfume.

"Bonsoir," he said, puckering his lips.

He walked for the first time into the club car wearing a well-cut jacket and a hat with no bird's nest on it. He'd borrowed them along the way from sleeping passengers.

Equally well attired behind his varnished wood counter, the starchy barman was wiping a glass so clean Monti thought he was miming to perfect his technique. Monti rapped his sword cane twice on the floor, and with a snap of his towel the server produced a coaster, an ashtray, and the glass he'd just polished. You couldn't even see it from some angles, depending on the streaks of light. Monti stroked his raw, almost scarlatina face. He promised himself to shave as soon as he could.

"Grand Marnier," he said with his best English accent.

He'd noticed the bottle among its peers and found it matched his swank disguise. Not even a Morse code expert could have deciphered the novel he was writing on the counter with his knuckles.

"*Tout de suite, monsieur,*" the barman said in French, with no English accent.

The Grand Marnier rose in the glass as his fluid fingers played over it. Three ice cubes silently sank into the liquor. Monti had no time for such ceremonies. He fished out the cubes and let them melt in the ashtray.

"Another Grand Marnier," he said, pushing his drained glass toward the bottle.

The Pole at the Klondike may not have served you in high style, but with his language sounding like screws and nuts and bolts he whispered to your liver words apt to subdue it. Monti lifted his second glass to toast the barman and swore it was uplifting.

"To your health," he said.

He downed his drink in a long swallow followed by a few short ones in rapid succession. This loosened his tongue. Smartly attired, he babbled to the barman about fertilizer, smelt, the Canon family, a potato sack race he'd once attended. Perhaps he somewhat overdid the English accent. He started talking faster and louder whenever the barman turned his back or stepped away a little. Monti wanted him all to himself. Standing before the rows of variegated bottles, the barman was an entity of light.

"Would you pour me one more?"

After a while Monti's jaw began to ache from the effort of babbling on in Yankee. The barman talked to him in his native

French. With an air of knowing the whole story, he explained that the railway company had bought a supply of liquor from the White Star Line, the ocean liner company. Monti made as if he wasn't listening, to indicate he already knew all that, but it interested him and he bought drinks for the other clients who showed up. "Put it on my tab," he said each time. It was better to pretend he was on easy street to ensure that the archangel at the taps wouldn't turn off the pipeline.

"One more, 'f ya please."

I'm getting plastered tonight, he thought. For fear of running out of room in his notepad, the barman started to put the little strokes closer and closer together.

"We wouldn't be derailing now, would we?" Monti asked when the train jolted.

What's more, the car was spinning and he wanted to stand up to hitch his pants up as high as possible. At the same time, he called the Grand Marnier over to him, just as he'd called for the beast in the bushes before getting whacked with the shovel.

"Maybe we just ran over a couple of Indians," the barman joked.

Monti gave him a prodigious glare. Even worse than what the conductor had gotten earlier. He was up to his umpteenth glass and still hadn't paid. The barman did his utmost to change the subject, but over the next hour Monti constantly brought him back to the Indians. He wanted to know why he'd said that. He wanted to know also if he knew a guy called Billy Joe Pictou. When he finally realized the barman hailed from Limoilou, he dropped the accent he'd affected for the sake of style.

"Me too, I'm French," he said, still staring at the barman.

Monti's mouth was numb to the point where everything came out as if he'd just arrived from the tooth puller's. Orange blossoms were about to start growing out of his ears, his brain wasn't sending orders to the right places in his body, he wiggled his fingers over his glass in an attempt to fill it himself with an abracadabra.

"One of these fine days," he mumbled to the barman, "you'll come over to our place for supper. I'll tell you about the poker game when an extraordinary beast led me to my seam in a river I'd just won."

After that the barman decided to discreetly water down his Grand Marnier. Deadly serious, Monti fired his thumb-and-forefinger revolver at people who weren't really there.

"We could invite Bradley too," he said, blowing on his fingertip. "Do you know him, Bradley?"

Monti saw right through the barman and his water. He bought the rest of the bottle of liquor and drank straight from it. While the server searched for a way to get rid of him, Monti himself searched for a way to vanish into thin air when the time came to pay up. Because he'd checked on the sly. Not one red cent in the pockets of his borrowed jacket. The level of conversation wasn't getting any higher. Now Monti was playing the wise guy about the varieties of alcohol and testing the barman's knowledge. When the man defied him to name a liquor he didn't know, Monti said:

"My brain-wrecking alcohol—there's one you've never tasted."

After asking him to repeat the name a couple of times, the barman concurred that, no, he'd never tasted it. Luckily, said Monti, he had some on him, left over from his last batch. Why not, the barman thought, his shift was ending. Monti had him set two whisky glasses down in front of them on either side of the counter. Then he poured out some of the substance that was eating away the inside of his flask. It was his unmarketable attempt to reproduce Yukon using guesswork. When he was still in the woods, he'd tried to dissect the taste of the divine libation, to identify its ingredients, but he lacked the subtle palate this required. The barman, meanwhile, was shaken. A large tear ran down each of his cheeks. He drank his second glass in the name of science. Standing before his bottles and lime quarters, he couldn't immediately remember what he'd intended to do. His head felt like a cat in a bag.

"My turn," he finally said.

"Okay, your turn."

He served them a mixture, something injurious, and there was no denying that, having swallowed it, Monti saw the decor fly out the window when the train dived down a ravine.

"Gotcha," the barman said.

He belched with a thump to his chest, and you saw the air in front of his mouth ripple like an overheated roadway. He began to untie his apron behind the deserted bar when a hand, sun-baked yet covered in poorly healed frostbite scars, thrust up from the ground and gripped the counter, followed by another. The wrist tendons bulged in an effort to hoist up the rest of the body.

"Don't you start acting up," Monti warned, wagging a limp finger.

It took him a moment to recover his balance and stop sliding off his stool onto the floor. He drank the rest of the Grand Marnier and wiped his mouth on his sleeve. He let out a satiated "Ah." *Goods Satisfactory or Money Refunded,* he recalled. He reached his hand out over the counter for his change. His arm was mirrored in the polished wood. To Monti it was a fish surfacing belly up in dead water. The equally addled barman unthinkingly dipped into his cash box and handed him the money. Then he turned back to balancing the columns of figures overflowing the page of his notebook. As he drew a slash through the last group of four vertical strokes, it dawned on him that he had no business giving back change since this joker hadn't yet paid anything. He whirled around. There was Monti's stool revolving with no one on it.

Moving as if his shoelaces were tied together, Monti had run off after the beast. It had just climbed down next to him, its silvery claws clicking against the wall. The animal kept cooing sweetly as it bounded down the aisle to the far end of the club car and the passenger car beyond. *Out of my way, Jack.* Monti bumped a conductor, leaving him rattled. Then he opened the door and strode over the coupling, which shuddered as the cars rumbled on. Aeolus tore off his hat. The hat sailed spinning into the night behind the train. Monti crossed one car after another. His excitement flowed down to the tip of his sword cane. He glimpsed the beast once again, now coral, now translucent, racing down the train's fuselage, flattening its body to slip under the doors.

"Where did it go?" he asked a woman.

He stopped short under a hissing lamp. The woman shrank far back when a thread of drool dribbled from Monti's mouth onto the armrest. A pile of cardboard suitcases spilled into the middle of the aisle. The mocking beast sprang from a seat in a welter of dazzling flashes. Monti managed to tumble headlong into the baggage without slowing down. *Maybe there's still gold in there.* He was exultant now: before him, his prey was backed against the closed door of the last car.

"You're so pretty I could eat ya. Why dontcha come a little closer."

Tears welled up in his eyes. The other passengers were transfixed, motionless, wax figures in fashionable poses. The creature grew fearful in Monti's arms and covered itself with lilac-coloured stripes. It retracted its feathery plumes under its angora fur, which became riddled with neatly rimmed orifices that sprouted long, fluffy ears.

"Don't act so pitiful," Monti said, turning it every which way to see how it was put together. "Never in my life would I do you any harm."

Then it was the animal's pupils that contracted until they practically disappeared. Under a tiny teat on its belly Monti found a fleshy fold and explored it with a lover's touch. But he couldn't reach the bottom of this warm flesh, which he rippled from within, the skin pliant enough to glove his hand. *There's no meat in there.* He pulled his fist out of the beast as fast as he pulled his hand out of his pants whenever the orphanage priests walked in without knocking. He stepped back a few paces, his boots turned into anvils, and cast the beast a questioning gaze. It was pressed against the door, now sombre and panting. Its fragile colours shifted like oil on water. Monti uncurled his fist and discovered a piece of paper. The punched half of a train ticket. Car 8, Seat 12. The beast whipped out a reptilian pink tongue.

Monti regained consciousness on the floor in a corner of the car. He saw that his hands were daubed with black ink.

His flask, covered in finger stains, waited patiently against some brain-splattered wainscoting. *I'm never drinking that stuff again,* he thought. Someone had tried to open the door behind him. That's what had roused him from sleep. There was an immigrant family in the car. The two Camemberts that were his feet seemed very far away, unlike his oversized hands, which he examined incredulously with watery eyes. *You just had yourself some prime lunatic dreams, there, Honoré my friend,* he thought as he stuffed blobs of grey matter back into his skull through his ears. He stretched his limbs, his jacket sleeves rolled up to the middle of his forearms. The opposite wall receded and advanced at the same time, the aisle tapered away and gained in height. His posture needed minor adjustments as a result.

Monti put what he'd strewn about back in his pockets, not realizing that for the past two minutes he'd been trying to pocket his sword cane. He wondered what kind of disabled fencer could find such a contraption in any way useful. Then he set about rereading what he'd written on his typewriter before going under, until he began to list to one side, slobbering and seeing spots in front of his eyes. The writing was dreadful, but even so. There was a good side to giving up other things so he could buy this gadget: he'd had fun with it. He drained what was left in the flask, carefully licking the inside of the bottle's neck, and rolled himself a few. His memory was playing tricks on him: he jammed the stolen hat down to his chin even though he remembered losing it in the wind along the tracks. *Borrowed,* he thought. *Not stolen.* He had no liking for thieves.

He couldn't find the club car. Must have imagined it. A shame, because a Grand Marnier would have washed away the aftertaste of turpentine that his brain-wrecking alcohol had plastered all over the inside of his yap. He went out on the steps in the wind to brush his teeth with his fingertips. The arc of his jaw opened onto a lustrous bronze beach under the reddened sun of his eye. His eyebrow had turned into a gannet above the rolling waves of his cheek breaking against his temple, a clay cliff dominated by the concha of his ear.

His thoughts could no longer escape the trap they'd plunged into while he was having a pleasureless smoke under the stars. *Always start from the principle that people have bad intentions.* His tobacco had retained the taste of winter; he felt restless and lost as he contemplated the black-and-white fields of flowers cleaved by the locomotive. He began to kick furiously at the guardrail.

He awoke again, his palate chafed by his snoring. Someone was shaking his shoulder, pointing to the stub of his ticket— Car 8, Seat 12—to show him he was sleeping in their seat. *Well, well, ain't that peculiar.* But Monti remained seated, at the other fellow's expense. And he wasn't in the least distracted by this. In fact, he was wondering if those were gladioli or phlox in the field earlier, if it was the season. He didn't budge. The other passenger craned his neck in search of an attendant who might get this mule out of his seat. With streamers and confetti flying and to the sound of applause and cheers, Monti finally got up and walked away like a puppet with its strings tangled up. It had been a while since he'd dreamed of Dexter.

He woke up laughing to himself in the club car, his face forgotten on a table that didn't match the others. Behind the counter, the barman was tapping away on a typewriter just like Monti's. The barman shrugged as this man from Gaspésie minced his words, explaining that he didn't have the means to pay up. Monti walked through a few cars and got back to his seat, his repose, a more suitable latitude. His sword cane rapped against the armrests and the bars of the baggage racks. Even in a train he went around in circles. So he returned to the club car. The door at the far end was obstructed by a dead body asleep on the floor on the other side.

Monti about-faced and retraced his steps to the car behind. There was another attendant standing in the aisle farther down, getting lambasted by a voice at once haughty and animated. Only a bit of hat and a hairy hand peeked out from the compartment where the sorehead was lounging. The lad took the scolding without flinching. Then he wheeled around, a tray perched on fingers arranged in a pentagon. He marched toward Monti aping the boor's grumpy expression. Monti had to step aside to avoid being trampled. When he spun around, trying to snag the boy by his uniform, the door swung shut in his face. He wanted an apology and opened the door again. The tracks and ballast streamed by beneath his boots. He turned back in the direction of the whiner at the other end, who was playing solitaire on his table. The cards naturally drew Monti's attention. The man placed the jack of hearts on top of the queen of spades.

"Donald Bead?"

If his name hadn't been spoken out loud, the man would never have noticed Monti looking over his shoulder at his cards.

Donald Bead's neck just barely fit into the opening of his collar, from which the cool water of a lace ruff spilled out. His eye sockets hollowed his face out with windy caves that, through the bushes of his sideburns, were connected by the canyon of a mouth filled with rocklike teeth under the grainy moon shining on the tip of his nose. Whereas he should have flung back the panel of his jacket to draw his gun, Donald instead hugged the bag of gold next to him and shielded himself with his other arm. His flesh split like a tomato at the first stroke of the sword cane. Monti told himself that he might have caught just one of the three, but at least he'd caught the biggest one. After twenty strokes Monti was polite enough all the same to tell Bead to forget about the cattle he still owed him.

27

"OKAY, OKAY, WE HEARD YOU, WHY DONTCHA SHUT UP
this morning," Xavier Melançon grumbled.

Perched on a strut of its coop, the cock thought it was a
tenor. Xavier came out holding a newspaper and stumbled
over the watering can by the doorstep. He pretended to shoot
the cock with a slingshot through the openwork. His suspenders knocked against his thighs as he shuffled through the tall
grass to the outhouse on the far side of the yard, where the
sandy beach began. The loose pages of the *Vivier* fluttered
behind him like a pennant among the dragonflies and the
white dandelion blowballs. Due to the clap he'd caught at
Mrs Dubuc's place, he wasn't exactly eager to answer the call
of nature. It was going to be a muggy day, you could tell just
by looking at the dead-calm sea. The sun swelled up from one
minute to the next. Along the way, not so much to perform his
ablutions as to relieve his hangover, Xavier dunked his head
in the pigs' rainwater-filled trough.

In any case, at 8 a.m. the foreman would be no more pre-
sentable than him or any of the jobbers at the work site, which
is why Xavier, though hardly ahead of schedule, took the time
to have a breakfast of flowers and a raw egg. Back in the house,
he sucked it through a hole in the shell, along with the dregs

of some serviceberry wine he'd transferred into a soup tureen so he could fill his canteen at the well. Between two sucks, he stubbed his toe against a loose board as he reached out to grab his six-toed tomcat, which had no business lurking around the trap near a dank pile of laundry. A dead mouse sailed out through an opening and into the neighbour's raspberries. Xavier picked up his mite-ridden cap and his tarnished steel lunch pail and closed the door gently, so as not to bring down his little cottage, as he left.

To spare himself thirty-eight good mornings, he avoided the road to church and cut across the cemetery overrun with ryegrass. There were white crosses smothered under the foliage and a whole population of crickets chirring within it. Here and there, Xavier directed naval salutes toward the graves whose occupants he'd once mingled with; the gravedigger at the far end gave his spade a rest.

"We won't be needing our coats today!" Xavier shouted.

"Oh, y'know," the gravedigger answered.

He looked like an Albert, but that wasn't his name. Xavier had it on the tip of his tongue.

"So long as there's light in the daytime!" the man added.

Xavier hastily slipped through a breach where the wall, nicely overgrown with viburnum, had collapsed. Charging down through the apple trees, he narrowly made it across the rickety footbridge that served as a stopgap until the real bridge was rebuilt. The old one had been washed away by the flood waters of the brown, fish-filled river to which the town of Saint-Lancelot-de-la-Frayère owed part of its name.

"How goes it, Agapithe, old buddy?" Xavier said after arriving at the work site, his shirt buttoned askew.

Agapithe Guérette, that was the foreman's name. Right then he looked like his reflection in a tub that a granite rock had just fallen into. Known to be not much of a taskmaster, he and his men had closed the hotel bar the night before. Past a certain hour he had trouble keeping an upright position in his chair, let alone his position of authority. Agapithe wasn't an alcoholic, just a guy who liked to drink. Xavier knew perfectly well that even if he showed up late, there was nothing to fear in the nonsense the grumbling foreman scrawled in his dog-eared scratch pad. Each was the other's cousin's brother-in-law, and they'd been partners in mischief since Sunday school.

"Go and start calibrating," Agapithe instructed Xavier once they'd heard about the best shenanigans of the night before. "The connectors should be delivered right quick."

"Is it Du Deux doing the deliveries this afternoon?" Xavier inquired.

He asked the question though he already knew the answer. His shirt clung to his back. He went to join the rest of the team, Gabi's boy Abel, Émilien, Skelling, Jacques Nault, and the others, all in various states of the morning-after-payday. In the distance, the sea was like yogurt. A mongrel with no tag was capering about.

"Du Deux, ya."

The town, out of pity, had hired Agapithe to bring the water main closer to the lots newly cleared of rocks and more densely populated with each passing month.

"One, two, three!"

"Careful."

"Okay, let go of your end, let go, let go."

"Heave ho! Heave ho!"

A workday with nothing much out of the ordinary. The workers were short on vigour on account of the previous night. Despite feeling green around the gills, the men sought the faint breeze laden with the odour of seaweed. The conduit wasn't going to build itself, yet they would loaf around on the grass as soon as Agapithe's back was turned.

"The hours aren't flying by, at least," the foreman said. "Maybe we'll manage to get this done on time."

"Go fetch," Jacques Nault told the dog, which tried to catch the pipes whenever a labourer pitched one off Du Deux's wagon.

The church bells pealed twelve times. A connector rolled down toward the river in mud churned up by all the to-and-fro. The clonk of pickaxes on the rocky ground died away. The men, tuckered out, slumped down on the pipe. They went to sit on some silt-covered logs in the wagon and mop their brows with their handkerchiefs. No one spoke, but they understood each other. At least ten minutes had elapsed in silence when a sleepy boat came into view offshore.

"Well now," Skelling said as he scanned the bay. "That's Labillois coming back from hauling his nets up."

"Whaddya talkin' about," Abel objected, his eyes nearly closed. "That ain't his trawler, nope, it's the fishin' patrol."

The grass grew. The men chomped on parsnips as if they were apples and gnawed at crabs' legs. Now, Du Deux, he was a poker face. He stood up abruptly, catching everyone by surprise, crossly shooed the lazybones off his cart, and made ready to leave without so much as a goodbye.

"You're not going to get us more connectors, I hope?" Émilien asked anxiously.

"Me," Du Deux replied, "I've run out of patience for spats over a boat and such."

Du Deux's real name was André Saint-Onge. He'd been raised by the bogeyman on Deuxième Rang, but the trouble was another André, André Lebeau, lived on Premier Rang, and they were both called Dré. To distinguish between them, the students in the class of Mrs Bujold, Joséphine's late mother, had redubbed them "Dré du Un"—Dré of One—and "Dré du Deux"—Dré of Two. Du Un and Du Deux for short.

Agapithe ate facing the others. As Du Deux set off, he was busting his chops on a slice of quiche he'd tried to cook for himself. His wife shunned pots and pans. With the men making fun of him, he threw his lunch to the dog scrounging for leftovers. The animal gobbled the gift down whole and slunk off to the shade of an elm tree, where it set about licking its sweet spot.

"He's getting a different taste," Émilien quipped.

"The dog or Agapithe?"

Agapithe had just tilted his head back. He was swigging the barley wine he'd brought along to set himself up again. Then he began to shake, and Skelling was the first to lift his butt off his seat, thinking the foreman was having a stroke. Agapithe stared over the grimy foreheads at the river beyond while groping behind him as if to touch the church two hundred metres away.

"Monti?" he said, and they all turned around.

Yes, it sure was Monti. In city clothes, up to his hams in the river, his horse carrying a load of gear twice as wide as its height. The neighing had led the men to believe it was Du Deux coming back. Monti wrestled with a blanket to hide the satchel slung over his mount's rump.

"You didn't ... You didn't die in an avalanche?"

Monti had a nervous tic in his potato-skin lip. His face looked flayed but very clean. Not the slightest stray hair. A fish jumped in the river.

"Up north, there, where you were? Wasn't there an avalanche? The letter that Bradley had us read said you ..."

Many things became clear as their eyes met.

"For Chris ..." Abel began, but Agapithe cut him off and, taking him aside, pointed at the church.

"That damn fucker Bradley," Émilien said.

Recovering from the shock, he stepped toward Monti, arms spread wide.

"Whoa, whoa!"

The workers shat themselves when their old friend, on seeing Émilien come too close, drew a revolver so massive they assumed its weight was why Monti's hand was trembling.

"Monti, it's us!"

They didn't have pistols of that sort in Gaspésie. They had hunting rifles and even some military antiques under glass in the town hall lobby. But no gems like that. A bone-cracking sound welled up in Monti's throat.

"Are you ... Are you thirsty?" Agapithe offered with feeling, and held his bottle of barley wine out at a slight angle.

The story would later go that Honoré Bouge, a.k.a. Monti, slid like he was stealing a base to keep the drop suspended from the bottle's neck from hitting the ground. Having lowered his gun, he drained the bottle in one go and hurled it into the flowing Fray river. As his buddies embraced him to make sure this was no ghost, he chuckled quietly. It tickled.

VII

THE LAST MORNING

28

SOME WHO'VE COME BACK FROM THE EDGE CLAIM
that you see your life replayed when you die. For Patapon,
there must have been parts that dragged on. Not that he'd
been resuscitated, but his remains had disappeared; they were
nowhere to be seen when François, oblivious to all that, stood
up in the field where the Volvo had come to rest. The windshield had shattered and the miraculous survivor concluded
that he'd been propelled into the snow when the iPod triggered the explosion. *I would be dead had I not unbuckled my
seat belt.*

Rock was gone. The snow had covered whatever tracks may
have been left. François, cramped and shivering, wrapped the
front panels of his jacket over his bony ribs. Hunching his
shoulders, he walked back through the snow. Lodged under
one of the windshield wipers, a kind of escalope fluttered in the
wind against the taxi's pleated hood. A button on François's
pants had come off. When he reached the middle of the road,
he took stock of the overpass's condition, confident that the
publication of his book would be a boon for the region. *Sub-
sidies, private investments.* He'd spruce up the summer camp
across the way. His toes, his whole left foot, were cold. The
abutments of the overpass, battered by gales and budget cuts,

were crumbling at the top. He was eager to get home. Imminent glory wasn't going to make him snub his old companions, and he added asking after Patapon to his agenda. He managed a few painful, hobbling steps.

"The Canons' field," he said.

He scooped up a petrified potato lost between two snow-filled furrows and pitched it against the fence. An icy clink rang out. The wind whistled.

François walked back to the car, holding his pants up. *The prodigal child, everyone,* he thought. *Oboes play, set bagpipes sounding.* He was a tad disappointed. It wasn't a matter of being oversensitive, but he'd nevertheless been naive enough to hope for a more welcoming reception committee, a banner, whatever.

"I am the chosen one," he declared when he saw what the taxi had been reduced to.

The bottle of Yukon was broken. François leaned into the crumpled car to retrieve his briefcase. A spray of sharp-edged flowers had sprung up where he'd been seated before the explosion. The airbags dangled over the seats, uninflated. He had survived through divine intervention. François walked around the Volvo feeling wet in his perineal region. He was drunk, but it didn't show. He acted normal when he was drunk. Snow mixed with glass crunched under his feet. Under one foot in particular. He stretched and contorted his body inside the already-cold wreck, his arm bent out of shape in the plexus of twisted steel. His vertebrae must have separated from all the stretching, but he was able to graze the briefcase and then grasp the handle. He eventually managed to work it loose. He shook it from left to right amid the metal dentures and shards of plastic and drew it closer. The gusts of wind grabbed each other by turns and at the edge of the field rushed off again through the jumbled trees. The Mi'kmaq reserve was to the west, La Frayère to the east. François blew a fuse and pulled with all his strength. He fell on his behind in the snow and the briefcase popped open. Pages of his manuscript flew away in an aerial carousel. On ribbons of wind. They scattered haphazardly in the forest. *Drat,* he thought. *But then, I did have to make some cuts.* Clamping the briefcase between his knees, he buttoned up his jacket.

"*Tabarnak,*" he said.

François didn't often curse. But he'd just noticed he had only one shoe. That's why his foot felt so cold. He must have lost the other when he went flying. Or the driver had absconded with it. Searching around, he spotted a sneaker that stood out against the whiteness of the snow. A crow was pecking at it, and this likely wasn't the bird's first encounter with a scarecrow, because François had to beat it off.

"Victory!" he said. "Go back to your nunnery."

François wasn't too keen to put the thing on his foot. His beige sock clashed with the lavender of his frozen ankle. He cursed for the second time that year as he removed the bits of human lasagna from the laceless sneaker. François wore a size seven. He had very small feet. The sneaker was a size eleven.

François unenthusiastically opened the envelope he'd taken out of his hip pocket. His eyes spun furiously in his head, like a slot machine. One eye and, seconds later, the other stopped on the dollar sign. But when he looked inside the envelope, he clearly saw that it contained pieces of newspaper. For a moment he failed to understand. *Now, what did I do with that money?* There were stalactites of frost hanging from his eyebrows. He tried to recall the events of the night to see where the foul-up had occurred. He interlaced his arms. After a while, somewhat embarrassed, he wrote his telephone number on a fake bill, along with a note for Rock to call him later, he'd pay up once his advance arrived. He inserted the piece of paper between two plastic scalpels shaped by the mangled dashboard. Then he walked away in the cold, a smile frozen on his face.

He was a couple of hours from the town on foot. It would have been less boring had Poupette been there with him. The snow falling on the overpass was ashier than before. François had forgotten to mentally prepare himself for the possibility of seeing Yannick again. He stopped short underneath the structure and turned back toward the Volvo, still holding his pants up. In the spring, pussy willow branches would sprout inside the taxi and the seats would get covered with soil. François noticed a muddled set of footprints the powder snow was in the process of erasing. They went from underneath the car to the edge of the woods; he began to follow them. The sneaker he'd put on refused to stay on his foot. When he came to the middle of the field, he looked around and then returned to the car. He removed his piece of paper, crossed out his telephone number, and wrote down Poupette's instead. François's line had been disconnected.

That's when the snowplow breached the horizon alongside the field. The dirt road nearly levitated in its wake. *Quick! Quick!* François thought as he bounded over the fence. *That will be Rock coming back to rescue me.* He was waving his arms on the shoulder of the road when his pants dropped down to his knees. His pecker peeked out. Maurice Foster sat gaping in his cockpit, unsure of what he'd just seen. A spinning wheel had told him in a dream to start his run on Route Sainte-Cluque and Rang Saint-Onge. The big machine dematerialized in a swirl of white atoms.

François went back across the tilled field. He would have to do without Rock's blitheness and his taste for things that really mattered. He felt bitter and his thirst welled up again. He rolled the waist of his pants so they would stay up. He pitched his briefcase across a fence painted with less pride than in days gone by and jumped over. He clambered up the embankment to the top of the overpass and set out on Rang Saint-Onge.

29

STRETCHED OUT ON THE COUCH SINCE THE NIGHT before, her boots jutting out beyond the armrest, Lorraine decided she'd gotten over it. She sat up. She smoothed her skirt over her thighs and righted the photo of them that she'd laid flat in its ornate frame adorned with curlicues and chubby angels. It was their Niagara Falls vacation picture; they'd promised to go back there for their honeymoon. Laganière's face had been crossed out with a pen. A dried-out pen. Stabbed with a pen. But right then, her eyes horribly puffed up, it had just occurred to Lorraine that maybe something had happened to her Joël. That Joël might not be asleep and spooning with someone else. *What would Gwendolyn d'Artémios do?* she thought. She picked up the phone, wondering who exactly she might call. *Forget Old Marcel. No phone. I mean, the old guy makes his own clothes.* She called the library, but the line was busy. If she'd had the car, she'd have braved the storm and investigated first-hand, except that Joël had taken it to work yesterday. A half-hour later she called the library for the thirty-seventh time. Still busy. She called Cynthia.

"Hi, you've reached Yannick and Cynthia. We're probably doing something really crazy, such as giving birth, but leave us a message and we may get back to you someday, if Yannick feels like it."

She called the Perraults and they answered even before the first ring.

"Hello?"

"Jacinthe? It's Lorraine."

Harmonium was playing in the background. Lorraine told herself she liked that album too, and it would do her good to listen to it.

"My god, sweetie, I thought you were a man. What's going on, you're not at the shop? You sound all outta kilter."

Lorraine worked at the Perraults' homeopathy and natural products store. She was also their best customer.

"No, I didn't go in. Things aren't great at home right now, Joël was supposed to come get me yesterday, remember? He had a surprise for me and that's why I took today off. But he never got back from the library, and now I don't know where he is. Did Romain go into town yesterday? Could you ask him if he might have seen him around?"

On a mis quelqu'un au monde. On devrait peut-être l'écouter. Na-na-na-na, na-na.

"No, no. Hey, look. Romain's still sleeping. He stayed home last night after his curfew, took it easy. I'll ... Look, I ..."

"Jeez, I'm worried, you know."

"Listen, I'm up to my elbows in Budwig cream, but gimme a few minutes and I'll call Mrs Foster. Maurice was out on the snowplow this mornin', he might've seen the car somewhere."

"You're a doll, bye."

The moment Lorraine hung up, the telephone rang.

"*Joël?*"

"No, sorry, it's me again. I meant to tell you. Do yourself a favour. A capsule of ginseng and a spoonful of royal jelly in a hot cup of verbena."

"You're a doll, Jacinthe."

Instead, though, Lorraine went to the freezer. She pulled out an ice cube tray and rapped it on the counter. She rapped it until it was empty and all the cubes had slid down onto the floor around her. She flumped down on the floor. She scooped up one of the ice cubes, full of hair and dirt, and bit into it.

30

OH, TICO-TICO, TIC...WHISPERED A MILDLY NEUROTIC voice in the drowse Laganière was basking in. It was over. The nightmare at the cottage was over. No fouled bath, no third-degree burn, no man-eating weasel. He lay in bed, wallowing in satin. Daylight filtered through the little Cellophane hoods that were his eyelids. "Oh, Tico-Tico, tac . . ." Not ready to open his eyes just yet, he savoured the warmth, the security, the comfort, the delectable monotony of the cradle after dreams somewhat too taxing for his sensibility, his settled life. In spite of his headache, not much bigger than the eye of a needle, he let himself sink into the mattress, be absorbed by the mattress, and began to nuzzle his darling's hair abandoned on the cloud of pillows. How could anything feel this good? *O Lorraine, barley queen, my Guinevere, c'mon over here.* Laganière *became* the mattress. He snuggled up to the creature beside him, all moist and palpitating, albeit a mite fusty this morning. *Because at some point, I have my needs.* Then he wriggled his pelvis to jimmy his fiancée's chastity belt. His hand moved up her thigh, swept over her groin, and very ergonomically wrapped itself around an altogether tangible seven-inch sin.

"*Lorraine?*" Laganière gasped, jumping back six feet from the bed against the corner of a piece of furniture.

This was when he realized it wasn't Lorraine. And that the sheets were fit to be incinerated. It was Marteau, not so much asleep as conked out, and he turned toward Laganière. His lips were a conspicuous cherry red, as though he'd put on makeup. He was smooching right where Laganière, now hugging the wall, had lain a moment ago. Marteau began to jiggle his white, swollen tongue, French-kissing the air and filling the room with his putrefied-liver breath. Laganière's headache suddenly flared up. He raised his eyes heavenward to ask for God's forgiveness, and to get Marteau out of his field of vision, except that Marteau kept on billing and cooing in the ceiling mirror.

Everybody was really proud that Laganière had drunk the night before. He more than anyone else. He just would have liked to have been briefed on the facts about hangovers. The clothes in the dresser drawers were scattered over the floor, and Laganière slipped his braised leg into his uncle's twilled cotton pants, his arms into a beige shirt with still beiger stripes, which he was careful to tuck into his pants. H-e-a-d-a-c-h-e. Leaving Marteau to his languor in a dress that his aunt could cut up for rags, he took his migraine out for a walk, down the angular hallway with its rigid corners, its hard straightaways, and was struck by the, to say the least, blunt opacity of the drywall in his face.

The first thing to draw Laganière's attention in the kitchen, the *only* thing to draw his attention in the three-dimensional automatist painting the kitchen had become, was the big bottle of Aspirin on the table. He let out a sigh of relief as he already pictured himself shovelling down the thousand tablets floating in milk instead of his usual oat flakes. But when he opened the bottle, he was disappointed. Thanks to some glutton, there were none left. Not a single tablet. You could hear the sea in the background. Laganière was about to stoop to sucking the cotton ball left lying on the table when he noticed under the footrest Perrault's label-stripped Aspirin bottle. It nearly popped open on its own, and the pills magically cascaded into his mouth. He ate a whole lot of them and turned toward the patio door; there was the spectre of Steeve standing in the blizzard.

"Danny never came back," said the spectre.

Its outline was ethereal, its skin stomach-turningly transparent.

"Who?" Laganière asked.

The spectre came away from the glass door and reappeared next to him, more substantial but just as cadaverous. It was actually Steeve's reflection on the patio door, but through an optical illusion he seemed to be outside. Steeve too had dark-red lips. He brushed his fingers across Laganière's face.

"Danny . . ."

Steeve swallowed when he saw the Aspirin bottle that Laganière still clutched with all his strength. His mouth smiled, but not his eyes. His eyes wept. There were stars deep within them, dark matter.

"Oh, yes!" Laganière exclaimed, slapping his forehead so hard that he reeled back into the weasel's crushed remains on the carpet. "You mean the Montreal dude. Our coureur de bois of urban developments."

You'd better not get pricked with a needle, he thought, having surmised that it was Steeve who'd gotten into the big bottle of Aspirin. *You'd bleed to death, that's how thin your blood must be now.* He looked at his foot in the animal entrails covered with a white powder. Then he scanned the room in search of a spatula, a plastic bag.

"Did you get any sleep?" he asked after a few minutes.

He grasped Steeve by the shoulders and invited him to stretch out on the couch. But Steeve resisted. Laganière's muscles weren't up to it.

"You guys, last night, you didn't hear. Danny won't be coming back. Yannick can call me a wimp all he wants. He can stay here if he likes, I'm not his mother, but I—"

"Hear what? Where is Yannick?"

Laganière stood opposite the window over the sink. Seeing Steeve's eyes follow something on his neck, Laganière gave himself a slap there.

"Yannick's looking for Danny outside. And, *no,* I won't calm down, I…I…"

While Steeve was catching his breath, Laganière stole over to the front door, next to which his uncle had installed a rack of key hooks at the right height, with the right tool, so that in wintertime you wouldn't have to stretch your arm out too far to reach the key to the shed when you'd just devoted ten minutes of your life adjusting your Gore-Tex coat sleeves over your Gore-Tex gloves. But the key to the snowmobile, which was always parked in the Tempo shelter, wasn't among the other keys on the rack.

"…that's nothing, right now," Steeve rambled on relentlessly as Laganière, listening with half an ear, began to search elsewhere. "The weather eased off. At six in the morning the trees were dancing the lambada something fierce. It wouldn't have surprised me if we'd stepped out of the cottage in Natashquan…"

The thing was, the tips of the titanium hooks, for which Laganière's uncle had gone up to Chandler because they didn't have the sort he wanted—titanium—here in, as he put it, their "two-pit" hardware store, the hooks, then, they had tips exactly point eight centimetres in circumference, which for his uncle guaranteed the indestructibility he sought in all things, especially since at that diameter there was ample room to hang any average set of keys—a copy of the car key, the key to the shed, the riding mower key, the key to happiness—all to say that the snowmobile key—sometimes, those Japanese, well—came with a frigging dinky sissy ring, like, point six centimetres, so, that day, after the rack had been all neatly installed, it wouldn't fit on his titanium hook, and luckily his wife begged him, because it wasn't just the key rack the old fellow was about to rip out but the entire wall.

"...then the Jeep moved too, it's half-sitting on the mound where your uncle must be planning to build his crypt..."

Babbling on without a pause, Steeve tapped the side of his nose to let Laganière know he still had something there. Steeve himself, at the very same spot, sported a magnificent, juicy boil girded with a sort of inflamed prepuce. Laganière had the impression his burned leg was grafted to his brain. A patentable pain travelled from one to the other in a loop. Not sure anymore of what he was searching for, he kept searching anyway in hopes that a plan, a procedure would end up occurring to him. He came up empty-handed. After a while he opened the drawer where the night before he'd found the remote control of what used to be the sound system. He equipped himself with whatever might be of use—batteries, a hand warmer, a map of North America, a golf tee, a flashlight, and some…A shimmering Kawasaki key, which he discreetly slipped into his pocket.

"…growling and clawing at the cottage outside. I don't know what it was, some monster, but I heard it. Go see for yourself, it left scratches on the logs. You'd have…Laganière, seriously, you've got something there, a red dot."

Laganière finally saw what Steeve had been trying to show him for a while. The red beam of a laser was visible through the floating dust and motes. *The laser sight,* he thought. He pivoted toward the window in time to see Yannick posing as a hardwood tree in his camouflage gear and acrobatically disappearing into the firewood-to-be.

"Sorry to interrupt, Steeve buddy," Laganière said, "I'm…"

In his mind, *not* came before "sorry." The countless times he'd been beaten up as a boy or called faggot ran through his memory like those films with a bunch of scenes happening at the same time in little boxes.

"I'm telling you…" Steeve said, he too rubbing his temples despite a massive dose of analgesics. "As soon as Yannick shows up, we throw Marteau under a cold shower, we set him up in the truck with a sap bucket between his pins, and we haul ass outta here in fifth gear."

31

"MAMA!" JACINTHE PERRAULT HEARD HER SON YELL from the house.

Caught off guard by the weather like everyone else, she hastily crammed the milk crate with parsnips, rutabagas, and Jerusalem artichokes from her kitchen garden.

"Romain's awake," she said.

With frost on the inside of her scarf, all healthy and balanced in her sheepskin-lined jacket, she thrust her shears into her pocket.

"Mama!" Romain yelled again.

"Yes, yes, Romain, I'm coming, okay, I'm outside."

You could tell she knew how not to injure her back. She hoisted her vegetable-laden crate like a weightlifter.

"You aren't going to keep feeding us roots until the spring," Romain said when his mother came into the house loaded down.

He might have held the door for her, except that he hadn't asked to be born, had he.

"I'm gonna cook us a stew for supper, with the pumpernickel your father made. Perfect for this weather."

"You mean the pumpernickel he *tried* to make. Normal food would be okay too sometimes."

"Oh, stop it."

Jacinthe gave her boy an affectionate poke in the belly and put the water on to boil. Perrault hadn't yet entirely come back down from his night out and stood there, levitating, fascinated by the sensation, hoping his mother would poke him in the stomach again.

"Pizza pockets," he said, "Dixie Lee, microwave stuff you can eat in front of the TV."

"Except we don't have a TV, and it makes me sad when you say awful things like that."

"You're right, Mama. And your soup's good for our poop."

Romain squashed his mother's cheeks into a grimace so she would find this funny.

"I'm hungry right now. What's for breakfast?"

"If you get outta my way, I'll fix you something."

While she was improvising a country-style dish, which allowed her to use up some leftovers, the phone rang somewhere amid the empty egg cartons stacked up everywhere, the smoothed-out sheets of aluminum foil, the blocks of beeswax, the jars of kefir grains, the compost bin, the cucumbers and beets, the balls of wool speared with knitting needles, the bottles draining upside down and those soaking in the now-tepid lemon water meant to sanitize them.

"Hello," Jacinthe said, after she'd made the mess even messier digging out the phone.

"Hi, how's she doing?"

"Very well, thanks. Who's speaking?"

"Come on, Jacinthe, it's Paule."

"Paule? Do I know you, Paule?"

"Paule Foster, you called me this mornin', I was at the community clinic."

"Ah! Paule, course, sorry, I—"

"I called you back a couple of times, Romain didn't give you the message?"

"No, no…"

She craned to see what her son was up to in the solarium. Romain's brows were knitted together in a V shape. Wearing the same clothes as yesterday, his shoes placed below the window through which he'd stolen back into the house an hour or so before his parents got up, he was rifling through the pockets of every coat within reach, rummaging behind the plants, under his mandolin, in the baskets, in the gaps in the couch. His malamute was asleep on the floor, yelping in a dream.

"Anyway, it doesn't matter," Paule said. "I—"

"What can I do for you?"

"You're the one who called me, Jacinthe. Hey, are you all right?"

"Yes, yes. I'm sorry. I talked to—"

"Mama!" Romain shouted.

"I talked to Lorraine Arsenault earlier, she—"

"Mama, I'm *talking* to you!"

"Hold on a second, Paule. Romain's talking to me. What is it, Romain?"

"I lost my bottle of Aspirin. You wouldn't have found it, maybe?"

"No, I don't think so."

"Well, if you do, don't look inside, okay?"

"I won't look, Romain, I trust you. Paule? Yes, so like I was sayin', I spoke to Joël's Lorraine earlier. Seems Joël hasn't come home the last few days. She wanted to know if Maurice hadn't spotted their car somewhere. He was on the snowplow this mornin', right?"

"Yes, but then, with this big snowfall, he is not getting back before noon, one o'clock. Joël didn't come home?"

"Looks that way."

"That's not like him, is it? What I'll do is I'll give Nadine Chabot a ring, I minded her kids yesterday. I know she went over to the library, maybe she—"

"She—"

"Do you really think that…Nadine…I found she looked quite a bit tarted up when she came back to fetch the children."

"Joël and Nadine?"

"Y'know, you think you know someone."

"Joël Laganière—hard to believe."

"I dunno, but…"

"And Nadine's little ones, how are they doin'?"

"Oh my god, girl."

32

WHILE HE INCREASED THE DISTANCE BETWEEN HIM-
self and the Canons' field, François harked back to a story his
uncle Baptiste would sometimes tell. Baptiste was the eldest
Bouge, fifteen years Henri's senior, and one of the few, though
not the only, Frayois to have fought the Nazis in Europe. He
wasn't quite sure how it had come about, but shortly before
the armistice he'd found himself in the same brigade as Jumbo,
one of Onésime Canon's four sons, Onésime himself being
the son of Pancras. Between them the four youngsters probably didn't have more than a dozen years of schooling all told,
but that's beside the point. When the Allied victory was
announced, Baptiste and Jumbo's platoon commander decided that his troops were eager for champagne and, since they
were deep in the scrub, it was no longer in anyone's interest to
hang on to the two sauerkraut eaters they'd held prisoner for
too long. He therefore ordered the Gaspésiens to take them
into the woods and come back without them. But along the
way, when Baptiste began working Jumbo to convince him
the war was over and no one would be the wiser if they set
free the Germans they were holding at bayonet-point, Jumbo,
irascible by nature, grabbed him by the chinstrap and said:
"Do what you want with yours, I'm gonna kill mine."

A Heritage Minute brought to you by Historica Canada, François thought as he continued along Rang Saint-Onge, lost in his patriotic remembrance and the few abject recollections he'd retained of the television world. He not so much walked as skied. As he advanced, the powder snow covered his asymmetrical tracks behind him. He felt luckier not to have encountered a Canon in this field of theirs than to have survived the taxi explosion. He caught himself occasionally shouting Rock's name. "Rooo-ooock!" he cried. The gas station sign that Patapon had gone by in the opposite direction during the night faded behind him, quite pale for something so energy-intensive. The sky seemed to contain more than its fill of clouds and overflowed around the edges. François came across the same coyote his friend had seen lying in the ditch a few hours before. This prompted him to fantasize a cash-prize quiz where he'd be asked to explain the usage of the verbs *lie* and *lay*. He turned the half-buried animal over, and at the sight of its entrails laminated by the cold, what he'd drunk that night rose back into his throat.

He continued on his way. The white plume of his breath trailed behind him. He walked past the spent cartridges, the cans, the bottles. They were strewn across the shoulder of the road, having mysteriously surfaced despite the ongoing precipitation. If such a thing as a second freezing point below the first existed, François was approaching it. His clothes bent nowhere but at the joints, making a noise like chips between a set of molars. He imagined Rock getting his paunch tanned, flipping burgers on the barbecue, with Elvis in a hammock nearby, plucking on a ukulele. The more he walked, the more he froze, and the more he froze, the more he yearned to get drunk again. Thirty metres on, he stopped. His blood stopped circulating too. He rocked from one foot to the other and then retraced his steps to the cans. *Talk about a waste,* he thought. *People are dying of thirst the world over.* Hence, out of humanitarian considerations, he drained the dregs of beer not yet turned into Popsicles. It wasn't that François refused to confront his father sober, no, only, he needed calories if he was going to . . . *Why am I justifying myself?* he thought. The snow had taken on the appearance of meringue.

"It's the curse," he added out loud.

"Curse, curse, curse . . ."

There was an echo at the spot where he'd just arrived, amplified by rotund valleys and callipygian hills. For a second he mistook the cement plant quarry for the bay, before reminding himself he wasn't on the 132. The meteorite that had wiped out the dinosaurs could fit into the quarry with barely a centimetre to spare. A feeling of lightness—not recommended in such a wind—took hold of him in spite of the anxiety he was prey to at the thought of returning to the family nest after he-didn't-know-how-many years. Come what may, his book was almost done, the mirror image of his life, at last complete. He would give Mama a big hug. Hold himself erect as he shook Papa's paw. How very touching their reunion would be. Together they would have a fruitful conversation about his work as they perused photo albums or played a board game. Everyone would be in a jolly good mood. They would share a family moment without the slightest tension. There would be something contagious about his passion for writing, and with all the blessings accruing to him, François could afford a suite in paradise, and then he'd spend the rest of the evening in his father's record and book collections while stuffing himself with whatever the pantry contained. The next day he would sit down at the desk with his pad of lined pages. He would place a bottle of Yukon close at hand but not touch it. Just to understand. Then he would toil over the final touches to his book while his mother did his laundry and served him cookies. To help him concentrate, his father would keep proudly, protectively silent, save for some gratifying remarks or ever-constructive suggestions whispered on occasion.

He walked, walked, walked. François walked. Either he'd managed to go astray while following a straight line or he'd gone around the world, because the gas station he'd put behind him earlier was now ahead of him again. He could make out its telltale flamingo-pink sign through the snow of which no two flakes were identical. A little later he wondered, as he cleared a path with a fictitious machete through the wood he'd just plunged into, if what was pink to him, the gas station sign, for instance, might be blue for someone else. The woods were dense, barely passable, visually complex.

"*To lay* is transitive, *to lie* intransitive," François raged, all the while swinging the machete. "For a million dollars, *lay* transitive, *lie* intransitive."

33

IMMEDIATELY AFTER HER PHONE CALL TO JACINTHE
Perrault, Paule Foster took out the agenda full of cut-along-
the-dotted-lines coupons where she kept her telephone numbers. She dialed Nadine Chabot's number and began doodling
over a winner's face on one of the ads. While the phone rang,
she fine-tuned in her head the subtleties of the interrogation
she had in store for that home wrecker.

"Hello," a pre-pubescent voice said at the other end.

"Hello, is this my little buddy Sébastien?"

"Yes."

Sébastien, Nadine's son, aged eleven. Paule babysat them
after school, him and his sister Manon. She sensed the youngster's alertness wasn't at peak level. His favourite game, when
he wasn't at home building his thumb muscles, was climbing
up door frames, ninja-style, or sliding down the stairs on the
big sofa cushions.

"This is Mrs Paule, will you be coming for a vis... Have ya
had your breakfast, Sébastien? Your voice sounds thin to me."

Poor Nadine, raising two kids alone on welfare, nothing
in the fridge three-quarters of the time. *Or ya had Ritalin
for breakfast,* Paule thought, having very few qualms about
gossiping all over town that the Chabots' place was in a pitiful

state while she herself, when Nadine was looking for work, "helped out" by skimming a hefty percentage off her government cheque for child care fees. Sébastien didn't answer. He'd probably wear the same track suit all week and was well on his way to flunking his school year. Right then he was too absorbed in an online war game to be interested in anything as social as talking on the phone.

"Are ya gonna come over to see Mrs Paule today?"

"I dunno."

Sébastien played as much with his mouth as with his joystick. It may not have been the latest computer on the market, but it was the most recent model available in La Frayère.

"We'll make snowmen, maybe, or fingerpaint like the last time."

How about some goo-goo gaga while you're at it? He isn't a baby anymore. He just blew a tactical squad to smithereens with an anti-personnel mine.

"Painting is boring. It's boring at your house. I don't wanna go there anymore."

"Is your mother there, Sébastien? I need to talk to her."

No answer.

"Sébastien, you still there?"

"No, she's not here."

That wasn't true. Nadine had been to an interview the day before and just learned she wasn't getting the job. She was urgently packing boxes and had asked the children to say she wasn't there if anyone telephoned because the collection agencies were after her.

"Where is she? When's she coming home?"

"I dunno."

"You don't know. Is it you minding Manon?"

Manon was six years old. She was in a world of her own. Dressed up as a fairy, she was in the laundry room, on the floor strewn with cat litter, directing a domestic quarrel between her one-eyed doll and her brother's robot, whose batteries were running low from bashing everything within reach.

"I dunno," Sébastien said.

"She wouldn't by any chance be with the man from the library?"

The snow digested the house a little more. The frost embroidered the windowpanes. The phone's dial tone was in the key of A.

"Sébastien?" Paule said. "Sébastien?"

34

"IS THERE SOMETHING I CAN DO?" LAGANIÈRE ASKED, his voice lost among the reverberations of his splintering skull.

The air hummed with energy. Preparations to finish up. The doorways became clogged with traffic. A slew of priorities to manage. There were just three of them, but it looked more like seventeen. Laganière was getting in everyone's way. He restlessly stamped his feet. As if waiting for a pass from someone. To take off on a breakaway. Sweet Jesus, was he ever desperate for his fistful of Aspirin to kick in.

"Move aside," Yannick advised him when he wanted to squeeze between Laganière and the wall to get to the firewood box.

The guns were laid out like a photo of a police seizure. Laganière got out of Yannick's way only to collide with Steeve, who pushed him against the grandfather clock next to the wine-stained suede couch. Yannick's pupils were seriously encroaching on his irises. His face was furrowed with wrinkles people usually don't have at that age. He tossed Steeve a pump-action shotgun across the living room. Steeve, nervous and emotional, caught the twelve-gauge and then several handguns and boxes of ammunition, immediately stuffing them one after the other into a gym bag or his pockets.

When he unstuck himself from the clock, his specs askew, Laganière had a plan. *Lorraine will have to wait, hang it all.* The two cousins shouted orders back and forth. Signalled to each other. They seemed to be on the same wavelength, both guided by a higher entity. They sent every cubic inch of air in the place swirling. *I've got a right to live a little too,* Laganière thought.

"I don't know what got hold of your chum," Yannick bellowed at Steeve. "But I guarantee we'll get hold of it before it gets hold of us too."

In the hideous visions engendered by the acid, Yannick had come to believe the beast that had gobbled up the Montreal dude during the night was the same abomination that had devoured Thierry Vignola fifteen years earlier. Steeve had heard growling. One plus one equals two. Yannick convinced himself he'd been waiting for revenge his whole life. Laganière was checking to see if he could get a radio signal with what remained of the sound system. He turned the tuning dial in both directions, his ear against the diaphragm, which sputtered and tiredly farted.

"Shh," he said.

He attempted to identify the sound coming through the speaker. Synthesizer notes playing in a loop through the interstellar crackle. *Prog rock,* he thought. *There's no way that isn't Marcel.*

"We can do without BSUC," Steeve said when he heard the vinyl skipping, while Laganière told himself his old friend must have fallen asleep or locked himself out—it wouldn't have been the first time.

"CBSU is what it's called."

Laganière followed Steeve up and down the corridor, lecturing him about the value of our institutions, explaining that they existed for us, that we were the ones who'd created them and we had to respect them. Each time Yannick's boots came down on the floor, the impact triggered an avalanche in their respective headaches. You'd have thought the black marks his soles left all over the linoleum were intentional. Steeve was now preparing coffee for them to take along. The cream in it would end up whipped if he kept on stirring it like that.

"Okay, do I have everyone's attention?" Laganière screamed.

He had the charisma of a parking meter. He said to himself he'd have liked to get to know other cultures, move through airports with proper signage, stay in hotels that accepted all credit cards. He'd have liked to be free.

"So what we're going to do now," he continued, "Steeve, you stay here to keep an eye on Martin, and Yannick and I, we'll take the Ski-Doo up to the CBSU station. They've just changed their program schedule, but I've reason to believe Marcel's up there this morning. We'll take a chance. We'll go and wake him up so he can warn the population over the airways about everything that's happening, and after that—"

"Laganière," Steeve said with a lump in his throat.

He was making more coffee because he'd just downed the first two. He stopped and turned toward Laganière.

"Old Marcel is dead for sure."

Just like the others, Yannick's lips were blood-red. He could barely move his eyes, which looked like they were mounted on a bar installed between his temples. He too noticed, as he swivelled his torso around, that someone had feasted on the big bottle of Aspirin.

"For Chrissake, Steeve, you're not alone here."

"Everyone is alone," said Steeve.

"You might have left me just *one*. They aren't Tic Tacs, eh."
Yannick started to circle around the other bottle of Aspirin—
Perrault's. He wasn't quite sure how to manage it and ended up
on the floor in the prone shooting position. When he finally
peeked inside the bottle and saw it was empty, he understood
what was going on. He swung around toward Steeve, who,
mouth agape and eyes wide open, was the spitting image of
a bowling ball.

Steeve straight away pointed the finger at Laganière. Yannick let out a womanish laugh.

"Better buckle up real tight, Laganière old buddy, you'll be
takin' off in a bit." It being a given, in his view, that an intellectual's brain was apt to spin out of control anyway.

"I can lend you some clothes," the librarian offered Steeve
the very next minute.

Laganière himself was preparing to prepare. He cast around
for pen and paper. He wanted to note down that, basically, in
La Frayère it seemed you always had to add "so to speak" after
everything a person said.

"Naw, I'll be fine," Steeve answered.

He was wearing his bomber jacket, no scarf, no mittens. It
was minus twenty-five outside. At least he had a toque on. The
fibres were stretched over his caveman forehead. *Get moving,
Joël,* Laganière thought. Yannick again laced up his Docs, as
snugly as possible. He tautened every single cord, loop, and
knot on his equipment and the survival gear he'd donned.
In the end it was all so tight he couldn't fully straighten up.
Don't stand there analyzing your headache like that, Laganière
thought as he watched him. They were just about ready to set
out, the two of them. The cottage, though buried deeper and

deeper in snow, was battered by the wind none the less. *First step, appropriate footwear.* Laganière dashed to the closet to get his uncle's rubber overshoes.

"You're not properly dressed, you know."

He waved his index finger at Steeve's bare spots, suddenly realizing, to his astonishment, that his finger was blue. His whole arm, his entire body, was blue, his woollen cap, shaped like an upside-down sock, was white, his pants as well; on his glasses, with their Coke-black frames, Yannick—he'd learned the trick from Henri, who'd learned it from Monti—had stamped his thumbprints as he went by.

"Oh, Smurf!" Laganière said.

Yannick walked through the trail of food and container debris and shredded wrappers spilling from the fridge, a scavenger hunting for provisions. Steeve followed him in lockstep, haggard and useless. Laganière was a good three inches short of filling the galoshes.

"A pair of woollen socks, that'll do it."

Make a beeline for the master bedroom, he said to himself, and headed for the bureau containing an abundance of socks of every description, including nylon ankle socks for trying shoes on in a store when you were barefoot.

"Our bard's on acid," Yannick said with delight.

Halfway down the corridor Laganière wasn't so frisky anymore, alarmed all at once by the gargle of a drowning man coming from the bedroom.

"Help!" he cried.

He did his best to run in spite of the fried-chicken skin of his leg and his irritable bowel syndrome.

"Hurry, guys! Help!"

Right in the middle of the nightmarish fuck factory the master bedroom had become, there was upchuck spewing from every orifice in Marteau's face. It was the stuff of exorcisms. Any moment now the lad would start talking dead languages backwards. And, because he was lying on his back and a thing called gravity exists, his reflux was on the point of obstructing his respiratory passages. In the background, the front door slammed shut. The roar of the wind swelled for three seconds and then faded again.

"Wait for me!" Laganière implored.

They'll end up busting that fricking door. He danced a peculiar sun dance at the bedside, doing his utmost not to regurgitate in his turn.

"Wait for me! I'm coming with you!"

Silence prevailed in the living room. There were golf and curling trophies all over the bedroom. Up to his elbow in Marteau's plumbing in an attempt to at least drain off his liquid and a few clumps of stew, Laganière couldn't keep from realizing things weren't the same anymore between Lorraine and him. There was nothing around to clean himself with that didn't belong to his uncle. But when you have to make do, you make do, and Laganière wrapped his hand in what, at this point in his tribulations, must have been the Golden Fleece.

Lorraine worried because of the admirers she imagined were constantly lining up at the library counter to steal her "man." She wanted him to wear a ring, too.

"My ring!"

Either the ring had slipped off his finger earlier in the bathtub or it had just gotten stuck in Marteau's esophagus. The bride's breath wasn't fogging up the little mirror anymore.

The window frame in the bedroom must have been made of ash wood. There were ponies on the print of the curtains. Or colts, more likely. A tasselled string opened them sideways to let in maximum natural light. A bird that had gotten its seasons mixed up flew past the vomit-streaked window. Yannick went by just after that with Steeve at his heels. Laganière hadn't wanted a ring, another pointless expense. He bent down over Marteau, in horror, to give him mouth-to-mouth.

Lifting his paintball glasses up over his balaclava, Yannick, meanwhile, bent down to examine some tracks. He'd decided they were tracks. After tracing the outline of a footprint with his fingers, he rubbed them together.

"Affirmative," he said.

Then, hearing someone moan, he swung around toward Steeve. Immediately the moaning stopped. Steeve's face was tucked in against the snow, his neck and wrists already gone red from the cold, which had a pretty mean bite to it. His burglar's toque was now completely white. Yannick bent down over the footprint again. The moaning resumed. He turned toward Steeve and it stopped. It went on like that. The Jeep had stayed there, abandoned crosswise on a wintry mound. One of the back doors was still ajar even though only the driver's door opened from the outside. The Montreal dude must have gotten in through the roof to take shelter in the car—that was the hypothesis—and opened the door from the inside to run away after he'd smashed it up. That's when the beast grabbed him. There was no chance of Steeve and Yannick going anywhere with the Jeep either. Yannick had his finger inside one of the many slashes they'd found on a tire.

"Go check in the shed for a jack and a spare," he ordered Steeve.

Steeve's moans, which nothing interrupted anymore, sounded like some bad news on a cardiac monitor. It wasn't as if they could get very far anyway in snow that deep. Except that the laws of physics had for them become highly relative and elastic. So Steeve obeyed, starting at the slightest noise, for fear that Yannick might leave without him. He entered the shed, actually a Tempo shelter. Square shovel, round shovel, plastic canister with spout. Several bags with various seed mixtures. Sack of salt, sack of earth. Paddles and snowshoes. Flexible tubing for Laganière's uncle's sugar shack project. Fishing gear. A chainsaw. A lawn mower and even an old remote-controlled model airplane. A still-unused gas grill. The unplugged mini-fridge, a legend of the bard's youth on account of the smutty magazines piled on its shelves. And, especially, the snowmobile. Steeve backed out of the shelter to estimate its size. It appeared larger from the inside than from the outside.

"No jack or spare tire," he shouted to Yannick, who was retrieving his cellphone from the Jeep.

"What?"

Steeve walked over to the snowmobile, a Kawasaki. He unscrewed the cap and saw the gas tank was almost empty. He tugged the starter cord as hard as he could. You felt it was hereditary, because even though he must not have practised this move very often in Montreal, he did it expertly. Out of sadness or indignation Laganière's uncle would have died on the spot, a thought-induced suicide, had he witnessed this: someone trying to start his baby without even having the key in the ignition.

"It won't start?" Yannick asked from the entrance.

He sucked on an icicle. He'd thought Steeve was pummelling someone on the ground.

"Zero reaction," his cousin replied. "Hardly a drop left in the tank anyway."

"I'll take the blue ones," Yannick said.

He'd just noticed the two pairs of polypropylene snowshoes behind the seed bags.

One pair was cobalt blue. The other was metallic fuchsia.

35

MRS FOSTER HAD HUNG UP PROMISING HERSELF THE Chabot woman wouldn't get off the hook so easily, and now the telephone was already ringing.

"Hello?" she answered, hardly containing her excitement.

"Jeez, Paule, are you all right?"

"I'm fine, just fine. What's the matter, Maurice? You're on your lunch break and don't know what to do with yourself?"

"I wanted to know how long I'm supposed to heat it up for?"

"Oh. So you've lost the instructions I stuck on the container again."

"Looks to me like you're goin' Alzheimer, woman. You didn't leave any instructions, cripes!"

"Oh my. Would that be a tear I just let fall?"

"Sooo I wanted to let you know, on this beautiful sunny day when I've been clearing the roads since four thirty in the mornin', that I ate my lunch cold. Thank you, Paule. Besides, how come you answered all keyed-up like that?"

"I thought it was Nadine Chabot calling, because it so happens there might be..."

She detailed that morning's melodrama for him two or three times, offering a slew of increasingly far-fetched conjectures such that she herself had no idea where she'd gotten them, eventually asking him—he hadn't been able to get a word in before his wife made it clear it was his turn—if he might possibly have noticed the Laganières' car on a street somewhere, maybe with two legs that weren't Lorraine's sticking up from the back seat.

"No, I don't think so, but you're reminding me. I was plowing in the early hours along the Canons' field when I spied something weird. Visibility was poor, what with the blowing snow, but standing by the roadside was, guess what. Half-naked, I tell ya. One hell of an animal."

"As in 'animal from hell'?"

"My boss is here. I'd better scoot."

36

WHAT THEY'RE VIEWING ARE SHOTS OF THE LA Frayère service station. The snow-covered gas pumps, the road barely visible at the very edge of the frame. This is the parking lot that Kevin Plourde, whom everyone on the case ended up calling Patapon, crossed going westward on the night of the events, and that François Bouge crossed going eastward a few hours later. The gas station owners had installed the security camera after it became trendy for locals to fill up and abscond without paying.

"Rewind, rewind," the detective says. "A tad more. He's looking at something behind him. I want to know what."

The technician zooms in on the frozen image of François in mid-jump. He's leaping over a vacuum cleaner in the parking lot. His jacket billows over his back, his tie floats above his shoulder. One of his knees nearly clips his chin while his other leg is hooked behind him. Shielding his briefcase, François has twisted around in mid-air to look at something on the ground that he seems to be running away from. It's impossible to zoom closer and see what it is. The picture breaks up into large square pixels. The detective gives the desk a slap of frustration, unintentionally activating the Play button. He misses seeing François disappearing into the forest adjacent to the parking lot with the beast, its muscles rippling, at his heels. Its fur is plastered down here and there by tarry patches and, when the wind blows through its empty orbits, it whistles like a teakettle.

37

KNEELING BESIDE THE JEEP, LAGANIÈRE COUGHED and spat in the loose snow. At his feet was a red can with maybe an inch of gas inside, and his gloved hand held the flexible plastic tube he'd used to siphon it from Yannick's tank. He'd just swallowed a mouthful.

After managing to revive Marteau, he'd pulled on a one-piece snowsuit adorned with the badges of clubs, tournaments, and more or less prestigious sponsors. There he was, the dungeon master, gone out into the storm. He didn't know how, but he would start up the snowmobile, even if it meant drilling for fossil fuel in the environs. He still had the key, but the tank was nearly empty. Laganière had examined the Tempo shelter and the assortment of objects inside it, which, without manuals, were basically of no use to a bookworm like him. Yet straight away something in his head had gone: can, tube, tube, can. He must have learned it in a spy novel. He unhesitatingly grabbed both the plastic container fitted with a spout and the piece of tubing the old boy kept in case he one day discovered a maple on his property. Never would it have crossed Yannick's mind to siphon gas from his own Jeep into someone else's tank. On that score the guy was not at all the sharing type. Laganière was in luck.

Dizzy from the vapours, he again began to suck on the tube inserted in the fuel tank. He spat another mouthful into the can. Given what a gallon of the stuff cost, he was not about to spit it on the ground or swallow any more. It took some time, but the can was filling up, certainly enough to get him to CBSU, and if he succeeded, he'd be able to make an emergency call for his leg, notify the Sûreté du Québec of the Montreal dude's disappearance, and possibly get police protection from the vendetta awaiting him when his uncle came back. He'd see later about lodging a complaint against the guys.

Attired in his racing outfit, which was as yet unused, judging from its plate-armour stiffness and the brightness of the reflective stripes on its sides, Laganière made his way toward the Tempo shelter. He walked like a deep-sea diver lost in Inuit country. He eyed the can in his hand and was pleased. He felt manly to the core. Still, he didn't feel quite bold enough to check out the snowmobile right away. Laganière was more familiar with Batmobiles.

He had a world of trouble—who would have thought, with those bionic gloves he was wearing—unscrewing the gas cap. But he didn't want to mess up and pour the fuel into the wrong hole. He stepped out of the shelter and scanned the woods from behind his foggy glasses.

"Yannick!" he called out, but holding back somewhat. "Steeve!"

Okay, there aren't that many options. He introduced the spout into the hole and poured the gasoline. He wouldn't admit it, but he was miffed. The liquid slapped inside the spout. Laganière would've liked for his cousins to wait for him, because deep down he envied those guys. The tank was filling up. Steeve and Yannick, they had something he would never have. And what he had, well, what earthly good could it be to them? The last drops trickled out of the can.

The engine started up under the snow-laden tarp, and Laganière's headache started up again too. He switched off the ignition, smiling amid the hydrocarbon fumes. *I'll go get my things.* He'd have a glass of grape juice while he was at it. There was at least one unopened carton left in the pantry. As he slogged through snow nine feet deep all the way back around the cottage, he made a mental note to warn Henri Bouge that he absolutely mustn't leave his house to Yannick if he didn't want Monti's modest heritage to rot in the hands of Bradley's descendants. The time for taboos had passed. Old Marcel would be there to attest. Additionally, he wanted to take advantage of his airtime to thank his parents and his colleagues, and to tell Lorraine he loved her in spite of everything.

"*Thierry?*" he cried.

Sometimes you bump into a person outside their usual setting and, for a slow second, you can't place them. Laganière jumped and finally recognized Marteau barefoot among the trees. The queen of ghouls. Long, crusted hair. Leprous gown. Laganière had mistaken him for someone fifteen years dead.

"Martin, you'll catch your death."

Marteau was as spaced out as ever. But he stayed docile and offered no resistance when Laganière brought him back into their quarter-million-dollar pigsty. You had to have gone out and come back in to realize how badly it stank of corpses and stale booze. Marteau was so limp he'd have collapsed on the doormat if his saviour hadn't shored him up at the last moment. At least his heart was still beating. Laganière led him baby-stepping back to the master bedroom. But the room hadn't automatically cleaned itself, and he was not about to put Marteau back into a bed with puke-covered blankets. He settled Marteau on the floor, propped up with pillows in front of the giant home theatre screen. With his chin turned to the right and his pelvis twisted to the left, he kept his balance pretty much on his own. Laganière hit twelve buttons before finding the right one. Soon layers of xenon melded with the argon moving across the screen. But no universe was born inside the TV. Laganière, in pushing buttons at random, had messed up the preprogrammed decoder settings and they had been erased. He turned to a DVD featuring car chases and explosions and then tiptoed away. Marteau was either silently enchanted or asleep with his mouth agape.

It wouldn't have taken much for Laganière to sink into the living room floor when he hoisted the bag he'd prepared onto his back. He sent a lamp flying when he swung around, but by then ... The guys had forgotten their canvas bag on the table. He stepped back out onto the porch, arms akimbo, his rubber boots gleaming in the snow.

As he went along the side of the cottage for the third time, the mystery of his incurable headache was solved.

Hey, this is dangerous, Laganière thought. The snow had fallen relentlessly since the day before and the wind had driven it so high along the wall that the air vents were blocked. At the library he'd read somewhere that your lips can turn cranberry red from carbon monoxide poisoning. In which case they'd been lucky as shit. He'd forgotten the detectors weren't working, and just from breathing fresh air he suddenly had the impression his grey matter was being aired out a little.

Touches of green emerged through the browns, touches of blue through the greys. He felt no pride at having forgotten the air duct. His uncle had made a point of it, looking him in the eye as if confiding his last wishes: "Joël, here it is in three words: keep the carbon monoxide duct free of snow." Seven words. No, eight. "This isn't about being a keener, eh. You've got to keep it in mind. I don't want to find you and Lorraine all dried up, snuggled together bare naked in satin for all time."

Laganière brought his gloved hand closer to the vent. He'd have had to strap Marteau to his own body with a rope in order to take him along on the snowmobile, something he had no intention of doing, yet he couldn't very well leave him to die there of CO poisoning. Although. His hand stopped. He pictured himself debating, an angel in an old chalky tunic on his left shoulder playing arpeggios on an untuned lyre, and on his right shoulder a red devil nearly a head taller. Laganière wasn't legally responsible for Marteau. Marteau had kidnapped, hooded, and handcuffed him. Besides, Laganière had nothing to do with this storm. Act of God, as they say. If he wanted revenge, now was the time. On the other hand, Marteau was a motherless child. And it takes a village to raise a child, right? The townsfolk, the Frayois, had they really done their share? Laganière had never done anything for a kid but give him a library sticker when he'd read a whole book without whining. *People don't read no more,* he thought.

He cleared the duct and went back inside. He turned the heat all the way up, banishing his uncle from his thoughts, and opened the patio door to let in the air. The pages of the wall calendar, the curtains, everything floated on the breeze. He went into the bedroom to say goodbye to Marteau and wrapped Aunt Sylvaine's shawl around his shoulders. *You'd better pull through, so I won't have given you mouth-to-mouth for nothing.* To make sure there was enough ventilation, he hurled the decoder through the window over the bed.

He'd been unable to open it with the crank. It was too heavily iced over.

38

AFTER TALKING TO MR RANCOURT AT THE CALL CEN-
tre, who had talked to Mr Guérette at Mrs Guité's hotel, who
had just had a conversation with Mrs Foster that he'd have
been hard put to summarize, a certain Mrs Gingras decided
she was in need of attention. She dialed the beauty parlour's
number.

"Hello, Chez Ginette Beauty Shop. Are you calling for an
appointment?"

"Hi Ginette, its Guylaine. You know, that's a good idea.
Have you got an opening next Tuesday?"

"Are you due for a dye job already?"

"Yeah, and I'd like some purple streaks too. It's all the rage
these days."

"Hold on, let me check."

Elevator music.

"No, I'm booked Tuesday. But I can take you now, if you're
free. Mrs Plourde hasn't shown up. Otherwise..."

"Yes. No. Some other time. Actually, I was calling about
something else, you won't believe this, I..."

Ginette of Chez Ginette Beauty Shop wasn't about to
start keeping secrets at her age; she put Mrs Gingras on the
speakerphone and went on with the blow-dry she was doing

while the other party recounted that morning's story to all and sundry in her shop—customers, visitors, husbands. Lorraine Arsenault and Joël Laganière were history.

"Men, they're all the same."

"Seems he's gone off with Nadine Chabot, but no one knows where they're at."

"We've got a pretty good idea of what they're doing, though."

Apparently, Joël's car was spotted in the library parking lot, but he wasn't there. And Nadine had abandoned her little ones.

"Ah, that woman."

"Yup. Two children, two fathers."

"Although I'd have abandoned them too, the little monsters. And long ago at that."

"But the scariest part," said Mrs Gingras, "is that Maurice Foster, on the snowplow this morning, was attacked on the side of the road by some kind of big ferocious humanoid beast."

"Say what? A ferocious beast?"

In the chair where she was getting a perm, looking as if she'd been outfitted with neural receptors, Thierry Vignola's mother wanted to know.

39

LA FRAYÈRE WAS HEAVEN ON EARTH. YOU'D HAVE HAD to be blind not to recognize that and to want to go anywhere else on the planet, if only on vacation. Except maybe Florida. Time to put La Frayère on the UNESCO World Heritage list. With its low wall of ballast stones, wreathed in climbing plants, running along the old cobblestone mill road—the mill now converted into a museum—snaking across the grounds full of silver-capped hundred-year-old trees, then disappearing farther on under the grey-green wood-shingle covered bridge and reappearing on the other side to encircle the pastoral slope of a hill, covered at springtime with fiddleheads, where some one must have vacuumed between the snow-blanketed roofs pierced by smoking chimneys that one might very well have come to believe belonged to thatched cottages of bygone days if one weren't perfectly aware this was the trailer park. Not a single mushroom that didn't look hand-glued to its stump with artistically entwined roots or its soulful fence post. Not one snowflake too many in that hundred-dollar postcard. It turned dull in the long run, but that's how they liked it in their countryside. When all at once the dark trapezoid shape of the covered bridge's entrance lit up. It bristled with light as though the sun were about to emerge from it. Instead, the tunnel spat out a brown Oldsmobile steered by Mrs Turcotte, the carping old library patron. The driver-side door was a different brown from the rest of the car. Even though she was prone to memory gaps, she'd stayed hopping mad at Laganière ever since he'd tried to control her mind over the phone while he was being held hostage at his workplace. Mrs Turcotte's car door had been torn off in traffic the other day because she hadn't looked before starting to get out. Her daughter Edwige, not as far gone, though it wouldn't be long, had phoned earlier, after getting her hair done. They called each other every morning to talk about things like who'd come down with which ailment, who'd won at bingo that week, or the librarian's car, which had stayed in the parking lot the whole night. Edwige hadn't wanted to worry her mother with the other rumours, but she'd told her about the car. Not quite sure if it was still snowing or if it was her cataracts, Mrs Turcotte was not about to notice the wretched-looking pilgrim who desperately vaulted over the wall and dashed toward her car in the ruts carved into the whiteness. The town hadn't yet salted the roads, and the Oldsmobile was moving at a snail's pace. Mrs Turcotte didn't hear the back door open either, nor did she see the briefcase flash across her rear-view mirror or hear the door being shut. She didn't smell the refrigerator odour suddenly permeating her car. Her face set, she hugged her handbag, telling herself he'd eventually have to come back for his car, that bespectacled library guru, always trying to indoctrinate her, ordering books she couldn't care less about.

"I'll be waitin' on ya," she said.

She fingered something through the leather of her handbag.

"I beg your pardon?" François said, teeth chattering, face thrust between the front seats.

Mrs Turcotte turned around toward him. Not certain, but not distraught either. Then she turned back toward the road. Then again toward him, at which point François had to swivel her head forward. He had a parachutist's hairdo, a little rain cloud above his skull. He hadn't had his Nescafé.

"You. I forgot you was there," Mrs Turcotte said.

40

THE STORY ABOUT LAGANIÈRE AND NADINE CHABOT kept on travelling from house to house throughout the town, with all manner of deviations, epiphenomena, and settlings of accounts. Seeing how it had been blown all out of proportion, it was surprising no one as yet had rushed to buy the film rights. Now they were saying Maurice Foster had taken the rest of the day off because he'd been attacked in his snowplow by a beast with sharp teeth and long yellow arms, which he should have run over when he'd had the chance next to the Canons' field. At least, that was the version his wife told his supervisors. It had reached the point where so-and-so said to so-and-so, who was going to play bridge with him that night, that he'd seen something in September at the municipal campground, something he'd never seen in the woods. Slitty eyes outside the screen door of his mobile home, a furry back, fleeing in the crossed flashlight beams. Next day, at the water fountain in the middle of the campground, they'd found a rotting Expos cap like the one Thierry Vignola was wearing in the picture circulating on milk cartons back then. Everybody repeated this everywhere, with embellishments. Luckily for them, Maurice Foster hadn't ended up as a turkey dinner, what with him vegetating in front of the sports broadcasts asking Paule for another cold one, which she wasn't getting him. Eventually, though, she did come over to him, but to ask for his signature on the card going around for Lorraine. Because Joël Laganière and Nadine Chabot, well, everyone was pretty much convinced they were toast. In overwrought households and local shops, people wondered whether or not it was best to call the police. For Jean-Guy Saint-Onge, the answer was no, Bilodeau's police shouldn't be brought into it. He said the La Frayère police was a big joke, and that he'd been the victim of a plot when they'd taken away his licence as he left Mrs Guité's hotel.

"Me and the other guys," he said, "we're organizing a search party."

After which Ruth Leblanc added she wouldn't bother herself going down to the station to sober up Gaétan Bilodeau, with his dust-brush moustache, except maybe for the satisfaction of throwing a few glassfuls of water right in his mug along with a *goddamn* and some hard slaps.

"Drives around in his patrol car lecturing us and never even manages to pay his alimony, poor Céline."

"Sooo, then, what do we do?"

"Well, we wait."

41

"I'LL MAKE NO SECRET OF IT," FRANÇOIS SAID TO MRS Turcotte. "You do me a great favour. It is, as they say, cold as the moon. I trust you'll oblige me by coming inside to warm up. I can assure you Mother will be delighted to serve us tea and snacks."

"An' your li'l girlfriend," Mrs Turcotte wanted to know. "When's the baby due?"

They were approaching the heart of La Frayère in first gear. François had climbed into more cars in the past twenty-four hours than in his last three years in Montreal. But he wasn't enjoying it, especially because he thought he'd heard, somewhere underneath the Oldsmobile, between the transmission crankcase and the differential, his predator's whistling breath. *It's going to end up driving me bonkers,* he thought. It was impossible to fool the beast, but François was doing things right. He forced himself not to think about it. He concentrated on the frigging synthesizer measure that had been skipping since the middle of the night on CBSU. Mrs Turcotte's perm boggled the mind. François had no idea what his rescuer was saying and talked over her as if it didn't matter. His jaw was thawing out and he rubbed his transparent hands in the space between the seats opposite the heater. Bread slices soaked in milk and sprinkled with brown sugar—his grandmother called it *panade*—was what he craved. He noticed a pile of library books on the passenger seat. He at once checked to see if they included something by him even though he hadn't yet published anything.

"You are aware no doubt that my paternal grandmother was the founder of the La Frayère library?"

"Would it be a l'il boy or maybe a l'il girl you're expectin'?"

Mrs Turcotte turned toward him. Her perm vibrated on her head. François realized she not only took him for a hitchhiker but was mistaking him at present for another of her acquaintances. She'd asked him a moment ago if he still lived on Jacques-Cartier, after François had painstakingly refreshed her memory and revealed that he was Henri Bouge's son. But now he made no special effort to clarify the situation. The streets of his childhood monopolized his attention, the modest houses, increasingly rundown, the weather vanes not unnecessarily alarmed in this sea of prefabs. They'd left the postcard zone. The old-fashioned hand-painted storefronts had gradually given way to signs on which you changed the big square letters yourself to announce your final closing sale.

"Buckle up," Mrs Turcotte said when she noticed he hadn't put on his seat belt.

"I would rather not," François said. "If you have no great objections."

In the taxi, the seat belt would have cut him in half.

A real estate broker who looked pseudo-familiar to him seemed to hold sway over the village like a demiurge. His idealized puss was cloned on For Sale signs everywhere you looked. *Cheese melts in the mini-oven with slices of bacon and*

Velveeta, François dreamed. Mrs Turcotte's prattle had turned to her departed cat. She wore its haloed photo on a badge pinned to the parka culled from her daughter's attic. To test her vision, François made faces at her, but was unable to determine whether or not she made them back. *Oh, come on,* he thought. In the end, he buckled his seat belt.

"Anyhow, little Romain Perrault that ya prowl around with on occasion, ain't he nice? Such a fine youngster, always tidyin' up my handbag whenever he sees me."

She launched into a panegyric, Romain Perrault this, Perrault Romain that, confusing community service with volunteer work. On the radio the same six notes constantly repeated themselves. As the most famous fast-food chain restaurants paraded past the window, Mrs Turcotte pulled out of her handbag, not a thirteen-ouncer of Yukon, but a taser. The column of hamburgers that François was mentally building to the moon collapsed. Mrs Turcotte jabbered away untiringly. She patted her perm, looking at herself in the rear-view mirror. *Be tactful,* François thought. The toy in her hand, he knew what it was. In the city, the cops gave Poupette a taste of it probably twice a week. But he hadn't thought even once and a half before asking the lady what she was doing with the weapon and already it had vanished into the folds of her parka.

"It's good to return to one's roots," he improvised. "Believe me, this is the jewel of the province, and I..."

It seemed like a good idea to butter her up.

"...from the pharmacy," Mrs Turcotte was saying at the same time. "But then I says, it's high time I popped in for a visit with Carole..."

"...and I see from these books here you are as voracious a

reader as I am. You are no doubt aware that I am currently writing a book on ...”

“... it'd been quite a while since I'd—how does that go?— had my cards read, sooo I heads on over, and I says, how's she doing, Carole, eh, and she was happy, I'd brung her a jar of rhubarb ...”

They'd have kept up their dialogue of the deaf until their destination if the keyboard notes on the radio hadn't abruptly faded out. Old Marcel's voice began to pour out a stream of apologies, and you sensed he was smothering his laughter and that other people at the back of the studio were splitting their sides, as if there was a party going on.

“Welcome back to BSUC,” said old Marcel. “We apologize for the technical problems.”

His laughter exploded. A pensive smile played on François's lips.

“Oh my lord,” Mrs Turcotte gushed, “he's got the most enchantin’ voice, that man does.”

Followed by a comment that left François not quite knowing how to react. Now Mrs Turcotte wanted to turn up the volume.

“Next up is one of Maxophone's most unforgettable hits,” old Marcel's voice piped, still laughing.

François noticed it wasn't the volume his driver had turned up but the treble.

“Um, Mrs Turcotte?” he said.

The Oldsmobile rolled into the library parking lot.

“I'm afraid you may not be at the right address. Or in the right decade. You know, of course, that this building once belonged to my family, before my grandmother converted it into a public institution and donated it to the municipality, which at the time was called Lancelot-de-la-Frayère..."

The breath was knocked out of him when the bumper hit the wheelchair ramp. The Maxophone singer was belting out his masterpiece in an empty auditorium with his head in a cooking pot. Mrs Turcotte switched on her high beams to see through the window if anyone was hiding in the library. Laganière surely hadn't taken the time to lock the doors or shut off the lights before leaving, but no one had come in the meantime. Then, without ever checking that the way was clear, she put the pedal to the metal and zoomed straight back to the other side of the road, where she parked in a lingering pocket of night alongside Pagé's garage opposite the library. She lowered the music but not altogether. She cut the engine, drew the taser out of her parka, and pulled up her hood. She waited.

"Mrs Turcotte?" said François.

The old woman sprang up in her seat, pointing the taser. *I'll give you a Mrs Turcotte.* She'd forgotten there was someone else in the car. The windows flashed blue. The interior filled up with smoke shot through with branching bursts of electricity. François managed to escape before his skeleton got X-rayed. He vaulted a fence and cut through the backyards, stepping on rakes and such along the way.

Mrs Bradley, who lived next door, saw all the goings-on from behind her curtain. Or sort of saw, because outside it was snowing entire snowman body parts. She got into a state at the sight of the creature bounding away and had to self-medicate with the sherry in the liquor cabinet before remembering that such a thing as a telephone existed and you could use it to call folks.

"Joël?" Lorraine's strangled voice answered at the other end.

For a second Mrs Bradley had an urge to play a trick on her by pretending to be Laganière.

"No, no, Lorraine, this isn't Joël," she said. "It's Micheline Bradley."

Micheline was truly sorry she hadn't played that trick on her.

"Now, get a grip, lock your doors and listen up. I just seen something freaky in my yard. I was at my window when I . . ."

She told her what she'd seen, embroidering, laying it on thick with special effects. The smoke shot through with branching bursts of electricity—that was hers.

"But, hey," Lorraine said, her Kleenex box and the jar of Vaseline to smear under her nose within reach. "A beast, a beast . . . Shoot the thing down, no hesitation, no regrets!"

VIII

LA FRAYÈRE

42

IT WAS TABOO IN THE VILLAGE TO DWELL ON THE
question of how exactly Monti had managed to provide himself and his own with such a comfortable lifestyle. Tongues
wagged, but not anywhere and everywhere. The subject was
off limits on line dancing nights or at corn roasts. But offshore in a skiff, ankle-deep in tomcods, yes, sometimes. Or
in coded terms at funerals, under a wreath fancier than the
rest, which the Bouge family had had delivered. Monti himself didn't talk about it, about his gold prospecting days, and
there were lots of townspeople, including him, who'd have
been unable to show on a map where his peregrinations had
taken him. Some believed Manitoba was a place you sailed to
by way of the spice trade route, while others had heard from
someone who'd heard from someone who was surely Victor
Bradley that you could take a train from nearby, just back of
Campbellton, and get to Europe in a couple of hours. The
younger generations had become accustomed to not calling
Monti Monti. Mr Monti, they called him, thereby showing
their due deference to such a good Samaritan.

Good Samaritan, because he was the main mover and
shaker of Lancelot-de-la-Frayère now. The "Saint" of Saint-
Lancelot-de-la-Frayère had been dropped, owing not so much

to secularism as to signage space. The town grew more prosperous than before. Which wasn't saying much, but, even so, Monti often paid out of pocket to get a host of projects off the ground. The mill—that was his doing. The construction of the seaside boardwalk too. The very first winter sports facilities. Not to mention the digs he had built for him and his wife. "One more address for Bradley!" Monti would say. He sure was fond of old Bradley.

The mountain and the bay, before he took charge, had mainly served to satisfy various needs. Food, housing, a place for men only. Before Monti, everyone did their bit. You gave whatever time or advanced whatever money you could according to your wherewithal. You didn't get shares in anything afterwards, that wasn't what motivated you. Back then in Gaspésie no one talked about long-term yield. Or real estate speculation or risk capital. Or market fluctuations. Business wasn't thought of in those terms. The point being, Monti wanted to ratchet things up a notch, so he planted his flags everywhere. He amassed wealth, unabashedly, yet more often than not found a way for others to profit from his dealings as well.

He never stopped learning his trade, just as he'd learned the rudiments of poker in the North. In a big city they might well have made mincemeat of him. In his neck of the woods, he was considered a visionary. And a sight better dressed than the average joe, to boot. His wife didn't do all her shopping at Berthelot's. Nevertheless, not one of the Bouges was swell-headed. As evidenced by Monti's hat, which was the same size as that of the fellow next door. Monti's hat was nicer, but this didn't matter in the least. The difference lay in the thinking that went on under that hat—it didn't proceed in straight lines. It worked like dominoes, through corollaries, in swarms. Monti always seemed to be several steps ahead, with a bottomless bag of tricks in hand. He relied on his intuitions, pulling off schemes the competition failed to understand until the opportunity had already passed them by.

For all that, Monti was mocked whenever he spoke of organizing a monumental event in the village, something the Frayois would remember, where all the facets of their lives would converge and crystallize in all-encompassing festivities that would bring them together as a community. The beer would flow at Mrs Guité's when he launched into those speeches. Or the times he decided to have certain areas zoned, while normal people viewed these places as quite useless. It always paid off in the end. Because the more Monti spent, the richer he grew. The logic of which was not within everyone's reach. Mayor Pleau invited him to come over for dinner and explain. As he'd promised himself, Monti had a sidewalk built. From his house to the church. The first half out of cedar, the second out of pine, because the sawmill had run out. He made it clear to the townspeople that it belonged to him but everyone could walk on it all the same. And, don't you know, the older women blessed him. No longer would they have to lift their Sunday dresses to keep the frills out of the dirt. The church at the end of the sidewalk also received the occasional anonymous donation. A couple of times a year, at Pentecost and Thanksgiving. That was Monti, that was, at the back near the font, devising a way to make his fellow citizens look like tightwads as he nibbled on his wafers. He was at home in the house of the Lord, and for many years a little Bouge would be chosen to incarnate the baby Jesus in the Nativity scene at midnight Mass.

The new priest, Father Isidore, wasn't too bad. Unshaven, curly-headed, he split the presbytery's wood himself, wearing a big woollen navy-blue turtleneck sweater with leather elbow patches. More than one Frayoise would cast him admiring glances as they passed by, lamenting his choice of vocation. The parish he was taking over was in good shape. The groom didn't like the unshaven part, but Father Isidore was still the one tasked with celebrating the nuptials between Honoré Bouge, a.k.a. Monti, and Joséphine Bujold, thenceforth Joséphine Bujold Bouge. A marriage made in heaven.

"You may kiss the bride," the priest said, and Monti wanted someone to pinch him. His and his new wife's teeth knocked together.

The account of their reunion had made the front page of the *Vivier,* which had four or five pages in all ever since the editorial board had discovered the publicity principle. The day Monti appeared near the aqueduct construction site on his return from the realm of the dead, his betrothed was at home in her father's house baking pastry so as not to waste blueberries. She sometimes went to bring victuals to the ailing, sometimes to the general store, and on her way back found shelter in a garret, where, together with Flavienne and Coraline, she smoked cigarettes purloined from Dr Bujold's cardigan, which hung by the front door. While Father Isidore healed souls, Dr Bujold healed bodies, and some ladies in the village had talked about launching a petition to have it the other way round. In short, Dr Bujold was the town's only accredited physician. The only one. If you were a visitor, say, from Notre-Dame-de-Liesse in Rivière-Ouelle, and during your visit you were beset by angina, you had better be careful. Someone else in the village claimed to be a follower of Hippocrates: Dr Maturin. You needed to watch out not to inadvertently end up in his barn. When it came to anatomy, a mare and a marquise were in his view both modelled on the same lines.

Joséphine laid the pastries in her picnic basket on a blue-and-white checkered handkerchief under which she'd concealed a novel from France deemed poisonous and hence illicit by the Quebec clergy. How very kind of her to go to Godefroi's wife Madeleine's bedside, was her father's response when she apprised him of her plan. His glasses perched on the tip of his nose, Dr Bujold reeled off his recommendations for stomach aches.

"Please tell her I'll be dropping by to examine her after nap time. And, I beg you, don't tire her out."

"I'll be back in time for my lesson, Father."

Sporting a boater under her parasol, Joséphine made her way down the elm tree–lined lane in front of their house and let her pumps skip freely along the roads fringed by flowers no wilder than she was. Bells chimed in the distance. Caps were doffed with slightly superstitious courtesy as she passed, and a great deal of respects were paid between her house and the cemetery. Monti's resurrection at the construction site had caused a commotion; once past the breach in the low wall, Joséphine saw people clustering on the riverbank. When she caught sight of her beau in the crowd, the basket of pastries was cast aside. Holding her shoes, tearing down the hill through the pollen-filled air, no sooner had she reached the bottom than she already had a bun in the oven.

His features flooded by a caramel glow, Dr Bujold leaned over his future son-in-law's half-open satchel. When Monti had asked for his daughter's hand, the doctor nearly severed it over the sink to make sure Monti would leave with it. And what a lovely wedding it was! Although Skelling, Sicotte, Labillois, Langis Allard, those fellows just didn't know what to do with themselves in the presence of their old chum Monti. He had adopted some surprising standards in matters of protocol. There was nothing pedantic or in any way presumptuous on his part, yet the wedding wasn't to his friends' liking. For those in his circle who'd known him as a kid—his pecker aloft in the orphanage locker room or, with a rope tied around his waist and a knife in his hand, diving into the salt water to cut clams off the pier piles—it was as if only his bodily frame had returned from the voyage. Inside it, instead of Monti, there now was an excess of drive, a cramped genius, a blend, a mixture that obviously couldn't have been brewed locally. It was: get out of the way, I've got big plans.

Monti worked tirelessly, without let-up, for years, knowing no other way to live, while their house glowed under his wife's influence. There were always visitors, a flock of kids waving wild manes and wooden swords. Joséphine served them fresh milk, and flowerpots brimming over with herbs adorned every step of her porch. The little scamps ran among the sheets, the clothesline spirits. Their frolicking shadows mottled the lilac trees. Mrs Bouge made check marks in the department store catalogues, and the furniture arrived on a train from Montreal or Toronto. For such things she sought her husband's approval, but Monti, well, whatever worked was fine. Indebted to his wife for her domestic enchantment, he remained unaffected by comfort and pleasure. What's more, everything tickled him. And when you tickled him, he completely lost control. Love, therefore, was made in the dark, through a hole in the night-gown. At times he kept his socks on.

Due to subtle aspects of her nausea, Joséphine sensed the good Lord would make her first-born a girl. She was mistaken. Her Baptiste was born with a beard. They took their time and watched him grow. The child learned to walk, to name the animals on the property, to gulp down liquor without blinking. He let out battle cries when the mailman came up the hill toward the house. One child wasn't enough, and the couple was all the while under pressure from friends and relations. But the Bouges procreated at their own chosen pace. They were going to do things their way. Besides, Monti hadn't yet established himself to his satisfaction in the village. Before the family got too large, he intended to bring to life some of the visions he'd nurtured during his months of pickaxes, rocks, and riddles in the North. In those visions, people flocked from all directions toward Lancelot-de-la-Frayère, drawn by omens, promises, and a prodigious swarming. And those projects, those visions, well sir, his plans for them covered a period of about three hundred years. He had more vitality than the average individual, Monti did, and he strove without pause to expand his empire. A regional empire, somewhat extravagant, built through bursts of activity, but an empire all the same, and the Frayois' name for it was respect. Thus, Joséphine mothered her Baptiste with no siblings or concerns that might impede their bond. His tin soldiers arrayed at his mother's feet, the boy, in androgynous attire, carried out the execution of deserters.

When of an evening Joséphine detected incipient doldrums in her husband's mood, she encouraged him to head over to the hotel for a toot with the boys. She had no problem with these appetites, which every man owed it to himself to satiate. She tolerated behaviour decidedly more dubious. But now, darn it, the transcendence born of intoxication eluded Monti. What's worse, he could never fully slake his thirst. No matter what you served him, it never failed to leave him unsatisfied. Yes, he drank his aquavit—what dishwater! Or vermouth— pure ersatz. He drank to keep his hand in while awaiting the only drink apt one day to grab his palate for good. The only drink he knew capable of shrinking the inside of his skull, where there was too much room for rumination.

"I'll break you, I'll break you," Mrs Guité growled behind her bar as she concocted poisons for him.

But Monti didn't break so easily. Animals, on the other hand, touched a tender spot in him. Not like Maturin, but get a load of this: The warehouses on the New Brunswick shore, obtained through barter, were starting to pay off. Monti rent- ed land to farmers and used the rent money to build himself a barn behind his house in his spare time. He made it all pretty inside, and his filly, his cow, and his ewes ran their tongues over his mouth. He also inquired about ostriches and a llama. What's more, the necessary maintenance gave him the chance to hire people less fortunate than him, including veterans of the Great War. His grooms, he called them, and their faces were a sight to see when he popped into the barn to boss them around, mangling Racine-style French in a harangue full of laboriously phrased orders that, at bottom, were as simple as ABC. The fact was, Joséphine laid traps for him. She planted literary classics everywhere under the cushions, on the easels and occasional tables, at times to make him read something that would convince him she'd been right on a previously contested point, but mostly to lend their home a spiritual dimension.

Fortunately, Monti derived amusement, an outlet for his stress, from the supreme stinker that now, more than ever, Victor Bradley had become. Still a tenured postal employee, the Paspyjack had become an institution. If you wanted to learn more about the usefulness of tolling bells when the need arose to drive out some pestilence, or the risk of shifting tectonic plates when using dynamite, he was your man. The fellow licked the glue on envelopes just for the taste. And while representatives of the female persuasion railed at his lack of class and the inappropriateness of his turns of phrase, throughout the mailman's territory, in the hovels and houses touched by widowhood or estrus, red-headed tots proliferated.

It wasn't long before the hostilities between him and Monti resumed. One dealt a low blow and the other retaliated with a blow below the belt. Bradley was an incorrigible snake. Being a barfly, he had more friends, people like him, but naive and suggestible. Whereas Monti was a loner at heart. He needed his nemesis for recreation. Regardless of what he was up to, there was always a scheme taking shape below the surface of his mind. It kept him fit and titillated the masses—folks followed the goings-on. Especially because a kind of ethics had been established between the adversaries, a moral imperative, a code of honour that was hardly lacking in absurdity. Not only were they forever trading insults, but the slightest provocation on one side was interpreted on the other as a challenge impossible to ignore. Needless to say, it was the talk of the town when Bradley, after a morning prodigally spent sleeping in, showed up at the Bouges' with a parcel, only to find Monti had repositioned his letter box at a height of twenty-five feet.

Bradley would have to borrow a ladder somewhere in the village. Not that ladders were scarce in that town of manual workers. Only, nobody trusted him, not even the nitwits he hung around with. The mailman ended up looking for his ladder at Mrs Guité's in a bottle of plum liqueur, pondering over his raison d'être and his role in the community. He went to Monti's place in the afternoon, more than a little in his cups, with *part* of a ladder: a solitary side rail, with just a few rungs, pulled out of the garbage. He leaned it against the front of the house at a practicable angle, wedging one end into a gap in the porch. He rolled up his sleeves, sadly eyeing the letter box up among the clouds, when Monti, his head protruding from an attic window, sneered at him. The mailman's response was to gesture *shove it*. He didn't get very far up.

After about a week of convalescence, Bradley had a night-mare in the armchair where the Dubuc woman tucked him in at night when he was being impossible. The stuffing was coming out in tufts through tears in the upholstery. The mail-man awoke with the springs creaking, his sour candies spilling onto the floor around him. His neck was as stiff as ever. Dr Bujold had given him a brace to soothe his lumbar region and advised him to use the homemade antiphlogistic he'd rubbed all over for pest control purposes. All Bradley could remember from his dream was wrestling with job complications, with non-existent forces.

If he was going to work in his sleep, you could be sure he'd be billing overtime hours. He belched as he got up, weary from idleness, let out a fart at his other end. He was itching to move again despite his aching neck; he was going to work, a good excuse to get away from his girlfriend and drink himself cock-eyed. His feet left sticky tracks up to the declining Empire mirror propped against the wall. Bradley had never hung it up and the tools gathered dust on the floor. On seeing his reflection nicely framed like that, the mailman thought it would make a knockout stamp. He scraped the tartar from his teeth while smoothing his hair back with his other hand. He dipped his gap-toothed comb in the small tub of grease where gnats had gotten stuck ever since he'd misplaced the lid. A special twist of the wrist—worked out over a long period of time—and the punkish wave in his forelock rose like mayonnaise. His silly goose slept on, a brood of redheads nestled against her.

Bradley drew on his boots, which, as he never bothered to untie the laces, were misshapen. He kicked his way through toys to the middle of his crookedly fenced yard. A patch of bayou in a damp continental climate. It was full of junk and dead leaves, with heaps of brushwood that sometimes on his sabbaths he watched burn. His dogs barked after him, pulling on their chains. They chomped on their empty tin bowls while their master performed his physical therapy, scrupulously airing out his entire person. This was how he washed, standing in the wind, arms spread wide, legs apart. He'd had shooting pains in the tendons of his thighs ever since he'd tried to prove to a couple of fellows, in a field used for baseball, that he could do the splits.

"Mrs Berthelot, Mr Berthelot," he said, pushing open the door of the general store.

The slightly loose floorboards shivered under his dirt-caked soles, he being too proud to walk on Monti's sidewalk. He took care to leave the greatest possible mess behind him as he made his way to the nook where the mail had piled up during his week off.

"He's not to blame," said Mr Berthelot.

Perched on his stepladder, stocking the shelves with his perennial canned foods, the shop owner turned his whole body around toward his associate, who happened to be his wife, as if he too were wearing a neck brace.

"M'thinks he might've lacked affection as a child," Mrs Berthelot added over her columns of figures and her abacus.

To Bradley, people like them were ciphers. He didn't give two hoots about them. He went about his business, sorting the mail, starting with the lightest because he wasn't one to deal with the hardest stuff first. *Well, looky here,* he thought. He nearly snapped his neck back into place again. *Another parcel for Monti.* It had just come back to him. A voice had talked to him in his nightmare. Bradley cast a malicious eye, the brown one, behind him. Mrs Berthelot was counting on her fingers something that would have required a few more of them. The mailman shook the package against his eardrum in an attempt to guess its contents. It was from the USA, as indicated on the delivery slip. He recalled that the orders the voice shouted at him in the nightmare were in English. Again he glanced back over his shoulder, this time with his blue eye, and noticed Mr Berthelot momentarily juggling with his cans and about to lose his balance up on his ladder.

Bradley had dreamed he was arguing in his creative English with what turned out to be a talking spinning wheel. The spinning wheel ordered him—though the mailman objected that Monti's house was located in another dimension—to go deliver the parcel being woven with every turn of the wheel.

On the sly, Bradley drew out of its cardboard case the ratchet box cutter he used on heavy-duty adhesive tape. He cut the string and the package opened. The voice had promised him he'd get his due through effort. A bottle of something bearing the name Yukon breathed in the box. *That dream I had was an omen.* There must have been verities written on the enclosed note, because it too was in English. *Like the voice.* The Paspyjack started to find all manner of connections with other dreams he'd had in the past and things that had happened afterwards. He put the bottle back in the box, but then he hesitated. Though not for long. He took out the Yukon again but, before he uncorked it, turned around a third time and found himself face to face with Mrs Berthelot. She was taking a break from bookkeeping to put a stop to his monkey business. Bradley pretended he'd dropped something in the box and put the bottle back, for good this time, in its tissue paper wrapping. He tied the whole thing up without making a fuss.

"This came for you," Joséphine said to Monti as she swept in and set the parcel down on the desk in his study.

Monti was writing on his typewriter. He wore a cashmere dressing gown over his pyjamas—not made of denim, but just about. It would have tickled too much to wear the robe directly against his skin. Gnawing non-stop at his strip of salt pork, something he'd taken up of late, he let out a single burst of laughter when he took out the bottle and saw its label.

"My, my. Yukon. Well, if that don't beat all."

He smiled without a hint of bitterness, the way you smile on recalling the exploits of rogues who once brought you joy aplenty. Besides, what reason could he have had to be ticked off? He was making money. Making it at that very moment. The note enclosed with the bottle consisted of a few ceremonious remarks. In it, Charles Bead stated that this gift, to be renewed on a weekly basis, was meant to honour his poker debt. *"The taste of gold,"* Monti thought. *Yup. That's right. My gold. Mine.*

Little Baptiste tugged at his sleeve to show him the warplane he'd drawn. He might as well have been talking to the paperweight. Monti had smelled the cork of his gift and metamorphosed into a herd of buffalo ranging the prairie. *Never again will I be thirsty.* He shouted to Joséphine to come get Baptiste and baby Toine. The toddler was building a marina with blocks his father had fashioned out of remnants of his sidewalk.

"It's gonna take me a demijohn of this stuff," Monti said.

Once he was all alone, with the door locked, he reached out toward the cabinet he kept near his chair. He grasped two tumblers with a hand practised from his years of helping out behind the hotel counter. *Is this your evil spell, Dexter m'boy?* Oblivious to the gravity of his gesture, he poured two identical glasses of Yukon and slid one toward the empty chair in front of him.

"Well, cheers, Donald m'boy!" he said to the neutral, immobile glass.

Leaning back, legs crossed, Monti swallowed the drink like a pill and instantly curled up, quivering with pleasure.

IX

THE GREAT WORK

43

FRANÇOIS TRIED TO STOP AS HE RAN UP THE WINDING
lane at the far end of which stood the disfigured facade of the
house Monti had had built in the previous century, before his
son Henri rebuilt it to his taste piece by piece. Through the
powder snow interlaced with phosphorescence, the fangs of
the extraordinary beast snapped behind him. François didn't
take the time to muse on the mutations of the family property
sitting on its hillock, as far as possible from any traffic. His
mismatched shoes slipped on the flagstones, already shovelled
and more salted than the Canons' hogs even though it was
still snowing, and he dropped to his knees as if he'd just scored
a goal. He pitched clumps of ice haphazardly behind him in
the beast's direction.

He got back up and shook his limbs, whooping like a monkey after driving it back into the trimmed hedges bordering
the grounds, a sight that made him nostalgic for the punks of
his Montreal neighbourhood. Beyond the wall of greenery
were trailers tightly aligned on streets surveyed and registered
to the nth degree. The garden hose was perfectly coiled, a perfectly domesticated thirty-foot-long blindworm. The house
was unrecognizable. François had to poke around in the mailbox to make sure he wasn't about to show up unannounced

at a narcotics lab or some such. The mailbox, now located by the roadside, contained a few bills, a credit offer, and the current edition of *Le Vivier* with dozens of circulars between its pages. It was yesterday's mail, indeed addressed to the Bouges. Tucked inside the mailbox there was also a bottle of Yukon that had turned into granita. François had to chew rather than drink his swig. His eyes rolled up and went white. His mouth was edged with crystals.

"Hello!" he shouted as he walked toward the house.

The mailbox had been moved because Croquette barked too much at the mailman. The bag of salt lay on the steps of the porch, where François's shadow preceded him as if to say, *I'm not with him.* The door knocker was gone. *What have they done to the house?* The new doorbell with programmable chimes, this François didn't see. The door was locked. He pushed against the panel, to no avail. The beast was lurking out there, half-buried in snow that would soon need to be exported. François stepped off the porch and backed away, to take in the building and learn to love it.

"It's horrible."

Maybe so, but these weren't the old days anymore. At the slightest thaw the roof would leak, and the place cost a fortune to heat. Now, at least, it was clean and tidy.

"Well, you see . . . the reason is that . . ." François tried to rationalize.

He walked around the house, his indignation rising once more when he noticed that the antique shutters which gave the windows so much character were missing. He brushed a peevish hand over the cement blocks covering the original foundation stonework, over the fresh stucco on what had formerly been brick walls. An entire outgrowth, a whole wing, had developed on one side, where the flower boxes had been removed for the fall or forever. There was a gigantic SUV parked in the driveway.

It would have suited him, after he'd climbed up the weeping willow, for a squadron of sparrows to swoop in and help him cover the rest of the distance to the window. The willow in the backyard, what with all the pruning and tail ends of hurricanes, didn't weep much anymore. Down among the roots, the beast ruffled the snow and let out its unnatural hawking noises. It had come back to pursue François, its tongue an alkaline green, its metamorphosis in full swing, like the house. The gazebo had disappeared. François wasn't even sure now if there had ever been one. With the tip of his foot he managed, centimetre by centimetre, to push the upstairs window open. But, with his leg at an obtuse angle, he found himself stuck in a Spiderman position, briefcase between his teeth and eight purchases on different branches. One of the beast's corneas fell out from all its preening.

"Perhaps if I unknotted my arm in order to transfer my foot to…"

The beast pounced. In a spray of froth, its maw clamped shut on the seat of François's pants. The branches on which he'd been perched a second ago continued to shake. Their last leaves sailed away on the wind.

Having torn down the blind and the sheet of plastic insulating the window, François landed on top of a metal file cabinet. He rolled down another notch onto a melamine table, then the carpet, and immediately stood up sneezing, as if the whole thing had been choreographed. He stepped back in surprise.

To all appearances the office had been moved upstairs. Outside, the beast flew off as a swarm of versicoloured beetles.

"Atishoo!" François went again.

It seemed to be his allergies. Remarkable, as there had never been any pets in the family. "Now, as for me, oh yes, I'm all for it, I like dogs," his father would answer when François begged him as Yannick looked on, sneering. "Medium rare on the grill." Or Henri would tell him to go ask his mother, who told him to go ask his father, who told him to go ask his mother, ad infinitum.

When François stroked the mouse, the computer screen, making the same noise as the taste of cream soda, turned on. It displayed an Excel spreadsheet, and François started changing the decimal points at random. From the ground floor came a polyphonic hum produced by several TV sets playing in various parts of the house, interspersed with more or less hostile vibrations. François poked his runny nose into the paperwork: invoices for tools bought in Plattsburgh, half-finished bids, a depleted chequebook where only the stubs were left to flap on their rings in the draft from the window. The Yukon buried in the filing cabinet under a veritable tarot of business cards, next to a Rubik's cube and an old puck with tooth marks, didn't stay buried very long. It's really something, the way a bottle is designed: you hold it there, the neck is here, you drink like so. Right away François felt looser and among family. He looked for something to look for. The calendar on the desk had paid for itself long ago. Among other notes, there was a Post-it stuck to the computer monitor. *A sticky note,* François thought. On it, in an unfamiliar script that made your blood run cold, were the words: "Understand your accountant." The vibrations in the floor resumed. *Fifty hertz,* François guessed.

"That's not what I'm looking for," he said.

He picked up the deed of conveyance of the house, nota-rized, the whole shebang, but didn't notice anything. He hadn't seen a thing. His throat and eyes stung. Squeezing a stress ball he'd found who knows where, he skimmed through a severely marked-up poem inserted in an atlas that also served to collect dried plants. In the poem, which didn't scan properly, Henri expressed the view that the older he grew, the younger he felt. The stress ball emitted faint whiny squeals.

The layout of the upstairs floor had changed. Disoriented, François wandered down the hallway that now ran through an open space. Propped against the walls were scores of folded boxes. As he slushed his way across the rug, François detected the sound of the beast scratching on the other side of the wall; he really would have to get rid of it in order to work. *Now what might this room be?* The various TV sets in the house were all trying to tell him something at once. Looking for the stairs to the ground floor, he took a chance and opened an enigmatic door.

"Oh, I beg your pardon," he said to the scarecrow standing before him.

It was a blue nursery. As yet without a baby. The scarecrow, at the same time as François, recoiled in surprise into the gloom among the flimsy furniture of his childhood, next to a handcrafted crib over which hung a tinkling mobile full of stimulating baubles that were choke-proof for when you put them in your mouth to cut your teeth. François was about to shut the door again when he realized the other facing him in the room mimicked his every move simultaneously. *Could it be that* . . . It was him in the mirror. He stepped closer to his reflection. He had the same chin as the rest of the Bouge dynasty, the same dimple, which in his case was peeling in scabs through a patchy beard like Velcro full of fibres, denser on one side than the other and rising to a tic-ridden eye highlighted by a pink crescent above cavernous circles that branched and blurred into cheekbones sagging below the knobby brow that made him look like a sunfish.

"Oh my," he said, stretching the skin of his face with his hands.

He left his reflection behind and continued down the hallway. His face slowly drooped back to its normal shape. François finally found the stairway to the ground floor. He set his foot down on the first step. His mother walked by below with an axe.

44

STEEVE AND YANNICK HAD GONE TOO FAR IN THE
storm for Steeve to be able to make it back to the Laganière
cottage on his own without a compass. With his rifle barrel
leading the way, he forged through the harsh, whistling woods,
his face buried in his collar. He somehow managed to breathe
despite the ice-up. Wishing he were home surrounded by his
stuff, wishing everyone would leave him the heck alone, he
looked at his gun, looked around himself, and then looked at
Yannick's back disappearing into fir trees like car wash rollers.
I'll bet you five bucks, he thought, *Danny's gone back to the cottage and is taking it easy without for a second wondering where we
might be. Right now he must be bouncing around in the vibrating
armchair yelling for someone to come and unplug it.* Without
warning, Yannick's face reappeared amid the branches.

"Why don't you make more noise, friggin elephant."

His balaclava bristled with needles. Steeve felt the blood
pulsing in his carotid.

"I... You sure we're going in the right direction?"

"No, but hey, go for it, trumpet away so they can hear us
coming all the way to Cap-Chat."

Steeve could see himself in his cousin's paintball glasses and
pitied his reflection. Feeling hurt, he wedged his gun into his

armpit. His bare hands cast a shadow full of accidents onto the snow. His hands cried out for warmth, clothing, linings. There was nothing much pointing in that direction. He hunched up against the wind. His hardened little finger dipped into the bag of powder he'd forgotten to share.

"You owe me an apology," he told Yannick.

The dope had just sort of slapped him in the back of the medulla. He readjusted his anatomy inside his inadequate clothes.

"Apology for what?"

"For calling me a pachyderm."

"Calling you what? Hey, check it out. See that burrow over there? Okay, now go hibernate in it for four or five months."

"Wait for me! Wait up!"

Steeve slipped on the icy crust as he tried to salvage his spilled coke and rub it on his gums. But white on white— good luck with that. He cursed as he stood back up. The trees had become more defined, their branches riddled with pale, shifting gaps. Yannick, meanwhile, was in his element, getting his bearings by craning his neck above tall grass vitrified by the wind or bowed here and there by the built-up weight. Each time their snowshoes sank into the snow, they sounded like food falling into hot oil.

"It could have been whatever," Steeve said over the gusts once he'd rebalanced his faculties.

The scratching he'd heard during the night, the possibly hallucinated tracks around the cottage, the claw marks on the logs—he ultimately didn't know what they were, if indeed they were something.

"Your existence, *that* is whatever," Yannick shouted up ahead.

The way Yannick saw it, he was doing Steeve a favour. After all, it wasn't *his* guest who'd gone and gotten himself lost in the wilderness. With each stride his snowshoes skimmed his ears. Steeve, more at home in a metro car or at an IMAX theatre, struggled to keep up. He recalled very little of his otherwise notorious time with the Scouts, though they definitely remembered him.

"It could have been whatever," he said again.

In spite of his surplus lactic acid, he did his best to catch up with the costumed head, that rippling camouflage ahead of him. He advanced, jaw slack, slightly dislocated, arms held out in a V to push aside the branches. He stopped paying attention to the snow sliding down his neck and into the sleeves of his orange bomber jacket, torn on one side. He was going to break down crying if they didn't right away come out onto a path or a clearing. The cones shook on the branches. In a gap, he collided with Yannick's back. Yannick, stopped short, informed him they were lost.

"What?"

Steeve began to stomp around heavily, seeking a way out through the vegetation and the galaxies of maddening snow, ready to charge in any direction. A cramp twisted his thigh and he dropped down on one knee.

"Relax, for Chrissake, I'm kidding."

During their trek, each time the trees blurred and faded again, each time the snow lost its glitter under their snowshoes, the cousins rewarded themselves for their trouble with a snort of coke. Otherwise Steeve would have collapsed. Screaming almost at the top of his lungs, he was reminding Yannick of all the joys of their childhood. Yannick stopped so abruptly the powder snow flew up like when you're skating and hit the brakes.

"What is it now?" Steeve asked anxiously.

Yannick removed his gloves by shaking his hands like a hockey player. Pressing down with all his weight, he bent a still-impressionable sapling under his foot and broke off a switch. Then he prostrated himself in the snow hollowed out around a brown ring, before an adorable coiled turd studded with seeds and undigested bits of bark.

"What's that?" asked Steeve.

"Your twin brother."

Yannick flipped the turd over with his stick.

"No, seriously," Steeve insisted.

"Don't you shit turds?"

"I didn't do anything, I swear."

This set them laughing for a few seconds. *That's my cousin,* thought Steeve. The tree Yannick had taken his switch from never entirely straightened up.

"What do you think the shit came from?"

"Something fairly big that smells bad."

"Is it fresh?"

"The stick says it's soft."

"But is it warm?"

Yannick stared at his kinsman.

"You can just forget it," Steeve protested, adjusting his grip on the rifle. "Not on your life. I will not poke my finger in that."

45

HIS STOMACH SPRINKLED WITH GREYISH HAIRS,
Henri Bouge lay inside the cabinet of the bathroom vanity.
The vibrations his son had detected were from his lithium-ion-
powered drill. The device was cooling beside him in a shiny
tool box. François crept closer and straight away noted the
thirteen ounces of Yukon lying in the tool box among the
Allen keys and washers and sockets. The ground floor apparently had also undergone its share of transformations. François
tapped Henri's knee; Henri, groaning like a didgeridoo, peeled
off half of his back trying to climb out from under the sink.

"Hello," said François, squinting his eyes in the beam of his
father's headlamp. "Well, here I am."

His arm, briefcase swinging at the far end, was stretched out
at a hundred and eighty degrees toward the nearest exit. He
looked up at Henri, now standing before him. Henri punched
himself in the heart. His son wouldn't have recognized him
if not for the delicate contours of his face, overflowing with
joy on a balloon-like head.

"Good timing," his father whispered with a zigzag smile, his
eyes watering. "I could use a hand."

Throughout the ground floor, televised voices, all on different stations, competed with each other.

"Liette!" Henri bellowed emotionally.

He hugged François, who inhaled in the nick of time before being crushed. He breathed in the swarf from the drilling. *My baby,* Henri thought. *Thank you, Lord. My baby.* François, too short in the arms to clasp hands behind the giant's back, smeared a little snot on his father's shoulder. He made a mental tally: *François, one, Henri, nothing.*

"I thought it must be Yannick. What are...Come tell us..."

A ferrety snout withdrew farther inside the inlet of the central vacuum cleaner in the corridor. François hoped it wasn't his mother barking like that in the living room.

"Liette!" Henri shouted. "Liette! Come on over here, come see our special guest!"

As if pulled along by the TV remote, amid a shuffling of slippers followed by the clicking of eager claws, his mother careened around the corner of the corridor but was still overtaken in the final sprint by her dog. A rectangular prism perched on four toothpicks, a purebred mutt evincing its masters' manners. Liette had a cigarette stuck in her beak and was wearing a geometric print blouse that turned your pupils into asterisks. Along the way she somehow conjured up a shirt to cover her husband's semi-nudity.

"Oh, my god! Oh, my god!" she repeated.

The dog rolled at François's feet to show him what a nice smooth belly he had. Then he went to position himself, sitting or standing—the angle was nearly the same—and growl in front of the vacuum inlet. The briefcase with the manuscript was on the floor, making an incognito getaway at three millimetres an hour.

"It's François!" Henri yelled over his wife, jiggling his boy as if to shake out every bit of François there was inside.

As particular as ever about her appearance, Liette had purple fingernails and chandeliers for earrings. *My, how they've aged,* François thought. *The pistil and the stamen.* His mother smiled at him, to the extent possible. Completely panicked.

"Oh, ma gawd!"

She needed to touch him, needed to touch her François. Okay, that's fine. You can let go now.

"Have you eaten?" her lipstick asked him.

The guy was wearing a suit from the Sally Ann. A bloody sneaker and what was left of another shoe. He had streaks of dried wasabi under his nostrils. A twenty-sixer in his system, and then some, since the day before. There was puree bubbling from a knife wound and patches of soot everywhere from almost being tasered. "Have you eaten?"

"I . . ."

"Look, Henri, he's way too thin!" Liette said.

"Jeez, Liette, let's not make it out to be worse than it is. He's not about to shrivel up and die tonight, but we'll fatten him up, woman."

Liette pushed past François and hurried to the kitchen, instantly generating a domestic din with seventeen appliances switched on at the same time in a cloud of cigarettes.

"Do you think you'll have time to go see your aunt Mireille?" she bawled from her racket at the other end of the hall.

"He's just arrived, for pity's sake!" Henri snapped. "And she's not his aunt, she's his cousin!"

"And your cousin Steeve, he's in the neighbourhood too, and Yannick's gonna be real glad to see you!"

"Can we have him to ourselves for a minute, dammit? Would that be okay, eh? And, by the way, Steeve's his second cousin, not his cousin!"

There was a pause between the two men. All that was missing for a candlelight dinner was the dinner and the candles.

"I . . . I don't know what to say," said François.

His father gestured for him to come closer so he could smooth him out, adjust his tie, his posture. Henri examined him at arm's length. Maybe it was contagious.

"Don't waste your saliva. You're going to need it in a little while to drool over your supper. Liette! That poached game Yannick brought us, take it out of the freezer, will you?"

He stooped down, pretending to gather up his drill, but his true purpose was to close his tool box, snap the clasps shut, hang sixteen padlocks on it, and then bury it six feet underground in a safe full of progressively smaller safes. In short, he closed his tool box with the bottle of Yukon inside it.

"We'll have a quiet supper. Not entirely legal, but we're under no obligation to invite the game warden either, what do you say? Listen, I was about to drill a hole in the cabinet to run the pipe through there."

"Do sit down, Papa," said François as he led his father toward the toilet.

Henri sat down on the lid. Another punch to the heart.

"But my chuck rolled away somewhere over there, I looked everywhere for it. You, you're slim, you've got nimble fingers, why don't you get underneath there and see if you can't find it."

Chuck, chuck . . . François knew this sense of the word was a variant of *chock*, from the Old French *çoche*. Nothing else, though. No idea what it might look like. He bent down under the sink and took his chances among the vanity's entrails. They didn't ooze as much as the undersides of the sinks at his place. This wasn't the same bathroom he'd known as a youngster.

Henri stood up again. He'd never been able to stay put longer than that. He blathered on distractedly, his down-to-earth logic disrupted by the paranormal disappearance of his tool. The telephone in the kitchen started to ring. With every ring, Henri, gripped by anxiety, took a step back against the wall. They had three square metres to search. No chuck anywhere.

"Hell's bells, it didn't fall through some multi-dimensional portal!"

Solemnly devoted to its self-imposed mission, with its feather-duster tail and its need for a diamond-pattern sweater, the dog was still standing guard beside the central vacuum cleaner. François was inclined to ascribe the tool's disappearance to a kind of ambient senility. The telephone rang, rang, rang, ever louder.

"What on earth is going on?" Henri shouted toward the kitchen.

He wiped his face in his shirt, which he inspected as if it were the Holy Shroud. As for François, nothing came to mind but *red telephone.*

"Who is it? What does it say on the call display? Why don't you pick up?"

"It's the hair salon," Liette shrilled. "I'll call back in a bit!"

In the meantime, François disinterred himself from under the vanity. He was holding what looked like a pearl necklace, an antique, but brand new.

"Let's see what you've got there," Henri said. "Why, it's your grandmother's necklace. We gave it to Yannick a while back. For Cynthia. But I was meaning to ask you: How did you get here?"

François really didn't feel like going into detail. He didn't want to worry his parents with the accident, much less get judged for his spending. At the microwave's third beep Liette reappeared in the hallway. Coppery sparks shot out from her chignon, her violet streaks. She was holding an infomercial tray on which the last slice of a sugar pie was smothered in half a litre of ice cream.

"I've got something else too," she told François, or someone behind him.

"I don't like ice cream," he replied.

He set the plate down on the rim of the bathtub, and the dog, Croquette, straight away abandoned his vigil in favour of his dessert of choice. Liette wheeled around. When she was young, she would dress like a dowager. Now, middle-aged, she dressed like a college kid.

"How did you get here?" Henri asked again.

"Gimme a moment and I'll make a crust!" Liette said. "I'm gonna bake you another pie."

Her voice receded as she stepped away. A few minutes later she came running back to the bathroom, same scuffling of slippers around the corner, same tray with everything leaning into the turns.

"Here you go, my men ... For heaven's sake, where've they gotten to?"

That floor—she was going to wear a hole in it.

"We're in the living room, marshmallow!"

They were talking road conditions, forecasts of sleet after the snow. Also the advantages of a glossary. Crossword problems. Just looking at the dog was enough to set François sneezing. Croquette was sitting sphinx-like on the knees of his great love, Henri, who offered his son the occasional evasive reply. The pater, his mind wandering, scanned the room. He still couldn't get over the disappearance of his chuck.

"Trandolapril!" Liette exclaimed as she entered the room.

With an aerodynamic sweep, she handed her husband a glass of water together with his capsule.

"We were in the living room," Henri said by way of thanks.

"For your old papa's heart," Liette explained to François, and served him his second slice of sugar pie.

He wouldn't have minded popping a couple of those capsules himself. His slice of sugar pie was even more generous than the first. Topped with the other half of the ice cream bucket, it tasted of cigarettes. He sent the plate bouncing on the coffee table without paying attention, instead scanning the shelves screwed directly into the plasterboard and lined with books and vinyl. On the floor along the baseboards a portion of the records, largely opera, was stored in cardboard boxes that had been labelled *Music* with a marker pen. There were rolls of packing tape scattered around and everywhere more boxes crammed with all sorts of stuff. The boxes were stacked up in structures sturdier than the building where François lived. He was struck all at once by the, well, bareness of the decor and the stencilled outlines of objects gone from the walls and furniture.

"Coffee?" Liette said with a belch as she returned again from the kitchen.

She was still holding the dessert plate licked clean by Croquette, which she'd removed from the coffee table to put in the dishwasher.

"Ah, just in time," François said.

"Decaffeinated for me, my dear. And for François add spice, wouldn't that be nice?"

Liette burst out laughing. As if this was the funniest thing she'd ever heard. A rhyme always made her laugh, and she gave Henri a wink. She gave François a wink.

"Did you take the game out of the freezer?" Henri asked her.

"Yes, yes."

The mater scurried back to the kitchen, which was immaculate except for a swarm of fruit flies.

"Atchoum," went François, peeved to see his father pampering a furball.

"Bless you."

The briefcase had faded into the background. The good thing about the mini-Cerberus Croquette being there was that the polymorphous beast seemed loath to hang around in the vicinity. The wild images spilling from the TV were getting on François's nerves. No matter where he turned, they chafed the corner of his eye.

"I wasn't aware that dogs purred too," he said.

"Oh, look," Henri said. "I'm driving him crazy. Croquette, poochy. Look at Daddy, Croquette. Did Bradley the mailman steal your little bitty bone? Bradley the mailman, did he steal Croquette's little bitty bone?"

Croquette had zero reaction. Even so, Henri marvelled as if something historic had just taken place. In the basket next to François lay a sweater for a newborn. The infant would have to be strangely put together to fit into it. Watching his parents, François came up with ideas for a second book. And, boy, was he ever making himself at home, shoes up on the table, doing a visual autopsy on his father to understand what had caused his brain death. Still, he was comfortable, with room and board to boot. It would have taken a square shovel to pry him loose from the sofa. But then, of course, Liette had to warm up his coffee. It overflowed into the saucer. Just enough to trigger him.

"I'm going to check the mailbox," Henri said, roused from a snooze that he categorically would have denied had anyone mentioned it.

He got up from his armchair, hands pressed against his sacrum, and eyed François's brandy coffee. Plenty of calming brandy. François scanned the books on the shelves.

"The mailman hasn't come yet," Liette said. "Croquette didn't bark."

"I'm going to see if there's any mail," Henri said.

"He likes this show, Croquette does," Liette said.

She rested half of her behind on the arm of her easy chair. She turned up the volume in the living room to drown out the soap operas playing in the kitchen. The spoons jingled in the cups and the cups rattled in the saucers.

"I'm expecting a parcel!" Henri called out from the front entrance.

Liette, nearly twenty years her husband's junior. Almost in ecstasy before the miracle of the holy cathode. Yet she used to be such a bright young woman. Her brain wouldn't have dried up so much if she hadn't spent her life trapped under Monti Bouge's roof. There was a fusion cuisine show on TV, of which the dog was a loyal viewer.

"Yes, yes," said François. "I'm doing just fine, Mama, thanks."

Henri walked past the window outside. The blood vessels in his nose were bursting at the mere thought of the expected parcel. François could guess what it was—yes indeed.

"No," he continued. "Not this term, no. I'm not teaching any courses. Thanks for asking, Mama. Not next term either, no. Yes, I'm still single. Silly you. I'm working on a major writing project. Yes, that's right. An in-depth study. I'm making progress. Thanks. I…"

"…will be right back after the commercial break," the TV promised.

"Sooo then…" Liette said, as if returning from an astral voyage. "Yannick must have told you Cynthia was pregnant?"

François hadn't spoken to Yannick since the paleolithic age. *We become our parents,* he thought. Fuming, he stood up and brushed his finger over the Pléiade collection aligned on the uppermost shelf. The gilding had been completely rubbed off. One of the volumes was missing. François got lost in his father's wall of books. His collection of *Moby-Dick* editions had taken on bibliophilic proportions. Henri had always promised himself to do a decent retranslation of Melville's masterpiece if he ever went to prison.

"Now, don't tell him I told you this," the mater said under her breath. "But your father…he's stopped drinking."

She uttered the word *drinking* with a wide grin.

46

THE DOOR FRAME OF THE HUT THEY'D JUST FOUND shook for thirty seconds each time Steeve kicked the door.

"This is for Danny," he sputtered, his cheeks studded with white prickles.

He let fly again, and the hut's entire structure trembled. The snow fell away from the edge of the windows. A tornado of powder snow swirled off the roof. The door was locked from the outside with an anti-theft combination cable. When they were young, no one would ever lock a hut in the woods east of Rimouski.

"This is for my stepfather."

With each blow, strands of dust spilled down inside the dirt-blackened room awaiting them. It rained down from the struts unwitnessed. The sawdust danced on the beams. Yannick yawned.

"This is for Thierry."

The cable didn't give way, but the door did. It snapped off its hinges and the room was instantly pervaded with a failing-battery light mixed with excitable powder snow.

"Are you going in or not?!" Yannick demanded.

He shoved Steeve over the jagged broken wood in the doorway. It wasn't Laganière's uncle's cottage in there, but so what.

The mere fact of arriving somewhere, of being in contact with something made by humans—Steeve had to pinch the bridge of his nose to choke back his tears of relief. Still, you couldn't see very far inside the cabin, so he lingered near the threshold. Once Yannick had stepped inside Steeve grabbed him by the coat, but his hand was too numb to keep holding on. His cousin pushed him away and, with the nude-girl lighter he must have inadvertently filched from Marteau, lit the candle stuck in a Jack Daniel's bottle. Steeve shut his eyes, afraid of what might be brought to light. Because in La Frayère you could never tell. There was always a chance, when you ventured like that into an unlit cabin, of bumping face first into the shoes of a hanged man.

"This here is Chénard's cabin," Yannick decided.

Steeve opened his eyes again. The candle flame, spouting black smoke, grew very tall and thin. No dead bodies. Steeve pulled back a fossilized muslin curtain, which dissolved along the length of the curtain rod.

"Who's Chénard?" he asked. "Do I know him?"

He started putting away the dishes that had been left to dry on the rack since maybe the nineteen fifties.

"A low-life from Saint-Omer," Yannick said. "Hangs around with Perrault."

But talk about quaint. All you needed was to stick a sign out front saying TYPICAL FRENCH-CANADIAN HOUSE and you'd make a bundle renting it out to Parisians.

"I can't see how you can be so certain."

Having put a potful of snow to melt on a camping stove he should have dusted off with an archaeologist's brush, Steeve set about undressing. He was going to add some layers by helping himself to a bag of clothes rotting away in a corner.

"Are you telling me I don't know where I am?" Yannick asked. "This effing mountain has got four cabins pretty much like this one per square kilometre."

He slipped on a sepia sweater vest and felt like he was dressing up for a re-enactment of early settler life. He couldn't suppress a shriek when Yannick unsheathed his Rambo knife.

"I'm sure of it," said Yannick. "Right here is where Chénard keeps his stash of weed."

He split open the camp bed mattress from side to side. He flung clots of down into the air, growing more and more distraught as he failed to find what he was searching for.

"This isn't Chénard's cabin," Steeve mumbled.

Yannick stood in the feathers next to the bed and at the same time in the woods twenty feet away. That's how beside himself he was.

"We're lost," Steeve continued more softly, hugging himself and rocking as though wearing a straitjacket.

"Christ!" Yannick eurekaed.

He took out his company cellphone to call his girlfriend.

"What are you doing? Do you think you can—"

"Marie-Jeanne—a damn good name for a girl."

But the reception in the area hadn't improved since the day before. The storm, as it happened, had toppled the cell tower. Steeve pulled out his little bag of cocaine again. He snorted enough of it to mistake himself for a demigod. He rubbed the residue over his gums.

"Isn't that finger the one you poked into the shit a while back?"

Five minutes later Yannick was relaxing on the gutted bed. Steeve remained standing, unable to keep still for a second. He felt compelled. He had to touch, fondle, caress every single civilization museum exhibit in the cabin. He had to appropriate those objects. From today on they were going to live like hunter-gatherers. Possibly owing to his supine position, Yannick started to blather. It began with the memories his cousin had recalled earlier, the stunts they would pull with their other cousins when they were even more brazen than now, the atrocities they would pin on François. Steeve paid no more attention than if a pair of mechanical dentures were chattering away amid the mutilated stuffing. It went in one ear and out the other, as Steeve, despite the minimalist interior, was too busy redoing the place. They'd been lost. Now, they were no longer lost. *A matter of attitude,* he thought. Now they lived here. Yannick, watching him without seeing him, kept up his monologue. The high school shrink would have given anything back then to witness this. He dredged up everything he could remember about Thierry Vignola. He wasn't about to start crying, but he'd never opened up this much. Steeve, meanwhile, plunged into his own scenarios. The cabin's owner shows up. He realizes there are people squatting his place. He's the violent type. Steeve decided it was a good idea to put all the artifacts back where he'd found them. He realigned the four legs of the only chair with the four dust-free circles on the floor. Suddenly less focused, he was on the verge of blocking his ears and singing la-la-la to keep from hearing Yannick. It was Laganière's cabalistic midnight storytelling that had dragged it all up, like a drowned man, to the surface of his cousin's mind, dislocated in various points. Steeve was doing his best to fit the pieces of the door back together so that nothing would show. Yannick talked about what's-his-name's first big dope trip, someone else's constant nightmares, lost ambition, plans put off to other lives. A real good guy, Vignola, he was saying, and that's when his words began etching themselves in Steeve. A live wire at the very back of the classroom, that was Thierry. He would traumatize the substitutes. Yannick had already gone through their graduation album when his cousin realized he was purging himself of his own experience. Steeve came to sit down beside him on what was left of the bed. Hands pressed together between his thighs, he nodded yes emphatically, letting his demeanour evince all the stereotypes of the mentor, the big brother, the baseball coach. Outside, there was a very distant buzzing. No doubt a snowmobile, or a giant mosquito.

"You know," Steeve said, now confiding in his turn. "Me too, when my stepfather bought it in a Cessna, you, you didn't really know him, but my mother, you know her, she's your godmother, you can imagine what the mood was like at our place after the accident. I'm sayin' accident, but between you and me . . . There you are, tryin' to stay strong, you've gotta take care of your mother who's out of commission, and . . ."

Yannick stood up without a word and collected his gear, his guns, and his snowshoes. Before his cousin had finished his sentence, he was already outside.

47

LEFT ON HIS OWN IN THE FEAT OF REMODELLING THAT it represented, François cased the bathroom like a burglar, coming to terms in his own time with the amenities his basement apartment in the city, twenty thousand floors below the earth's crust, so cruelly lacked. A lotus-shaped soap dish. A deodorizer you just plugged into the wall outlet. Synthetic products for every part of your body, right down to the follicles. A flush toilet where you didn't need to reach into the tank to lift the flapper. François removed his jacket and unbuttoned his shirt while his fingertips tested the velvety two-ply toilet paper in its seashell dispenser. It almost worried him to feel good. *Everything is going smoothly,* he thought. *I'm home.* Semi-good is how he felt. He ran himself a bath with four litres of eucalyptus-scented foam and a little yellow plastic duck. *I think I'm home.* He sat down on the edge of the bathtub and pulled with all his might until he finally managed to get those things off his feet. Faint television voices seeped in through the partition. *Shadows on the walls of the cave,* François thought. It wouldn't have taken much for his jockeys to start running in circles when he took them off. The bathroom was a masterpiece of design and functionality. The drugs in the medicine cabinet were grouped in order of expiration date. The anger management effort it must have required for Henri, while under the influence, to wield potentially dangerous tools without maiming himself. *It's not my fault,* François told himself. The lad was all thumbs. The plumbing often backed up at his place, but it wasn't his fault. All his life, his father would get rid of him by sending him off on fanciful missions whenever he set to work on a do-it-yourself job. François wrestled with what he called his *gaminet,* his cotton top, unable to find the way out. The T-shirt ended up crucified in a corner, and the environment immediately woke up, endeavouring to eject the foreign body. The coffee began to have an effect on a certain colon. What a potful his mother had forced him to drink. The bathroom's overriding theme? The great explorers. The bathwater was temperature controlled. François didn't know where exactly his parents' illness might be lurking, but he was taking no chances. He completely overlaid the toilet seat with TP. The toilet water was bluer than Lake Louise. François "sluiced down" the bowl, even though there was nothing in it, no number two, nothing. He would never have said "flushed." The water went down instead of rising the way it did at his place. Thighs aquiver, François sat. His first moment of relief since the beast had appeared before him. He could hear Croquette existing on the other side of the door and, farther away, in the kitchen, the clatter of Teflon and specialized utensils. Supper came early for these folks; the morning reunion over and done with, his parents were already busy with the preparations. His father, anyway. Ah, the tribulations of creativity. Culinary and otherwise. Henri had quickly lost patience because he couldn't find what he needed for his recipes. Half of the utensils had already been packed away in boxes. François heard him scolding Liette.

"We've got a guest, for pity's sake! I . . . Tricky as hell, my Belgian endives. No! Stop! Give me that, give me the apron! These vegetables are delicate things!"

Liette's hands flapped as if taking flight. Then she bolted, on the pretext of going shopping.

"And your lectureship," Henri yelled to François from the kitchen. "Is that going your way?"

Henri, the man with sixteen hands, eight fingers each. Chief jack of all trades, able to put up an interior framework in an afternoon. Or tell you how to do it, anyway. The fellow could raise your telephone poles, assess a mineral deposit, tow any boat gone aground in the shallows. And he cooked into the bargain. Held his own in the face of the most finicky eaters. Even Europeans. While Liette was probably waving her discount coupons up and down endless white sanitized aisles, he was putting together mmm-good dishes for the three of them. Appetizers of smoked salmon roses with fennel and watercress stems and greens, and garnished with capers—make way for the artist. He wore his wife's apron.

"Your seniority must start to . . . Because, I mean . . . at some point . . . Lecturing . . . It's a little . . ."

Even if lots of fellows of Henri's stripe, not overly equipped with diplomas but having enough strings to their bow to play the harp, viewed academics like François as a species of protozoic blobs that reproduced themselves by dint of lofty speeches . . . Even if guys closer to concrete reality, as the Frayois often were, tended at times to scorn the kind of "work" François devoted himself to, well, not Henri Bouge. Never. Henri Bouge didn't scorn his children.

"I hope you at least find the time to focus on your dissertation?"

"Well," François shouted back from his bath, "that is part of what led me to make this trip. I wanted to talk to you about…"

In much the same way that he'd abandoned his doctoral ambitions years ago, he now abandoned the conversation. Instead, in the foam and lapping bathwater, with a wholly unsuspected knowledge of the corpus, he continued to leaf through the magazines he'd discovered in the rack next to the large toothbrush standing near the toilet. There was a message in a bottle. A model caravel on one of the shelves.

"Yes, no, the doctorate, I'm done!" he shouted, and Croquette gave a pugnacious bark on the other side of the door.

Framed in those terms, it wasn't a lie, and François kept on leafing through his *7 Jours* magazine, taking great pains to avoid his horoscope. Then he tossed the poor periodical onto his T-shirt, which instantly started to digest it. He reached out toward the magazine rack, but his arm was something like three feet too short. He couldn't help it. Here was yet another reason to hold a grudge against his mother. She was surely the one who'd placed the magazine rack this far from the bathtub. His favourite was *Paris Match*. He had to stand up. He splashed water everywhere. While rummaging for his magazine, he stumbled on a whole other kind of megalith. The Pléiade volume that was missing from the living room bookshelf. Full leather cover, Bible paper, Churchill red edge. The tome, without a trace of selfishness, let itself be handled by François, who, thanks to this contact, regained a grace full of surprises. *Le Père Goriot, Le Colonel Chabert, La Messe de. La Messe* whatever aside, it was clearly *Le Père Goriot* or *Le Colonel Chabert* his father was reading. It was also clear that the reader *was* his father. *Papa does not scribble in his books.*

There were sticky notes scattered throughout, the same as in the upstairs study, blackened with annotations and codas, rewrites, snippets of a stillborn work.

"I'm writing a book!" François barked, and now it was Croquette who shouted.

"You're writing a book," Henri echoed in the kitchen.

He thrust a fork into his slab of meat. It was thawing out on a rustic, bloody plate. An hour later, Liette came home carrying thirty-six bags, which her husband took off her hands. On account of keeping his bathwater warm, François had drained the tank in the basement. His skin was all pruney. He was on the verge of growing gills. Bubbles floated up from his knife wound and bloomed at the surface.

"You're not wearing your new coat?" Henri asked his wife.

He wasn't angry anymore. He didn't even remember being angry. Behaved more like a gentleman than on his wedding night.

"Didya record my show?" Liette asked. "François! François!"

Henri tasted the marinade he'd prepared for his meat.

"For heaven's sake, where is François?"

"And I'd like you to wear your glasses," Henri said.

"I don't like my glasses, I've gotta go and get new ones."

"Your lenses hurt your eyes, you said."

"François! Where is he?"

"He's relaxing in the tub, imagine that. Now, me, I'm going to check the mail."

Henri opened the door and called Croquette from the porch. But Croquette didn't come.

"Shut the door, goddammit," Liette said. "The drafts! The flu!"

"The flu is a virus!" François bawled from the bathroom.

"Nothing to do with drafts," Henri added.

He soon came back from the letter box exuding good cheer and fumes of Yukon. He set about examining his wife's purchases amid the rustle of plastic bags. He was about to delight in the clothes she'd bought him when she snatched the pile from under his nose. Henri glared at the shopping mall cake on the counter. Liette scudded like a hovercraft down the hallway, where the dog was still standing guard.

"François?" she whispered seductively against the bathroom door. "I'm putting some clean togs here for you, okay?"

"Would it be *possible*," François said in a tight-lipped voice, "to get *one* minute of privacy?"

He opened the door a crack, enough to slip his arm out and grasp the clothes in different shades of beige, which Croquette kept sniffing three seconds after they were no longer there.

"And it seems to me," François said, still shouting, "you could at least sew this button back on."

The bathroom door opened again and his suit pants, grimy and threadbare, knocked against the corridor wall. They slid over the floor, leaving a trail of slime in their wake like a snail. Henri, seeing how upset his wife was when she came back to the kitchen, left off rechecking her receipts and approached her.

He enfolded Liette tenderly, pretending to close the imagined floodgates at the corners of her eyes. Then he snatched away the whisk she was about to use on his sauce. He had his very own special technique.

François put back the Balzac, of which he'd read a hundred pages, now completely warped. He stepped out of the bath wrapped in steam and fragrances. Or perhaps it was his aura evaporating. Next came dental hygiene. Vigorous cleansing with an electric toothbrush. Distracted by the list of ingredients on the back of the biggest tube of toothpaste he'd ever seen, he spat half in the sink, half on the countertop. There were barb-like wisps of enamel left on his teeth. The foam gave him a goatee. The washcloth he'd used to wash himself parachuted down next to the laundry hamper. Time for the dental floss, time for blood. He brushed his teeth again to eliminate the taste of iron and bacteria. Garamond type size 9. The Pléiade font. It had literally liquefied his thoughts. Things of beauty like that, they rattled your neurons, and François took a gulp of mouthwash to kill the few surviving germs in his body. But there was no mouthwash in the bottle. Instead, there was Yukon—bingo! *Papa, you old rogue,* he thought. He felt cleverer than the best processor on the market. His cotton swabs stuck to the inside of the toilet bowl, glued there by enough earwax to fashion a large yellow candle. He sucked his mouthwash while his scissors took themselves for Pac-Man. He evened up his bangs, unevenly. He worried at his boo-boos with the tip of the nail file to scrape off the scabs. Once purged of his impurities, he weighed himself on the scale. The device was accustomed to worse loads than him, but François already saw himself as corpulent, easygoing, and droopy, like Rock in his taxi. His mind, however, was uplifted by the divine proportions of the Pléiade's layout. He felt more Rastignac than ever. A huge door had opened in his intelligence. He could have cracked tournament-level crosswords on his knees. Yet for all the poses of famous intellectuals he assumed in the mirror, he was as unphotogenic as ever. He brushed his teeth again, tongue and palate, uttering almost a battle cry. He brushed

his innards with redoubled intensity, down to his pancreas,
unable to dispel the dromedary stench rising from his depths.
The bar of soap disgusted him. There was a curly hair stuck
in it. Here was a man who slept every day in a bedbug colony.
He sometimes washed with dish detergent. Poupette was his
last remaining friend. But that soap—wouldn't touch it. There
was a hair on it. Another gulp of mouthwash. He unscrewed
every top of the surrounding lotions. Bottles and jars slapped
the palms of his hands. François blissfully slathered his epidermis with cream. Shea butter by the shovelful. His pores
thrived on aloes and emollients. His revitalized hair billowed
under the dryer. But at that very moment his beast might be
swimming up the pipes to reach him. François re-plugged the
bathtub and put the stopper in the sink.

The TV in the kitchen was holding forth, following a wave
of barbaric acts, on the need to review standards in hog
slaughterhouses. Nearby, a knife made long, smooth, deeply
felt slashes as Henri sliced his endangered species steaks into
medallions on the cutting board. François, in his new apparel,
a veritable two-legged rainbow of beige, sat down at the table.
His mother smoked with a vengeance. As if she were being
punished—she had no business in a kitchen where she wasn't
entitled to touch anything—Liette held her baby's hand while
her free hand swatted at a squadron of fruit flies over a coco-
nut bowl crowned with a few bananas. Now the TV showed
a couple of laid-back, physically fit seventy-year-olds against
a background sunset, grandchildren riding on their shoulders,
generously covered by their life insurance so that when they
died, they would explode and drift back down in a shower of
green, red, and brown banknotes.

"I'll get you another coffee," Liette said.

Henri's knife struck a hard lump.

"With a kick to it," he said.

His disappearance in the bath, the eucalyptus, the mouth-wash had left François enervated. Yet the amount of coffee he'd imbibed since the morning kept him in the pink. His nerves would keep him from collapsing if everything else fell apart.

"I'm going to need the cleaver," said Henri, wrestling with the meat.

"I packed it away in the boxes," said Liette.

The other TVs in the house harmonized with the one in the kitchen in a schizophrenic surround sound. Henri brushed sauce on the meat, over which he'd finally prevailed. He sea-soned it—scientifically. He set the timer for two hours. Put the pan in the oven at very low heat.

In the living room, the hallways, the carpet grew taller.

"Well, I'm going to check the mail," he announced, and he went out with his toque, his apron, and no coat. "Come on, Croquette! Come out for a little pee!"

He went out. But Croquette stayed put under the table and went back to where he had left off, sniffing François's new pants. Outdoor cargo pants, with eight pockets and pock-ets in pockets and snaps, trademarked fabric, lighter than any gas, with a moiré outer layer, waterproof, fireproof, the works, ventilation eyelets everywhere and various drawstrings to adjust the fit and the hems, so that snakes can't get inside you through the urethra when you sleep under the stars in the woods because you like to.

"You think you'll have time to go see Kevin next door?" Liette asked him.

"Cripes, let him settle in!" Henri shouted outside.

The seconds ticked by on the timer. They felt like finishing nails planted all around the top of François's skull. Pretty soon the migraine, the obsessions, the hang-ups would start to simmer in there.

"Lord, he's going to catch his death, that man."

Outside, at the far end of the lane, the pater, as it happened, was in the middle of a conversation with Monique Plourde, Patapon's mother. Delicate, illicit aromas escaped from the oven. Croquette thrust his snout into François's pants. Tormented by a stinging sensation, François dropped what he believed were bananas in the centre of the table, in a sweat because he couldn't remember where he'd left his manuscript.

"Monique was telling me," Henri said, brushing off the snow by the front door a few minutes later. "Seems Kevin's gone missing."

As he removed his shoes, he looked at François, sitting now with his briefcase pressed against his chest. Henri looked at the briefcase. He looked at the dog's leash on its point-eight-centimetre titanium hook. He looked at the briefcase.

"Tie it up," he told François, "if you're so worried it'll run away."

Then he confiscated the meat thermometer from his wife. He half opened the oven door and checked to see if the meat was done. François, for no reason, blurted something out to his mother, something gross, too shameful to be repeated here. Had Henri, at any age, said the same thing to his mother in front of Monti, he'd have ended up in the garden as fertilizer. François broke a banana off from the bunch and peeled it to take a bite.

"You eat them like that, do you—plantains?" Henri asked him.

Meanwhile, he'd sequestered the remote. He zapped around for the news and happened on an actor in a smock, with his stethoscope, his prescription pad, and his dime-store credibility.

Liette flashed her men a triumphant smile when the doctor on the screen asserted that the flu virus was activated in drafts.

48

AS FOR LAGANIÈRE, HE WAS HAVING AN UTTERLY FAS-
cinating day.

"Yahoo!" he whooped as he negotiated a curve like a stunt-
man that morning, not very far from the hut where Steeve
and Yannick had stopped.

His visor fogged up and the speed machine dropped back
on one ski, then the other. His librarian's bum landed back on
the snowmobile seat and started bouncing again. There was
a guipure screen, a semicircle of snow, constantly spraying up
before the windshield. Behind the vehicle the tracks packed
down a trail studded with yellow leaves and small round turds.
Ever since he was born, Laganière had always been careful
about everything and everyone. He counted every penny.
Fretted over trifles. Didn't want to be a nuisance. Let himself be micromanaged. He gunned the snowmobile and the
acceleration disintegrated the thoughts nagging at him. Legs
braced over his seat, he charged toward the fork ahead. With
the handlebar practically his only point of contact with the
machine, he went over the steps of the plan he'd devised. *Step
one. Siphon off Yannick's truck to fill the snowmobile tank. Check.*
His headache had dissolved without him realizing. The vise
had come off his cerebellum. Either there really was a carbon

monoxide problem in the cottage or the pills he'd crunched were beginning to kick in. He hadn't felt so alive since city hall had decided to bequeath its archives to the library. The snowmobile leaped ahead in a hungry surge. The driving snow crackled against the plastic of his visor. The atoms of the snowmobile's shell, overexcited by friction, were seconds away from self-reconfiguring as a leopard.

"Yikes!" Laganière gasped, giving the handlebars a twist.

If not for the visor, his eyes would have yo-yoed out and back when he nearly collided with the pine standing where the trail forked. *Get a grip,* he thought. *Where was I? Focus.* He veered left toward the muskeg not a moment too soon. Had he turned right, he'd have ended up in the Canons' field. He slowed down a notch. *Step two. I zoom over to CBSU to see Marcel. Chances are he's still asleep, with the mixing console stamped on his face.* The mountainside station was remote enough to be accessible by these trails. He'd put the tingling in his body down to the cold, the mechanical vibrations, the equestrian posture he'd maintained for too long. And anyway, it wasn't half bad. *The man's on his way, gang, he's on his way.* He opened the throttle again, bellowing the notes from the record that had skipped all night over the airwaves. That's when he noticed the initial fraying of his euphoria. At that speed, long diamantine planes slid away on either side and broke up at the foot of the trees. Throughout the forest something throbbed under the snow. *Step three. I wake old Marcel, I seize the mic, and I warn the Frayois of the dark and dirty stuff going on.* His kidnapping, the Montreal dude's disappearance, two tripped-out killers on the loose in the wilds. The trees around him had acquired a more plastic quality. The remaining leaves didn't seem real. *Besides, it's a matter of heritage. I'll have to convince Marcel to reveal the true identity of Yannick's fath— What the hell is that?* He jerked his head aside. Nothing there. Perhaps he ought to say something to Lorraine as well. The snowmobile hood was flecked with black stains. A muscle-like ripple travelled under the ice. *Okay, there's too much oxygen going in, I think.* He slowed down a lot and recapitulated his plan. *First. Siphon off Yannick to put the tank in the snowmobile's truck. Next, zoom on my radio, remote enough on the airwaves to be accessible by the station mountains.* Something wasn't right. He blinked very hard a couple of times to clear his head. This only heightened the tingling tenfold. He slowed down further and then cut the engine even before coming to a halt. The semicircle of snow in front of him slowly collapsed on his helmet. *Animated the old record on its Marcel, sleep mixed under the faces' table because the time keeps skipping.* He wasn't advancing, but he felt his body continuing on, propelled in all sorts of directions at once. He removed the key from the ignition and dropped it in the powder snow. The key wouldn't stop falling into the snow. Laganière shook himself behind his visor. He bent down to look for it and when he straightened up—his eyes sans whites, sans irises, just two fathomless pupils—he noticed the branch transpiercing his side. He didn't know why, but he was holding a drill chuck. Blue, green, turquoise paint oozed from his hallucinated wound. *Too much oxygen,* he thought. He calmed his breathing, but the balloons in his chest began to swell all the same. *Announce to Yannick's hands that the dark and dirties have kidnapped the village mic because of the heritage of disappeared stuff in the Montreal dude.* As if from a distance, he witnessed the disintegration of his self with a blend of dread and curiosity. Attracted by the glyphs on the bark, he dismounted. He took a few astronaut steps and began to sink into the snow, up to his knees, his navel, his teeth. The surrounding trees, forest, ground, all quietly rose into the air, turned perpendicular to the normal orientation, and descended in his wake like a carpet pulled into a bottomless pit.

49

IN THE NASCENT DARKNESS OF THAT LATE AFTERNOON, the fleshless table legs cast illogical shadows on the kitchen floor tiles. The goblets were filled not with wine but with fizzy water. There was something unbearable, whenever his parents took a timid gulp, about the liquid's effervescence. Liette had her nose in her plate. Henri wasn't laughing. François was mute. The chairs creaked under their constantly shifting buttocks. The diners sipped, browsed, swallowed the fishy flowers of their appetizer on a bed of greenish leaves with translucent veins. A ladybug stood out against the crunchy green of François's iceberg lettuce. The drip of the sink faucet made an awful racket. In its frame by the window, the portrait of Monti in ski wear stared at his kinfolk with his eyes that bulged as if from an overactive thyroid.

"Is it to your taste, darling?" Liette asked François.

Cue the canned laughter of a comedy show. François's tongue explored the scallop that he'd just discovered in his mouth. He answered his mother by separating the different foods on his seashore-design plate so as to be sure they wouldn't contaminate each other. He scraped the tines of his fork on his grandmother Joséphine's china dinnerware. His parents took the set out of the dresser once every ten years.

Yannick was pregnant and would be getting the house. François found the news hard to swallow. Likewise the quantity of food his mother had overzealously stuffed him with since he'd arrived. An arrival not altogether finished yet, not fully accomplished. "He's hardly arrived!" Henri kept repeating to his wife since that morning. "I've arrived," François said. Liette just *had* to drop the news like a ton of bricks when they'd all teamed up to set the table. Holding a bouquet of knives, she'd announced to François they were moving, she and his father, to a place quite a bit smaller, but clean and without too many stairs.

"Is that so?" François had said.

He'd placed the spoon where one of the two forks should have gone. Things went sour when Henri informed him that Yannick was taking over the homestead with Cynthia because they, he and Liette, wanted to devote their latter days to something other than keeping up the house.

"It's become a burden," Liette said.

"It's my heritage too," François protested. "Granddad's house!"

Having wiped the three goblets with a cloth, Henri filled them with Perrier. Straight away, the sound of insects rose up.

"We'll have something for you," he promised with summer-theatre cheerfulness. "When we die. Or when you've completed your studies."

"What about Yannick? He never even finished high school," François said.

"Or when you've given us a grandson," Liette added.

She flashed a painfully broad smile. Right then, François understood why one of the upstairs rooms had been redone as a nursery.

"You must have gotten the invitation to the baptism, eh?"

"The letters I receive generally invite me to get out."

"You've no doubt already realized that you and Yannick are the only members of the family able to pass on the name of Bouge? Charline is childless, Lucie had Mireille, who had Steeve, but the fact of the matter is all my brothers' children are female."

"Or gay," Liette put in.

"Oh, what difference does it make?!" Henri snapped. "This is the twenty-first century... Here, look, your nephew."

Henri had taken a picture of Cynthia's last ultrasound down from the fridge. There was no ambiguity about the child's sex.

"Okay, it's ready, now let's sit down," he suggested once his appetizers had been served.

The others were already seated. They were waiting for him.

"We're real fond of that girl Cynthia," Liette said.

"The Cynthia Yannick kept under his thumb," François went on, "through tyranny and ever more degrading humiliations, until her beam broadened to the point where she was disqualified from the dating market, which, of course, gave him another reason to bully and humiliate her and chase women from Dalhousie to Matane and come home with STDS, accusing *her* of cheating on *him*."

"François, please. Not in front of your mother."

"'Not in front of my mother,' he says!"

This was followed by the long, arid silence described earlier. There were nervous and awkward clinks as each of them put down their goblet or cutlery.

"Is it to your taste, darling?" Liette finally asked.

Henri watched his boy spoiling his appetizer. With the finger he'd just had Croquette lick under the table, he rubbed the

rim of the goblet, making it sing monotonously, with no mod-
ulation. *Not in front of your mother,* thought François again,
and took advantage of his father's meeting his gaze to push
every shred of watercress off his plate with his knife. *Quite a
convenient leitmotif. Not in front of your mother!* Since that
morning, he'd had enough time to map out the circuit in detail,
to connect the spots inside the house and on the grounds to
which his father ducked out every twenty minutes to slake his
not-very-under-control thirst behind his wife's back.

"Your mother is talking to you, François. Is it to your taste?"

François stabbed a caper with a tine of his fork. He opened
his mouth as wide as possible and, turning toward Liette, overdid the act of chewing.

"Come now, Mama . . ." Henri sighed.

"I'm not your mother," said Liette.

"You might have served his lettuce in a separate bowl from
his smoked salmon! As far as I'm aware, there's no dearth of
dish soap at the grocery!"

The alcohol made his father's gestures fuzzy, but his diction,
on the other hand, had grown sharp-edged since a moment
ago. More elastic, too. When he started to seed his sentences
with "no dearth of" and "the fact of the matter," it signalled
that he was no longer just tipsy. *He's gaining strength,* François
thought.

"If I came to pay you a visit," he said, "it's in part because of
the project I've undertaken and which I'd like to share with
you."

"*You're* the one who packed the dishes away," Liette muttered.

She wriggled her toes under her chair.

"That is beside the point," Henri said in defence.

He faintly dabbed the foam at the corners of his mouth with a corner of his napkin.

"The point is that it repulses him, our François, when his foods touch. You were saying, François? Your dissertation?"

"No, no, not the dissertation."

Liette stood up, theatrically clearing her throat, and used a huge pair of bronze-coloured oven mitts to take out the main course, which had been kept warm. At the very same moment, François stuffed his mouth with the leaf of iceberg lettuce from which the ladybug was screaming, "Don't eat me!"

"It's his school stuff he's talking about, eh," the mater said, "not your whatchamacallit dissertation . . ."

And he was off. For many minutes, hopeless minutes, Henri explained to his wife that a dissertation was something you did in school. Croquette whined under the table, tail tucked between his legs, frightened by the six feet shifting around it. *Run far away from here,* François thought, lifting his chin, ready for takeoff.

"I've stopped going to school," he attempted to make clear over the controversy.

He was increasingly vexed by the muted television on the counter, where the curved trails left by a rag were visible on the illuminated screen.

"So you see, he's doing his doctorate," Henri said, his hair now curly on one side.

It's moot whether he said it to have some fun at his wife's expense or because he'd managed to confuse himself. François looked away, the TV screen was too annoying, though it was either that or the blinking diode of the fifteen-hundred-dollar coffee maker. Liette stopped short, holding the spatula, from which a slice of meat dripped on the hand she'd placed beneath it, which in turn dripped on her slipper.

"I thought," she said, "the subjects you're studying were more—what's the term?—like, mental. Because, take a look, right here, this beauty spot on my neck, I find it's shaped a bit too much like a—"

"Not *medical* doctor!" Henri bristled. "*Ph.D.* doctor, Jiminy Cricket!"

He laid his face on the table, arms folded over his head. François emerged from his meditation. Croquette was sniffing his feet. A ball of tumbleweed rolled through the kitchen.

"Excuse me?" Henri said indignantly as he detached his face from his plate, his lip deep red in the shadow of a Gallic nose rhizomed with burst capillaries.

"I didn't say anything!" François answered, rearing up.

"But you thought it," Henri said, upright again.

"Okay," said Liette, almost lying on François's face as she served him. "Can we have lunch without squabbling? Careful, it's hot."

On the TV was a very sober, codified scene of hara-kiri.

"We're having *supper,*" Henri said, correcting them both, even though François hadn't spoken.

"Lunch-supper, then. It's still fairly light outside."

François once again sorted out the foods on his plate. It was rather meagre, he found, for a main dish. Two or three boiled, more or less decorative vegetables. A side dish of orzo. A juicy bit of animal, seasoned just so. *Lynx?* he wondered. His father motioned no with his head.

"I can guarantee," Henri boasted, "you are the only ones in Gaspésie eating this tonight. Genuine local gourmet food!"

"You're drunk, Papa."

Liette's eyebrow went knocking against the ceiling. The house's framework felt the strain farther down in the hallway.

"Drunk on love, my dear, drunk on love."

François pressed down on the meat with the back of his fork. A brownish liquid bubbled up between the tines, and the telephone rang. It rang again. Half-standing, Henri sighed:

"Hell and damnation, we're lunching, eh, do you mind?"

He at once began to imitate the cry of the fish, casting all around for something to drink.

"We're lunching-supping," his wife reminded him.

But the pater wasn't listening. *It's his fear of the red telephone,* François thought. Henri was listening to the silence between rings, hoping for an interruption, his eyes fixed on a cabinet handle. Croquette remained unfazed.

"Now, who on earth could that be?"

With each ring the surrounding space splintered a little more. A first-class guardian, that dog. Fresh from the taxidermist's. Henri tried to keep Liette from getting up. She was already on her feet. She stood there, dazed, before the call display.

"Well, I do believe that's Cynthia's work number, that is."

"Madame *Bouge*'s work," said François, and when he speared his steak, the steak gave him the slip. "*Madame* Bouge, *mistress* of the house."

Liette didn't answer either the telephone or François. The telephone fell silent in mid-ring.

"I'm going down to the mailbox for a drink," Henri announced, and headed toward the hats, umbrellas, canes, flashlights.

"For a *drink*," Liette said, laughing. "Oops, slippy tongue, your old foibles are showing, my dear."

"A *blink*, my darling. Be back in a blink, pardon my malapropism."

He called Croquette as he went out, but the dog didn't budge from under the table next to François's foot. Liette took the opportunity to bring her son up to date on distant or deceased relatives. She confessed to him that she'd been down in the dumps of late, nothing interested her, and it did her a world of good to see her boy there in front of her, although she wished he had more flesh on his bones. François had his mind on other things, and Henri soon came back covered in a sort of gaseous snow. He methodically eliminated it with a portable vacuum, having shaken himself beforehand. Then, starting from the front hall rug, he made for the table, wobbling like someone returning after a long stretch at sea.

"It's really delish," Liette said with a full mouth.

François unconsciously shook his leg to get rid of the hot mass that had just enveloped it.

"I just saw three camouflaged hunters in the ditch across the way," Henri said. "Their rifle barrels were sticking out between the bulrushes. I hailed them. They stood up. I came back."

The wordless plying of cutlery gradually uncovered the idyllic landscape depicted on the plates. An angler, painted with a one-bristle brush, sporting a goose-shit-coloured toque and a jovial pipe, in the middle of the North Atlantic equivalent of an atoll, under a flight of hybrid birds, part gull, part dove. *Possibly horse meat,* François thought, while the conversation waded through the topics of the day: employment in La Frayère, local politics, and the latest city hall jokes. One thing led to another, and Henri was now expatiating on the region's decline, reminiscing about a more authentic, fun-loving Gaspésie. With a latent fado in his voice, he decried the fact that the only new government-funded regional project that quarter was a bayside landfill site. It was hard for François to listen to him. The flow of images on the screen at the edge of his field of vision tore away half his face. *Scram,* he thought. He shook his leg.

"The US should deal with their own trash. This is no garbage can here."

François, napkin on his knee, cut the now-subdued piece of meat, while his mother deplored the recent closure of her shops. Even though she adored the Walmart in Campbellton, it was, well, in Campbellton, a long way to go at times to buy something you needed right quick.

"It's not just our stores," Henri said, correcting her. "It's all our tradespeople. The ski centre. The thalassotherapy centre. The Aquamer festivals. All the jewels of our identity. We're not about to have our hunters' fest when even the church is for sale! Because it's been discussed, you know. La Frayère will end up like Murdochville, a ghost town, and I'll tell you something. It's largely because of the brain drain. People here with a modicum of education, they head off to Montreal saying that's where the money is."

"Here we go again."

Much to his wife's displeasure, Henri had managed once more to bring together in a single supper all the conditions needed to get riled up without even realizing he was referring to François, who, in a final effort, cut even smaller the piece of meat he'd just cut. *Or maybe farmed ostrich?* His father repeated in a loop the four cultural institutions, including *Le Vivier* and

CBSU, that François himself and the Gaspé intelligentsia could have worked for in La Frayère if they'd been less selfish and patient enough to wait fifteen more years for the senior staff to get pensioned off or croak. François finally trapped the morsel of defeated steak between his asparagus and his knife. He gave the *coup de grâce* with his fork, which he held like a microphone.

"The likes of Mayor Pleau and Monti—those days are behind us," he grumbled.

Liette burst out laughing.

"That's a good one!" she said.

She hadn't yet finished eating and already she was lighting her digestive cigarette. The warm mass under the table climbed back onto François's leg and began to frig. There was a miniature torture chamber in Henri's eyes as he scrutinized his son.

"I mean," François said, pushing Croquette away with his undefiled leg. "Far be it from me to be defeatist, especially since I myself have returned here with a number of strategies to turn the situation around. But isn't that a little passé— major developments, totalizing visions?"

"*Full*," Henri said from somewhere far, far away. "Our mountains are *full* of gold."

"What are you blathering on about again?"

In that case, shouldn't we exploit it? thought François. He had a good idea of the episode his father was alluding to.

"Exploit it to what end?" Henri asked.

He can read my mind.

"Whether it's in the ground or not, that gold is ours! Let's enjoy it, that's all."

François held his morsel gingerly between his teeth. Didn't taste too bad. He forced himself to savour it, to chew it the number of times recommended by the obscure authority he always submitted to in such matters. Cattle, game, fowl? He gave up and chewed over his question as he asked it.

"It's placenta!" Henri said point-blank.

Liette placed a cooing hand on her man's forearm. A forearm bigger than François's thigh. The mater coiled the arm hair around her fingers, slightly tilting her head, with local gourmet cooking stuck everywhere between her teeth. A certain steak unobtrusively plopped down on the floor.

Henri cleared the table while mentally revisiting the mystery of the chuck. He washed the dishes perfectly clean in the sink before putting them in the dishwasher. Then, as if with the tip of his foot, he switched on the coffee maker. He poured cream into the creamer and tossed off a few spoonfuls, congratulating himself for not draining the whole quart. *Anyway, I've got my doctor in my pocket.*

"What did Cynthia want a little while ago?" he asked his wife.

"Whatcha mean, what did Cynthia want?"

Liette had another of her lipstick-stained-white-filter cigarettes in her mouth. Croquette was licking his bruises next to the ejected steak. The meat stayed there, shaken by infinitesimal tremors rising from the furnace through the floor. *Ten hertz at most,* François estimated, distracted by the smoke right in his face.

"Can we turn off the television?" he said, rubbing a temple that had too much skin.

"It wasn't Cynthia," said Liette. "It was her shop, and I didn't answer. How should I know what they wanted?"

She stirred her coffee with her dessert spoon.

"And did she mention when she'd be dropping by?" Henri insisted, and then he snatched the dessert spoon from his wife and proffered the appropriate instrument as if it were a rose. "She promised to help me transfer my record collection to my portable gizmo."

"I *didn't* answer, Henri. Hello. Henri?"

"Your record collection to your portable gizmo?" François interjected.

"My iPod," Henri said with a measure of smugness.

He'd pronounced the *i* like a Brit, the *Pod* one hundred percent à la Québécois.

"You and your machines."

"You have to keep up with the times. I've moved up to digital. I'll show you the listening room I've set up in the basement. I haven't yet packed the boxes down there. Ah, I believe the mailman may have come."

"Croquette didn't bark!" Liette noted.

"So," said Henri as he sat down again after checking the mail.

The cup of coffee he'd taken along to the mailbox had been topped up.

"Uh-huh."

"Will I finally get to know why Cynthia called?"

She called, François thought through the turmoil of his soul, *to let you know she's found you a charming cozy nest in a nursing home, and that the time has come to pack your bags, clear the hell out of her house, and go get undernourished and treated like half-washed babies as you look for the pocket money that's disappeared, while being abused by health care professionals.*

"Yannick and Cynthia . . ." his father began, bent over his placemat. "Yannick and Cynthia live in a kennel over a bunch of drug dealers. They're going to have a child. And we, we're no longer able to keep up the property as we should. Now, your mother would like me to retire. Retirement, that's out of the question—never. But we've always been generous to you. In due time, we ..."

François had had enough. He got up from his chair, went over to the TV, and pushed the power button so hard it didn't turn off because he in fact had pushed the volume button. He hit buttons at random to turn down the sound. Henri, who was nodding off in front of the hard, cold, sullen cheeses Liette had taken out *after* the coffee, bounced up as if jolted by a defibrillator. He flat out unplugged the television and made a show of picking it up in order to heave it away. But it was too heavy and he didn't feel like it anymore.

Outside, dusk had fallen; inside, everyone had sat back down.

"Speaking of generosity," Henri resumed.

Using the tip of his knife, he licked a dab of the butter sitting next to the cheeses, which, judging from the smell, were returning from the realm of the dead.

"Ah, yes," said Liette. "It's sharp of you to think of that."

"My accountant recently pointed it out. Those dividend cheques the company sends you every year, is it true you never deposited them?"

"Which dividend cheques?" François asked in surprise. "The bailiff calls me by my first name. If I had received any cheques, I would have deposited them. Or I would have cashed them at the store, since I'm not certain of still having a bank account. Actually, in my book-in-progress, I disclose certain disturbing connections between the Saint-Lancelot-de-la-Frayère postal service and the Yukon company, which, back in the day—"

"Are you getting by, with your lecturing? I mean, the rent in Montreal..."

The light bulb in the fixture over the table burned out. Once the lighting was restored, Liette applauded.

"Hey, where did you get that?" Henri asked François, whose eyes were always slow to adjust to the light.

The pater was standing on his chair, his belly spilling out of his too-short shirt. The spent light bulb in one hand, he pointed the forefinger of the other hand at the bottle of Yukon that his son had just produced, it seemed, from under his placemat.

"Here and there," François answered.

Liette heard none of all this. She didn't want to hear and gazed at the TV. The unplugged TV.

"As I have already mentioned," François said forcefully while pouring himself a shot, "I'm not teaching any courses this term. What's more, I won't ever again. By the way, my dear old Papa, *malapropism* isn't used the way you did a little earlier."

"Oh, but I can assure you that it is."

Throwing his shoulders back, he sat down again without ever taking his eyes off the bottle. He looked exhausted from doing more exercise than usual in a single day.

"I don't think so, Henri," Liette said distantly.

"I played that word in Scrabble just yesterday! Triple snore on the *q*."

"Snore?"

"*Score*, triple score. Now, François, I realize this goes without saying, but when it comes to loans and bursaries, prudence is well-advised."

"*What* loans and bursaries? Hello. Is anybody listening to me? I, am, done, with, *school*. How can I make that any clearer?

In any case, I reached the maximum loan amount long ago."

"Doctors," said Liette. "With the salaries they make."

"Maximum amount?" Henri said with a jump, twenty-five seconds late.

The whole table jumped with him when his knees hit the underside.

Liette hastily straightened the skewed cutlery. Then another silence descended on the Bouge family, heavier than the ambient air. It hovered over the floor, where Croquette barked without making a sound.

"Soon I'll have finished my book," François ventured. "That's the reason why I'm here with you. My publisher will give me an advance, an advance against royalties, to be exact, and you know what a fierce negotiator I can be."

He made as if he were elbowing his way through a crowd. Or doing the Chicken Dance.

"Time for dessert?" Liette suggested, and Henri sat up in his chair with a yawn.

There was chocolate everywhere, and François hiccupped over the documents that he pulled out of his briefcase one by one with a sweeping movement of his arm. His motormouth had seriously loosened up, and he finally and very emotionally explained to his parents the nature of his book. Mama sank down in her chair, her hair brushing against the fabric of the back. Papa, meanwhile, wondered why his son was almost crying as he dissected the slice of Technicolor cake in front of him with an exploratory fork, in part because he liked to know how things were put together.

"Which capital discovery?" Liette asked. "What are you talking about? Tell me *everything*."

Dessert was a pitch-black triple Styrofoam chocolate cognac cake topped with a polyester coulis. Henri ate only the cognac part and finished his wife's. With more than a little lubricity, he drew the spoon out of his mouth to smooth the foamy mousse, noticeably diminished but more lustrous and tapered after each penetration. He listened to François's convoluted sentences with softened politeness. They weren't devoid of interest for a history buff like him. He even raised the occasional little question to bring his boy back when he got lost in too many digressions. The presentation's intelligibility soon gave way to the sort of enthusiasm that's best medicated. To François's credit he at least had retrieved a few mothballed parchment documents concerning Henri's father that Henri himself had never had the chance to peruse. Among them the title deed for a parcel of land located in the Klondike. One William Dexter had transferred it to one Henry Bouge— Henry, with a *y*.

"Here is the intriguing part," François averred. "Mr Dexter, for reasons that will never be known, transferred to Granddad a concession that had belonged to him fifteen years earlier. Of course, nothing in the archives of Dawson City or the neighbouring municipalities confirms the presence of a Henry or Honoré Bouge. The shift in his given name suggests a side of Granddad I have yet to explore."

"My, my," Liette said, her hair floating in the air from the static electricity on her chair back. "Would you pass me the milk, teddy bear, that cake sure is sweet."

"One can't rule out the possibility," François announced, "that I'll go to the Far North myself to do some field research."

Henri, with a sliding gesture, passed the milk bottle across the table to his wife. The armada of fruit flies took off in anarchic formations. They soon returned with a vengeance to the cake left on the table and the half-peeled plantain of which François had taken a bite. Her neck tendons bulging, Liette unscrewed the cap, which Henri always over-tightened. The glumness now showing on Henri's face didn't portend anything especially festive. Liette poured herself a dollop of the nice and rich, barely skimmed, farm-fresh milk. She drank and poured some for François as well. A cottony whiteness uncurled lazily in the Yukon left at the bottom of his goblet.

François read them bits of chapters, scattered words written left-handed in no particular order through arrows pointing toward nothing on pages full of crossed-out lines still needing to be written out cleanly, pages with red wine or coffee stains, pages he smoothed out as he reframed his theories. There were things in there that had been drafted in another life and he couldn't always recall what he'd meant to say. His disjointed, ornate prose didn't help.

"It's not finished yet, you know."

He intermittently twisted around and uncorked a decompression jab against the back of his chair. Henri, the man who'd always maintained that the only work entitling you to disorder was intellectual work, watched his son thinking out loud the way he'd once watched the mite hockey games he sponsored when the kids were still small, featuring the occasional fretful breakaway from the swarm or shot at the wrong net deflected toward near-empty bleachers.

"And your advance?" he cut in. "Who is your publisher, François? What's your plan? The production schedule? You need a plan."

"Oh, it's Gallimard," François declared, his fingers rolling under his chin like a ruff. "Le Seuil. Their major series in the humanities"

"We'll help you," Liette said.

"But the Klondike story," Henri said, switching gears. "That's the missing piece in your novel. I have trouble seeing where the Yukon fits into the narrative."

"First of all, it's not a novel," François said. "But look, Papa, look, this is what I was searching for."

François separated two pages stuck together by something akin to cockroach marmalade and launched into a sort of incantation before what little text was left around the tears. *No wonder he's thin,* Henri thought. *He writes.* François was saying it was all the same a weird coincidence that this Dexter person—he tapped his finger on a poorly faxed photo in which the three men were hard to tell apart from the background of trees—transferred his concession to Monti and also turned out to be, how about that, the founder of their favourite brand of liquor.

He pointed to the bottle on the table like a six-foot-ten blonde in a quiz show presenting the prizes to be won.

"It's so exciting!" Liette exclaimed.

Henri, in turn, poured himself a shot.

"So that is where, as you put it, the Yukon fits into my narrative," François said, laying it on as he looked for a passage in a part of his manuscript that, in the end, didn't seem to exist. "Listen, I can't find what I'm looking for. Even so, look at this: on the *same* date, drawn from the logbook of the *same* railroad company, two tickets registered respectively in the names of Honoré Bouge and Donald W. Bead."

Exultant for a second of somewhat premature glory, François ran a finger over the man in question in the picture of the three Americans. Tricked out like that, they had to be Americans. Donald was the one in front of the fire holding a bunch of squirrels by the tail. His face was a grainy jumble of faded folds. Henri poured himself another shot, a double. Triple.

"Donald Bead, wait. I have a copy of his birth certificate, which I ordered from Vermont. I had to pass myself off as a ... I'll spare you the complications, but, basically, he was a farmer's son, known to the authorities because of his clandestine fights in New England. I can't remember where I put the other certificate, but what I meant to say is that Donald Bead was the brother of Charles K. Bead, this man, here. Charles K. Bead, together with William Dexter, invested in starting up the distillery."

"And?" Henri asked.

"The day after Granddad's and Donald's train ride, look at this, it's incredible: the death certificate of Bead, Donald, signed by a Canadian medical examiner. He must have died on the train, the dates coincide. We can skip the macabre details for Mama's sake, but the autopsy report suggests he did not die of natural causes."

"But, hey, will it be all right?" Liette asked in alarm.

A long run appeared in her tights. Henri's brow was so furrowed, the spoon in his fist threatened to bend on its own. His son sprang out of his chair and began to walk around.

"So, if I follow you correctly, you're insinuating that Granddad may have killed Donald Bead?"

"I'm not insinuating anything at all," François said as he sat back down at the table, where he repositioned his napkin, this time tucking it into his collar, but he immediately yanked it out, stood back up with his milk, which he then poured down the garburator and flipped the switch. "The facts speak for themselves. Look at this, a few weeks previous. A statement made by Granddad at an RCMP station in Timmins. His gold had been stolen!"

Liette nodded in approval. She turned toward Henri and nodded. She hadn't understood a thing. Henri poured François another shot, ignoring the milk at the bottom of his goblet.

"And that isn't all. Here. Newspaper clippings galore, by the score. Ha ha. Seattle, 1919. Charges of…I hope those are fresh batteries in your pacemaker, Papa. Charges of sorcery were brought against William Dexter at a Washington State courthouse. Sorcery, no less!"

Liette had her hands over her mouth, manga eyes, and taut legs locked at the knees.

"Enough said," the pater sighed. "It only adds to the absurdity of your book."

He had a sudden urge to build something right away. *To the absurdity of my life's work,* thought François, his head bowed.

"Of your life's work, yes. What you assert isn't impossible. Papa could have collaborated in some way with those men. They may have co-operated, pooled their resources."

"Wrong. I have evidence here—"

"That Granddad travelled alone to Toronto, and that he travelled on a very low budget."

"Yes, but that isn't all, it's only when—"

"I know what you're about to say. The luxury hotels began when he reached Montreal. According to you, then, Granddad supposedly found his gold on the train. Part of his gold, at any rate. The other part presumably went to the west coast to finance the beginnings of Yukon."

"I … But … The thing is …"

"That proves nothing."

Henri's arms were spread to the fullest extent. The ram whose wool had served to weave his shirt seemed to want to burst out of it.

"I must admit to feeling somewhat ill at ease," he continued. "I sense that you're on the defensive. I see that you yourself are struggling to reassemble the pieces of your puzzle. And even more to justify such a project. You come here, after all these years, with your ragbag conspiracy—"

"A curse," François blurted.

"A curse?"

"Or a conspiracy. Call it what you will."

"You come here with your piles of germ-ridden documents and your Liquid Paper fumes, trying to convince us that *my father* took the train with the person who robbed him, and this same person was murdered along the way. Is that right? And that the Yukon distillery is somehow mixed up in these events? The 'taste of gold,' right? Mother, call Dr Dugas. We've got someone here who needs help."

"I'm not your mother."

"Why, in that case, and this is only one out of a thousand flies in your pretentious ointment, would the Yukon people provide us, as it were, with a lifetime supply? It seems to me there must have been some friendship in there, because when you kill someone, usua—"

"Well, Papa, that brings us to Bradley the mailman."

The remainder of the cake went flying against the wall. François glanced at the glaring, greasy stain it left on the plaster. Then at his father's chair—empty. The table moved. Liette's feet were where her head had been a moment ago. François started to spin. The telephone rang. *Red telephone,* thought François.

50

STEEVE'S HANDS WERE CLINICALLY DEAD. SHIVERING despite the mouldy embroidered quilt he'd borrowed in the shack earlier to use as a cape, he tried to release the safety catch on his gun while Yannick did a series of sideways rolls in the purplish snow mottled with darting, crooked shadows. The two cousins had heard hungry rustling in a denser copse. They thought they'd spotted a creature in what they assumed to be its lair. It wasn't wildfowl, judging from the sound it made. Yannick flattened his back against a tree a little too hard. The snow shaken loose from the branches powdered the top of his balaclava. With his camouflage reduced to the most tenacious leaves, he intended to flush out the creature on the flank so Steeve could man up and blast it like a pro. He hooted like an owl on steroids to get his cousin's attention. Steeve, his eyes trapped in circles of frozen rheum, was now unable to make anything out in the underbrush. He stifled a cry of joy when he saw Yannick crawling toward the copse, holding his weapon like a soldier. Yannick gestured to him to hush up. He sent catcher's signals with a glove reinforced, it seemed, with a Day-Glo skeleton hand. Baffled, Steeve skirted around a sort of accidental dolmen to be ready to run if ever a wildcat or something…

In a flurry of snow, the animal leaped from one branch to another and the fireworks began. The quilt was a square suspended in mid-air. Cheeks puffed up, mouth puckered, Steeve dived to one side, firing his twelve-gauge on the fly. A geyser of snow mixed with ochre and leaves turned into chips spewed up from the ground. The spent shell sailed past his face when he pumped the gun and the second recoil drove the butt into his belly. It sent up a wave and Steeve landed in the cockleburs. He screamed, shooting all the while, even though a twelve-gauge has just two rounds. On the far side of the copse, Yannick stopped firing too. Steeve got up on his knees, howling the whole time without let-up. He fumbled in his pockets for ammunition. But his fingers refused to co-operate, he had monkey wrenches instead of hands, and the little bags of ketchup and mustard he'd filched from the bus depot restaurant the day he'd arrived fell out all around him on the snow, along with the shells. He grabbed his shotgun by the barrel and flung it into the bushes.

"Come take a look!" Yannick called out to him. "Come here and have a look!"

"Did we kill it?" Steeve asked. "Fuck, fuck, fuck. Did we kill it?"

"The monster, my man, check it out."

Talk about a ferocious beast. They'd just finished off a garbage bag swollen by gusts of wind and snagged on some branches. The gunfire had shredded the bag and the bark. Yannick fired another shotgun round at the tatters. An ambulance siren went off deep inside Steeve and he decided to go back to the cottage to hide behind Marteau's skirts. He headed out in no particular direction, crying ice cubes and sinking down with every step.

"Where ya goin'?"

It took Yannick a few strides to catch up with Steeve. He knocked him down on all fours with one of his snowshoes. Steeve did his best to get away, but his feet were all snarled up in the bindings of his pink snowshoes, one of which was askew on the side of his leg while the other lay straight along his calf. Yannick threw snow on his back, on the naked skin between his belt and the elastic of his bomber jacket. It was playful at first, but soon turned aggressive. Steeve was hopelessly entangled. He attempted to push the high-tech snowshoe tormenting him out of the way, swiping the air as if shooing flies away. A jumble of memories, things repressed, the debris of instincts formed and deformed in the stroboscope of his consciousness.

"Sorry!" he said as his fist shot out.

Paintball glasses awry, not dazed so much as surprised, Yannick let the blood drip from his split cheekbone through polyhedrons of mist. He did nothing to staunch the wound.

"Did you just *hit* me, you fucking jerk?"

"You can hit me back! I won't put up a fight."

Steeve proffered a cheek that you didn't necessarily want.

"Oh, go play in traffic."

Yannick collected the bags of condiments from off the snow, his lower jaw thrust out over his upper teeth.

"I won't put up a fight!" Steeve whined. "Shit, Yannick, I'm *sorry,* forget about the ketchup and mustard, why are you picking them up?"

"To eat you with."

"You said ... You said we weren't lost."

Scads of orange ribbon pieces were knotted everywhere on the surrounding trees. Steeve felt encouraged. He started to follow his cousin, who'd already set out.

Later, having fallen far behind, and worn down by the stinging snowflakes, he again shouted, "Are we lost?"

Yannick, shut behind his warrior mask, in a cheerless gloom, had stopped talking to Steeve. From time to time he swept his laser sight over the forest. The beam bumped into obstacles thrown up by the terrain in ever-greater numbers. The wind gusting between the trees wailed like ghosts. Steeve's face was reduced to a blue hole deep inside the quilt he wore like a hood. He'd lost all hope. Yannick, through his silence, persisted in denial, but there must have been a reason he stopped more and more frequently, as the evening descended around them, to assess a potential shelter, the dampness of the wood, the edibility of anything besides his cousin, displaying all the survival techniques he'd learned from action films, the Scouts, and the freebase dealers in his neighbourhood. *Pure swagger,* Steeve thought. Neither of them was going to survive. Steeve should at least have indulged himself and given Yannick a good thrashing once and for all. He'd have liked to hang him by the collar from a high branch, making sure to take his gloves before abandoning him to the predators. But too cowardly by nature to defend himself, he was ill-equipped to take revenge. The to-and-fro of the snowshoes had somehow numbed him and he followed Yannick with no will of his own, until they arrived at a dead end.

Any of the paths they might have taken would no doubt have led them there, because the vast forest converged toward the rocky bottleneck where a steep, winding pass rose up ahead of them. They advanced and soon discovered that the path ended abruptly. It gave way to a rather narrow ledge running along a sheer rock face. Steeve didn't feel like venturing up there; there was no purchase on the cliff, and he was afraid the ledge would crumble under his weight. But there was no alternative, and the path continued on the other side, a few feet beyond, high on a plateau that stretched away as far as the overhang allowed them to see. A mountaineer had been kind enough to secure a chain to the rock with pitons, providing a handhold when you climbed onto the ledge to reach the far side of the abyss. Okay, maybe not exactly an abyss, but high enough to get you nicely smashed on the rocks below. What's more, given the rotund shape of the rock face, retracing your steps across the void once you'd reached the terrace wasn't really an option if it turned out to go nowhere.

"Right," Yannick said.

He pulled out the small flashlight that hung in a loop on his chest. He shone it on the void and then beyond the void on the path leading upward. He removed his snowshoes and flung them to the place where the path began again.

"Yeah," Steeve said, shivering in his quilt, his hands tucked as far as possible into his jacket sleeves, the cuffs dangling dejectedly. "Let's go back."

Different strokes for different folks. A few goatlike leaps and Yannick was already past the end of the chain. Standing on the plateau now, he stretched his lower back. Steeve sighed, dazzled by the beam of the flashlight his cousin held above his shoulder, his arm bent at a right angle, just the way Steeve dreamed of holding the handrail in the metro on his way home, where he could quietly shut himself off from life. He stepped nearer to the abyss that wasn't one, but no matter. He tested the chain. Sweet Jesus, did it ever feel good to touch something factory-made.

"Catch!" he said to Yannick.

On the count of three he lobbed him his quilt rolled up in a ball. The blanket had hardly travelled a quarter of the way when it popped open in mid-air like a parachute and ended up hugging the contours of the rocks below. *Oh well.* He would get it right with his shotgun, which he proceeded to hurl, also on the count of three. But Yannick apparently couldn't count that high, because he didn't even begin to consider the possibility of making a move to catch it. The gun fell twenty-five feet and got wedged between the juts.

"Thanks, eh."

Then it was his turn. He didn't even bother to throw his snowshoes. He'd make do without them. He grabbed the chain in both hands and concentrated on clenching his fingers. He pictured himself bludgeoning Yannick with the flashlight as his body swung out over the void and rolled against the cliff. At the far end, the sole of his shoe skidded over the terrace, except that he never let go of the chain. He was too fond of it. To keep from swinging back in the other direction or dislocating his elbows, he had to let himself drop onto some wobbly rocks. Most of his bulk landed on his leg, which twisted into an S. Before he could even wonder how he'd managed it, Yannick was there, arms folded over his chest, examining Steeve's big shin bone, which flexed where it wasn't supposed to.

"Nice," he said.

The fractured bone had perforated Steeve's pants. Clearly, he'd done a bang-up job. The snowflakes, as they neared the rip, melted in the heat of the dark blood.

"Don't leave me all alone here," Steeve begged in a spent voice, his face whiter than the snow in the starlight streaming from his cousin's fist. "Yannick, are you kidding me, for Chrissake. Yannick! For Chrissake! I'm your own flesh and blood!"

Wrong. Yannick backed away and dissolved into the storm along with the last photons. Steeve's veined eyelids soon closed on a face on which the frost prevented any expression. The moon above the peaks followed its arc through clouds transforming at speed.

"Wake up, you big slob," Yannick said when he returned.

He poked his cousin with the muzzle of his gun.

"Huh?" said Steeve, half-buried. "Who's that?"

"I dunno, must be Monti."

"Am I dead?"

Yannick didn't give him the time to rise from the grave. He drew out his Rambo knife and cut three strips out of his cousin's pants, which he used to cobble together a useless splint. Steeve shrieked in agony. There were practically dotted lines marked *Cut here* on his wrists. Yannick tried to sling him over his shoulder like a potato sack. *I ain't twenty anymore,* he thought.

"You need to help yourself a little," he said over the sobs. "Hold on to me. I went to reconnoitre. We're not far from the Canons' field."

51

FRANÇOIS CLUNG TO THE TABLECLOTH TO KEEP FROM being blown away. Everything else on the table had been blown away. Henri held him by the face, a time bomb deep in his breast. François felt broad fingers crushing the bones of his skull. Liette jumped on Henri's back, manuscript pages flying in every direction. A three-headed hydra, panting and spitting, trampled the remains of dessert, shards of china, cutlery, while a pack of hunting dogs composed solely of Croquette circled round. And *thok!*

Thok! Holes appeared in the plaster walls. Henri used his son's briefcase to fend off a jab from a serving fork. Then he exerted all his strength to cram François headfirst into the cabinet next to the sink, where they stored oils and vinegars and the hot sauces the missus didn't eat on account of her heartburn.

"Down, Papa, down," François mumbled, his mouth puckered like a cleaner fish.

It was all a little hard on the digestion. François, groping his way to the faucet behind him, managed to grasp the side sprayer and splash his assailant. That's when he discovered another twenty-sixer of Yukon, sealed, between the balsamic vinegar and the reserves of sriracha. Even as he was being killed, he tried to open the bottle of liquor with his teeth. It didn't work, but he must have drunk by osmosis, because, much revived and armed with a wet, slightly sticky rag left dripping over the faucet, he began to blindly lash his mother.

"Ouch!" she said.

François needed to grab hold of something. Twisting his body, he seized Liette's hair and then went sliding across the floor, like a sort of meditative curling rock, toward the basement stairs. With the collar of his new polo shirt stretched and his head cube-shaped from seeing every corner of the cabinet up close, he gasped for breath on the steps, unsure of the order in which to have his bones fused back together.

"You good-for-nothing," Henri said at the top of the stairs.

Liette, her cheeks streaked with mascara, was already cleaning up the mess in the kitchen. François climbed up a few stairs, feeling bad. In his grey, cracked fist he'd just found a tuft of his mother's hair. Not quite knowing what to do with it, he watched Liette bustling about in utter silence.

"You *ingrate* you," Henri said. "You miscarriage. You mistake."

"Mama," François whispered reluctantly. "I'm sorry, Mama, okay?"

From the staircase, he proffered the tuft of hair, wanting to give it back to her. But Henri blocked the way. He gestured "come here" to François. As welcoming as a customs officer.

"Hitting your mother?"

François, on tiptoe, again looked past his father, over the cannonball of his shoulder. Liette was on her knees weeping, not for herself but for her men.

"You can clean up later," François called out to her.

Between Henri's legs he saw her collecting the manuscript pages, certain that any moment now she would crumple them up and dump them in a garbage bag, never considering they might be important to him.

François gave his parent a mumbled command: "Let me through."

"Come," Henri said, egging him on from the landing. "Right through here. Through the machine."

"Let me *through*," the son repeated.

He pulled himself up the stairs, holding the handrail to propel himself forward when he charged. Henri, shedding a tear, pressed all his weight down into his woollen socks and adopted the sumo position.

"It's for your own good, young man."

A cast iron fist closed around a chicken neck. On the verge of fainting, unable to focus his eyes on his blurry mother, who was yelling and waving her arms like a referee overwrought because no one was listening anymore, François had the good fortune of tumbling down the stairs. As he fell, he experienced an epiphany. The secrets of the universe were revealed to him. The solution to every sudoku in the world. But when he dropped into a heap of polystyrene chips, the kind you put in boxes when you move, he lost all his ideas. Then he lost his breath when his father landed on him. Croquette's legs were too short for him to follow the wrestlers down the stairs. He chased his tail in the door frame up above.

"Yanni . . . Croqu . . . Henr . . ." Liette said, testing the first step with her foot. "Oh heck! Get it right. François! You're going to give him a cardial attack!"

She hung on to the handrail. Her tiny sequined slippers scampered down at a slight angle. Even though nothing hurt, she kept on squealing *ouch* as she outdid herself to separate her men. Here she was inflating François so he would regain something like a normal shape; there she was guiding her husband's breathing exercises.

"Cardial *arrest,*" Henri said in the middle of the scuffle.

"Cardi*ac* arrest," François said.

All hell broke loose. Liette went flying in a sort of misty flip. Henri ricocheted all over the walls. Croquette, at the head of the stairs, had half his own body in his mouth. François, his throat tattooed with whitish fingermarks, was about to rip out a sheet of plasterboard when his mother said:

"Ouch, my eye! Hey, wait, everyone, for real. I've lost a contact lens. Ouch. Damn. My eye."

François plonked himself down on a stair, drained of all strength. It would have been time for a coffee refill.

"I can't take it *any longer,* understand?" he cried, his head hanging between his thighs.

The bad vibrations had faded. Henri and Liette combed the floor looking for the contact lens. After a few bland remarks and timid *sorry*s were exchanged, François slumped down on the staircase.

"I've had it up to *here!* With everything! Which in my case actually doesn't amount to much . . . My apartment certainly is spacious, eh. Lots of room. Been a long time since any girlfriends came around. But that suits me fine. That's how I like it. Lot of room for my strolls from the bedroom to the living room. Blank walls to hurl myself at. Ample space between the furniture for my ratiocinations. Because, when I see them, with their degrees, their careers, their credit. They'll never fit the universe into their computers. Did you know the calculators that college students buy at their co-op are more powerful than the technology used to launch the first space rockets? We live in our air-conditioned palaces, in condos as big as warehouses, with brick walls looking out on the Old Port. We make love to each other with objects. But inside your head, that's where you live. Make it nice in there. Because it's easy to be forever clicking on icons. You'll see, once I set my mind to it. I can score points too. Soon I'm going to slip into people's heads. One of these days my life will begin. You haven't seen me on the news? Ah, the news! I've given it up. I'm no mere receptacle for background noise. I buy the *Itinéraire* magazine from street people, to promote knowledge. The city trash cans are overflowing. I can't find anywhere to chuck my paper on the way home. It piles up and spills out and I, well, I try to stay afloat when the wave rolls in. But that's not all. I don't get up in the morning anymore. It's the things around me that get up and start streaming past so that I have the illusion of walking. Why? Can you tell me that, can you? I see them slip by on the bus, when I go off to do fieldwork with *X*s instead of eyes. The Canadiens let me down this year. François for president. Even when you want to stay healthy, you get screwed. But when I drink, oh boy. I'm a saint. Poupette dressed as a monk speaking in tongues. When I'm drunk, I have substance. Otherwise, transparency takes over. We got shut out in the seventh game. The problem is nothing gets me drunk anymore. I've lost the intoxication. I'm immune. You know that good old paradox, don't you? If a tree falls in the forest with no one there to hear it, does it make a sound? Well, the tree doesn't make a sound, even when it falls right in front of me. I live in another era. I live at a point frozen in time. In a single dimension. A little while ago I lost my way near a school. The children passed right through me at the pedestrian crossing. I was still in the middle of the road when the crossing guard lowered his sign to let the eight approaching buses roll right over me. That's the reason I drink. I drink in the sky, in the crush at the metro exits. In raw emotion. I give courses to animals in the park. It's on the program of all the Montreal variety shows. A sidebar in the special edition of the *Vivier.* I don't know what I'm saying anymore and I'm sorry. I don't even know anymore why I'm writing this book. Who is it that said, 'At least I don't need to write to drink'? What a strange piece of machinery memory is. Why did they do that to us? We white folks, we're the ones who brought alcohol to the Indigenous peoples. I've dug too deep. Like Monti. With my lead pencils, my lined notepads. With my sharpener, my eraser, my scissors. I wanted to make the air circulate in my own way, with my tools, take down a few bad guys, dig my own shafts. I buried myself too deep. I had too much ambition. Without anyone or anything else, I got lost in my own labyrinth. There was nothing but echoes to keep me company. I want to die, but I'm already dead. Sometimes I get the feeling I've surfaced somewhere in the world where I don't speak the same language as the people there. Where are they, the people? Did I miss something? I found gold. My veins are just full of gold. Has it made me happy? 'I sing *La langue de chez nous. Our* language!' I drink and get closer to the truth but never reach it, I open another bottle to keep from getting lost, to keep writing. There are things wanting to surface from my scrawl. The page rips. I lose the thread of my ideas. I lose my friends. They say my mind is poisoned. I refuse to stick my head in the sand, and I don't say that to flatter myself. We've been receiving a bottle of Yukon every week for three generations.

At least, what's left of us, of our old dried-up genes, plunging into the fog with our arms held out. There are limits to pleasure. Not that it's all that *good,* the Yukon. 'The taste of gold.' I've seen their agents. Someday, somewhere, the facts will coincide. The wondrous beast will spring from between the empty spaces. Are you being followed too, Mama? Papa, what were you told that fateful day when you picked up the red telephone? At least have the courage to see me for what I am. You would always tell us, Yannick and me, that we'd talk about it again when we grew up. Well, I've stopped growing. We're ripe for a very long conversation. 'You'll understand when you grow up.' I don't understand a thing! I wanted to write that book to . . . I'm on my way now, I'm on my way. I wander over the fields, howling in my rags and my chains. I kick away the spells cast on me. Poupette said he would help me. *He* understands me. I owe him money, but no matter, I came here to finish and I've finished. I don't even need to write it anymore, my book. I'm free, I think. You'll say I'm too young, but I distinctly remember Granddad sharpening a knife on a rat-tail. He said that if he kept on, the knife would eventually disappear. We're not going to open the suitcase to check, but inside there's a lovely soft-bound tome with unguillotined pages and my name in capital letters printed on it. And on the flap, the awards I'm winning at this very moment. I'm famous, but I couldn't care less. All I wanted was to say something true."

Transfixed, Liette must have stepped back ten metres from François. You could hear the fruit flies hovering in the kitchen.

"All Gaspésiens are liars," Henri concluded.

"What did he say?" asked Liette, not yet half-blind but pretty damn close to it.

She gave her husband pleading looks, and her son awkward smiles.

"Hey, it's not just me," Henri said. "It wasn't super clear, right?"

He had his wife's contact lens on the tip of his finger and roguishly slipped it into his pocket. He signalled to François to come with him.

"But, well, it's just that I—"

"I, I, I. I said come on."

"Is it to do with his doctorate, you think?" Liette said, persisting, as she followed at their heels down the hallway.

"And bring me my hat, too!" Henri shouted to her a minute later when she stepped out of the listening room to remove her remaining contact lens and slip into something she wanted to show François.

Seated in the corner of the sectional sofa, François made a blatant display of indifference as he was handed collector's vinyls. He was seriously pissed off by his father's way of handling them like plutonium. Between albums, Henri asked him hyper-finicky questions about his presentation earlier, obviously sidestepping the crux of the matter. They both looked as if they'd come out of the dryer. There were cigarette burns on the upholstery and the rug. The museum of a room was a notch above chaos. *A time capsule,* François thought as he assessed the listening room. *Or pandemonium on standby.*

"Here, do you remember this?" Henri digressed, interrupting his pointers on how his son could better organize his line of argument to proffer a vinyl, which he held by the edges between his palms and shifted under the light to show how completely scratch-free it was. "I had this on a cassette back then. We'd listen to it whenever we took you on holiday to Shédiac, surely you remember? The vinyls are impossible to come by. You have to kill to buy one."

The times François had been to Shediac in his life were even fewer than the holidays Henri had taken in his; what's more, the musicians on the sleeve, which his father now held open so François could slip the record back in, all had the same haircut, satin jackets, and quasi-identical faces.

"I've got two copies," Henri said.

He'd also bought the jukebox that was of no use anymore at Mrs Guité's, other than to get kicked around. The drunkards jumped each time the tom drum began on the jukebox, which day after day they mistook for a cigarette machine or a one-armed bandit.

"Please don't put your fingerprints on the record."

"Ta-dam!" Liette sang as she came back into the room.

The *daaaaam* was stretched into a long fanfare. The mater had put on the striped mink coat her hubby—for the pleasure of splurging and, above all, to keep his wife from freezing in the winter—had bought her earlier that week, along with Croquette's diamond-pattern sweater.

Blind as a bat, Liette advanced, taking care to put one foot in front of the other, as though walking a line. She pirouetted, somewhat shaky, shaky, very shaky, her stiletto heel nearly buckling under her still-pretty leg.

The walls, ceiling, and rug were speckled with the shimmering light from a disco ball that must have once belonged to Yannick. Sporting a Russian-style fur hat, also mink, because families mustn't be separated, Henri stood behind his "dry bar." That's what he called the padded and studded faux leather counter where he'd installed a turntable—and other electronic gear for effect—connected to a mixing desk sprouting a whole bouquet of wires. "I'll treat you to some music tonight," he'd said. He drank like a prince, crooning under the silvery flecks gliding over him, not even bothering to hide from Liette, who was so glad of the renewed peace she didn't notice a thing, nada.

Wrapped in her long mink coat, she did a slow dance, holding her François very close. They awkwardly trod on each other's feet to the sound of a poignant sax solo. Those heels weren't called stilettos for nothing. Beads of condensation formed on the door frames. François, with a measure of tenderness, adjusted a few locks of his mother's hair to cover the recently plucked square of white skin at the back of her head. *The black wire next to the yellow,* he thought as he mentally untangled the connections spilling over the dry bar. *Or did he . . . No, that's the turntable terminal, but the other one, the yellow, it goes . . .* Soft, the fur coat. A languorous throb distorted the space in front of the various speakers of the surround-sound system. Liette danced with feeling, her cheek resting on her boy's chest, where she could hear his heart beating out of time.

"I dreamed of this moment," she said. "You, you dreamed of it too, eh?"

She hugged him.

"I can never remember my dreams," François answered.

Henri, a single earphone pressed against his ear, made a vaguely Sinatra-like gesture. He took a splendid swig of his Yukon while François continued to visually isolate the path of each wire hooked up to the mixing desk.

"And now . . ." the pater announced as he changed records.

Under that lighting he appeared to be dressed entirely in white, with white hair, and white nail polish.

"A perennial classic to get the youngsters moving."

Liette took off her high heels. Her jerky steps speeded up. She clapped her hands and swung her hips.

"Make your mother sweat," she told François, quite a bit shorter without her shoes. With mink hairs on his tongue, François couldn't quite manage to loosen up, despite his mastery of some pretty wild dance steps. Liette lifted her eyes up toward him. The light-speckled ceiling turned slowly beyond the full moon on his shoulders. *The other black wire is connected to the speaker above the volunteer firefighters plaque. The blue wire next to it goes to* ... Over a four-four beat and plagiarized vocals, François finally untangled the cluster with his eyes by following the red wire running along one wall and behind the jukebox and then within an inch of him. Liette sighed with contentment when he pushed her down on the sectional whose sections had slightly moved apart. Between a stuffed gopher and the neon sign for a brand of beer, on a shelf made of paddles, at the end of the red wire, was the gizmo Henri had mentioned earlier. An iPod fresh out of the box, inserted in a kind of launch pad. François dashed out of the room stammering unintelligible apologies. He imagined the device suddenly lighting up behind him with a countdown on the screen. His parents heard him charging up the stairs.

An unlit cigarette between his fingers, Henri savoured his drunkenness. He was drowsing on the reclining sofa in the living room in front of a deadly report on nothing very specific, dozens of sharks cut up in the surf, a minaret peeking out on its rock at low tide, people not like us. After their fiesta Liette had asked him what the matter was and he said he was "sick."

"We'll pamper you," she responded, already in her nightgown but newly made up. She swapped the fur hat on her spouse's head for a hot water bottle.

As there was nothing else her husband needed for the moment, she went upstairs to enjoy a few peaceful minutes sitting in the kitchen with the *Vivier* crossword puzzle, which her son had easily solved. Almost at once, coincidentally, François's oh-so-familiar smell set her nostril, somewhat less translucent under her foundation, aquiver. Liette turned toward her habitual window, which for her framed the known universe.

52

WITH STEEVE HANGING ON TO HIM, IN A HEROIC
effort lacking only the soundtrack of a big-budget movie, Yannick climbed up the side of a brimming irrigation ditch, its
water sprouting arborescent crystals. The snow fell even more
insistently. Here and there in the gloom it exploded in volatile
particles above the Canons' crumbling field. Steeve's dried-up
hypothalamus had stopped producing endorphins some time
ago. The halo of warmth lingered around his fracture and the
approaching snowflakes melted before they could pepper his
epidermis.

"Try not to squeeze my throat like that," Yannick wheezed.

He was exhausted as he freed himself at last from the hardened bulrushes.

Rock's taxi was disappearing under the snow. From afar in
the darkness it could pass for one of those bales of hay resem-
bling giant marshmallows that the farmers sometimes leave
on their land. The traces of the accident had been covered
over long ago and neither of the men noticed anything out
of the ordinary.

"I won't let go, you dirty dog," Steeve said, breathing hard.

"Believe me. If I want you to let go, you'll let go."

They were nearing the edge of the field and the road was

coming into view when a yellow dot appeared in the night. The dot blinked intermittently. It grew larger behind the trees.

"The light at the end of the tunnel," Yannick said.

The dot spread out between the tree trunks. It stretched into an ever-broadening cone, a funnel Steeve felt was sucking him closer. He expected the hand of God to reach out from it and grab him by the scruff of his neck. Yannick made him let go with a self-defence move.

"Hey!"

Yannick ran toward the road. Supine on the snow, Steeve experienced the moment in slow motion, as in a nightmare. His whole being wanted to gush out through his wound. He and Laganière now had one good pair of legs between them. Don't go toward the light, he wanted to shout to his cousin. Then he realized the light came from snowmobiles. Yannick leaped and let himself topple over the fence alongside the road.

"Hey! Over here! Stop!"

The snowmobilers stopped on a dime. Steeve smiled and his face became crazed with cracks. Around the distant headlights he reconstructed moving silhouettes. Two figures had just stepped off one of the vehicles. They ran toward Yannick. A smudge, a streak of black ink, lengthened the shadow of one of them. *A rifle,* Steeve thought. *Hunters.* Soon a third snowmobile pulled up with a single rider. Steeve thought he could make out Yannick drinking from a bottle. Around the machines a whole operation was getting under way. Yannick, shielding his face from the snow with his forearm, pointed toward Steeve with his other arm. More rifle barrels moved through the headlights and the fumes. *It's over,* Steeve thought. He shifted his broken leg as Yannick mounted one of the snowmobiles behind the driver. It must have been jet-powered to take off like that. The snow churned up in its wake blended with the falling snow. One of the remaining hunters was using a CB radio while the other two strode over the fence. They came across the field in the general direction of the casualty. *I'm nothing but a lousy wimp,* Steeve thought again. Flashlight beams swept over the snow ahead of the men. *Please, a stretcher. A helicopter.* Treading on the footprints Yannick had made, the hunters advanced toward the invalid.

"It's over," Steeve said out loud.

Just speaking was enough to send pain shooting through his leg. The guys called out to him. They had a blanket that looked like aluminum foil. One of them set off a flare. They hadn't yet reached him when Steeve, dragging himself through the powder, struck something hard with his good leg. His face contorted as he turned toward the object.

In the whiteness there was a head. Not understanding, Steeve nudged it with the tip of his foot. The head rolled, snowflakes sticking to the red-slicked hair. The chubby, bloated face was a mask of stupefaction.

"Patapon?" Steeve said.

It was the part Rock had forgotten in the snow upon leaving the Canons' field with a few limbs under his arms. The hunters quickened their pace when Steeve began to shriek uncontrollably. In his attempt to hurl the head of the boy he'd bullied all through their adolescence as far away as possible, a piece of the face had come off in his hands.

X

BILLY JOE PICTOU

53

FOR WHAT MUST HAVE BEEN THREE-QUARTERS OF AN
hour, Yannick had been waiting for his father in the company van. The windshield was as wide as a bay window and a
spectacular sun flooded the interior. Fearing that little bits
of himself might stay glued to the black leather seats, Yannick didn't dare move. He'd tried to convince himself Henri's
errand would give him a chance to drowse, to relax after a week
of lawn mowing and remedial classes by rating from one to ten
the sun-creamed women going by in swimsuits after their dip.
But that would have meant living in denial. Because, unless
you were endowed with a probably unhealthy capacity for
autosuggestion, you couldn't really miss the blankety-blank
shopping mall the private sector had had the bright idea of
building last May right on the beachfront along the 132, just
opposite Chapleau's fish shop, where the Bouge & Fils van was
parked. You couldn't see the bikinis from Chapleau's parking
lot anymore. You saw uncles and aunts pushing shopping carts
or bone-weary parents behind strollers. You couldn't see the
water anymore. Instead you saw a Rossy store, whose cladding
coincided with the boundaries of Yannick's field of vision. He
must have been, what, at the time—fourteen, fifteen years
old? Acne, limp goatee. He had no wish, on such a beautiful

weekend, during a record heat wave, to be roasting like a lamb on a spit in his father's van.

"I'm going to swing by the fish shop for three minutes," was the lie his father had told him forty-five minutes ago.

The sun beat down at an angle on the shopping mall's white-hot roof, a prism of pure energy. Even with the windows open Yannick could have wrung out the T-shirt stuck to his flypaper skin. The only thing that kept him from fainting was the char-nel house breeze, the brain-damaging stench, the sad, apoc-alyptic reek of fish trying to flee from itself through the fish shop's blowhole and into the van. *The lesser of two deaths,* he told himself. He was about to roll up the windows again and be smothered by the heat in the van—any remnants of air con-ditioning had long ago petered out—when the doors locked all at once, then unlocked, and the alarm system emitted a couple of desultory beeps. The lights on the dashboard turned on, then off. The doors locked again. The engine started up. The doors unlocked again. Yannick saw Henri appear in the rear-view mirror, reddish face, teeth as white as pastis. Patch-es of sweat darkened the chest and underarms of his shirt. The pater put a box of wood chisels in the back and installed himself behind the steering wheel, which was so hot a drop of saliva would have made it go *tsss*. It was his first remote starter and he wasn't used to it. But, seriously, when your kid has already wasted half his Saturday riding all over town with you while you shop around for new conveyor belt rollers, you might have the decency not to stink of liquor quite so much after every stop.

"Okay, co-pilot, ready to go?" Henri asked after sucking in a sideways belch.

He filed away an invoice in the Duo-Tang where he kept anything tax-deductible, blew his Saint Christopher medal a kiss, and gently, very gently eased into first gear; his van was not to be mistreated. The asphalt surged in thick waves. Yannick was seeing mirages.

"I just spoke to Mr Perrault," Henri continued.

Helluva cornball, Mr Perrault, Yannick thought. *With his round glasses and his cosmic consciousness.*

"And sit up straight while we're at it. Or you're sure to wind up with scoliosis by the time you're twenty."

Henri couldn't make out a single word of what his son answered in defence. He couldn't make out any of the oxygen-deprived monosyllables that occasionally jostled their way through Yannick's clenched teeth. *An invertebrate.* Yannick's mullet swung like a pendulum in time with the roadway's wear and tear. *You want to wreck cars in the dunes, go ahead,* Henri said to himself, *smash yourself up at thirteen. Drop out of school. But keep your hair short.* He let out a sigh of discouragement. Swirling somewhere in the centre of La Frayère was the white-red-and-blue spiral of the barbershop.

In a huff, Henri began to poke around in the grocery bag he'd brought back from the hardware store earlier that morning. He slurped a periwinkle into his mouth. His chewing sounded like love. It was always the same with Henri. He'd go into the fish shop and come out with tools. If he drove by the hardware store, he would veer into the parking lot. Systematically. He was programmed that way. Then he'd suddenly get back in the van holding something improbable, say, a short-nose sturgeon wrapped in a pound and a half of saran wrap. This time it was periwinkles.

He offered one to Yannick, but the boy jammed two fingers against his uvula as if to make himself retch. *Poor little thing,* Henri thought. *Be better off dead.* He adjusted his side-view mirror so as to admire both his new brush cut and the words BOUGE & FILS that he'd painted in latex on the side of the van. *Keep your hair short,* he insisted in his head. Sixteen, that's how old Yannick was. He'd just passed his driver's test. The kid may not have been talkative, but he took notes. His father had them all down pat, those moves that make you fantasize about driving when your navel isn't dry yet. The arm behind the passenger headrest when you back up, and so on. *A C-note he repeats himself,* Yannick thought as he darted a glance at his father.

"I just spoke to Mr Perrault."

Henri always repeated himself and, what's more, he was in his cups. *Double or nothing he comes out with the same old bad joke,* Yannick thought.

"I know," he said, "you just told—"

"Holy moly, it talks!"

The pater threw in a few heart attack theatrics, to which Yannick responded with a yawn. A prolonged yawn that got strangled toward the end and turned into a whine of frustration. His fist shot out on its own against the polymer over the glove compartment.

"Hey, you need to rein it in," Henri said.

The van cruised unrushed toward the intersection of Rue Principale. Zero chance of showers. *Blue sky, calm sea,* Henri said to himself.

Yannick couldn't get over it. His father had no right. He didn't own him. While he was wasting his youth in slavery, his friends were preparing for their camping trip. Heading for the Malin, a river inland from Bonaventure. The Perseids had begun, it was going to be absolutely insane. Vignola had his mother's car. So what good did it do Yannick to have passed his driver's licence? That was the worst part. The old man never let him drive.

"Mr Perrault assured me we wouldn't find the kind of rollers we need in Chandler. He went up there day before yesterday for a milking machine and some shelving."

What? Yannick thought. *How's that?* Did this mean they weren't going to Chandler? Someone must have lit a votive candle for him, because when they came to the corner, the van turned left. West equalled home. East equalled Chandler. After a quick calculation, somewhat skewed by the barely controlled excitement that started to look like a heat stroke, Yannick figured it might not be too late. *Maybe I haven't missed my lift. Wouldn't be surprised if Marteau wasn't ready yet.* All of a sudden his Saturday turned into an ad for the joy of living in a healthy community. A jogger marked time at the green light while waiting to help an elderly woman cross the road. Children abandoned their impromptu car washes or their lemonade stands to run after the ice cream truck through rainbows sent up by lawn sprinklers. Yannick could already picture himself doing a cannonball dive from the rocks to purify his system in the flowing Malin river. But right then the van's interior was shaken by a red alert ring that made you want to duck down with your hands on your head and look for the closest emergency exit.

"Yes, hello, Bouge et Fils, Henri Bouge speaking, how can I help you? Oh, it's you, darling, I was about to call you."

It was the cellphone. One of the earliest models, too. At twenty-two pounds it was a mean piece of hardware. Fifteen hundred bucks at Radio Shack.

"It's your mother," Henri whispered to his boy, one hand over the mic.

But Yannick was already swimming where he sat, in expectation of joining his crew of "freebooters," the term his father used to tease him. The hand over the mic was the quirk of a secretive man. On the rare occasions when he answered the cellphone, very much on his guard whenever it rang, Henri was anything but a paragon of brevity, especially since he'd just bought that bit of technology and hadn't yet had much chance to use it and justify the expense. Judging from the tone of the conversation, Liette had been separated forever from her husband by the tragedy of his leaving the house that morning. Yannick imagined his friends Kim and Marie-Pierre stretched out on their warm towels, getting an even tan on the riverbank, with Vignola's mother's car nearby in the background. Ah, the good life. The drive would be a whole lot better than riding in Patapon's rustbucket Chevette. *But, hey, get a load of this.* Henri had forgotten where they lived. Instead of turning right on Jacques-Cartier when he was supposed to, he headed up Rue Pleau on the tail of a Winnebago with Nova Scotia plates going west on the 132. *Mayday, mayday.*

"We'll be coming home late, honeybun," Henri said. "I have to drive down to Rimouski for my rollers, otherwise, come Monday at the work site ... Yes, that's right, we'll get lunch somewhere past Escuminac, I guess, the kid has to eat."

All the while sublimely ignoring Yannick, who was having an epileptic fit right beside him, Henri gave his wife a detailed description two or three times of the dicey Monday he risked having if he didn't first take care of this roller business. *Rimouski,* Yannick thought. He hadn't seen that one coming. And he knew which snack bar his father was talking about. It was where they always stopped to eat, a place that didn't seem to have a name but where the sign said CHINESE, ITALIAN, AND CANADIAN SPECIALTIES. Every time, Henri ate his two egg rolls and let his Caruso hamburger get cold in its canned sauce. He drained one brandy coffee after another over the crossword puzzle in the newspaper while Yannick gulped down his *galvaude* or his stack of predigested pancakes and mock maple syrup. CANADA'S OCEAN PLAYGROUND, said the Winnebago's licence plate in front of them.

"And enjoy your bridge party tonight. Tell Gaston I'll look forward to his revenge game."

Unbeknownst to Henri, his honeybun had hung up three minutes earlier.

"Couldn't you," Yannick said, "ask François to help out for once in his life?"

Henri, his hand over the mic, gave his boy a squint that meant: *François, seriously?*

"I'm speaking with your mother," he muttered.

"Lucky her."

"Tell Gaston I'll look forward to his revenge game, so, yup, okey-doke, darling, I'll see you later, bye-bye, big kiss, how's our François doing today? Anyway, talk to you again soon, bye now."

Unable to set the telephone back in its cradle, Henri ended up wedging it between thighs dappled with blue fuzzballs, the keypad facing him as if he were about to dial another number. He lit a cigarette with the van's lighter. The vacationers around them rode on a bleached road that extended into the panorama all the way to a sun whose diameter could only have been contrived by SFX artists. Henri held his cig in the middle, between his stout, quasi-jointless fingers. Each time he took a puff, his hand covered half his face.

"Maybe if I was allowed at least to drive . . ."

"It talks!"

Kittens squashed in a vise, Yannick thought. *Cute little bunnies worked over with old nicked shears. Chicks dissected in . . .*

"And it's 'if I *were* allowed'—subjunctive mood for hypothetical situations," Henri corrected. "I haven't changed my mind, big fella. You can't drive and you know why."

The eleventh commandment. Thou shalt not drive the paternal vehicle so long as thy hair a barbet water dog resembles.

"The hitch is going to stretch in the straightaways."

Henri was pointing at a trailer in the other lane farther down the road. What he meant was the weather was hot, but what he really wanted was to break a silence that he felt served no purpose. A sign indicated three hundred and twenty-eight kilometres to Rimouski, a number Yannick latched on to as the van made its way among more and more station wagons, minivans, SUVs, the occasional kayak mounted on a roof, hardly-ever-used bicycles, a host of vacationists with layered or mushroom haircuts, or hair combed to one side, undoubtedly going to spend the weekend in rivers streaming straight out of *Blue Lagoon* with their girlfriends and buddies and their girlfriends' friends and bucketfuls of beer and Frisbees and tons of packaged sausages to roast on the fire.

Yannick had felt it coming for a while. In the middle of the news bulletin, Henri turned the volume down on the radio.

"How are your summer courses going?" he asked, offering his son the cigarette sticking out of the pack.

"Pretty scholastic," Yannick replied.

"Hey, what in the world am I doing?" Henri said.

He drew the cigarette of temptation out of the pack and crushed it in the ashtray even though it wasn't lit. There wasn't the slightest likeness between him and his son. In fact, in all of La Frayère, no two people were less alike. Henri took a deep breath. His belt went taut. *Oh no,* the son thought when the father's lungs began to deflate.

"My boy, sometimes we have to do things in life that don't appeal to us. Because they're somehow for our good."

Ill at ease, Henri obsessively adjusted his mirror and twiddled buttons here and there on the dashboard with an air of expertise. Yannick groped under his seat as though searching for the ejection lever.

"Builds character. Yes, I know, you're wondering how."

Most of all I wonder when the heck you'll leave me alone, Yannick thought.

"Take Mr Turcotte, for instance. He didn't feel like having a hip replacement."

"He never walked again, either."

Rimouski, three hundred and forty-one kilometres. Yannick had just seen that on another sign.

"That's not the point," Henri said.

The deepest pains are sometimes the most silent.

"Oh, and hey," Yannick muttered. "Pick two cards and lose your turn."

"What did you say?"

Yannick padlocked his trap again. There wasn't a single car on the road, not a jalopy in sight. Mountains reared up around them. A valley fell away before the van.

"One fine day," Henri said, "I'll always remember it, my

father told me something. He said that everything he owned, his money, his properties, the big car in the front yard, the lucrative handshakes, he'd have traded all of it, any time, for a glove save against the Paspébiac Crolions forward who robbed him of a piece of his destiny in a hockey tournament when he was a kid. Billy Joe Pictou was the guy's name. He was Mi'kmaq."

Meanwhile, a slender thread of black silk, the scudding shadow of a stratus cloud, slid down between the shaggy peaks to the foot of a mountain slope where the wind seemed to be produced. They entered the Matapédia Valley, as Monti had seventy-five years before on the horse he'd appropriated from the Saint-Lancelot-de-la-Frayère mailman with the whole crowd at the hotel looking on. Monti won the horse in a mythical wager—no one ever figured out how. In any case, his stunt worked, because the horse, after all, hadn't teleported itself. Somebody one way or another must have hoisted it up and into Mrs Guité's hotel through an upper-floor window. Different versions of the legend still circulated among old-timers throughout the peninsula. Youngsters like Yannick were also familiar with the anecdote, having heard it from their parents and grandparents while still in diapers. But his generation had had their fill of such stories. To Yannick and his friends they were nothing but fabrications, figments of drunken imaginations, stratagems that like so many other things had taken on irreversible proportions through word of mouth.

"Possessions cannot satisfy every want," Henri said. "There's some truth in clichés."

Lost in thought, he opened the van's console. Without even looking, since the cassettes were arranged in alphabetical order, he pulled out the third one from the back. He blew on the magnetic tape, dropped it into the blaster, and rock on. It was opera.

"Have I ever told you how it got started, Bouge et Fils?"

Only seven hundred and ninety-eight times, Yannick thought. A quarry a little farther up in the northeast. Deeds transferred to get all his ducks in a row with city hall. Buyback of shares from Pleau and Labillois. Backhoes bought on the cheap from business people in Murdochville. And boom. With every blast of dynamite, investments showered over their necks reddened by the sun and hard work.

"I mean how it *really* got started. When Granddad Monti once came to wake me in the middle of the night, when I desperately needed to sleep. I was about your age. And I was quite a handful. Or maybe I was a few years younger than you, more like thirteen, I guess. Anyway, Baptiste had gone off to the war, I remember that. My father, did he come to wake me that night to punish me or to reward me? Back then I wasn't the most capable member of the tribe at our house."

Henri confessed that it had been his very first drinking spree.

"And it was a bender."

On the day he was referring to, his parents had taken the children for a visit to Uncle Gédéon's in the backcountry near Saint-Elzéar where he had a stand of sugar maples. Gédéon wasn't anyone's uncle, yet he still enjoyed spoiling the little devils that he himself had never had. He had a powerful personality and Monti suspected they were friends. The family would visit him in spite of these amiable feelings, which Monti usually found too insistent. The fact was, he could not say no to his offspring, and they had no problem with going to the woods to gorge on sweets. There was always cause for a tummy ache there, even when the maple sugar wasn't quite in season.

Still, this was how it had to be, and that Sunday Henri had to resign himself to watch through the judas hole as the Ford Super Deluxe, still regarded by part of the populace as the devil's machine, drove off. Churning up the reddish dust in the driveway, it left him and Toine behind. Charline, the baby of the family, an afterthought, consoled herself behind the steering wheel on Papa's knees. Papa must have overdone the beating, because Henri's memory was pretty hazy. He sensed it was because of some incident involving her that they'd stayed behind, he and his brother, with a list of chores this long as punishment. When it came to Monti's two daughters, it was hands off.

What's more, it appeared that Henri would be getting no help spreading all those wood chips over the muck from the hutches. Toine had entitled himself to lounging unrepentantly in the wheelbarrow full of still-frozen tufts of earth and grass, reading the funnies in the shade of a mouse-eaten straw hat. His gangling carcass lay there, seemingly lifeless, with his long shanks poking out over one of the handles. It was one of those early spring days that gave you the illusion of sweating, and Toine had ordered his kid brother to drop his chores for a minute and go inside to fill a pitcher with water, to which he was to add a measure of brown sugar and some quartered crabapples, and to be very careful not to spill anything on his way back across the forty yards from the house, unless he was in the mood for a serious thrashing. But just as Henri, having not sliced so much as pulped the apples, was putting away the kilo of clumped brown sugar on the highest shelf in the pantry, the telephone began to ring. It rang with a spirited quiver. Henri stepped toward the device, a little closer with each ring, utterly embarrassed without really knowing why.

"We're stopping to fill up."

He'd just turned on his flasher. They'd arrived at Lac-au-Saumon. The tank was half-full.

"It was quite a conversation I had on the phone that day. I don't feel like talking about it, you'll understand when you're older. In any case, the thing I remember the most is what I did after."

Henri had hung up the red receiver. He'd forgotten the sugar water. Instead, he took out a bucket, some rags, and the stepladder. He went about in a daze washing every single window in the house—including the skylights and the oeil-de-boeuf—with tallow soap and a horsehair brush until everything was spic and span.

And now thirsty Toine was banging on the door frame behind him with the flat of his hand. Henri gave him a blank look and then turned toward the forbidden cabinet where their parents kept the wine and liquor and the grey jug of what Monti called his "brain-wrecking alcohol." The jug itself wasn't grey. The jug was transparent. It was the alcohol inside it. It didn't take long once they'd uncorked it for the brothers to cascade like two-legged fountains into each other's arms, wailing in disbelief. They tumbled, as it were, up the stairs to the second-floor room they shared according to a formally established pecking order. They sank into comas on their respective mattresses, Toine in the privacy of his alcove, Henri against a wall that stayed icy even in August.

He realized the rest of the family had returned from Saint-Elzéar when, as he rolled away from the round, bluish stain he'd left in his bed, he caught a dizzy glimpse of Charline eyeing him. His sister, with her dirt-smeared mouth and her ringlets, was sitting on a footstool next to the bed. She dangled her handmade bootees while darting a wary tongue at her maple sugar cone.

"A sorry sight," she said.

Monti came in to wake sonny-boy with a kiss on his curly head and served him his meal on a tray to atone for chastising him so vehemently earlier that morning. No, not quite. Monti yanked the blankets off Henri, biting his other hand till it bled to keep from killing him. Then he yanked Henri off his mattress and the tyke dropped on the floor, immediately assuming the fetal position. His mouth opened and closed like a chicken whose throat had just been severed. Shooting stars rained down in slow motion in the window behind his father.

"Haul ass."

It wasn't a suggestion. Monti was in his prime and nothing remained of the pipsqueak in the old photos taken before his departure to the Klondike that adorned the walls of his anteroom. The man was a bruiser.

"You're comin' with me."

Henri nodded. There were maracas rattling in his brainpan.

"You are coming," Monti corrected himself.

Never had Henri seen his father so riled up. Had something happened to Baptiste on the battlefield? Monti left the bedroom and went back and forth in the corridor, skating on the floor wax in his flannelette pyjamas. He held a bronze candlestick and the flame flickered terribly. Henri thrust his left

leg into his right pant leg and jammed his face into the sleeve
of his sweater. He heard his father going by again, struggling
to roll up a canvas bag. The household roused, keeping pace
with the calamities. From the lawn one could see the facade
lighting up here and there in an irregular checkerboard as the
lamps began to shine through the spotless windows for which
no one had seen fit to say, "Well done, Henri."

"Mother!" Monti shouted.

And he burst once again into the doorway of his boys' bedroom with a good length of skin-rasping rope coiled around his
arm. He took three steps back, and his exploded face disrupted
the rectangle of the opening. Henri smiled at his father, his
eyes rolled upward. He clenched his teeth to hold in the gobs.

"You," Monti told him. "Go down to the cellar and fetch us
our whole stock of salt pork. Mother!"

Henri, his pants around his knees, dozed off again for a
second on his footstool. Monti reappeared, seized him by the
biceps, and shook him, lifting him almost over his head. He
roared into his ear to go get the cart in the barn, and Henri
hopped to it without stopping to hitch up his trousers before
he was out in the corridor.

Things were bad all around. The youngest were sobbing
under their blankies. Toine in his alcove dreamed he was a
beached whale or something.

"Don't forget the salt pork!" Monti bellowed once more at
Henri, who was thumping down the stairs. "And grab five or
six twenty-six-ouncers of Yukon while you're at it."

On returning from the cellar with the pork and the alcohol,
his cochlea still unwound from his father's roar, Henri over-
heard a conversation on the ground floor.

"But what will you do when you get to the mountain?" Joséphine was saying.

There was a note of exasperation in her tone, whereas gentleness and tolerance were her stock-in-trade. Henri had never seen his mother so combative in the face of her husband. The flame in the candlestick Monti was still holding had gone out.

"I'll do it myself, Joséphine."

"You'll do it yourself?"

Joséphine, still in her nightgown, felt an urge to laugh.

"Well, yes, that's about the size of it!"

Henri didn't make the connection right away. But he was blasted out of his sleepwalking in the living room, where he was preparing to lie down again, when he noticed the gun was missing from above the mantelshelf.

The rope. The bag. The gun.

The pigeons in the attic drew their necks in between their wings. Henri, meanwhile, was unaware his parents were referring to the cart. His father didn't want to use the horse to pull it, but that part of the conversation Henri hadn't heard. He'd inferred, rather, that he was going to the mountain to be done in. Resigned, but with enough dignity not to make an issue of it, he put on his shoes near the front door. He pulled his earflap cap down on the future hunting trophy perched on his shoulders and took it on himself to go out the back way and make sure they had whatever was needed for his execution. The light spilling from the house had turned frothier because of the fog that had rolled in from sea. Henri started and snapped the screen shut against a neckless stranger who made the porch creak under his feet.

By way of greeting, the stranger slowly brushed his fingers

against the rim of his hat. There was a moment of uncertainty. The weather vane shimmered atop the barn at the far end of the yard. The stranger's shirt gave off a whiff of starch when he stepped back from the doorway. Henri, alert now but stammering unintelligibly, scampered out between the handrail and Billy Joe Pictou. He glimpsed the petroleum-coloured sheen of the locks slipping out from under the hat. An Indian on the porch of Lancelot-de-la-Frayère's most respected businessman in the middle of the night. There was a chance that tongues would wag.

Henri entered the barn, nervously kicking at the hens in front of him. *Indians,* he thought, *there's stuff we don't know.* Simply put, he was scared shitless. To the point where he nearly set the forage ablaze when he lit the lantern hanging from a nail on the lintel. He right away sensed the radiance of the horse in its stall. This wasn't Bradley's horse anymore but a colt that Monti had affectionately named Pegasus.

Leading the horse by the bridle, but without the cart, Henri went back toward the house. In the dark he played a peculiar game with Billy Joe, hiding from him while taking care to make enough noise to be heard. The horse's musky breath perked up the nape of his neck. From under the willow where he'd taken shelter, he couldn't catch what was being said on the porch, but his father, hair parted in a zigzag, was doing a veritable St. Vitus's dance in front of the visitor. Monti's suspenders were all that kept him from jumping out of his skin through the top of his head. Billy Joe gazed at him with alabaster eyes set with ebony and sunk in somewhat fleshy sockets. He must have given Monti a minute or two to make up his mind, because he was timing him on a pocket watch. He clicked it shut.

"Ah, Sonny, it's you," Monti said, looking discouraged.

A shaft of moonlight through the willow branches had given Henri away.

"I didn't tell you to harness the horse, I told you to go get the cart. No matter, we're not going anywhere, go back to bed."

Henri made to go unsaddle the horse and apologize to the hens. He couldn't quite grasp what was behind the disagreement between his father and Billy Joe Pictou. But instead of doing an about-face, he spun all the way around on his heels.

Billy Joe had just drawn a gold nugget out of a ball of newsprint. Monti, at once covetous and stupefied, wiped his mouth with his sleeve and adjusted his non-existent tie. Billy Joe remained impassive and silent. He looked at the nugget in his leather-padded hand not as a promise of fortune but as though the forest where he'd chanced on it had wanted to teach him something. The twists and turns of his life had led him back to Monti, whose prowess as a prospector he too had heard of. Henri disentangled himself from the weeping willow, smiling like when you're waiting to be photographed but the camera never goes click.

"It's a deal," Monti said, having dropped back into his shoes.

He shook hands with Billy Joe Pictou, whose large face flashed a smile as well, though minus the big incisors. They both felt a jolt of static electricity.

The crew set off toward the mountain at Billy Joe's leisurely pace. He was quiet and seemed in a good mood, moving with a loose, lumbering gait. He cast good-natured smiles at Henri, who was hitched to the cart. Henri told himself that if things went sour with his father, at least he'd have Pictou. After an hour Monti was walking way ahead of his partners in an alpine skier's posture. Billy Joe watched him with a frown but didn't quicken his pace. When Henri asked him where he'd found the nugget, not knowing if he spoke French, Pictou twirled his fingers over his head, drawing something like figure eights in the air.

"Kind of all over?" Henri said, bothered by the effort he had to put into towing the cart.

Billy Joe pursed his lips and stretched out his fingers. His hands swung from left to right. Then he traced a huge ellipse with his arm, indicating to Henri all that surrounded them. After which he beat time with his forefinger, perhaps to represent the passing seconds. Still befuddled by his father's brain-wrecking alcohol, Henri understood diddly-squat. *Something to do with the present moment?* he thought. He wasn't in the right frame of mind for riddles. Pictou burst out laughing at Henri's bewildered expression and wrapped an arm around his shoulder with a friendly shake. It made Billy Joe happy to meet the offspring of someone who, in his Grisous sweater in front of the net, had played a part in one of the rare moments of fame during his lonely outsider youth. The nugget was a pretext. Pictou had knocked on the Bouges' door out of curiosity, prompted by an urge to see what sort of man his erstwhile hockey rival had become. Maybe the memory of his triumph would feel even sweeter now in face of such an important person. Here Monti turned around to put the screws on his boy. He hollered for him to get a move on. But his bellowing was smothered in the oiled cloth of his hood, which hadn't turned with the rest of his head.

Once the excitement of setting out had faded, Henri struggled to keep up. He brought up the rear, green about the gills,

leaning on the cart while Pictou lent a hand. In the only corner
of his mind that hadn't been roiled by his headache, he cursed
himself for not having greased the axles, as he'd been instructed to do before the family left for Gédéon's place. Because
you're punished by way of your sins, and even though the windows at home were as clean as could be, the slightest grating
of a hub sent pain shooting from his brain stem to the tips
of his limbs. Walking ahead, Pictou guided Henri's thoughts
and his shifting spirits followed Pictou's lead. He focused on
the man's back, which evinced something substantial and harmonious. *I don't quite know how to put it,* Henri thought. His
fascination wore him out.

They paused on the mountain slope. Henri's queasiness was
compounded with vertigo when he saw a couple of kilometres
below the assortment of small houses and sheds whose boards
sometimes had clusters of mussels still clinging to them. From
this height Lancelot-de-la-Frayère looked like a scale model
built by city hall for a presentation of its electrification project.
The sea, at this distance, was rippled with minute, soundless
movements and fretted with foam. Monti was taking his break
a hundred feet farther along, on his feet with his packsack
still slung over his shoulders. He shouted to Henri that they
were going to develop the spot he was pointing to on a distant
crest. Billy Joe, shirt sleeves rolled up, gave him a placid stare.
It was because of the escarpment that the horse had had to be
left in the barn. His breed wasn't reputed to be as sure-footed
on the ledges as other hoofed animals. When they left the
cart behind, Monti made his son promise never to tell his
mother. The bay would have fit in the cup from which Henri
was drinking his broth, one eye covered while the other eye

scanned the Canons' field, an ochre kerchief on the horizon, a parched scab among the expectant truck farms and the garlands of trees whose leafage would soon be as dense as broccoli. He slapped himself lightly in the face a few times.

"Hey! Don't yous leave without me!"

Whenever they stopped, the energy Henri needed to get up again was greater than what he'd managed to regain.

"Don't *you* leave without me!" his father's voice answered him.

Henri clutched his stomach, which squealed like a braking train. He bolted down his ration of salt pork all the same, scratching his arms and face on clumps of thorns, which their guide negotiated with more grace than one would have suspected. It was clear to Henri that Pictou was disappointed, that his microscopic reactions betrayed his disapproval of Monti's obvious haste and growing exasperation. He was afraid the expedition might end in failure. It gave him a strange feeling to see his father, who was beside himself, expecting something from Billy Joe, depending on him, always willing to go blindly wherever Pictou told him to. Mr Bouge no longer had a will of his own. His boss man's assurance was gone. Mr Bouge would never entirely grow up. Henri removed one of his boots and shook out a whole moraine of pebbles. He was feeling more and more sick. Without even stopping, his father came out with an assortment of completely baffling metabolic hypotheses to explain that the best remedy for a hangover was to stay drunk. This threw Henri off balance, and one of his boots slipped off in the slush. The men began to drink faster than they were able to piss.

A temple of Monti's eyeglasses bounced on the topographic map that he'd grudgingly decided to take out. He grasped

Pictou's hand so as to get a better idea of the seam's exact location. Billy Joe recorked the bottle of liquor. His mouth full of alcohol, he took hold of the map. He let a gust of wind carry it off. Monti had brought two and he pulled out the second one. Henri would have liked for Billy Joe not to drink. Pictou pointed *beyond* the mountain, sort of. Still not speaking, he plotted long, swift lines in the air and then sublimed the route by letting it drip off the tips of his fingers in the wind. Monti nodded in agreement. His white calves flashed fluorescent in the greenery. It didn't take him very long to get fed up with the tourism. The more the man drank, the more impossible he became. Even in his soliloquies he proved to be too cantankerous to keep from quarrelling with himself. A lens of his eyeglasses was all crackled now.

"Y' understand French, dontcha?" he asked Billy Joe farther on as they rolled cigarettes from a shared tobacco pouch.

No matter how much he'd have liked to kill Pictou, Monti didn't think twice about sharing his alcohol and tobacco. He wasn't cheap about it. Alcohol and tobacco provided a foundation. The basis of relationships. After that you were free to harbour as many hard feelings as you liked. To Henri, the unadorned salt pork at the bottom of his bowl looked profoundly sad somehow. His own snout was chapped all around the edges like a crisp-fried slice of lard. He almost wished his father would finish him off as he was supposed to at first.

"Stop your dilly-dallying," Monti fumed at Billy Joe, "and hurry up and tell me where you found that gold!"

Covered with bits of salt right down to his glottis, arms spread wide, Henri vowed to eat nothing but legumes until the Saint-Jean holiday if it meant never having to take another bite of salt pork. He dropped face first into a creek to refresh himself among the grilse. Except that it was actually a long vein of mica with a rough surface. The distance opening up between his father and Billy Joe Pictou was also opening up inside him. Pictou seemed to grow less substantial with the alcohol, whereas it hardened Monti even more. And the father's torments were the son's as well. The man wouldn't leave him alone anymore. *Chew, chew on your strip of pig meat,* Henri thought. He'd resigned himself to the possibility they might not find any gold. If only he weren't so sick, he might have been satisfied to merely imagine there was some on the mountain. *In the ground or a bank account, what difference can it possibly make?*

"Savage need civilized, need method and gear to prospect shining rock without shake up too much not always helpful earth spirits," Monti said, and it hurt him to say it, he didn't like to talk that way.

Henri felt Monti was being a jerk. And petty. He searched for the inner strength to tell Monti he was way off base, a prisoner of himself. Pictou hadn't sought Monti out for his prospecting know-how. A falcon dived from the sky into the brush. Even before Henri could put his overly warm woollen socks back on feet chockablock with blisters, Billy Joe bolted, two sheets to the wind. He would run sometimes, impelled by panic or a powerful emotion. Monti's face sank as if something dreadful was happening. He hollered after Pictou, asking why he was angry, and thundered at Henri to step on it. It had taken two and a half centuries after the settlers' arrival for a local to discover riches in these mountains; the competition wouldn't be lining up any time soon.

"Okay, you unsociable so-and-so, just wait and see, I'm pulling out with my expertise and my boy if you don't hurry up and show me some shining seams in the rock."

Getting smoked in front of the fire while the pater barked at the smoke to blow somewhere else, Henri stroked a miniature horse in the palm of his hand. Pictou shook a tamarack; there was a dull thud followed by a swirl of floating feathers, and a pheasant dropped out wondering what in the world. Not even bothering to snap its neck, Billy Joe ripped the bird apart in hands aglow in the dancing flames and moonlight glittering with dew. Flashing a gap-toothed grin, he offered Henri the raw liver and invited him to switch places so the smoke would leave him be. A moment later Henri was pummelling his father's chest.

"You're the one driving him raving mad!" Monti complained to Pictou.

He struggled to wrap his son in a blanket. Nonplussed, Billy Joe kept mum. That his mere presence could arouse such inner turmoil in his companions—he wasn't sure this was something he enjoyed.

"Friend in need promise Mi'kmaq firewater and big warm girlie if he say nice words," Monti said, and his eyes begged Billy Joe to give him a good slap in the face to shut him up.

Sprawled on his back, his head having slipped off a lumpy cot, Henri recognized his father upside down on the ceiling. He had no idea how, but the three of them had ended up in a cabin. At that altitude the cabins belonged to everyone, provided you tidied up and replenished the stack of firewood. Henri could taste the salt pork right up to the back of his eyes. He had ganglions the size of golf balls. Monti emptied the rest of a can into a sooty oil-burning hot plate, and skewered opossum meat lay close at hand on a lattice of branches tied up with broad blades of grass like the ones you stretch between your thumbs for a whistle. His suspenders hung down along his sides, his pant legs were rolled up. Rain seeped in through cracks in the floor and trickled up to enamel basins on the ceiling. Nearly dead, Henri moved his head back as best he could to the corner of the wall his cot had been squeezed into. The room righted itself. A wet cloth lay in a corner amid boot tracks. Pictou was there grinding plants and spooning them into an empty Campbell's soup can, Henri would always remember the label. Billy Joe motioned to him to stay quiet while he finished preparing the makeshift ointment. It was either that or his father's mustard plasters, which had given him second-degree burns that time when Monti had diagnosed consumption on his own to avoid dealing with his father-in-law. Henri passively let himself be anointed with heavy corrosive stripes across his chest. Under a butcher's hook, his shirt unbuttoned, Monti smoked a pipe. He watched the procedure with great interest. Pictou gave Henri a drink of water, rainwater no doubt. But when he saw his healer with a snout and hair sprouting from the tips of his toes, the child wanted to scream. His mouth sank down into his throat, his throat dilated, and then his entire head sank into his throat. The mouthpiece on Monti's pipe got all chewed up.

The cabin rang with howls of laughter the next time Henri resurfaced. His flesh was boiling, but he managed to turn just enough to catch a glimpse of Billy Joe toppling into a cord of wood that was uncorded in short order. The twenty-six-ouncer he'd dropped rolled under the cot. The nugget he'd lured them with sat on a corner of the table. Feathers stuck in his curls, war paint on his face, Monti displayed more vulgarity than usual. He was drunk as a skunk. A tea bag hung from his mouth. He was acting silly to impress his audience.

"How's it going, big fella?" he inquired of Henri, scarcely interrupting his show.

Henri would have liked to answer, but he didn't have enough breath. His chest had melted under the ointment. A corkscrew tail peeked out from under the cot, where there was quite a stir going on. A hallucinated piglet was mucking up the lower walls.

In the midst of the merriment, Pictou, out of bravado, covered the nugget with his hat.

Monti's mood instantly changed. Billy Joe, full to bursting with existence and with Yukon, wasn't waiting for his reaction so much as challenging him with his unwavering spirit. Monti put his feet on the table, his forehead now just one big knot.

"I'll tell you something, Pictou... The Crolions shouldn't've won that tournament, not in a million years. Your goal never should've counted."

There was a pause three minutes long by forty years wide. Billy Joe, with no small effort, rose to his feet without putting his hat back on. Henri never would have believed you could go that long without blinking.

"Never should've counted, never counted, *never!*" Monti bawled, twisting his face.

The starlings were screeching. The sun came in through the milky windows. Crosswise in his chair, in a fairy-tale slumber, the pater had a dung fly at the corner of his mouth. Henri felt better. He promised himself he wouldn't end up like the old man. He lowered his father's eyelids, listened to him snore. He sipped the liquor left over in a broken-handled cup next to the collapsed cord of wood. His blankets were draped on his cot like a sloughed hide. *He took off,* Henri thought. Indeed, all that was left of Pictou was his hat on the corner of the table. He suddenly remembered and snatched away the hat, intending to nab the nugget. There was no nugget, there was a hockey puck bearing visible toothmarks. Henri pocketed it without really knowing why. There was no waking his father, no matter how much he shook him. He drained the cup of liquor and rolled himself up in a ball on his cot.

Not once during the entire trek back did Monti mention Billy Joe Pictou or any Eldorados somewhere back of Lancelot-de-la-Frayère. His deaf ear, his denials, his reworked versions conspired to persuade his boy that Henri himself had concocted the whole enterprise while in the grip of a fever or DTs. It did that sometimes, the brain-wrecking alcohol, after a few days. Going down the mountain, Henri wasn't happy to discover some rarely used muscles, while his father took his bearings by relying strictly on his topographic map and clues gleaned in the forest: the side on which a certain kind of rusted khaki moss grew on the aspens, the direction of big game tracks relative to coffee-coloured ponds dappled with water lilies where grey, hollow trees thrust up from the water.

"This way," Monti asserted. "We'll land smack dab at our place."

Then he crawled over the humus to estimate the freshness of the ground turned up by a creature that, to his knowledge, he alone over the years had spotted in the area. Unable to slow down on the steep forest trails full of treacherous rocks and shin-threatening roots, Henri's hunger was so great he no longer cared anymore, a blessing in these climes. What he craved was eggnog. Sugar pie. Cabbage rolls and bread pudding. Maple syrup dumplings for dessert after a generous helping of pea soup. Venison without a speck of salt. When they finally emerged from what Monti called a copse, their eyes finely hashed by the all-pervasive light, they realized they had strayed into the Canons' field.

"And if you *think* . . ." Henri shouted, his leg repeatedly pumping an imaginary brake pedal on the passenger side ever since Yannick had taken the wheel. "If you think today's Canons are nasty, that's because you never met the patriarch. I guess these days you'd call him a paranoid schizophrenic."

Onésime. Whatever flesh was left on Monti's and Henri's bones was liable to be pulverized by a musket blast just for their setting foot on his rock-strewn acreage. Anything growing there was fit to grow in purgatory.

"We'll skirt around behind the pigpen," Monti decided.

He shook his head at his map, signalling in no uncertain terms his indignation at anything so third-rate. But when they reached the back of the building, who did they come eyeball to eyeball with, kneeling in the muck? None other than that old s.o.b. Onésime in the middle of repairing a fence bashed in by a sow slightly befuddled after farrowing. Pinkish suckling pigs were rolling in the mire and oinking, you'd have thought Legion had just jumped in there. Monti's hackles rose when Onésime, wielding a crowbar and wound up to the breaking point, tilted his head as if about to charge. Henri stepped back out of his reach and upset a bucket of nails salvaged from barns. Pointing at the piglets, he said:

"They're some salty, those little creatures."

Sprawled on his bed in his underwear with adult-sized boots on his feet, Yannick turned over and over in his mind the one-liner that had immortalized Henri in the collective imagination and that Yannick had heard served up over the years at any and all occasions. He puzzled over the moral of the story. And, hey, wouldn't you know it, shopping for the conveyor rollers had taken longer than planned. So, Henri being none too fond of driving at night, they'd ended up in a very vacant riverside motel room badly in need of a paint job and unintentionally decorated in a retro style. Yannick examined the watercolour on the wall, a majestic lighthouse amid crashing waves, surrounded by seagulls soaring freely. *It's a joke,* he thought. He refused to accept his fate. Henri, once he'd showered, soon lay inert in his bed. After drinking every drop of Yukon in the mini-bar, he'd grabbed the TV remote, took a couple of minutes to figure out how it worked, and zapped Yannick's program in favour of a history show. He'd turned up the volume to make quite sure all the TVs in the neighbouring rooms were drowned out. Three seconds later, the man was asleep amid swastikas and regiments in pinpoint formation. His leftover pickled eggs were crumbling at the bottom of the jar on the nightstand. For Yannick, after that, it was good luck falling asleep with the combine harvester snoring on the pillow nearby. He began to putter around. He opened a complimentary bottle of shampoo in the bathroom, smelled it, emptied it in the bathtub. With an opera melody stuck in his head he fiddled awhile with the buttons on the strongbox. Bop, bop, bop, a bit of footwork. He shadowboxed in front of the mirror. But he quickly dropped his arms in boredom and stepped closer to his reflection to inspect his gums and pocks. Then, looking out between the slats of the blind, he admired the perfect alignment of the van he'd backed up in front of the room. Through the window the river stretched out its dark, teeming tongue, on which the motel would be set adrift if the tide kept on rising like that. With the remote wedged inside the waistband of his boxers, Yannick knew all too well that the boss, asleep in a terry cloth bathrobe steeped in stale smoke, would never notice a bottle more or less in the company books. So he in turn lined his innards with a bitter coating. And then one more bottle. The gaps in the mini-bar shelves multiplied in time with the snoring and the intermittently unscrambled scenes on Super Écran. Henri had learned to drive under the influence, and all the police in Gaspésie would wave to him when they crossed paths on the boulevard. But this here was the city. *Rimouski. Yay.* Which is why, when the red-and-blue cherrytop had lit up in the rear-view mirror earlier, the pater ordered Junior to put on his best good-boy smile while he hastily slipped the flask of homemade hooch under the Duo-Tang with his tax vouchers.

"Thought you'd promised Mama," Yannick said.

"My boy, you'll have to take my word for it. This stuff I'm drinking, it doesn't count as liquor."

The police had passed them on the right and sped away to other adventures. After that, Henri pulled over. He stepped out of the van. Without deigning to look at his son, who'd also gotten out, he tossed him the keys. The flying set of keys jingled like a glockenspiel. Even so, what a sucky day! There was nothing on TV but the infomercials his mother liked, and Yannick guzzled another bottle and grimaced and checked the label to make sure it wasn't aftershave or molten steel or something with a skull and crossbones on it. *Jägermeister* it said, under a sort of heavy-metal logo. And to think it must be midnight-swim time at the Malin…A Bible, a charred ironing table, three twisted hangers on their pole. *All your party needs, right here.* Yannick opened another bottle with his teeth—a Yukon that had miraculously survived in a hidden corner of the mini-bar—and chugged it in one go and a half in front of the watercolour vibrating on the wall above his father.

Still, it bugged him, that business with old Marcel the other day. They'd bumped into each other while hunting, on the trail of the same prey. Marcel had said to him:

"You, you've got your father's eyes."

Then he'd explained how to tell the female's droppings apart from the male's. Yannick wondered which of his two eyes this friend of the family was referring to, the brown or the blue, and it amused him to think he might have shot the hermit in the woods, with his Daniel Boone cap and his moccasins. *No one would have known.* He thought he'd finished the Yukon. Nope, not at all, there was plenty left. He was roaming around the room, shooting down all kinds of enemies with the bathroom hair dryer for a pistol, when he became paranoid about the little empty bottles everywhere. He gathered them up and crept on all fours over to his father on that excuse for a mattress. One at a time, he slipped them into the pockets of the bathrobe in which Henri had snuggled down. What were a few bottles more or less to the old man?

Henri turned on his side, calculating budgets and bids out loud, and in a flash Yannick was supine and immobile, not breathing or taking any chances. He stayed there reciting in advance the lecture with which Papa would favour him if ever he caught Yannick following his own perennial example. Yannick felt an urge to laugh at the irony of the situation, and to contain himself he tried to focus on the English program he'd accidentally turned to when he flopped down on the remote in his boxers. While the dregs of Yukon dripped into the bathrobe pocket, saturating the terry cloth, the mattress, the rug, and all the building's foundation beams, Yannick mentally replayed the earlier scene of himself parking the van. He stared at the waves rippling across the TV and waited for the programming to resume. Wave by wave, a television mantra eroded the contours of the room and the furniture. Henri's snoring was muted now, and Yannick wondered what Canadian Specialties might actually look like. He blinked. When he opened his eyes again, his father was gone. A sun twice as spectacular as the day before must have consumed the blind, because in its place was a blue rectangle where seagulls fattened on snack bar leftovers winged their way above the river. The traffic, from the sound of it, seemed to flow through the room. A bit hungover, more tired than when he'd fallen asleep, Yannick sat on the bed cross-legged, regaining his bearings. Then he came face to face with his friends. They were on TV. Before going out, his father had tuned in to the local news, the news from La Frayère. On the screen were Marie-Pierre and Kim, mopheaded. Their makeup had run. Patapon showed up, in shock, his wet T-shirt sticking to his body. In the background Marteau was beside himself because he didn't have the means to give the first responders even the slightest explanation. When Yannick finally took hold of the remote control, he raised the volume only to hear the reporter saying into a mic too large for his small noggin, his small journalism, that a rescue party was searching for Thierry Vignola. In a corner of the screen was the picture of Thierry that would end up on the milk cartons.

XI

MISMATCHED EYES

54

AT THE BOUGES', IT WAS THE MORNING OF DECEMBER 24.
Joséphine, her hair filigreed with silver, had kinfolk visiting
from as far away as the tip of L'Anse-Pleureuse and from Gros-
Morne, formerly Gros-Mâle. Lots of relatives on her side had
made the trip to celebrate Christmas Eve at the home of Mr
Lancelot-de-la-Frayère. The children were enchanted with the
big, ostentatious fir tree standing in all its imposture in a living room lit up by candles festooned with arrangements of
red berries. "Imposture" because it was in fact a spruce. Monti,
with the help of his boys, had felled the tree himself at the
edge of a nursery he'd acquired for no special reason, giving
even the youngest a turn with the axe. The tree was luxuriant
enough for the children to get lost in the woods right in the
living room. At the top, the robed angel with no naughty bits—
Henri had checked—had a twisted neck because the ceiling
was too low. Otherwise it was all very pretty, the candles, the
miscellaneous presents, the ornaments that Monti, insisting on
the real McCoy, had ordered from Germany. "That's where it
comes from, this here tradition!" he'd been saying since mid-
November. The Germans didn't have a very good reputation in
those days, but history wasn't exactly where Monti lived. The
macaroni garlands that Joséphine had her nieces and nephews

make each year, the gingerbread men the girls had forgotten in the oven—these he hid in the branches at the very back.

Outside in the soft snow, sleighs could be heard going by with their bells and the singing of folks on their way to celebrate. Folks were bundled up in their seats with woollen blankets over their knees. It was freezing cold that morning. Ice-fishing huts dotted the iced-over bay. They were cooking up a storm in the Bouges' kitchen.

"*Sehr gut!*" Monti exclaimed.

An aroma of citrus and cloves wafted up from the pot of *Glühwein* purring on the fire. Woollen stockings full of barley sugar and little toys adorned the chimney mantel. Monti had even promised to put a tiny nugget in those belonging to the children who proved the most deserving at midnight Mass. For the house was swarming with kids. Some of them had become dangerous in their rush to rip the wrapping paper off their gifts. And next! No thank yous, no nothing. The youngsters ran one behind the other all over the house, a long worm of flounces and frizz whose ringlets uncoiled in the curves.

"*Guten Morgen!*"

Monti, not the least bit angry—he just couldn't help it—*shouted* at each arriving guest. He had them go in through the back, this was important.

"There won't be anyone coming through the front door today," he said. Monti, if you did without the wet kisses and the hugs that tickled under the holly, liked the holidays just fine. Monti liked to share. Indeed, he was always giving people stuff and the others would say, "Why'd you give him that?" Yet no one knew where he disappeared to every quarter of an hour starting in the early morning, and each time he came back into the house, with the pail he'd once again gone out to empty, he would go to socialize in the living room, the boudoir, the office, which the men had instinctively taken over.

"Hey, Monti, the fun's already started, c'mon and join in!"

They were in-laws, close relatives of his wife whom he'd rarely seen, if ever. Mingling with the crowd were three or four beggars from the village who he suspected had no business being there. *Oh, well, it's Christmas!* he thought. They were breakfasting on *Glühwein,* talking smut. Soon it would be lunch, and the troop of little tots swept into the living room, split up to slip between the canes of the hazy gentlemen, and merged again into a single earthworm in the hallway.

"Hold on, sweet pea, easy, easy, I want to show you," Monti said to the passing two-year-old he'd managed to snag by the seat of the pants, who was now flailing about in the air and snivelling.

Monti held him out at arm's length to make sure this was one of his own.

"Everybody, I ... Could I have your attention, folks."

The conversations trailed off, and while Monti ran his fingers through his catch's hair, not really knowing how you're supposed to hold a child, the boozy gazes converged on him.

"Yes, well, anyway, all right, thanks everybody, eh, for being here with us in our home. Much appreciated. I ... I won't be making a long speech, now. I wanted you to meet my little boy Léon, right here, he's my fourth, he just turned two ..."

"Your fifth!" piped up Siméon Bujold, the pharmacist and Joséphine's brother, who had one leg shorter than the other.

Everyone laughed at the mistake. The ladle never touched the bottom of the bowl of *Glühwein.* Someone was always looking for his glass somewhere. Monti found his on the side table where he'd mislaid it. He perched Léon on his hip to free up his hand.

"Yes, one, two, three, yup, you're right, Siméon m' friend, he's my fifth ..."

"I'm his godfather!" Siméon added, pleased with his wisecrack, and slapped Monti on the back just as he was taking a sip.

"Ha-ha, yup," Monti said, trying to dislodge what had suddenly got stuck in his nose. "Sooo, anyhow, I wanted to let you know that my little Léon right here, he'll be the baby Jesus in the Nativity t'night at the church. And, well, I'm mighty proud, and now we're gonna ... Is that right, Siméon? Are you the godfather?"

By dint of much squirming, Léon managed to wriggle out of his father's grasp. Monti, at any rate, wasn't too sure anymore where he was going with his rigmarole.

"Hot to trot, our horny little hare is hot to trot," the obligatory life-of-the-party murmured, lewdly demonstrating with his pelvis. "One, two, three, four, *five!*"

With his Neronian eyes, Dr Bujold, Monti's father-in-law, cut the joker a venomous look. He knew the man well. And he knew exactly where his next injection would go.

"A real fine family, Monti, my friend, and it does us right proud too!" someone said.

Monti turned away to blow his nose. A clove quivered amid the secretions in his table napkin. Carrying his bucket, he'd slipped away once again to add another sheet of water to the front porch steps when Henri alerted him from the top of the stairs:

"He's coming, Papa! He's coming!"

Henri, minus a few milk teeth, must have been six or seven years old. Red and roiled faces swung around in his direction.

"Well, well," Monti said, as if momentarily lost in thought. "Who?"

"Who's coming?"

The living room windows looked out over the front lawn while affording a view of the porch stairs. Henri's announcement sparked a commotion. Everything went topsy-turvy. Monti hastily assembled his guests, whistling with two fingers like you do when your dogs won't listen. He picked up athletes three times his weight in order to get all his people into position. Everyone was soon stationed by the windows. Toine, who'd initially been assigned the task, had Henri bring the paternal armchair to ringside.

"Now that's what I like to see," a great-aunt gushed. "Obliging boys!"

Some in the crowd were acting smart-alecky. No one listened to anyone else.

"Ah, that's my Henri," Monti replied to the wrong aunt. "He's my cleverest, but he's also the one who'll give us the most trouble!"

The group was starting to wonder what sort of entertainment lay in store for them, Joséphine included. Ensconced like a viscount in his Voltaire chair, Monti relished the disaster in the making. He was already laughing even though nothing had happened yet. His wife, worried about the state he'd be in come suppertime, tried to take the cup of *Glühwein* from his hands. But Monti was stronger than her.

"What are we—"

"Shush!"

Settled in his armchair, tightly crossing his legs to keep from pissing himself, Monti laughed so hard the laughter spread around him by contagion. And that's when they saw.

"Over there, isn't that someone coming this way?"

"Yes!"

From his lookout on the upper floor Henri had recognized Victor Bradley as soon as the tip of a musical bonnet appeared at the bend in the road.

"Wouldn't that be the mailman, there?"

"*Yes!*"

The postal service incarnate emerged in all its splendour from behind the trees, black and spidery against the pale sky, that rimmed the Bouge seigneury to the west.

"Saint Nicholas looks a sorry sight this year!" said Monti, laughing fit to bust. His relatives, not so much.

Monti had an evil glint in his eye. The Paspyjack made his way, but not along the lane. He cut across the lawn, non-negotiable, even if it meant snow up to his hips.

"Miser!" Monti raged. "Squabbler!"

He laughed and fumed at the same time. Bradley wore the red bonnet with white fur fringe and bell-tipped white pompom the children knew for having admired it in pictures in their Advent calendar. But the ginger beard spoiled his disguise.

"This isn't Ireland, by Jove!"

Bradley couldn't hear Monti. He was too far away. But the jury of guests inside heard him.

"You're no *Viking,* you're a mail . . ."

The end of the sentence skidded to a cough, but no sooner had Monti finished coughing than he had a big fat Havana between his lips. Alongside the arbour, Bradley noticed he was being watched. He squinted to see who was inside there in the living room.

"Your mailman can't possibly be at work on the mornin' of the twenty-fourth, can he?" someone asked.

"No, no," Monti said, puffing on his cigar. "He's bringing the gift that's my due."

Then Bradley spied the entire company behind the garlanded windowpanes. He stopped frowning. His face twisted by a smile that entirely swallowed up his cheeks, he started waving a bottle of Yukon in the brittle cold air. Certain of stealing the show, as he now was close enough to hear the laughter, the mailman approached the house. He flexed his biceps, doing a few somewhat rustic dance steps. Here, just as Joséphine realized why her husband had come to bother them in the kitchen while he filled his bucket with water about eighty-eight times, Bradley, striding over the first two, set foot on the third stair of the porch.

The veranda stairway was coated with blue ice.

Bradley executed a beaut of a figure skating move and still somehow made an *attempt* to get back up without anyone noticing he'd just been killed. Monti was tired, so tired in his armchair that he didn't have the muscle tone needed to applaud. Unable to find his cup, he borrowed a nearby grand-uncle's glass of *Glühwein* to drink to his health.

"Spoiling for a fight, are ya?" he challenged the Paspyjack.

The bonnet bell jingled enough to make the air crumble. Little Lucie buried her face in her mother's skirt. Monti scooped the last drop of tannin from the bottom of his glass and sucked his finger. Even Baptiste, Toine, and Henri, old enough to know that a Bradley deserved nothing but scorn, were shaken by the scene. The mailbox. The ice. The persistence. All of Paspébiac's honour rested on the mailman's shoulders.

"Come on, come on, climb those stairs, Victor my boy!" Monti shouted again.

His limbs went limp in his armchair. Bradley had adopted the position of a lamb learning to walk. The bottle of Yukon, the belongings fallen from his pockets, everything slid over the ice around the mailman. Looking calm and focused now, he drifted on all fours. *You're pretty in red,* Monti thought, casting a cautious glance at his better half. When, in an improbable stunt that produced the loud clack of a pair of claves, making the audience turn their heads away, Bradley finally managed to grasp the iron handrail—a bad idea—straining all his muscles not to do the splits between two stairs and be sundered from his crotch to his well-nigh-unhinged chin, Joséphine closed the curtains with a definitive tug. Chewing on the utterly disgusting tip of his cigar, Monti rolled his eyes. People moved away from him, muttering indignantly. Bradley was heard howling outside as he yanked his hand away from the freezing metal.

A few munchers were nibbling at the buffet without much appetite. There was enough chow to feed an army.

"Mr Mayor, Madame," Monti said later in the afternoon when Pleau and his missus arrived. "Come in, come in! The door! We're glad to have you for Christmas Eve, bring your people inside."

Mayor Pleau made the introductions. He'd come with a few relations belonging to his inner business circle, straight away consigned to the "doll" category by Monti. He figured the one with the moustache and the good-looking lad must be the potential investors of whom the mayor had said Monti wouldn't need to twist their arms to sell them the project he was concocting. Joséphine pretended everything was fine, that her husband didn't smell like a tavern when the sun hadn't even finished setting. She collected the coats and went to put them on the bed. Monti had told her about the project. A library, in the village, could never be feasible without the mayor's involvement. Her lips twisting in every direction, Joséphine received the newcomers with a maniac surfeit of kindness. The fingers of one of the guests were busy at the living room piano and people wanted to dance.

"Sing, sing," the lady encouraged them over the long strings of frolicking notes.

Having pride of place on a baroque sideboard at the back of the hall, the bottle of Yukon that Bradley, with help, had finally succeeded in delivering stood untouched.

"Now, Honoré…" Mayor Pleau whispered to an increasingly histrionic Monti. "You're aware that there's an armchair in your front yard?"

"An *armchair?*" Monti answered with a clumsy show of stupefaction, handed the mayor a glass of Chartreuse—that's what was going around now—and escorted him into the hubbub.

What had happened was that after the accident Joséphine had invited Victor Bradley into the house so he could recover and relax. That, historically speaking, was a first. What's worse, being a good Christian, she had served him a Yukon, saying he'd worked so hard for it.

"This should warm you up," she said.

But the mailman, with a bump on his forehead and a skinned hand, abstained. Joséphine insisted. Bradley repeated no, point-blank. On the other hand, he might have a taste of *Glühwein*. Sitting in the armchair in the hall, he swilled a few cups of warm wine, peeking on the sly through the doorways of the adjacent rooms. He voiced his little arrogant "harrumphs" to signify the decorations weren't all that great, in his opinion. He finally left, and Monti descended from the corner of the ceiling where he'd wedged himself the whole time using only the pressure of his extremities. Drumming his fingers on the back of the armchair Bradley had occupied, he signalled to Henri to open the front door. Then he, as they say, heaved the damn chair with all his might. The piece of furniture dropped into the snow with a muffled little poof.

The festivities got into full swing again. Monti always felt such circumstances were just right for making big deals. He signalled once more to Mayor Pleau, half-seated in the Christmas tree, to round up all his moustache wearers and good-looking lads and follow him. After the armchair-heaving episode, he expressed himself mainly through signs. It was all hush-hush because he'd promised Joséphine to put a lid on business if they had guests on the twenty-fourth. The mayor and friends followed their host. Inattentive, not to mention tight, Pleau entered the study thinking this was where the meeting would take place. Well, no. They exited the room as though leaving a labyrinth. Monti, with no explanation, ushered them on tip-toes through the cellar. He lent them his own boots and some old coats. Then he pushed open the bulkhead door leading outside and guided the suckers through the snow to his barn.

The animals were going crazy in their boxes. From a padded chest, a luxury piece now filled with hay, Monti drew out a jug of his brain-wrecking alcohol. The good-looking lad, his chin curled into a cedilla, took a slug and immediately started giggling. It tasted as if he'd chomped on a piece of iron. One shot of the booze and the mustachioed fellow's right eye opened wider than the left.

Mayor Pleau took the floor. But after his turn with the jug he had to outdo himself not to lose his train of thought. He essentially set out the grand project with which a prophet must have entrusted Monti, one that would allow them to profit from the region's resort activity. Monti fixed him with a keen, devilish stare. Their lips moved simultaneously, a ventriloquist and his dummy. The moustache and the good-looking lad listened, drank, tried to listen, drank some more, stopped listening, went off on a tangent. Each time the mayor sought the approval of his "associate," as he called Monti, some good words to corroborate his own, Monti confined himself to taking a long, hammering swig from the jug.

"So whereabouts do you envisage it, this cable car?" asked the moustache wearer.

He had to look for something to hold on to. *Envisage,* Monti noted. He still hadn't said a word.

"The installations would be based at the quarry that my associate here has acquired on the point behind the rail depot."

"You don't mean in the *hole,* do you?" the good-looking lad belched, momentarily distracted by Monti, who all at once had shaped his hands into a telescope to follow something through the window.

The hole, yes. Clearing of throats. No one would ever dare laugh in his face, but behind his back Monti sure as heck was called senile after he'd signed a cheque with a few too many zeros for the aforementioned lot. A spot at the foot of the mountain, unfit for development. It abutted the road leading to the sea, so the private sector had quarried it for the rocks and sand needed to build the system of dunes and breakwaters that would protect the new seaside promenade. Nothing was left on the site but a pothole, the aftermath of concerted shelling. Youngsters would go there to shoot muskrats. But in Monti's head it was: sea and mountain plus access road equals a whole host of possibilities. A cable car, ladies and gentlemen. This was his grand project. Even so, Pleau's buddies' eagerness suddenly shrivelled up. "The hole, the hole," they said. The opulence went stiff inside their clothes.

"I don't in any way wish to discomfort you," said the moustache, "but it so happens your property has no ground on which to put your cable car."

Monti noted *to discomfort*.

"We need two months to prepare the ground," said Pleau, one arm stretched out to hold up the walls he sensed were about to cave in.

He explained that Monti had foreseen this sort of objection, which is why he'd arranged with the company in charge of any and all excavation work in the environs to have them dispose of the numerous mounds of earth—up to a quantity set by contract and duly compensated—resulting perforce from the expansion of the water supply network.

"Huh? Say what?"

"Simply put, they scoop up the piles of earth lying around everywhere for a fee, and fill the hole. So the ground practically pays for itself. After that, you shore up the sides and presto! A cable car! Well-maintained footpaths! Lookout points. Ski trails."

"Okay, okay, okay," said the good-looking lad as he started to get it.

"Honoré!" Joséphine called out through the kitchen fanlight.

"To the Lancelot-de-la-Frayère cable car!" said the moustache, and raised the jug. "It seems to me we here are going to be rich!"

Mayor Pleau had an urge to shed a tear. What was taking place was so very important. There were awkward handshakes all around.

"*Honoré!*"

"Looks like your wife is asking for you, Monti my friend."

They made their analgesic way out of the barn and back toward the house. Little ones were drawing with their fingers on the condensation-coated windowpanes.

"Everyone wins with projects like this," said Pleau.

"What's more, we'll create jobs!" the moustache enthused.

"I've been thinking about that," Monti said. "We ought to launch a raid in NB, a kind of safari, nab ourselves some slaves."

That was the only thing he said during their entire huddle. "Envisage," "discomfort." He was too canny to let that pass. Filled with shame about his origins, without even knowing why, the moustache lowered his eyes. At his feet were scads of sunflower seed husks. They were falling from the bird feeder onto the snow.

The squad of debauchees went in through the kitchen door, and Joséphine had second thoughts on seeing her husband's condition, as Monti cracked even more when he leaned against the oven, its sides near the melting point. But the woman had no other choice. The commitments she'd made to the priest predominated.

"Now," she said to Monti, "the children and I, we're going over to the church to help set up the Nativity. The bishop has arrived and Father Isidore must be at sixes and sevens. Supper's ready, just need to take everything out after Mass."

Including the magnums of champagne, thought Monti.

"All told there will be about forty of us, if I'm not mistaken. Léon's still napping, but he's already in his Jesus costume. Give him his bottle when you wake him, say, around eleven twenty, and be sure to get to the church by a quarter to midnight. And, oh, speaking of bottles. Maybe it's time you switched to milk too."

Expectations for that year's midnight Mass were even higher than usual, because the last time the *curé* had stepped aside in favour of the bishop . . . that had really been something. Onésime Canon, in the midst of a breakdown, had crossed himself when he saw the clergyman appear in the nave, with his purple robe, its echoing swish, his totem-pole helmet. Sicotte and Skelling at one point were unable to stifle their peals of laughter. Sitting in the back, they started to act like cardinals, sprinkling Mrs Dubuc with holy water. The bishop, with his kitchen Latin, had to rein them in, but no sooner had things begun to calm down than Onésime—God knows what he was imagining—decided something had to be done. "Shut those doors tight!" he belched. "Take it alive, the big purple critter!"

"Lemme tell you, the parish once again made a great impression," Monti recollected out loud as he stuffed his face with tourtière despite the prohibition.

Soon after his family left, he sat down at the table with the other men, total strangers, to while away the remaining hours with a few hands of whist. The mustachioed fellow was there.

They played for money and guzzled tonics. Bujold the pharmacist came back from his snooze on the corridor floor with, in one hand, a tall, shaky stack of enough glasses for everyone and, in the other, the bottle of Yukon from the sideboard in the hall. Monti was quick to put his finger in the most generously poured glass, thus lending more authority to his claim on it.

"Prost!" he cried over the clutter of playing cards.

Dentures were tilted toward glasses under the holly branches. A number of dry heaves punctuated the awkward silence. The moustache spat his mouthful of Yukon into his palm and hid the mess in his pocket. Meanwhile, a very mellow Monti poured himself another. In the thirteen distant cards he'd just been dealt, he held fabulous full houses, straights that stretched from his home to the buoys off the marina. As far as Monti was concerned, he now was playing poker, too far gone to distinguish the taste of liquor from the taste of piss.

The story went around from Cloridorme to Saint-Zénon-du-Lac-Humqui. A couple of weeks earlier Monti had scored a point against the mailman by forcing Bradley to turn back in front of his house before ever reaching the letter box. Standing at the oeil-de-boeuf in his attic, Monti flung tools at the Paspyjack's feet. He never would have hurt him—he needed Bradley too much—but the mailman nevertheless thought it prudent to turn around. He didn't feel like winding up with a screwdriver stuck between the eyes.

When they crossed paths again at the hotel that evening, Monti sat down at the bar next to his buddy Bradley. *His* Bradley. His very own. Their dispute, you see, wasn't founded on some trifle, and they were able to sit together. Soused from top to bottom, his back bent over the counter, Bradley began to rub the last bottle of mead Mrs Guité would be serving him that day. He was going to rub it until an amenable jinni popped out and fulfilled the sinister wishes he'd been mentally formulating in an invented language since the afternoon. His neck looked just like that pipe under a sink. There was the letter he hadn't been able to deliver to the Bouges. Before him on the counter. All he had to do was to slide the envelope over to Monti. That would've settled it. He couldn't bring himself to do it.

"That dead letter isn't about to be laid to rest," people said.

On the night before Christmas Eve the mailman had dreamed he was making his rounds when he realized he was buff naked in the middle of the village. He dreamed more and more as he grew older, but for once the English voice wasn't in this particular dream, nor was the spinning wheel. To shield his modesty, which never occurred to him to do during the day, he grabbed everything within reach, half in his dream, half in the real world. The sandwich board in front of the ice cream parlour, the shawl of his latest conquest. His phantom fingers ached unbearably when he awoke, and he made doubly sure he was dressed before heading off to work. Mr Berthelot, wearing a plaid smock that made him look like bagpipes, was shovelling the snow off his roof.

"It won't be caving in like two winters ago, no siree."

"Hey, was I talking to you?" Bradley said.

He barged into the building without closing the door—not part of the job—behind him.

"We ain't open today," said Mrs Berthelot, who was busy changing the labels on expired items.

Through the invoices the draft sent floating above the counter, she saw it was Bradley.

"Sakes alive, Victor, surely y' can't be workin' on the twenty-fourth of December?"

Bradley stopped short. *Is it the twenty-fourth, then?* Talk about an excellent bit of news. A holiday. But he couldn't possibly admit to being off base, so he went anyway to the nook where the mail came to rest.

"No, no," he shouted as he climbed up the boxes. "I'm not working. Something I needed to check and since I was in the neighbourhood..."

And, besides, mind your own beeswax. He applauded himself for his procrastination when he caught sight of all the late parcels the Frayois youngsters wouldn't have the pleasure of unwrapping after midnight Mass. Monti had received his weekly package, and seeing the coast was clear for once, Bradley decided to give himself a Christmas treat. He ripped open the box and uncorked the Yukon. He drank to his heart's content and got plastered. "To his heart's *con*-tent," is how that phrase goes. At least that's what he'd once affirmed to the editor of the *Vivier*. After that, putting one hand in front of the other, then hand over hand another couple of times, like when you slacken a rope, he fished out, amid stomach-turning fumes, his dick from his fly. A slimy member as muscular as an eel, which half the village had already seen because Bradley had the charming habit of marking his territory anywhere at all. His sphincter relaxed and with a sigh of relief Bradley refilled the bottle. Then, after roughly resealing it, he gave the concoction a few shakes. And off to Monti's. As he left the store, he threw into his pouch a handful of unpaid-for sweets.

Back at the party, the whist players must have been too afraid of provoking their host's ire to say anything.

"Where might my mittens be?" they said, eager to leave the table.

"My toque, my furs?"

The first ones to get outside ate pieces of snow to wash away the bitter taste left in their mouths by drinking the mailman's water. Siméon Bujold, out of pity for his brother-in-law, sat back down next to him on the pretext of shoeing up for the Mass. One of his boots was built up to compensate for his short leg. Monti poured himself another piss-and-Yukon cocktail. Bujold felt bad, not knowing what to say.

"Look who's here," said Monti.

With a lingering smile on his lips, he stared at a spot farther down the corridor.

"Who is it? Who's there?" asked Siméon.

He followed Monti's gaze to the far end of the corridor, but that's all he saw: the far end of the corridor.

"Come on, my bitty-beast," Monti called out, and patted his thigh.

He's starting to look more like a drunk than a guy who drinks, the brother-in-law thought, darkening. He wrapped himself up in his scarf. Léon was awake. His father had had the child brought to him to be mummified in his swaddling clothes. He rubbed gin on his mouth while he himself drained the glasses of Yukon abandoned amid the jumbled cards. He re-corked the bottle, which disappeared into his reefer jacket.

"Go on," he said. "We'll join you shortly."

He drove the stragglers away with kicks to their behinds. Now he was alone in his house with his son, his shotgun over the fireplace, his personalized beast. He'd decided it was time: time to kill it.

The folks of the *guignolée* charity drive were the ones who found Monti the next day in an overheated cabin of Gesgapegiag. His butt parked on an upside-down pail, shotgun over his shoulder, and the Messiah in his arms, he'd spent the Christmas Eve celebrations on the Mi'kmaq reserve binge-drinking Bradley's piss. Apparently, come morning, he was still bugging whoever was around to go find a certain Billy Joe Pictou. He needed to see him, really needed to see him.

55

THE *VIVIER* PHOTOGRAPHER STOOD STOCK-STILL behind the camera perched on its heron-legged tripod. The Lancelot-de-la-Frayère library was being inaugurated that day, and the people involved were gathered around Monti for a group picture. Monti wasn't smiling. Against the red ribbon stretched in front of the counter he held open a filthy pair of shears that someone at the last minute had hastily borrowed from a neighbour's garden, without permission, on the long-standing but increasingly neglected principle that if it was outside, it belonged to everyone, so long as you returned it afterwards. The photographer took the shot and the click continued to click in the air, clicks within clicks, because the shelves were still too bare and the building's acoustics were crappy from the start. The shears crunched and the ribbon flopped down on either side of the counter. Monti examined the books to make sure the flash hadn't imprinted his shadow on the spines. The photographer, wearing glasses fixed with adhesive tape, realized he'd forgotten to remove the lens cap. Hugs and congratulations were dispensed with. The participants hung around, not quite knowing what to do with themselves while they waited for refreshments. Monti felt someone brushing against his side and, tucking his arms in, turned around to see who was tickling him like that. No one there. He did an about-face, and there was the new mayor-elect, what's-his-name Fortin.

"I was looking for you," Monti said.

"We're up next," Fortin answered.

Despite being twice Fortin's age, Monti shook his hand, once, and a sine wave rippled all the way up to the man's shoulder blade. Outside, curvy, gleaming automobiles were parked higgledy-piggledy on the lawn. Another flash out of nowhere made Monti shield his head with the forearm on which he'd hooked his umbrella. He dropped the shears. They lay on the floor, a hazard for the little ones, who'd been promised a bit of fun after the formal proceedings, which the adults also found tedious. Henri was busy inside the hall. His adolescent sloth had dissolved forever with the development of his testicles. He was finishing up the installation of the dais along with other cheerful fellows less naturally inclined to find pleasure in exertion. While he worked, he talked music with his friend Marcel. Marcel, for his part, was being helped in setting out the folding chairs by young Léon's two hundred and fifty pounds of muscle. The Frayois of the more liberal professions rushed over to reserve themselves a seat by placing a personal item on it.

"Come on, Papa," whispered Lucie, one of Monti's daughters.

She entwined her arm in her father's. He was burdened by the weight of an elegant boater with a shiny silk band. Joining her sister and father, Charline, a young woman in full bloom, was delighted at Monti's scant resistance when they steered him outdoors.

"It will be your turn to speak after the mayor," she said.

She wetted her finger to wipe the dried tomato juice from the corners of her father's lips.

"Do you really need your umbrella?"

Once outside, Monti tossed the umbrella. On the roof of the building. The sun beat down. Looking very chalk-white in the sunshine, Honoré Bouge could not stop chuckling. With its high collar and long sleeves, no skin peeking out, Lucie's dress tickled him to death. He walked quickly, and his daughters could barely keep up through the maze of cars, some of which were going to be a pain to get out of the parking lot mess.

"And your speech, do you have it? Papa, you have your speech?"

Monti set about telling his daughters how proud he was of them. Quite the ladies they'd become.

"Never mind the compliments, it's your turn today."

"Well, well, Monti, my friend, nice companions you've got there," the notary Langevin called out to him from his car.

Indeed, Monti was escorted by the most attractive matches on the peninsula. He gave the notary a hostile wave in return.

"Anyway, that girl Lucie, if I were two-three years younger," over-the-hill Rémi Chiasson muttered behind them.

He was thirty-five years older than her. Monti wasn't laughing anymore. Not at all. His tickles had just been cut short.

"Quite the ladies!" he repeated loudly over his shoulder, with an urge to whip out his sword cane, but he'd lost it ages ago.

The tops of his shoes were dragging through the grass now. Charline and Lucie ushered him alongside the library toward the staff entrance. Chiasson's youngest had just given birth, and the infant looked so much like the old man that people were wondering if he wasn't both the father and grandfather.

"We two are going to hurry inside to help Mother with the children," Lucie said, entrusting Monti to her brothers.

They were smoking on the doorstep, having secreted the

bottle of Yukon they'd been passing around a second ago. Baptiste, as he did at every formal occasion since returning from across the pond, was wearing his decorations. Toine wore the suit on which he'd spilled some plonk at Dr Bujold's funeral. All three of them, Monti and his boys, went in. Hidden behind a tasselled serge curtain, they spied on Mayor Fortin. The mayor had mistaken a pat on the derrière for his cue and prematurely began to shower himself with praise on the dais in front of practically empty chairs. Squeezing each of them on the nape of the neck, Monti demanded his sons give him something for what he'd decided was stage fright. They pretended not to understand.

"It's not a suggestion," he insisted.

Toine and Baptiste looked at each other. They knew what this day meant to their mother. The rest of the Yukon was shared three ways.

"The municipality has truly thrived since the change of administration," Mayor Fortin reiterated for the fourth time, in different words, on his dais, "and we would be remiss in this address were we not to adequately and amply thank Mr Honoré Bouge for the devotion he has always displayed in keeping with his consideration for the community of Lancelot-de-la-Frayère."

At the front entrance Charline invited the townsfolk to proceed to the main hall for the speeches. Henri and Marcel were bringing the buffet from the locker room. Grumbling between the rows of chairs, Mrs Blanchard, an octogenarian, looked for Joséphine, whom she worshipped but who didn't have the time right then to attend to her. Chunks of Fortin's blather were lost in the disturbances and preparations.

"It is my great honour today to inaugurate a building, and also the collection of books that goes with it, all for the towns-people's edifification, sorry, efidication. We will become more cultivated for it, and perhaps you'll think of me at election time in six months."

Those in the front rows laughed, thinking this was meant as humour. It wasn't, and the mayor adopted a more pompous pose, which he'd practised in his living room the day before. Joséphine and Lucie hurriedly got the kids sitting on cushions in a semicircle between the first row of chairs and the dais. They bent down so as not to block anyone's view.

"But jokes aside," Mayor Fortin went on, a hint of touchiness in his voice. "Without the generosity, as I was saying, and the opportunities the town has always extended to Monti Bouge for him to invest here, because today we certainly won't shy away from calling him Monti…My friend, my associate. Hey, I see you there, Monti, I see you. Sooo then, there it is, we at city hall, we're going…"

A slight detail the mayor had omitted from his speech was that the town owed the library almost entirely to Joséphine. It was her project, but she wasn't one to complain about going unmentioned. She took a seat to Father Isidore's right. Spilling from the priest's unbuttoned shirt was a thick salt-and-pepper growth on a chest the colour of blond wood. Monti lifted his knees high as he walked between the children toward the dais, where the mayor was endlessly concluding, all the while saying "in conclusion." His wife, sitting in the hall, signalled to him with throat-cutting gestures.

"And who might you belong to?" Monti whispered to a little girl on her knees.

"To a Bouge, Granddad."

"Oh, of course, for heaven's sake, sorry, sweetie. Are you Baptiste's or Toine's?"

It wasn't that Monti's faculties were on the wane. But he always had too much going on in his head. And the family's proliferation, he followed that at a distance.

"Are you going to buy us our horse?" the little girl inquired. "You said you were going to buy us a horse."

"Monti, thank you," the mayor concluded, "thank you, let's give him a round of applause. Thanks to both of us. In conclusion, I'd simply like to add one thing."

Fortin was off again. Monti's foot whistled past his ear when, in a whirl of faces, he mounted the three steps of the dais in a single stride. Joséphine had asked him earlier, "Are you nervous, my friend?" Monti had replied by asking her if the horse was hitched up. She was the nervous one after that. Not for herself, but for her husband. First, because, though they hadn't had a horse for eons, the scribbler from the *Vivier* next to them jotted it down in his notepad. Second, Monti once again had slept in the hay in the barn a few nights previous. Everything else, the foul-ups, the people's bewilderment, the snags, Joséphine would always laugh about. Never in her life would she be ashamed of her husband.

Fortin would have liked to exit with a bit of prestidigitation, to fly over the assembly, up to the skylights, in a hidden harness, and sail away to the ether and fame. But he was simply pushed aside. Monti took the floor thinking this would be the ideal moment to own up to his shortcomings. In the tumult, the front door opened without anyone noticing. The latecomer summoned the buffet to come to him. Unbelievable, the acoustics in that hall. Amid the amplified rustling of papers, Monti unfolded a speech full of holes. He'd drafted it on his precious typewriter with several keys missing. Toine and Baptiste, leaning with arms folded and one foot flat against the wall, were talking rather loudly. There was never a dull moment for Joséphine with her men. From where she sat, she could almost smell the Yukon on her spouse's breath. Casting an accusing eye at his compatriots, Monti took a long time to begin.

"To be here today, in the company of my better half, is for me..."

At this point, from the back of the hall by the buffet, came a mighty slurp. Something would have to be done about the acoustics—this just wouldn't do. The slurp reverberated through the skein of ceiling beams. The hats in the room swivelled one hundred and eighty degrees toward the back. Find the intruder. Holding a crustless, triangular sandwich in one hand, Bradley was tasting the punch straight from the ladle. He scanned the audience out of the corner of his brazenly blue and magnified eye. The dais creaked under Monti's over-polished shoes. He straightened his stack of pages with little taps on the lectern.

"My fellow Frayois," he resumed. "This is an occasion for my wife and me to celebrate..."

The reverberations of the second slurp were even more powerful. People booed the mailman. Stretching out his ten fingers, Monti inhaled until there was no air left in the hall for the others.

"Have I ever told you the story of the bitty-beast?" he asked once the wave of protests had died down.

He stepped away from the lectern and sat himself down on the edge of the dais near the little ones seated in front of him. Among them were his Baptiste's blondies, his Toine's swarthy nipper, Nault's lassie, an assortment of cherubs, tots, and tykes. Marcel gave Henri a nudge and stepped closer to listen. The parents were forever telling their progeny not to pester Mr Monti about his adventures of yore because he didn't like talking about them. So more than a few were caught off guard by the story he related that day, miming and seamlessly conjuring up evocative settings with simple props gleaned from the gentlemen's fobs, the surrounding heads, the attire of several representatives of the gentle sex, and by enlisting the children's participation, forcibly for some, but at least he was entertaining, this man who for them had always been connected to the grown-up world with every hair of his body. He recounted that once, in the North, he'd sat at a table with three buddy-buddies. His buddy-buddies came from a foreign country. While the four of them were drinking root beer and eating snow-filled jelly beans, the idea of playing cards occurred to them. Now, children learn by playing, but at one point, probably because of all the sugar being consumed deep in their brains, the game they were playing became very dangerous, and in a flash Monti's three buddy-buddies turned twenty-eight years older. They didn't feel like playing anymore and wanted Monti to give them back the little bits of themselves that he'd cut off. As for Monti, he hadn't finished playing, and since he was the only one who spoke good French, the decision was his. He said okay. One last round for kicks. And then something fantastic happened to the cards. Four royal flushes. With the very first hand.

"And that," Monti said, "four royal flushes with the very first hand, is as if your schoolmistress were to swallow her chalk and start strutting on your desks like a hen in the middle of the arithmetic lesson."

In the castle where they'd gathered to play, there were lots of fireworks. Everybody got so worked up that a supernatural beast arose amid the root beer, the jelly beans, and the enchanted cards. The beast looked like a ball of candy floss with all the flavours. Yet it ran terribly fast, and you surely had to be very special to see it, because no one but Monti went chasing after it.

"I was jubilant!" he said to his Joséphine.

She gave him a loving look, telling herself that anyway the library wasn't about to crumble because of a breach of protocol.

Monti described how he'd dashed off in all directions at once. One of his legs raced that way along a crest. The other took a shortcut through the woods. His arms hopped along on their hands. Whenever the beast got too far ahead of him, it stopped and waited. It gambolled in the luminescent trails left as if in plankton-rich waters each time it wagged its tail. Then it actually frolicked in water, leading Monti to a half-frozen river he plunged into without feeling a thing, so great was his urge to cuddle it.

"The beast turned smooth as an otter as it swam along the bank, its fur was like a magic magnifying glass where I could see the seams of gold running through the ground, and I realized this was where I had to come back the next day to dig for my fortune."

It took a good hour to tell the story. In the end it was Liette Nault, a doe-eyed three-and-a-half-year-old, who asked whether or not he'd caught his bitty-beast. She filled the gaps between her words with guttural syllables. Monti asked a nearby interpreter to translate her question.

"I did capture it, yes. But just the once, and then it ran away. And now, children, listen up."

The billfold he kept in his jacket appeared in his hand and, presto, now the bills were dancing in his other hand. A tidy sum. Monti rubbed the corners of his twenties to make sure there weren't two stuck together. He waved the wad under the kids' noses, saying this was what he had on hand and he would easily pay, either later or right away, if they accepted cheques, five times the amount to the boy or girl who succeeded in capturing the beast.

"Because if no one nabs it," he said, "Mr Monti's gonna blow a fuse right quick."

The money disappeared into the folds of his clothing. Immediately, little Gilles, another of Rémi Chiasson's kids, began to hatch a scheme to steal it. This same Gilles had once shattered the window of the shoe repair shop. He'd crashed into it aboard a tractor tire launched from the incipient mountain slope. His father and Dr Maturin had dared him.

Joséphine stood behind the counter for a first symbolic loan. She was touched to see that her husband, having scanned the shelves as though he needed to account for something, had opted for Homer. He'd started the Greek saga in a Toronto boarding room and was curious to see how it ended. After the book was entered on a card, Monti wedged it under his arms, between his legs, then between his jaw and shoulder, and finally wrapped his arms around his wife to the applause of the Frayois. After the punch and the line, square, dodecagonal—

whatever—dancing, the event drifted over to the hotel. The men tried to contain their spouses' disgruntlement. Guité had just brewed another batch of his famous beet beer, they said. If you drank enough of it, you could see into the future.

Mrs Guité of the hotel, God rest her soul, was in heaven now, serving their usual beverage to the dead whom she'd loved when they were alive. Her nephew had taken over the establishment, and Monti showed up there holding the punch bowl in front of his stomach. The punch splashed everywhere when the new swinging door slapped him on the back. A red hair was discovered in the first glass he poured himself. The party was on, a huge crowd, old and young alike, palling around regardless of age. Henri was there too, in his beige coat with the sheepskin collar and a toque rolled above his ears. Though he wasn't about to start bawling over it, it bugged him to see his old father there so late. Monti was telling one of his favourite anecdotes about Léon, the time he'd sent him to work in New Brunswick to smarten him up. The labourers were hauling two bags of cement at a time. But Léon was strong enough to load three of them on his shoulder. After a few trips, the foreman must have told himself this Quebecer was going to wear himself out, because every time Léon passed by him, he'd shout, "Take five! Take five!" Léon didn't understand what he meant and almost dislocated the fellow's pelvis when he put him in his place. The hotel regulars split their sides laughing, but it wasn't as funny when Monti began to repeat the joke step by step to make sure everyone had really got it. Someone started in with the puck story, which by this time had Monti needing a tracheotomy for the object to be extracted with machines. The old man and Marcel went out at the same time to piss toward the gloom and the crashing breakers off the edge of the dry-rotted porch.

"Instructive, that story of yours this afternoon," Marcel said, and out streamed his piss, red from the beet beer. "Monti, this enchanted animal, would it by any chance be the same beast you caught on the train coming back from Ontario?"

The two men could scarcely make each other out in the dark. But Marcel knew, from the sound of a switch slicing the air, that Monti had just swung his head around toward him.

"You wouldn't by any chance have made me say something I don't seem to remember telling you?"

Monti's mouth sparkled in the shadows. There was a moment of truth. Marcel's spurts of piss grew more sporadic.

"What happened to the thief," he wanted to know as he gave himself a shake, "after you found him, Monti?"

"Never stole anything again," Monti said icily.

Marcel closed the beige fly of his beige trousers. The stars all rotated together overhead.

"Never again, as in never again?"

"And it's Mr Bouge from now on."

Wondering if Monti was being serious, Marcel stayed there for a minute, facing the night. *It's Mr Bouge, Mr Bouge . . .* Monti had known him since he was small. He'd even provided the initial funding for their community radio project. But if Monti was serious . . . Poor Marcel went back inside, and when the new swinging door slapped him on the back, he spilled his beet beer. Right then Guité announced there was none left.

Alone, finally, Monti was able to relieve himself of all that punch tossing him around. He never had been able to piss with another guy standing beside him.

56

PERHAPS IT WAS A WAY FOR HIM TO DENY HIS SHARE
of responsibility for the phenomenon, but Monti believed
the growing indulgence in an every-man-for-himself attitude by what claimed to be a community coincided with the
advent of the small screen in Frayois homes. The TV wasn't
so much the cause of the malady as a symptom; either way,
there was something about it that irked him. He had one of
his own—a television, that is. It was a UFO, a treated-wood
chassis mounted on chair legs, around which the entire living
room was arranged. Without even taking the time to sit down
sometimes, Monti, his features etched with a chisel, watched
the televised twaddle intensely. Which didn't mean he was for
it. Standing on what he termed "the respectable side of the
screen," he seethed at his fellow citizens' inertia, but Joséphine
cautioned him.

"Don't push our townspeople too much, they're good-
natured and that better not change," his wife said.

She added that not everyone had cable like him, then she
turned off his program because their children and their children's children had just trooped in for a Sunday visit. Gone
were the days when the couple would take their brood out to
Uncle Gédéon's.

"Stop that noise," Monti shouted when the kids were going wild in the living room. "Or you'll wake up the miniature folks napping in my TV."

There were nights—and this was true at their house—when distant neighbours would return something your father had lent their father before you were even born as an excuse to come and enjoy your picture box.

"What will it take them?" Monti fretted.

Driving through La Frayère at dusk, he saw the perfectly synchronized flashes in the windows of the more affluent houses or the homes of poor folks with misplaced priorities. Even if the town's population was mushrooming, there was more and more distance between the houses, which was why Monti disliked Mr Plouffe on Radio-Canada. Besides, he looked like Bradley, who, say what you will, had stayed quite a bit peppier than Monti on the cusp of their seventies. "It's because I fuck!" the mailman asserted, no matter where or when. He would make a spectacle of his still-uninhibited vigour before swim-suited women or, why not, Father Isidore's flock. The men of La Frayère couldn't stand him anymore. Asphalt was gaining ground on even the most gorgeous stretches of sand.

"Is it my fault?" Monti asked his wife one sleety evening.

He was jumping on their bed while Joséphine folded a sixth pair of pants all the same size, brand, and beige colour.

"Mentalities are changing," she replied.

"Or maybe I did something not right? Me, what I wanted was to build, not shut ourselves inside four walls, unfinished to boot, and watch black-and-white pixies prattling on. Everyone's me, myself, and I. Chuck a fistful of pennics on the ground in front of the shops in the daytime, you'll see!"

The laundry basket bounced at the foot of the bed.

"It's affecting your language, husband. But isn't that a bit easy for you to say? After all, you've got money. I know you had big plans for La Frayère, but—"

"Big plans, big plans. I wanted us to become a little more of what we are, that's all."

"Honoré Bouge, if La Frayère had grown at your pace, it would look like Montreal now."

"Sherbrooke."

"Rimouski."

"Matane. The problem is that myths aren't possible here anymore."

Unconcerned by either his wife's smile or the hens marching down the corridor single file, Monti stopped jumping. With a tendon bulging in his neck, he made futile gestures in an attempt to convey the precipice inside him. At moments like this he often whistled something in a panic. Music was the only thing that could express what he felt. Except this was nearly his eighth go-round with the tune—he'd forgotten how it began—and he formed a T with his hands like when you ask for a time out. He fell into an unwelcoming slumber. Gear noises escaped from his head onto the pillow. Dreams came to him of grizzlies, machine rooms, slides with nowhere to land. Monti emerged from them not rested so much as in a state of manifest neurasthenia. He was becoming not especially pleasant for anyone in his circle. His genius in those periods was applied solely to gallows humour or practical problems such as the ignition of the potato gun of which Chiasson, during the mill strike, had made a prototype to shoot at men like him. All the existential demands that Monti harboured for the village, his consuming desire to break free or to carry off sensational projects, were turning against him.

"You're disappointed," Joséphine said.

"I find it disappointing, the end of the world."

"The people here are simple, Honoré. They like to drink their own way. And I can't see what you've got to complain about, people have work, and that is what matters."

"We're each of us in our corner! And all the corners are being cut!"

One Saturday in the fall, his cute, well-shaped paunch impeccably framed by his suspenders, Monti had Henri take him back to the mountaintop where Billy Joe Pictou had guided them—badly, but anyway—ages ago. He was going up to inspect the ski centre, the one he'd built, before the new season got under way. He counted the yellow stripes in the middle of the road while Henri, a beer wedged between his thighs and paint all over his pants, tried to play up his accomplishments for the patriarch. Because things had really taken off for Henri since he'd struck out on his own. Yet, even with ten employees, even having to turn down contracts since he already had his hands full—insulating buildings, clearing snow off roofs, landscaping parks, you name it—for his father, who right then was disdainfully eyeing the daubs of paint on his pants, Henri remained one of those manual guys who were a dime a dozen in Gaspésie. Monti advised him to open a fence factory, which he thought would soon be the best way to make a buck in these parts. Or, better yet, go back to school. Coming from Monti, this was as close as it got to a compliment. Still, as much as he loved books, for Henri knowledge was something on the order of an abyss. At the same time, though, he was always lending Mr or Mrs So-And-So a helping hand. And despite his uncommon penchant for the good food and drink, no one else in the Bouge clan had the wherewithal and the drive needed to keep the house in one piece once their parents were pushing up daisies. Actually, Henri was the only one who stuck around to watch over them in their dotage, along with Léon. But Léon, well, you know.

The truck hadn't even come to a stop in front of the ski centre when Monti jumped out and scurried from one pole to the next, from the ski lift to the handrail of the ticket booth, while pointing a finger at the gables of the chalet. None of it had been repainted in spite of the horribly detailed orders given to the slackers he had no intention of paying for twiddling their thumbs. Henri, on everyone's behalf, received the lambasting peppered with bits of dialogue from the TV series *Les belles histoires des pays d'en haut.*

"Look here. It's not brain surgery, *viande à chien*. You take your can of paint. You open it. You dip your brush in it, then you coat your surface until you can't see the old colour underneath."

But, at the end of the day, having coloured splashes on your pants doesn't mean you're in charge of every paint job on the peninsula. Monti didn't give his son any contracts. That wouldn't be doing him a favour, he said. He tore flakes of paint off the ivy-smothered poles as he looked around for something to demolish.

"Well now," Joséphine said a while later when they were sitting on their porch surrounded by perennials and empty Yukon crates. "You'll have to explain to me how the average Frayois is supposed to 'transcend'—or whatever highfalutin word you prefer—when you throw fits like you did with Henri at the ski centre the other day."

"He's got a nice big trap, that Henri does," said Monti.

A piglet was asleep in his lap. His glass of alcohol stood off to the side in a slice of shadow.

"He's worried about his father, eh. He may not have gone off to war like your Baptiste, but you have to stop getting on his case all the time. Léon's the one you ought to lean on a little."

"Léon's the baby. Leave him alone."

"He'll be twenty-three soon! And the baby is Charline."

"Okay, the baby boy."

There was a pause. The slice of shadow, together with the sun, continued its slow rotation until Monti's glass gleamed in the light.

"You see," he said, "I'm the one who made this town. And I want the colour of the sea to keep matching the colour of my poles. Because it's as if a whole bunch of conditions had to come together for what was meant to happen to happen. You follow me, Joséphine? Four players show four royal flushes right off the bat, and boom. A beast pops up in the middle of a table. *That's* what I want. But on the scale of the town, understand?"

Joséphine wasn't sure if her spouse was going through a more extreme internal crisis than usual or going off his nut for good. He would sail on his stream of consciousness at ungodly hours with his beat-up typewriter. It was risky, but she had him read a slim metaphysical treatise that had solved many things for her. *Transcend, transcend. It may help him straighten out his thinking a little,* she mused. A simple booklet, as dense as iridium. What went on between Monti Bouge's ears when he read it was bizarre.

"I have an idea," he said.

Under a sky sparkling with all the stars in the universe, he got into his car. Realizing he'd inadvertently sat down in the back when, as he looked for the ignition, he poked the key into the back of the driver's seat instead, he pondered his insurer's recommendation: "You mustn't drive anymore, Mr Bouge." Monti drove off. The Cadillac was limply mirrored as it rolled past the, in his view, gaudy shop windows on Rue Principale. The electrification of the countryside had partitioned the sky with electric wires. Looking up, Monti told himself that at least there weren't price tags yet on every patch of blue. He flashed his headlights to greet an oncoming pickup with its high beams on. But because of the three-dimensional moon in the windshield he was unable to identify the person behind the wheel.

It was the pickup Péo had left behind when the cirrhosis carried him off. Even more tragic was that he'd taken his hooch recipe with him to the grave. At any rate, the keys always stayed in the truck, which could be found anywhere in town come morning. The pickup, as Péo would have wanted, was available to everyone who needed it. Young people used it to practise driving and leaving tire tracks on the wharf.

There was just one traffic light in the village of La Frayère. It was, predictably, red. Monti waited, his front wheels a hair's breadth from the line. He scanned the front of the former dry goods store, where a row of plastic mannequins now stood armless and faceless in a ready-to-wear shop. Green light. Monti couldn't keep from noticing the half-rusted propane tanks alongside the last restaurant where he still liked to go for his plate of shepherd's pie. He slowed down in front of the bowling alley parking lot. The neon sign burst like a nova on his freshly waxed hood. The good-for-nothings hanging around there,

Marlon Brando types in their twenties, hailed him when he stopped for a while to talk mutual acquaintances, good hunting spots, chrome hubcaps. With their overlong sideburns, the boys were wasting their best years propped against their bikes all night. While they talked, Monti tried to see if he might recognize a grandchild in the crowd. Tired of the Newfie jokes and especially their drinking exploits, he hit the gas, snatching along the way the flask that the ugliest among them was holding out to a friend. He drained it completely, drove around the block, and came back to fling it at the loafers. He hated nothing so much as people who romanticized the act of drinking.

"You drink to exist," he said to himself in the rear-view mirror, and headed down the Chemin du Réservoir.

He cut the engine under the overpass. As he closed the door behind him, his mysterious beast disappeared under a mound of burnt rubbish. He went the rest of the distance on foot through the underbrush, then he cut across the yards. On Mayor Fortin's balcony he wrapped his fist in his tank top and shattered one of the glass panes in the door. He reached in and opened the door without ever checking if it was locked. He then tiptoed, with an eighth note that rose higher with each step, like in the cartoons, to the refrigerator, which he half opened to shed some light. He leaned down. In the light his face was just a set of crude facets in different shades of yellow. He wanted to assess the state of his hosts' marriage. The absence of red meat and home-cooked dishes confirmed what in any case was an open secret. Everybody in La Frayère was aware that Mrs Fortin cheated on her husband.

"It bothers me that there's no sense of morality anymore," Monti confided to some leftover white rice.

He opened a beer with his lighter. Once it was empty, he put it back on a shelf and slipped another one in his pocket, then he reappeared upstairs and moved in the opposite direction from a woman's snoring that could have registered on the Richter scale. You didn't even need the rumours to realize the Fortins slept apart. It was enough to see the gentleman walking like a penguin. Gagging himself with his collar to keep from laughing, Monti ventured into the sort of darkness where you stub your toes and never saw it coming. He came to a tiny bed in the centre of a vast room, where the mayor lay in a position calculated in accordance with all the precautions taken by insomniacs. Not that he intended to wake Fortin, but Monti crouched down next to him. He began to whisper in the man's ear to sway him through suggestion.

"We're going to organize a hunting festival."

A barely audible whisper. Just enough to vibrate the eardrum. The mayor's brain, strictly through nerve impulses, would unconsciously convey the idea to the hand that signs the cheques.

"Yeah, okay," Fortin said, turning onto his back to stretch. "Got it. And you owe me a pane of glass."

Monti mistakenly dashed into a closet. He stepped out with an innocent look, as if he'd just arrived.

"I hope I didn't wake you."

"No, no, I wasn't sleeping."

"So, how's the marriage going?"

Fortin drew a corner of his blanket over some tissues.

"Peachy-keen," he sighed. "I didn't know you'd gone into marriage counselling."

Here, without Fortin being able to get a word in, Monti

set out his idea of a festival. The event would take place under a big striped tent, blue and white like the Quebec flag, and would be organized around a hunt on the mountain. It would put La Frayère on the map, and while he wasn't worried about the funding, he wouldn't mind either if the municipality were to grant him a budget.

"So that we can nab it once and for all," he said.

"For Chrissake, Monti," Fortin seethed, "I'm not the mayor anymore, haven't been for seven years. So do me a favour and go hassle Valiquette with your insanities at three in the mornin' when honest folks are in bed."

"Valiquette? I ... But ..."

"And nab what, anyway? Monti, hey, come back here, I'm talkin' to you. Nab what?"

At the far end of the corridor the tractor stopped snoring with a laryngeal implosion. In her nightie, Mrs Fortin stepped like a sleepwalker out of the master bedroom and headed for the can, never noticing the shadow flattened against the wall that slipped behind her to go lie in wait under her imperial bed. Her partial dentures swam in a glass of water on the nightstand. She came back to her adulterous sheets. She was on her way back to sleep, cut off from her surroundings by her eye mask and earplugs, when the whole bed, box spring, canopy began to shake like mad.

Monti couldn't remember where he'd left his car and wandered around until he stumbled on Péo's pickup. The keys were gone.

The reason there were so many people at the town meeting later on was the fence crisis. As usual, Monti had been spot-on in advising Henri to open a plant. It had all started with a land dispute in which the entire town soon became embroiled. The meeting centred on this and this alone. The room was packed. Monti found the crush especially unbearable, and he brandished his cane in front of him to keep the partisans of democracy at bay.

Victor Bradley was there as well. Politics was turning into a hobby of his, not since he'd retired but since he'd just about stopped working while continuing to draw his full-time wages. Not that he honoured the Frayois with his gracious presence very often, yet that day he'd apparently deemed it to be in the public interest to make a display of his knowledge in matters of zoning and real estate law.

Seeing the mailman in attendance rankled Monti more than it did the others. In situations like this Monti always dragged some of his boys along in order to harden them against boredom and to ensure his interests would be safeguarded in perpetuity after his demise. But on this occasion Léon nearly fainted even before taking the floor as his father had instructed him to do.

"Forget it, I'll do it myself," Monti chided.

Which begged the question of where Henri went hiding whenever his loquaciousness was needed. Chuckling, Monti began by telling his assembled neighbours not to take it personally. The purpose of his fence, actually, was to mark a boundary between their respective houses, his and Bradley's, a tad more than five kilometres apart. The mailman lived in the trailer park, which was expanding at an awful rate. The general mirth that ensued made short work of the land dispute, and when it was time for miscellaneous business, Monti announced that a hunting festival was to be held in La Frayère.

"A festival?" asked Ronald Pagé, garage owner and hunter by vocation, on the Bouges' blacklist since long ago for having snitched on Toine to the police when he once left the hotel with a pint too many in him for someone about to drive a plow.

Pagé was looking to take over the snowplowing contracts that would become available should Toine ever lose his permits. If your name was Bouge, you tanked up at Melançon's even if it meant a twenty-minute detour.

"A festival," Monti confirmed.

From then on it was the Mr Bouge Show. He needed only to arch his arms for his audience to envision a big tent full of tobacco smoke and activity. Then two or three tap-dance steps gave them all the urge to dance. While spelling out the word *sponsors,* s-p-a-w-n-s-o-r-s, Monti wiggled his fingers over his forehead by way of evoking hustle and bustle and the subsequent economic spinoff. It would be held during the hunting season, he said.

"With a shooting contest!"

Agapithe Guérette approved. The folks of La Frayère were all ears. Monti took his time, leaving them hanging on his every gerontic word while he uncorked his sterling silver flask to rinse his mouth and nip in the bud the laughter rising within him. *My, how it tickles,* he thought. There'd be an awful lot of grub, horseshoe throwing, plush toy prizes.

"A shooting contest!" Agapithe suggested.

His Alzheimer's wasn't getting any better.

"Yes, and potato bag races like when we were young, and mascots."

Buttered popcorn, taffy apples, pinatas chockablock with baubles and gold frills for the children.

"To give back to the region," Léon said excitedly, because right then Monti was howling with laughter.

Everyone thought it made good sense. The one exception was Victor Bradley. Of course. He'd never given anyone anything but the crabs. Even though he didn't agree, he immediately started looking for buyers for his yet-to-be-hatched chickens. He was wondering where he'd put the trophy for the rarest of preys, which he'd already practically won. It wasn't very nice, but with a sleight of hand a few rascals pretended to sever their own thumbs to make fun of his infirmity.

"I'm gonna bring yous back a wapiti!" Bradley crowed.

He was mocked left and right. Aiming at one of the jokers, the mailman pulled an invisible trigger. At the very same moment, Léon deposited on Valiquette's desk a typewritten project proposal with all the budgetary details. Certain corrections had been pencilled in here and there.

"Ain't no wapiti's been seen around here," Chiasson cried, "for must be ninety years!"

There followed a heated polemic concerning the populations of *Cervus canadensis* in the essentially boreal climate of the Gaspé Peninsula. On the basis of the schools being formed, the groupings, you could identify all sorts of demographic divisions in the herd. It amused Monti to see his fellow citizens' psychological profile revealed in this sample. In the end you had Mayor Valiquette standing next to his chair. He motioned to Bradley to come take his place up front. The mailman couldn't stop fidgeting with the bunch of keys he'd lately begun to wear on his belt.

"Must be they've got wapitis over in Paspébiac," Gabi's son Abel said.

"Yes," Monti added. "That's the name they use for what we here call a cuckoo."

He immediately flipped his lower lip over his nostrils. Rémi Chiasson burst out laughing. He licked his fingertip and touched the mailman, supposedly his friend, hissing like water on a hot skillet.

"You there, Honoré Bouge, listen up," Bradley barked over the near riot. "I'll betcha whatever y' like I'll bring yous a wapiti in the back of my pickup before this summer's end."

He threatened the backstabbers around him with his car key, wielding it like a cavalry sabre. Sitting in his chair placed slantwise in the corner, arms folded, chin thrust out, Monti looked like a boxer between rounds. Léon stood behind, not coaching but fanning him as needed, massaging his muscles.

"You don't have a pickup," said Monti, still able to put two and two together.

"If I bring yous a wapiti," the mailman went on, quickly slipping the key in question back in with the rest of his bunch, "I'm gonna head to your place one Sunday night and sit me down in *your* place and eat the supper made by *your* wife. Then with my boots on *your* footrest, I'm gonna smoke *your* tobacco whilst I watch *your* TV until *your* shows are over. Whaddyous say t' that?"

"I'll even give back your horse as a bonus!" said Monti.

Too bad there were just a few old-timers left to appreciate that zinger.

Dammit, anyway, how the years had flown.

"Never had no horse," said Bradley.

"So it'll be a bet for honour," Monti shot back.

On the one hand, Bradley owned absolutely nothing Monti might have wanted, especially since he already owned Bradley's soul as a result of a previous wager. On the other hand, what could be worse for Bradley than to lose his honour to Monti Bouge? The two sexagenarians shook hands at a distance of twenty feet. Their arms snaked through the tangle of bodies.

The town did provide the grants, but even so, the Bouge family injected a considerable portion of the funds needed for the project. The trails were cleared on the mountain and marked with an indecipherable colour code. Drains as well as chemical toilets were installed on the site, and the big tent was rented from a company in Mont-Joli, which Monti deliberately called "Mongolie" whenever he spoke to the man. They stored the tent, meantime, in a stockbreeder's warehouse under a renewable monthly lease. The carpenters were flush with lucrative contracts: erecting the bleachers, the fence, the booths. Joséphine had forced Monti to have Henri hired or at least afforded the same chance as the other bidders. "Come on," Henri said to Liette Nault, aged about ten, on a vacation day that she was wasting following him all over the site. "She's my helper!" Henri boasted, before giving her enough for a soft ice cream cone to get rid of her.

"Don't you fret now, Mr Mayor, everything's been weighed, considered, calculated," Monti bellowed through his megaphone when he and Valiquette recognized each other from afar.

Then he started to hop about again, tapping on the briefcase he toted around everywhere in those days. But should some snoop manage to poke his nose over Monti's papers, he would jerk back so sharply that he often started coughing his lungs out and, with a sprig of ragweed in his buttonhole, get away from the spy. Anyway, Mayor Valiquette, the treasurer, and the insignificant shareholders in the Festichasse, the hunt fest, were better off not knowing what the briefcase contained. There was nothing in it that might ease a businessman's mind. The list of sponsors consisted of Mrs Guité's hotel, the Yukon company, and the village barber, followed by a series of fictitious entities.

"Not yet, not yet," Monti rationalized in front of his large Victorian mirror, chin raised, throat bared, razor at the ready.

Meanwhile, the mayor must have given his okay eight times to the various people's committees that had been established. The Festichasse would be held in October, which left them a good six months to prepare. In late spring the foot traffic between the new post office and the festival site began to swell to the point where Bradley the mailman would show up in the morning at the crossroads *in short pants,* with his pack of cigarettes tucked against his shoulder, his mailbag, and a deck chair that he snapped open using his feet. After that he sat lounging under the clouds and waited for the hellacious heat that he'd promised a whole lot of folks would come in May. Under a soft-boiled sun, during the rare sunny breaks that would soon be spoiled by more showers, he slipped on his dark glasses, the better to ogle the "wenches," as he called the women. The townspeople, whom he treated like pawns, picked up their mail themselves, since Bradley didn't even bother anymore to hand it to them. He lazily held the envelopes with a finger and a half and let his hand droop over the armrest. He kept a revolver close at hand in case a wapiti turned up.

The younger set had voted to have a rock singer brought in from the States for the night of the big show. Henri and Marcel were fans, they were into that kind of music. They'd even mentioned it to Monti. The old man ate his cereal with Pilsner, he took the frailest animals under his roof when the

weather turned nasty, he'd once gone to the jeweller's to ask
if he could make him some silver bullets, but there was no
question of letting some wiggler with slicked-down hair come
and bray into a mic. It would be a band from Rivière-à-Claude,
a few banjo-pickers accompanied by a pots-and-pans player
and a washboard virtuoso. They were very good.

Monti demanded that Léon and a handful of seasonal workers show him around the warehouse so he could personally
double-check the inventory of foodstuffs, fireworks, and nov-
elties purchased so far. There'd been a lot of rain over the past
weeks and it was feared the damp would saturate the building.
Léon lit a cigarette and his match nearly went up in a ball of fire
as they lifted the crossbar that barely managed to hold shut the
heavy door bulging under the pressure of the gas inside. Let's
just say it had been too early to lay in a large store of provisions
like corn and frying potatoes in such a damp place. These had
soon changed into a black liquid at the bottom of the crates.
In the foul air Monti began to cough his bronchial tubes out
in the crook of his arm while the others scattered with their
hands on their heads because of the bats flitting about amid the
goods. The old fellow was not overjoyed when he saw the canvas of the big tent ridden with long crackling streaks of mould.
Apparently he'd not been sufficiently clear when he'd ordered
that it be covered with tarpaulins. The immaculate tarps, still
rolled up, had been chucked any old way into a corner of the
warehouse. A great help. Monti coughed enough to leave his
sleeve spattered with blood.

"You had better see a doctor," Father Isidore advised him
during a friendly game of croquet.

This was in front of the café on the promenade, on the lawn

Henri was in charge of mowing while waiting to have children. The players' conversation about hunting was put on hold while Monti finished coughing. He soothed his throat with a few nifty swigs of pastis in rapid succession. After which the coughing immediately resumed. Around him, the players waited. They didn't come to play croquet to get stressed. There was a lowering sky, but at least it wasn't raining, for once. Monti coughed as he spoke. He said he'd been to the doctor's. Then he made his shot, holding his mallet like a hockey stick.

"Dr Maturin assured me that I was fit."

"We're in no hurry to put you in the penalty box alongside Pictou," said Fred Sicotte, former right winger of the Grisous de Saint-Lancelot-de-la-Frayère.

Monti propped his mallet against a tree that he gave permission to play in his stead. Without a word of goodbye to anyone, he and the pastis headed off toward the library. The others eyed Sicotte, suspecting that he'd just said something dreadful. Not everyone had caught the allusion.

It was months since Monti had last set foot in the institution founded by his wife, in part because he'd lost the book by Homer he'd borrowed the day of the inauguration. He'd scarcely read a couple of pages. Yet he'd found it more captivating than during his trip to the Klondike. He wasn't sure if Homer was the fellow's first or last name, but either way, the manner in which he said things, the scale of the events he recounted, his unusual expressions—it was all to Monti's liking. Just don't ask him about the volume's current location. Now that Joséphine had assumed the role of éminence grise, it was Mrs Cousineau who managed the library, and she invariably scolded Monti, saying he'd better return the book or else she'd take drastic measures.

"It's somewhere in our house!" Monti parried. Then he would add under his breath that he'd paid for half of the library's collection, which did nothing to mollify Lili Cousineau. Such a gentle given name. Monti was afraid of her.

As it happened, there she was at the counter when he came in. He zipped past her as she threatened to have him distrained. He answered that he didn't know any Honoré Bouge.

"*Honoré Bouge!*" she thundered.

The presence of books hadn't much improved the acoustics of the place, Monti said to himself. Once he'd installed himself at what had been his kitchen table, in the periodicals section, he turned to the obituaries in that week's *Le Vivier*. The paper had many more pages than before. You didn't read the whole thing. Monti right away saw the picture, possibly taken after Billy Joe Pictou's passing—talk about a facial expression! He was survived by his wife Marie-Agnès Tremblay and their son Étienne-Jean Pictou.

He's mixed race! thought Monti, a little sad.

Though he was at an age when he knew more folks that were dead than those who weren't, in a village culture where no one got too upset when a person expired, the news hit him very hard. He shut himself off in his office for a long time with his bottle of Yukon and a big bowl of snow peas from his garden. On the other side of the door, Joséphine could hear him in conversation with himself. He phoned his banker and had him transfer a deposit to an account in Chandler in the name of Marie-Agnès Tremblay. The lady was not about to see a bank open a branch in her town, Pabos Mills. After that he sent her the nickel medal he'd been awarded by the Knights of Columbus. It was something that meant a lot to him.

Guité was obliged to hire helpers to fill the orders for the Festichasse. A premium beer was brewing in barrels while Mayor Valiquette was eating his heart out going over the figures. With the shitty weather they'd been entitled to over the summer, the campground had been reduced to a frog pond, and the hotel's six rooms were clearly inadequate for the hundreds of festival-goers needed for the town to at least break even.

"Hello, Joséphine, Valiquette here. Might I have a word with your husband?"

Monti had changed since Billy Joe's death. He too was decaying. Lacking motivation, worn out, he abruptly gave himself over to incantations in the mayor's presence. Valiquette watched in disbelief as Monti conjured up motels here and there. On Yukon days Monti sometimes also asked an associate that he alone seemed to see to back him up. But the butchered ghost of Donald Bead kept mum. The light passed right through him.

"They're going to make you wear a dunce cap," Joséphine said when it appeared likely that the festival wouldn't take place as planned.

More worrisome still, one boozy morning aboard a pedal boat keeping a steady course to Île aux Hérons, Monti suggested to the helmsman, Captain Labri, that if, in order to catch the beast that had tormented him all his life, it were necessary to drag the whole village of La Frayère into his madness, well, so be it. To which Captain Labri raised his glass.

"Hmm," Henri paused.

It was one of his last afternoons working on the construction site. His helmet left a red band across his forehead. Bradley had wanted to make an impact, and while the men were rushing to take everything down before the storm hit, he drove across the lawn in Péo's pickup. He'd found a way to have the vehicle re-registered in his name and was moving between the piles of studs and boards and even over the canvas of the big tent that had been left to rot on the grass, the warehouse owner having refused to renew the lease after the event's fifth postponement. The village apparently was in the path of the tail end of a hurricane. Already the boats were jostling against each other off the marina, their halyards entangled along the length of their masts.

"Your father ain't here?" Bradley asked Henri.

He stepped down from the truck, his leg bent as though mounting a bronco. With his tongue in his cheek, he motioned toward the pickup box.

"Just a sec," said Henri, and then he looked all around the field, under his shoes, even lifting under a corner of the big tent to see if Monti were there.

One of Bradley's sons, Jason was his name, sat in the truck on the passenger side with his feet poking out of the window. He'd just been released from jail and was rapping his knuckles on the outside of the door. His hair was a flaming red mane. A goatee encircled his cleft lip. Next to Jason, in the middle of the seat, his son Bobby was picking his nose. Bobby. He wore his baseball cap *over* his ears. Three freckles on either cheekbone, his mug flecked with pink. There was dirt stuck to his cheeks because the chewing gum he'd blown into a bubble a little earlier had gone pow right in his face.

"What's the matter?" Henri asked when the mailman stepped closer and plucked a loose thread from his sweater.

The truth was that Monti had had himself admitted to the Notre-Dame de Chartres hospital in Maria. Fortin had carted him around in a wheelbarrow on Rue Principale, both of them hammered into an advanced state of impairment; the former mayor had then dumped his associate on the steps of the union office, where Monti had spent the rest of the day snoozing. And one thing led to another. But that was nobody's business.

Festichasse banners fluttered among the motionless seagulls above tilted stalks of wheat. Two men from the work crew, Slater and Marcel, had climbed into the box of the pickup. They nudged each other and hooted with laughter. The knuckles rapping on the steel door stopped. Bradley Senior held one hand on his cowboy hat to keep the wind from carrying it off, the other on the biggest belt buckle imaginable.

"Anyhow," he said, "give your mother a message at home. I eat supper at six and no green vegetables."

"Y' call that a wapiti?!" Slater sniggered.

Granted, a specimen of the deer family lay quartered in the back of the pickup, but not one endowed with the desirability of its distant cousin the wapiti.

"Christ, Bradley, it's a whitetail."

Almost a fawn, actually. Antlers like pieces of broomstick.

"Don't let them talk to you like that," said Jason.

Some sort of duel was happening between the mailman and Henri in the gusting wind. All manner of litter was sent rolling across the grass or whirling in the air.

"Look over there," Bradley said, "an airplane!"

"That's it, go home!" Henri yelled at the pickup already speeding off toward a biblical horizon. "Before your dogs start spinning at the end of their chains."

"All right," said Slater.

Carrying a sledgehammer, he headed toward the stage erected four months earlier for the big closing show. There were twisters of dust dancing on it now. As for the great hunt, the collective hunt, the grand gathering with ramifications so vast, so sweeping, as to leave everyone clueless whenever Monti got going on the subject—some other time.

"And I better not catch you trying anything with a Bouge woman again!"

Henri wouldn't calm down. He'd make underpants out of Bradley's honour. That his father had dug a hole in the village's finances didn't improve his mood either. Marcel wrapped his arm around his neck.

"C'mon, let's go help Guité liquidate his stock. He's clearly gonna have a surplus."

57

A SHE-TOAD JUMPED OUT OF THE BUSHES IN THE RAIN with rubbery leaps. It bounded to the middle of the roadway and frolicked in a brimming crack.

"Out of the way, I'm comin' through," said Bradley.

His rust-trimmed pickup with its one functioning windshield wiper bounced over the dirt lane and turned onto the main road. The exhaust pipe rubbed a speed bump, which the driver chose to ignore. The she-toad tumbled over and over. Its flesh took the shape of the tire treads that had just run over it. It left behind a multitude of tadpoles.

In the cab, Bradley whistled over the transistor radio sputtering bluegrass on the dashboard. At his venerable age, sleeping at night didn't appeal much to him anymore. His liver-spotted hands, ridged with prominent veins, nimbly steered a course to the wharf. *I'm goin' out for a li'l run.* His view of the church fell away from the windshield with a jolt and was instantly replaced by a sea both grey and choppy. All his fishing gear, which he'd thrown pell-mell into the box of the truck, slid to one side. Bradley dipped into the bag of candies stuffed inside his door pocket. A jawbreaker was soon rolling back and forth in what remained of his teeth. It was raining buckets. There was no one waiting in line at the wharf. Bradley made a U-turn. The squeaks of his windshield wiper would have irritated anyone but him. *I could maybe go to the girlie bar in Point Cross.* The jawbreaker shattered between his molars.

Bradley nearly unscrewed his head as he passed an ingenue, come out of nowhere, swaying on the side of the road.

"Jackpot."

His brake lights were two stretched filaments of light smoking in the night.

"Want some candy?" he asked the girl through the passenger door after he'd reached over to open it.

The girl didn't look too wary. Obviously soused, she did her best to negotiate the footboard. Her flowered blouse was soaked. As were her bell-bottomed slacks.

"Sooo, been out with your l'il girlfriends t'night, have ya?" Bradley asked.

He cruised along at his own pace. The little blonde wasn't going anywhere, she'd told him. The alcohol amplified her gestures. Early twenties, liberated, she launched into an account of her evening. *Boring,* thought Bradley. Francine, Suzie, Lotte, the names meant nothing to him. And how a chick of that age spends her evenings, when you yourself are going on a hundred and thirty-three, give or take . . .

"Your life's too complicated for me," he said, deciding to head back to the wharf, why not.

But there was actually more to it. Because after the movie a quarrel had broken out between her and her man when she'd insisted on joining her girlfriends for a milkshake.

"Ah, you've got a man, do you?"

The way she told her story was all mixed up. Couldn't even arrange events in the right sequence. She said she wasn't in the habit of tying one on like that, making him promise not to tell, so Bradley pretended to zip up his mouth. The girl explained that her man had half dragged her out of the dairy bar in front of her friends. *That's your version,* Bradley thought. To ruffle her fellah's feathers she had started downing a few drinks. She wanted him to feel the way she did when he got tanked up, so she began bending her elbow in the dive bar where he'd taken her in hopes of them making up. *She's not gonna start crying on me now, eh.* In the end she'd rung up a helluva bill for the guy, proving she too could embarrass him in front of his crowd. That's when he gave her an ultimatum.

"'You either come and live with me,' he told me, 'or we split up.'"

It seemed her man had had his fill of her dithering.

"Tell me, who's your father?" Bradley asked.

Such was his psychological insight that when the girl burst into tears, this seemed the right thing to say.

"Pierre Nault," she hiccuped, even more sloshed now that her nerves had given out.

She reached five painted nails across Bradley to help herself to some candy.

"He wants to shack up, but me, I'm too young."

"Ah, you're Nault's little girl. I know your father."

Don't overdo it, thought Bradley. Stirred by the callow hand that had just brushed against his thigh, he uncapped the flask of Chiasson's gooseberry liqueur that he'd slipped into his boot.

"So what's your first name?"

"Liette."

"Oh, Liette," he sang quietly, "when I see you, la la la …"

The girl laughed and sniffled at the same time. There was still no one at the wharf. The waves tried to climb aboard the anchored boats. Bradley turned the truck around again. Left or right, Liette pretty much appeared to not give a damn.

"But, say, are you old enough to drink?" Bradley asked.

"Yes, yes," the girl answered, slightly nauseated.

Seeing her already completely slumped in her seat, Bradley had her take a couple of swigs from his flask to get her to straighten up. The trouble was Chiasson's gooseberry liqueur was so sweet you couldn't taste the alcohol. He lit two cigarettes at the same time and showed his passenger how to smoke. The ride in the pickup was about as smooth as if it had cinder blocks for wheels. The bottle was almost empty, and Liette, her damp blouse clinging to her chest, stifled another hiccup while Bradley—it was his way of chatting her up—described the technical intricacies of weighing parcels.

"You're such an old gentleman," said the girl.

Leaning against him, she skimmed her fingers across Bradley's cheek, feeling its grain.

"So, then, d'ya fancy old gentlemen?"

Here, Bradley, pretending to yawn, put his arm around her. Pressed against him, she was half-asleep anyway, and to keep it from ever ending, he drove up a country road. His window stayed ajar because the glass had come loose in its frame. It was 2:30 a.m. The wiper swept furiously across the windshield. Liette growled in her sleep. At one point, the girl, all warm and vibrant against him . . . Bradley took quite a long time to convince himself it was worth spending his few remaining years in stir. His boy was serving another sentence; they would be cellmates. Back in the village he turned toward the snack bar. He went behind the shack, at the edge of the mud-bound headland. The bay seemed to be jumping in place. Mademoiselle was still slouched against him, and he struck a match with his free hand. Aglow in the red flare his face was etched with black creases. He savoured his cigarette in the gloom and the rain, which had started again. He then opened his door and climbed down from the truck without even having to worry about waking Liette. She was dead to the world. Dousing his cigarette on the sole of his shoe, Bradley flicked the butt against the snack bar and into the torrent near the gutter. He momentarily raised his mismatched eyes skyward. His shirt became transparent. The rain slapped against his teeth. All that was real around him clasped him tightly, giving him a keen sensation of existing. For someone his age Bradley was still possessed of remarkable energy. He walked unhurriedly around the truck to the passenger side. Along the way he scraped clumps of mud off the grille with his foot.

Afterwards, he drove around the village again, but with his headlights off, to make sure no one was awake yet. Truth was, he felt comfortable in wet jeans. Eventually returning to the bowling alley parking lot, he circled the building and headed toward the back door, where the youngsters sometimes went out to smoke a joint. Bradley aligned the truck perfectly and backed it up so that the box was just a few feet from the door and its wire-meshed windowpanes. He got out without switching the motor off or shutting his door and lowered the tailgate. Seeing the girl lying amid the rods and the rest of his fishing gear, he told himself this catch was a good deal better than a wapiti. Yesterday's perch had spilled out of their tin pail and were strewn across the floor of the box. Drooling a little, Bradley tugged the girl out by the legs and dumped her in the mud behind the bowling alley. Liette had gone out like a light and was in no shape to remember anything the next day. The building's hydraulic door closer cast a harsh triangular shadow on her bruised side. The mailman shoved off in no great hurry, whistling all the way home.

He woke up something like four months later. The sunrays streamed through the lenses of his dark glasses. His eyelids were still shut. He heard the wavelets lapping at his feet, the children bathing, the hoarse cry of the seagulls. *Cream,* he thought. *Sun cream.* He opened his eyes and slowly sat up. There was sand stuck all over the back of his close-fitting beige-and-brown-striped swim trunks. Their fibres were stretched and worn thin. Bradley removed his glasses to better assess his burns. Two white saucers around his eyes stood out against his cooked shrimp pigmentation. Brutal sunburns had also coloured his arms, his shins, his upper torso.

"Are you all right?" a nearby tourist inquired from under her parasol.

Only tourists and children with their babysitters were to be found on the seashore. Self-respecting Frayois didn't go to the beach. By the same token, they didn't wear shorts. Bradley favoured the woman with his surliest gaze. Why are we forever under the impression that old men are inherently nice? He jammed an over-tight painter's hat on his raw, bald forehead and uncapped a cold one poking out from his cooler, in which the ice had melted. The bottle cap landed in the fringe of algae at the water's edge with its teeth pointing up.

"Why wouldn't I be all right?" Bradley asked.

"You slept for a terribly long time, *oh là là.* I was about to rouse you, *n'est-ce pas.* One mustn't stay in the sun like that."

Damned Frenchwoman, he thought. He adjusted the rabbit ears on his radio and turned up the volume to stop the tourist from lecturing him. A rowboat offshore was heading back toward them. In the green, indifferent water, the children signalled to it with a jellyfish impaled on a stick. In the boat were Marcel and a friend of his. *A Chapleau, prob'ly.* A short while later the launch ran onto the beach. Its keel scraped along the sand. Marcel and Chapleau had gone out to haul in a couple of crab pots with the aim of cooking crabs for any takers on the marina patio. Chapleau was stowing some gear in the compartment under the seat of the boat when he noticed Bradley on his blanket. He got his friend's attention, and Marcel, when he saw this, began laughing too.

Bradley didn't just go to the beach, he colonized it. For starters, his base camp was set up not on a towel but on a king-sized blanket. His clothes were scattered all around, along with his flip-flops, amid the rubbish that he generated over the lazy hours he spent idling there. He had his cooler, his refreshments. Under the lounge chair he'd brought in addition to the blanket, almanacs and newspapers fluttered in the breeze. His radio grinded out the play-by-play of a baseball game, its antenna utterly incandescent in the sunlight. Marcel and Chapleau were dragging their rowboat across the grass when they heard Bradley sneering at the French tourist over the unbearably fraught radio account of an imminent strikeout.

"They come from Paris and don't even know it's an *island!* Hello, *Madame la comtesse!* So, then how come it's called Île-de-France? I tell ya, y' can't trust no one no more."

There was no stopping him. Despite the woman's efforts to stay equanimous, she soon grew tired of listening to his rant. Doing her best to joke about it, she put her snacks away one by one in her basket, closed her parasol, rolled up her towel, and headed back to her B & B while avoiding Bradley's gaze. Bradley kept up his soliloquy for a while. He stared ahead at the children in the water without seeing them. One of his balls dangled from the slack crotch of his trunks. Only when he ran out of cold ones did he stop shaking his head. *Paris ain't an island, yeah, right.*

Seeming all at once to have far too many teeth in the middle of his very red face, he touched the tips of his toes a few times. Then he painfully slipped on his flip-flops, heedless of the clutter behind him. Except for his keys, of course; these he collected and crossed the grassy strip between the beach and the parking lot. He climbed into his truck. The engine started with a shudder of the hood. Bradley hit the gas and backed up onto the beach. The children left off splashing about. It was disconcerting for them to see the driver uttering back-up beeps at his mirror. He stepped out of the vehicle, a licorice stick swinging from his chops. The flattened blades of grass tried to straighten up in his tire tracks. Bradley untied the rope that had held up the tailgate ever since the latch had given out. The same fishing rods still lay rotting there, all tangled up together. The perch as well, sun-dried and glued to the metal. Each fish was circled by a coppery halo. Blanket, cooler, lounge chair—Bradley pitched everything haphazardly into the truck together with his clothes. He didn't bother with his trash, which was already attracting some unsavoury seagulls.

Bradley cruised along Rue Principale a couple of times, whistling at the female pedestrians, holding his left hand against the top of his open window. He went all out with his hillbilly music, eager to give vacationers the benefit of his enlightened tastes. The tin pail from which the perch had spilled months earlier rolled all around the box. This is how Bradley killed time before making for home toward five o'clock. The town would soon be putting up warning signs: *Swampland—Crocodile Crossing*. Bradley slowed down when he caught sight of the new mailman, Pat, struggling in the bulrushes. His truck spewed rings of black smoke. He began following his replacement to intimidate him, but Pat was a really nice chap, yes indeed. He gave his predecessor a wave with a foreclosure notice held against the blue sky. There was roadwork in the left lane marked out with traffic cones, making it impossible to pass. Bradley, in the right lane, let his engine idle while he imparted tips and advice. The line of cars behind him grew longer—it wasn't his problem.

"Are the Bouges still getting a bottle delivered every week?" he wanted to know.

"Yessiree!" Pat answered.

Bradley touched his visor with two truncated fingers and went on his way at a speed well below the generally accepted limit. He wanted to piss off the drivers behind him. You didn't honk at Bradley. The beaver tail hanging on his tow hitch trailed along the roadway. He must have set a record for slowness when he swung into the scrapyard that Pagé's garage had become. He rolled back and forth repeatedly over the tube lying athwart the asphalt in front of the pumps. Inside the building the bell rang again and again.

"Fill 'er up," said Bradley, not deigning to so much as turn his head toward the pimple-ridden attendant.

He walked out of the garage a minute later with a crate of cold ones and some smoked herring that you bought not even wrapped. He kicked shut the fuel door of his truck. If he was fit as a fiddle, it was thanks to his lifelong love of sports.

When he got back to his house, he put an overflowing pot of water on the only element that didn't send up too much smoke from the baked-on crust. He nursed a beer, shirtless before the window, waiting for it to boil. His dog's snout had left thick white smears on the pane. When the water came to a boil, Bradley grabbed an open box of pasta from a cabinet in which half the containers were empty. Flour mites soared up from the noodles. Without salt or oil or any such thing he plunged the sacrificial pasta into the rolling boil. Having finished his beer, he drank the last of the Carnation milk going sour on the counter, then resumed his position at the window and nibbled raw noodles while supper was cooking.

It's ready. He stabbed a tarnished fork into the mound of pasta, which he set down on the counter long enough to empty the water from the pot while holding it with a hockey glove. Echo-laden gurgles rose from the depths of the sink. Bradley dropped the mound of pasta back into the pot and used a potato peeler to grate pieces of his herring into it. Finally he sprinkled everything with steak seasoning and went to have his meal on the throne. His leftovers ended up in the dog's bowl. *He'll be back from his jaunt by and by,* he thought. Putting on his short-sleeved shirt, he stopped midway to examine the sore on his abdomen. He suspected the tick was still embedded in his flesh. He scratched around it and shrugged.

He arrived a little late, but the good thing was that traffic at the primary school had thinned out. Even so, the parking lot was packed and he had to weave his way among the townspeople until he got the chance to nab a spot another latecomer was about to take. The fellow's turn signal kept on stupidly flashing.

Bradley's worn-down boot heels clicked on the asphalt. The sound was momentarily muffled by the mat in the entrance. The clicking began again on the concrete steps and along the basement corridor lined with student research projects. He could already hear the amplified spinning of the balls in their cage, interspersed with the numbers the caller yawned into his mic. The corridor opened onto a gymnasium loosely rearranged to serve as a community hall on bingo nights.

"I'll take four of these off your hands," Bradley said to Mrs Cousineau.

He pointed to the largest sheets, the ones with three by three cards.

"Hello," Mrs Cousineau replied from behind a cash box where she was playing with coins.

Bradley snatched his change and, slapping his cards against his thigh, stepped farther into the room.

"*B,* fifteen," the blasé caller said on his rostrum. "*B.* Fifteen."

There were basketball nets at either end of the room, stacks of blue gym mats along one wall, variously coloured lines painted on the floor. The usual retirees sat crowded around the metal-topped folding tables. *My my,* thought Bradley. *The nice family from up the hill.* Not that he really wanted to, but seeing that Monti was accompanied by his daughter Charline, he made for the unoccupied chair at their table.

"*N,* thirty-two. *N.* Thirty-two."

Charline turned all red, slightly less red than the Paspyjack's face, as he set his butt down opposite her. The only thing between them was a bowl of translucent plastic tiles in rainbow colours.

"Well, well," said a sickly Monti once he'd regained his composure.

Monti's hair was white now. He wore it straight up on his head. His hat was hooked onto a handle of the walker behind him. Everyone around them had missed the last number called. The greedy few who had heard hid their cards so their neighbours couldn't copy it.

"We were just talking about you," said a certain Bernier.

One of Bradley's eyebrows went up. When he exhaled, both sides of his moustache uncoiled. He spread his cards out in front of him. And in front of others as well. He drew the bowl of tiles closer to himself.

"*O,* seventy-five. *O.* Seventy-five."

The veteran players used a dauber. Better psychomotor performance, fewer accidents. They were easy to spot, those players. They applied themselves. There was some more talk about Bradley behind his back. Because, even though he was right there, he wasn't quite there. He had one eye on Charline and one eye on his cards. He wasn't keeping up.

"So, will ya be eatin' crab too, later on at the marina?" Jean Bouthillier asked him.

Bloodsuckers, all of yous, thought Bradley. As nonchalant as ever, he guessed that someone at the table must have bumped into Marcel or Chapleau, and now folks were busting a gut.

"What, we can't enjoy our beaches anymore?"

"*B,* fifteen," said the caller with a chuckle. "*B.* Fifteen."

A grumble went up around the room. The caller had already drawn *B* fifteen. Not very nice, but he was, after all, volunteering his services. Bradley took advantage of the fuss to focus his attention on Charline. *There's some unsettled business between you and me.* She was a beautiful woman, Charline was, in the flower of her life. *Still an old maid,* Bradley thought. *What a waste*. Ever since he'd arrived, she'd been fidgeting with her rings and bracelets, unable to turn away from her dad's one card.

"Fine, fine, okay. *N,* thirty-eight," the caller went on, even more robotically than before. "*N.* Thirty-eight."

Monti would always joke that he came to bingo nights to recoup his losses, except that he didn't even play. He was merely hewing to the principle that you sometimes had to get out of the house. Thirty-eight, someone said, must be about the number of grandchildren he had.

"Kidding aside, how many are you up to now, you and Joséphine?"

"No friggin' idea," Monti answered.

"Seven," said Charline, "eight pretty soon."

"I bought 'em a horse," Monti added.

"Got a bun in the oven, Miss Charline?" Bradley asked. If so, he'd have congratulated her, that's all. Believe it or not, even the caller kept quiet for two minutes.

"*V,* forty-thirteen. *V.* Forty-thirteen."

The number caused one heck of a stir among the elderly. Wild-eyed behind their coke-bottle lenses, they scanned the numbers before them. The nets on the basketball hoops were missing. The lines on the floor marked out unequal zones. The caller continued with a normal number, revelling in the confusion for a moment more. Over the mutinous mutterings and nervous coughs a conversation ensued. Bradley learned it wasn't Charline about to delight in the joys of motherhood, nope. It was Henri. He was four months pregnant.

"*I,* twenty-nine. *I.* Twenty-nine."

Truth was, bingo nights were somehow more pleasant when Henri was at the mic.

"I have trouble picturing Nault as a grandfather," Bernier said on hearing the news.

At this, Bradley dropped his tiles and, in an attempt to catch them, upset those already placed on his cards. *One, two, three, four,* he calculated. Four months. And there weren't ten Naults in La Frayère either.

"Pierre Nault?" he asked in amazement.

"Anyways, he sure takes 'em young, Henri does," said the notary Langevin.

"*O,* sixty-fourteen. *O,* sixty-fourteen."

"The wedding will take place in the fall," said Monti defensively.

There's no way it's not her! Bradley thought, holding another tile in his palm. His eyes mechanically swept across his thirty-six cards from one *O* sixty-fourteen to the next, but he did nothing.

"The beautiful Liette, married," Bouthillier remarked.

This knocked Bradley off his chair, which galloped away between the tables. It dashed back under his butt just before he fell to the floor.

"*G,* forty-two. *G.* Fort—"

"That's it!" someone cried out at the next table.

There was a sudden flurry of activity a few rows down.

"Is it bingo?" the murmur rippled through the room. "Bingo, bingo."

"Don't touch your cards," Monti shouted to the people around him. "Do not touch your cards, any of you!"

Charline was embarrassed to see her father get himself into such a state. But Monti, well, he hadn't forgotten what a hassle it could be to have all these Frayois replay the exact same sequence on account of a falsie. Bénédicte Blanchard, a rather spindly woman, stood up from her seat, always the same one game after game. She was aided by a caregiver. With her card all properly daubed and trembling in her hand, she, the most senior player, was somehow afraid to go have her bingo verified up at the front. Mrs Blanchard may have been the only centenarian in La Frayère. That would've had to be checked against the census.

"Anyhow, Bradley old boy, looks like you got some sun today," said Bouthillier.

"It suits you," Langevin added, "a raccoon mask like that."

Bradley heard nothing but a barely audible blabber. Muffled voices, as if under water. For two and a half minutes he'd been laying down the same moist tile on *O* sixty-fourteen. Everyone at the table was making fun of him. His swims, his notions about geography. Save Monti, who kept repeating that he was taking up riding again, that he'd told his wife the horse was for the grandchildren so she wouldn't gripe but it was actually for him, that he didn't want a horseless life. Charline pointed out that her mother never would have griped about something like that.

"*B,* twelve, yes," the caller confirmed into the mic.

Mrs Blanchard's caregiver enumerated the winning numbers. *Hey,* Bradley thought, if Henri was marrying Liette Nault because she was carrying his, Bradley's, child, that meant that a bit of Bradley would eventually infest Monti's house and corrupt the Bouge lineage.

"*I,* twenty-nine, yes, yes."

The gal didn't remember a thing, otherwise it would've already gotten around. She was wasted the night he'd picked her up. Or she'd thought it more credible to blame the louts that hung around the bowling alley.

"Wearing shorts in the middle of town," Langevin said amid faraway bursts of laughter. "You've got no honour, Bradley old boy!"

"Well, I should say so!" Monti interjected. "His honour, as it happens, belongs to me!"

Bradley stared at him, his head halfway in the clouds. Then his pout gave way to the same sugary smile he'd flashed, back in his referee days, at the Grisous' outraged coach.

"Free space," the caller repeated after the caregiver.

Bradley made no answer. Monti was alarmed.

"It isn't finished, I hope?" he asked, looking for reassurance. "Bradley, it isn't finished?"

"*G*, forty-eight, there it is, yes."

Bradley shook one of his boots off under the table. He scratched the side of his foot against the denim of his other calf.

"*O*, sixty-fourteen," said the caregiver.

Mrs Blanchard giggled on hearing that number. It made her squeak. Bradley's smile broadened almost to the point where the corners of his mouth touched behind his head.

"It's bingo!" the caller announced, and the cage spun on half-heartedly to not very enthusiastic applause.

XII

THE BAPTISM

58

LÉON BOUGE HAD JUST PARKED IN FRONT OF MRS
Guité's hotel. The doors were locked, making it impossible
to get inside, where Henri was wholly absorbed by his dart
game and the story he was telling his opponent. But his eyes
opened wide when his brother rapped on the window. His
opponent hadn't gotten the message either when the staff had
started placing the chairs upside down on the tables. Through
the window, Léon motioned to Henri to come quick.

"Is there an emergency?" Bilodeau asked.

Bilodeau, the local police. As usual, he was squandering
his paycheque on the poker machine without a thought for
his wife Céline and their children at home. Henri didn't
answer. He laid down his darts in an ashtray and knocked
back another shot of salt: in those days he always kept a
saltcellar next to his pint. Then he staggered toward all the
exits at once while unbuttoning his shirt so he'd be quite
ready when the time came to clasp the baby against his skin.
Guérette, the new owner of the hotel, raised his head from
the fridges he was filling for the next day. Things weren't the
same anymore in La Frayère. There weren't as many wondrous
occurrences. A scene like this would feed the rumour mill
for weeks. Right then, however, it put a stop to the prattle

of the few regulars still on the premises forty-five minutes after closing time.

"That'll be Liette giving birth now," said old Marcel, alone at his table in the glow of the jukebox and wreathed in the smoke from his bidis.

Marcel. People had been calling him old Marcel since he was thirty-five.

"Must be something like that," Bilodeau replied.

The policeman stepped away from his poker machine to take a swig of the beer Henri hadn't bothered to finish, amply salted, to be sure, so much so that Bilodeau went to ask Guérette for a refund, insisting it wasn't fit to drink and if he could have it in quarters that would be just perfect.

"Okay, breathe in, breathe out, push, push hard," Henri ordered Liette as she lay in her hospital bed.

François's birth was, shall we say, rather messy. "The place was plastered with it!" the parents would later boast. Through her agonized wailing, Liette had the impression she was birthing something like a picnic table. And yet the newborn had an itty-bitty little body, but the good Lord had issued him with a disproportionate head. There was a knot in his umbilical cord. The doctors took a picture, and Henri jumped at the chance to ask them to take another, of the family, with his camera.

"Your progeny, Mr Bouge," the obstetrician said.

Overwhelmed, Henri recognized himself in his gooey, shrivelled offspring. Liette, covered in bits of entrails, ate the banana meant to remedy her potassium deficiency.

Scarcely forty-eight hours had gone by and already Henri was off carousing again.

"And in spades," Liette's mother explained on the phone to Joséphine, who'd called to ask after her daughter-in-law and grandson and to apologize for not coming over right away as her husband was being difficult.

Henri, meanwhile, was pestering his father-in-law to help him finish off the rest of the twenty-six-ouncer of Yukon that a porcelain rabbit playing a porcelain guitar was keeping an eye on for him in the Naults' living room.

"It's a collector's bottle, I was saving it for this."

But Nault wanted none of it, and Henri stood up from the couch, arms stretched out as if someone were pulling on them. Liette was slumped in a heap in the armchair, at her breast her newborn wrapped in a blankie filched from the neonatology department. The naked little caterpillar would have to be baptized. The hospital officials had already written *François* on the certificate, but that was just in the meantime. Now they had to baptize their infant François for real. Yannick, a tad over a year old, squirmed and fussed in his grandmother's lap. No fun here. Henri had found a way to get his body more or less upright, and by hanging on to the rudder hanging on the wall he managed to strike an approximation of a speaker's pose. *Is this some sort of joke?* thought the father-in-law, who couldn't stand being there anymore. And to think this was his house. Henri's torso swayed but nevertheless stood like one of the mud-bound headlands facing the bay. It was ridiculous. There was testy foot-tapping in the living room. The father-in-law, increasingly on edge, was about to tell his son-in-law to si . . . But Henri was off, in a silvery voice made thinner by the liquor and his emotions, thanking everyone, announcing what he'd be announcing here tonight, his little

boy's name, a name already known to all, but first he wanted
to say a few words, and just saying this had taken five minutes,
while everybody there anticipated *the* monologue, a sprawl-
ing monologue, and, yes, it was pretty lengthy and massively
maudlin, and Liette lost it whenever Henri got stewed like
that, in front of her father to boot—give me a break, someone,
please—when suddenly, enunciating pedantically and precisely despite being seriously sloshed, because, dang it all, we're
entitled to be happy, aren't we, Henri opened the sluice gate
for good, taking a kind of *run-up* before churning out what
he predicted might be a historic speech, though meanwhile
it dragged on a bit—false alarm—with wishes, thanks, plati-
tudes, going around in circles and then setting off again in a
maze of convolutions, and Yannick in Gramma's arms began
to whimper like it wasn't even funny anymore, the father-in-
law getting steamed up to see his half-dead daughter enduring
such driv…*but, hey, hold on a sec,* even Nault was taken aback,
as though it had just hit him, what his son-in-law was prophe-
sying now, *go on my boy,* he thought, and Henri, glowing and
more and more articulate, deftly controlling his cadence with
little staccato pokes of his tongue between his pink, glazed
lips, had visibly relaxed his pose, softened it with a rustle of
cloth at the thighs and buttocks, his eyes on the absolute, he
kept working his chops while the others gaped at each other,
no one wanted to miss another word, borne along a second
later by the movement of his pink, glazed lips, Liette as well as
her parents, and it must have been purely out of magnanimity
that Henri repeated what he'd just imparted to them—how
very beautiful—that they might each of them better reflect
on it all afterwards; what's more, he took advantage of the

twist in his discourse to blend in a host of other veiled images, so very finely wrought, it was nuts, the place rang with loud wows, and all at once you felt the whole room was dislocated, you might say *reset,* as Henri struck a secretly sensitive chord and took another swig of Yukon—this was a celebration— and his speech, which for the space of a few alexandrines had become a blissful ode, thereafter radiated such energy that the TV turned fuzzy-like; "whoa" they all went in their arm- chairs and sofas, not fretful anymore but dazzled, bewitched by the orgy of eloquence of the immortal lush before them, high-wire artist of the toast, soaring on an improvisation that could have stirred multitudes and even lit up houses, but, look, now he wasn't even talking anymore, Henri was *singing,* mak- ing the language sing, at any rate, manipulating with ease an oh-so-supple, somehow dilated syntax, lovingly, smoothly pushing it to its most extraordinary points of tension and release, and shush, shush, "he's going to come out with some- thing," said the mother-in-law, and with the merest inflection, *immense* truths were spoken, just like that, everyone felt shiv- ers run down their spines, and even Yannick stayed stock-still, and Liette's face sparkled, and the father-in-law finally poured himself two fingers of liquor, while Henri, about to beat, in utmost glory, his own record of drunkenness, still found the strength, oh yes, to squeeze from everyday words tropes that gave them each such pleasure it had to be a sin, ooh, ah, all in honour, ahem, of a baby looking anything but exalted, what a shame, not exactly ungrateful but almost, like I-don't-give- a-hoot, yet for the oath of capital-*L* Love with which the bril- liant orator had honoured it even so, well, the little golden bell hanging at the very summit of the French language hadn't stopped chiming, chiming exquisitely, chiming so that even Henri could contain himself no longer and doffed his hat to his conspicuously absent sire, "Thanks, Papa, for being so hard," and even treated himself, why not, by duly baptizing, before his weakened and aching relations, the adorable button present among them, five pounds, nine ounces, his *child*—wasn't that something!—whose given name was *François,* lucky kid, and here Yannick whinged a little at this given name, which, simply put, meant *Français* in old French, "in *homage!*" Henri crowed, but with the voice he usually had the day after bottling Monti's brain-wrecking alcohol, and even if not everyone in La Frayère could have summarized, even if no one could have summarized or even grasped the complexity of the emotions that had just been experienced here, they were in raptures, the entire family embracing and saying they respected each other, promising it would be forever, "yessir," said father-in-law Nault, Henri having moreover made it very clear that he had very very high expectations for François, who, merely because he bore that name, was, linguistically speaking, subjected to Jovian pressure.

XIII

END OF HUNT

59

LIETTE TAPPED THE PANE A COUPLE OF TIMES, LIKE when you want to restore the reception on your TV. She was vegetating by her kitchen window. Outside, the ground seemed to be torn into long, spiral ribbons of powdered snow.

"I'm going out to walk the dog," François said.

He went behind her. Croquette, inserted beforehand in his diamond-pattern sweater, was at his heels.

"Are you dressed for the cold?"

François wore the too-wide, too-short fur coat belonging to his mother, who hadn't found the motivation to turn around as she asked him this. Flattened against his broad, glistening forehead, locks of hair stuck out from his father's fur hat, which he'd donned as well. Croquette eyed his rubber ball. François eyed Croquette. Liette eyed the roll of plastic dog-poo bags. Click! All set. François had clipped the clasp of the retractable leash onto the dog's collar, which matched his sweater.

Luckily, the door didn't snap off its hinges and go spinning to the other end of the kitchen when François turned the knob. The wind had grown even more muscular at dusk. The dog dragged François, head bowed, into the blizzard. Zero visibility. François edged forward on the porch, holding on to his fur hat to keep it from flying off. The leash immediately began to unwind from the case he held in his free hand. The bag of salt, the handrail, everything had been blanketed with a thick frosting. The bin that Henri had cobbled together with scraps of wood to store more scraps of wood was also filled with snow. With all the trips the pater had made from the house to the mailbox, there should have been some semblance of a trail, a minimally beaten path, boot prints to walk in. But everything had quickly been covered over. François ventured a shaky step, sinking knee-deep in the whiteness, and the leash went taut in front of him. He advanced with difficulty, leaning into the storm, his face buried somewhere between the crook of his elbow and the fur of his coat. The weather was so bad he couldn't see the dog at the end of the leash. They'd hadn't yet reached the perimeter of the yard and already the dog was unwilling to press on.

"Let's go, pooch, come on."

Again the leash went taut, but toward the house, toward the lights that kept the gloom at bay even as it settled all around. François gave a gentle tug. There was no way to reason with Croquette. He and François had very different plans for the evening. François pulled on the leash once more, this time with all his strength. He felt it slacken, then Croquette landed beyond him closer to the road. The dog's shivering alone was enough for him to make out its ridiculous silhouette in the night.

"I need you," he said.

He felt it was imperative to show the dog some appreciation. Because he didn't know for sure whether the curse had been dispelled, whether the conspiracy against the Bouges had been foiled by the pure and simple truth; what he did know was that his predator had never dared approach him while he was under Croquette's protection. He wasn't going to risk it. He would keep the dog at his side. But neither was he prepared to carry in his arms a creature that was pampered enough as it was. He would have liked the house to fold up behind him and zoom away to other dimensions. The leash grew slacker with every step he managed to take. Eventually he once again passed Croquette, immobile beside him, behind him, far behind him.

"François!"

Already exhausted, with the dog in his arms, he'd scarcely arrived at the bend in Rue Jacques-Cartier when his name reached him through the blizzard. Shredded frequencies he had to piece together in his inner ear in order to decode them. He swung around, eyes slitted against the wind, skin stretched tight over his face bones. His mother, a very pale grey, stood in the illuminated rectangle of their front doorway. François could just barely discern the house on the knoll.

"Leave me alone, dammit!" he shouted.

Carried off by the blasts of wind, his shout fell to pieces in the jumbled branches slashing the air behind him. There were several houses for sale in the neighbourhood. But François had no intention of putting down roots there, so off he went again, hurrying as best he could with the snow piling up. Croquette, on hearing his mistress's voice, writhed in his arms as if three hundred and fifty volts were shooting through his flesh.

"*François!*" his mother called again.

Her outline had faded for good in the distance gained at great cost. *Enough of this emotional blackmail*, François thought. *My god.* There was an alien invasion taking place above La Frayère. Unless what he saw were the street lights. They floated overhead, attached to nothing, their faint conical beams timidly slicing through the shadows now grown thick.

"Right. Croquette. Listen. I appreciate everything you've done for me. But, quite frankly, you wriggle a lot. I must therefore make do without you. Uncle François is going to tie you to this tree here. And your assignment is to intercept the beast—you know the one—should it come chasing after me. Understood, Croquette? Stay, dog, stay."

Animals—they understand more than we suppose. Croquette held his paw out in empty space while the one he considered a kind of half-brother, an ally against Yannick, moved away amid the swirling snow.

"I'll show you, just wait!"

Punching against the wind, François scolded the whole human race. The only light around him seemed to be imprisoned in ice. He heard Croquette's leash uncoil behind him, cracking like a whip. Too late, he was headed toward the centre of town and the seething swarms he guessed were buildings.

And what a thirst!

"We *love* you!" whistled the wind.

Alone on his ice floe, François turned one last time toward the house dissolved in the distance. The leash gyrated under his nose on the gusting wind. There was no dog at the end of it. Up ahead, a snowplow rumbled into view. It tore a few sparks from the asphalt, and Rue Principale slowly ravelled out behind it. François ventured down the street. He asked himself the questions that mattered. *Do the Canadiens have the first line they need to have a shot at the NHL finals?* Everything was closed. A few yellowish squares occasionally pierced the mosaic of opaque windows, the missing pieces in the puzzle of the night. He was convinced the defence would be reshuffled at the next practice sessions. He went by the beauty parlour, Chez Ginette. The paltry Halloween decorations in the street jarred with a setting fit for the Carnaval in Quebec City. François was close to tears as he remembered not seeing the slightest sign of a pagan feast at his parents' house. He continued on his way. Thought of names for his nephew. A siren wailed in the white-speckled darkness. The underside of the clouds kept going from red to blue a few blocks farther on. There now stood on La Frayère's Rue Principale a costly, elegant sculpture meant as a tribute to the good relations between the Mi'kmaqs and the settlers. François had never seen it before. He circled around the piece a few times to admire it, rubbing the snow off with his arm. This is when he found the bronze finger missing from the statue of Mayor Fortin down the road, welded at right angles to one of the Indigenous figures' cheeks. He went off in another direction chosen at random. Meanwhile, he blinked his eyes more. His life was all lightness. He recognized none of the storefronts in the village, not a single one, apart from the same fast-food or video club chains found in Montreal. Rock's image came back to him. The vacant commercial spaces prolif-erated as well among the few luckier businesses. *Darn,* thought François. Out of nowhere a bruise appeared on his face. He'd left the envelope full of money in his jacket pocket. No doubt they were right then turning into little stumps of paper inside his parents' washing machine.

Speaking of which, upstairs from a boarded-up laundromat a kid was calling his father to come quick. Richard Sainte-

Cluque, busy unwrapping slice after slice of orange cheese, hurried over to see what was going on. His son pointed at the animal in the murky street below. Richard wasn't sure what he was seeing. François, in furs, was digging fistfuls of snow out of the storm and pitching them against the walls of the buildings within range.

60

"HIDE ME! GET IN FRONT OF ME!" ROCK SAID, URGENTLY interrupting the Montreal dude's bragging.

They'd been glued to the bar since opening time, sheltered and sucking on the Yukon the waitress had brought them on her last rounds. Despite the storm, ice cubes with something like congealed smoke in the middle were melting in their glasses. François stood outside with a string of snot between his nostril and chin. He pressed his nose against the window to see what sort of life went on in Mrs Guité's hotel, which hadn't belonged to any Guité whatsoever since the late sixties. It was the youngest of the Guérette brothers who ran the place. And it wasn't easy. Because from Sainte-Madeleine-de-la-Rivière-Madeleine to Listuguj, every horsefly on the peninsula who'd ever leaned an elbow on that counter would to this day insist on calling the establishment "Mrs Guité's hotel." Each time he heard this, Guérette felt a six-inch nail stabbing into his heart. What else could he do but ask himself what his place was in the world.

"Is that *him?*" the Montreal dude asked in amazement. "The big ape in the window?"

He straightened up, sat down again, nearly stood up on his bar stool. He'd barely touched the Yukon in front of him, incapable of drinking it, incapable of drinking at all anymore.

"Hide me—I mean it!"

Hardly losing his cool, Rock grabbed the Montreal dude and planted him between the window and himself. Had you put the little guy's engine inside the big guy, you'd have demolished everything. There was canned FM rock music playing in the hotel. The Montreal dude threw his shoulders back, bracketing his torso between his arms. The handful of customers in the place were too busy enjoying his performance and sipping their beer to notice the primate behind them in the window.

"All clear, he's gone now," the Montreal dude said in an old-hand tone of voice.

Four or five customers were too much action for François. The storm had taken him elsewhere. The Montreal dude soon found himself jabbering at a couple of fellows seated farther away, saying he failed to see what could be so legendary about a hotel like this. Folks here should have seen the crazy bars on Boulevard Saint-Laurent in Montreal. The pool table felt was torn. As for Rock, he was telling the barmaid about his journey to Gaspésie.

"Can I get you another?" the barmaid asked over the music. "Should I set up a couple a cots for you somewhere?"

Heidi, her name was, looked at each of them in turn as she collected their glasses. They, meanwhile, leered at her. Chewing on gum in her jeggings and no-logo sneakers, she swayed her hips to the FM rock.

"We've got time for one more," said Rock. "Anyway, our lift will wait."

He walked his index and middle fingers toward Heidi's hand. She lifted it off the counter and placed it out of harm's way on her black leather money pouch. She may not have had much experience behind the bar, but she knew how to deal with a jerk. She was very careful not to encourage Rock. The Montreal dude had seen none of these goings-on. He was too eager to try out for himself the powers that Rock had promised him a couple of weeks earlier when they'd met in an electronics store. He poured his drink down the hatch in one go.

With his throat ripped out and his forehead ablaze, he asked the waitress, "Are you on the menu?"

Heidi offered him a fork and pointed toward the other end of the room.

"Here, go play in a socket with this."

The Montreal dude swung around. On the far wall one could still see the faded shape of the jukebox that for thirty years had had pride of place before Henri Bouge bought it. From time to time the lights on the sign above the pool table gave out. The L and the final T in LABATT disappeared. The Montreal dude rolled the sleeves of his T-shirt up over his shoulders and ordered a double Yukon, neat. He gave the barmaid a wink. His entire face winked.

"What were we saying?" said Rock.

He'd lost the thread of his taxi story and looked toward the window to make sure François wasn't wiping his feet on the entrance mat. He knew it was risky to wait at the hotel for their evacuation, but then, no one feels like spending the day in an apartment building doorway. The Montreal dude took advantage of his silence to start talking about his ambitions, but Rock watched him gesture without understanding a word. He was replaying in his mind that morning's pseudo-accident, his stunt. The whole thing had left him sore, and bitter as well. He recalled François, so endearing, with his cockamamie dissertation and his nervous tics. Heidi brought them their drinks with the same sway of her hips. A Yukon for the Montreal dude, two for Rock. He set one of the glasses down in front of the unoccupied stool beside him.

"Cheers, Granddad," he said.

"To the USA!" the Montreal dude added loud enough for everyone to hear, but, getting zero response, raised his glass alone.

Although Danny had never been to the States, he'd always felt it was made for him: the huge celebrity houses under the palms, the swimming pools, the money growing on trees. And, especially, the entire planet's respect. *Give me the means,* he thought, *and I'll show you I can get respect.* They didn't pussyfoot around in the States. They did things on a grand scale down there. You could be somebody. The Montreal dude could already see himself ruling the roost. He pictured himself going out with singers, cruising on a yacht. He was unable to string three English words together in the right order, but it didn't matter. He didn't have a passport either, but he'd been assured it wasn't a problem. Rock, on the other hand, hadn't congratulated him earlier when he'd explained how events had unfolded at the Laganières' cottage. Danny had strayed very far from the plan. But, in the end, it hadn't affected the outcome and Rock knew it. The detours, the improvisations, the slashed tires, that was all part of the plan. The ways of the grandfather were inscrutable. There wasn't too much traffic at that time of day, but they had loads of time to see the local hunters growing restless. They sensed the Frayois' mood gradually darkening until it was black. Rock turned around to look outside. A Greyhound bus had appeared in front of the hotel and now filled the entire window. Rock stood up and signalled to the waitress. Heidi, laughing out loud, whipped her rag over the counter in front of another customer near the unisex washroom and then came over with their bills.

"I hear voices," the Montreal dude said when she told him how much he owed her.

He looked all around with his most innocent air.

"Then you should have yourself committed," the barmaid replied.

"Angel voices."

A remix of La Bottine Souriante had just started up in the speakers, *dondaine la ridaine* with a disco beat.

"Don't give up," Rock told his sidekick.

He suspected his grandfather had a special fate in store for this pawn too. He had his VIP card for the Yukons, but he had to follow the waitress behind the bar to pay for the other drinks with his debit card. *She's using my buddy to get closer to me,* thought the Montreal dude. He saw Rock write something on the receipt with his pen. Rock had just given the girl his telephone number, and she found it amusing when he started rattling off numbers trying to guess hers. Heidi eventually took the pen and wrote her boyfriend's number on his forearm. Her boyfriend was a Canon. The Montreal dude stood up. He sauntered over to the pool table and sent one of the balls knocking into its mates.

"Let's go, Danny boy," Rock said. "It's all paid up, just leave the tip."

The Montreal dude wore his pants so low, he had to bend down to fish out his wallet. His arms looked like overcooked spaghetti. Stunned by his own generosity, he stepped toward

Heidi intending to slip five bucks behind the strap of her top. But she drew back. When she tried to take the fiver the usual way, the Montreal dude let go of it. They both watched it drift down to the floor.

61

AMONG THE HOI POLLOI A RUMOUR WENT AROUND
that a wild creature straight out of a top secret file was wreaking
terror on the outskirts of La Frayère. Apparently it had even
been seen in town. A group of Frayois pictured themselves
going on safari in the streets at nightfall. Yet most of those concerned were fairly down-to-earth as a rule. The likes of Raël or
Roch "Moïse" Thériault would have had to outdo themselves
big time for Nicolas Labri or Fernand's son Gabou to transfer
funds into their accounts. The people involved weren't the gull-
ible type; they had a penchant for tangibles. They fell asleep at
night reading catalogues for bolts or circular saw blades. Nor
would you have been able to get someone like Gilles Chiasson
or Richard Sainte-Cluques to wear pink shirts and sandals for
very long; they weren't inclined to extravagance. These folks
had pretty firm ideas about the difference between a man and a
clown. But while none of them would've taken the existence of
monsters seriously—Thierry Vignola notwithstanding—the
fact remained that some, starting with Foster, had seen what
they had seen. And the discovery of a dismantled corpse in the
Canons' field certainly didn't help. The local police were on the
scene but lacked the manpower to cope with the situation, not
to mention their even greater lack of equipment, especially in

those weather conditions. What's more, police chief Gaétan Bilodeau's mind was prone to seriously gangrene after his third rye. Reinforcements were on their way from the neighbouring towns, but in the meantime they had four or five guys searching over terrain that would have required two hundred.

The Frayois had certain appetites that nothing but a mobilization could satisfy, a mobilization that promised to purge them of their idleness and give them an excuse to dust off their favourite toys in the bargain. Thus, a posse was organized independently of the officers of the law. The ones who got the ball rolling were the snowmobilers who'd saved Steeve, who for his part was no doubt in his hospital bed drinking his fill of juice in little cartons through a straw and demanding endless pillows and adjustments. So much snow had fallen that the taxi hadn't been spotted by the emergency crew until it was too late for anyone to make the connection. And, besides, it wasn't unusual in those parts for someone to dump their old car, minus the licence plate, out in the open. Yannick behaved as though he'd recruited for his own purposes the snowmobilers he'd joined up with. He gave them the order, *after* everybody had already agreed it would be their meeting point, to gather at the base of the mountain, at the logging site not far from Chemin du Réservoir, on the edge of town. Half of the guys acted like racing drivers, keyed up on their irrepressible speed machines, which they were eager to get limbered up for the first time since last winter.

"Sooo, how many of us are there, more or less?" asked a hunter, hunched over with his engine revving.

The snowmobilers were trying to determine the best way to spread out across the territory, starting with the town centre because that was where the creature had been spotted last, opposite the old laundromat.

"There are fifteen of us," said Yannick, "eleven Ski-Doos."

These were the numbers that had popped into his head. He had no idea how many men there were, nor could he have cared less. Attached to their owners' snowmobile suits, the walkie-talkies crackled in the cold. Over the howling wind someone with a tuba-like voice suggested that so-and-so take up position at the shopping mall, two others at the Emergency Services depot up the hill, while the rest combed Rue Pleau, Rue Principale, and so on, that is, the streets leading out of town. With their snowmobiles angled so they were facing each other, amid the dismembered logs and stumps and snow-covered branches the skidder had left on the site, the troops passed around a bottle, looking at one another with a sense of unity as they drank. Save Yannick, who fixed his dissimilar eyes on the other two-bit strategist acting like an alpha male, half-hidden by the blowing snow. He felt like telling him they weren't in some video game, that if you found a length of pipe on the ground, it wasn't there for you to pick up thinking it would come in handy later. But he couldn't quite see why he'd have said that.

"No, that's not how we'll do it," he said instead.

Seated behind Gabou on their shared snowmobile, he laid out the very same plan, point by point, changing nothing except who would go where.

"Let's go," said Foster while the walkie-talkies communicated with posses assembled elsewhere.

The centre of town was vaguely outlined at the other extremity of the road that opened onto the artificial clearing where the rear ends of their speed machines skidded and spewed out snow as they tore off in different directions. Yannick and Gabou cast about for a while but found no clues. They drove down the street, on the sidewalks. You're not allowed to do that, but at one point Gabou noticed something. He couldn't tell for sure; in fact, it might just have been the floater that had been drifting around in the aqueous humour of his eye for ten years. Still, he definitely had the impression a shape was moving around near the public housing units, a kind of ectoplasm sundered every which way by the teeming snow. He saw it coalesce like a fluid under the awning of Gérald's convenience store and then flow around a corner. It was worth checking out. Wanting to make a detour, Gabou was overly cautious and drove too slowly to suit Yannick. The idea was to surprise the critter—assuming there was one—from the back, but just then his receiver sputtered. You'd have thought the device was made of paper and was crumpling up inside.

"Ten-four, ten-four. I . . . Gabou, y' there? Answer, y' there? Over."

It was Nicolas Labri. Speaking from his car, he sounded all wound up. The year before, his snowmobile had gone through the ice and sunk in the bay. He'd put it up for sale regardless, but at least was honest enough to make it very clear in the ad that it would be up to the buyer to salvage it. He'd buy himself another with the proceeds.

"Gabou here. I read you. What's up, Nico my friend? Over."

"I . . . Dammit . . . Breathe, I've got to breathe. Where the heck have you been? So, Gabou, we've got an affirmative over our way. Richard's kid wasn't making it up. There's something weird out here."

Gabou pulled his face away from his receiver. The device was writhing and spitting out grindstone noises. Yannick was losing patience.

"... in front of the store with the books," Nico just about shouted through the feedback.

"Roger that," said Gabou.

But he pronounced *Roger* à la française—*Rozjay*—and *that* like *dat*. His vehicle hadn't yet accelerated very much when Yannick jumped off, rifle in hand. He took a dozen strides, slightly lost his footing on the hard-packed snow, then recovered his balance and disappeared heading northwest.

"Now, where could he be off to?" Gabou wondered.

There. Proof positive. If you tilted the bottle, laid it on its side, turned it upside down, the alcohol inside always levelled out. Chiasson downed another swig after hooking his receiver back into the clip on his chest. Still parked alongside the Emergency Services depot, he too had just been alerted to the presence of something abnormal on the corner of Rue Pleau. There was another fellow with him, Robichaud, who'd joined him for the simple reason that he had his brand of beer. The circumstances made drunk driving permissible, they'd agreed on that. And even if Gaétan Bilodeau were to stop them and tell them to blow into the drunkometer ... Chiasson flung his empty against the side of his former employers' building, and, like Gabou, he and Robichaud went off toward the zone to be surrounded. The depot was located near the top of a hump-shaped hill, such that the rise made it hard to see what was down below in the town before you hit the crest. Luckily for them, they'd taken the time to finish their beer, because five seconds earlier, on reaching the point on the hill where the slope began, they'd have been run over by a Greyhound bus looming out of a side street. Stupefied, the both of them, they let their snowmobiles coast on their skis on down to the bottom of the gradient. The tracks turned freely in an infinite unreeling of rubber. In a town the size of La Frayère people knew the bus schedules, and no intercity buses were scheduled for that time of day; what's more, there was no Greyhound service in the area, only Orléans Express. A brown patch shaped like a string bean grew larger on the sidewalk below as they approached the bottom of the slope. Not that the visibility was good enough to let them see it was a couch, but Chiasson knew it all the same. There'd been talk on the wharf the day before last to the effect that so-and-so had helped his neighbour put his couch out on the road.

It had gotten so that this was the level of the stories folks in La Frayère were telling each other.

Then another dim shape, its outline chewed up by the swarming snowflakes, detached itself from the couch. Chiasson immediately saw two other snowmobiles appear at an intersection. He figured it must be Foster and someone he couldn't identify. They were coming back from the shopping mall. The shape dashed off toward the copse, a stand of trees as big as a couple of residential lots, between the commercial district and the rows of duplexes in the back.

"Chiasson?" his receiver exploded. "Foster to Chiasson. Do you read me? Over."

"Chiasson here. I hear you. Over."

"The animal's gone and trapped itself in the thicket. Move in *tranquilos* at your end, I'm coordinating with Gabou so we can corner it."

"Copy that."

To avoid detection the hunters left their vehicles behind and hand-signalled to each other to position themselves so as to cover all potential escape routes through the trees. Gabou was fired up. He could barely keep from shouting just for the fun of it. Foster, constantly checking his gun to make sure it was loaded, advanced under the leafless branches, which, despite their scrawniness, he found somehow festive. He wasn't the only one who had the impression the chamber of his rifle was filled with paint balls. Or that a little flag marked *pow!* would pop out and leave a cork stopper hanging from the barrel on a small chain. Some of the guys wondered what they were doing in the woods at that late hour, but the others around them moved forward and so they moved forward too, with the same smothered giggles. It was a night of celebration, a night of hunting and celebration that Monti had once dreamed about. All you'd have needed were garlands strung between the branches, pennants, fairground booths, sequins on the snow and tokens and packages of candy, for you to be right in the middle of the Festichasse. No one had any idea where Yannick had gotten to. The hunters plunged deeper into the wood. They couldn't make anything out in the shadows now but their silhouettes like construction paper cut-outs glued to Popsicle sticks. A guy whose name no one could ever remember shouldered his rifle before the life-sized scene outlined ahead of him. Through the intricate lacework of the branches he vaguely discerned a monster less prepossessing than the surrounding scenery. The creature grunted amid clouds of mist that froze in mid-air. Overhead, two birds chased after each other. What's-his-face wanted to fully experience the moment; he cocked his rifle. He was going to bring his loved ones the most extraordinary trophy. Around him they weren't even holding back from laughing anymore. The ruby tip of his cigarette flared up.

62

AT ABOUT THE SAME TIME, RUNNING IN THE COM-
pletely opposite direction, Yannick had almost reached the
edge of La Frayère. He was nearing the supermarket, which
stood alongside the 132. Following the trail of the prey that
had fled this way, he jumped the fence around the loading area,
not fully realizing that, down deep, he was chasing after the
right to do whatever he liked. He never again wanted to have
to stop from doing anything. With one eye on his rifle sight
and his mouth closed, he scanned the environs. He ground
his teeth at the snow under his soles, but he knew it wouldn't
last, that it would melt and reveal the world scarcely altered
underneath. With the muzzle of his rifle, he sniffed the cabins
of the handful of trucks in the parking lot. Romain Perrault
knew some of the warehouse employees and, in exchange for
his services, they sometimes left the alarm system disarmed
and the door unlocked for when it was time for a pig-out after
a night of carousing. Yannick found the door right away. That
wasn't hard, there was only one. It was, in fact, unlocked, and
as he pulled it open, it carved a quarter circle in the snow. He
let himself get absorbed by the gloom between the forklifts
and the pallets stacked with goods waiting to be shelved. His
finger squeezed the trigger of his rifle just short of actually

firing a shot. He entered a staff room with a table, a microwave, some green-and-white uniforms. The rifle muzzle preceded him each time he crossed a doorway or turned a corner, ready to flush out whatever was lurking in the spaces that made him dizzy when he saw them opening up before him. It had been a long day, but he wasn't tired. He would never sleep again. Stepping through a curtain of transparent rubber strips, he entered the grocery proper, the place where you bought your food. At age ten or twelve he dreamed of accidentally spending the night in a supermarket and stuffing himself full of whatever he fancied without restraint or anyone scolding him the next morning. He strode down aisle after aisle, chewing on a hot dog. The laser on his sight shot a straight line to the far end of the store. He went past the boxes of Vachon cakes and ice cream freezers. He plucked another hot dog from the package and devoured half of it in one bite. He propped his rifle against a shelf in the aisle with snacks, biscuits, and such. He pulled out his cellphone and rang Cynthia's number. So long as he was at the grocery, he might as well ask her if she needed anything. But she was in bed by then and his call went to voice mail. There was something calming about the stillness of the place, this world of objects, as if it contained the knob that put the universe on pause. Yannick began to open the refrigerator doors without closing them behind him. He took all the meat out of the display counters in the meat department, pitching tournedos and lumps of ground beef on the other products nearby. Same thing in the seafood department. Catching his breath near the cash registers, he started leafing through the *7 Jours* magazine, and that's when he remembered he was going to be a father. The celebrity on the front page talked about this in an interview. He nibbled some pepperoni sticks to relax his jaw while he read. Then, using his rifle butt, he proceeded to properly smash all the monitors and the glass over the scanners embedded in the counters. Like a professional wrestler, he followed up by clotheslining all the jars of olives, dried tomatoes, and hot peppers in the condiments section. He toppled the shelves as he went along, looking for those single-serving packets of crackers and edible putty with the little red plastic spreader. He was afraid of the house he'd have to warm as soon as his parents moved out. As he stepped out of the beer storage room, he admired the mess he'd made in the eggs, yogurt, and soft cheese section. He took a run-up in the aisle and then hit the brakes and slid across the slick floor to where it was still clean. He repeated this more often than one would have thought necessary for sheer boredom to set in. Anyhow, he'd have to be getting home soon. To wake Cynthia so they could go retrieve his Jeep. He just felt like having something sweet beforehand.

63

AT THE SIGHT OF THE ANGRY COLUMN OF SNOWMO-
biles approaching the end of the Chemin du Réservoir a
few kilometres away, François spun around on his heels. He
changed course and made for the sea rearing up in the bay.
There was no telling the sidewalk from the roadway under the
snow. His hands, his chameleon face, whatever flesh he had
peeking out from his furs, was erased against the grey facade
of the subsidized housing building, which he hugged despite
the sign saying TRESPASSERS WILL BE PERSECUTED. He
batted his eyelashes and found himself smack in the middle of
Rue Principale, at an intersection where the wind tossed the
traffic lights around on their wires. *I've been blanking out,* he
finally realized in front of Gérald's convenience store. More
snowmobiles were going crazy over by the shopping mall.
Though spent, François managed to quicken his pace. He was
deep in conversation with the tips of his boots.

The one thing that could stop him was the display window
of a bookstore. *Just you wait,* he thought, feeling increasingly
bitter. He didn't know who'd had the strange idea of opening
a bookstore in La Frayère, but the manager seemed to have a
penchant for cooking, judging from the display, where a couple
of other inert and faded books lay dying. François felt an urge

to rub his woolly palm over the bright-yellow splashes covering the window. He wanted to make sure his book was clearly visible once its turn to be on display came around, unaware that he was rubbing at the reflection of the SUV headlights behind him. Once again he thought he heard someone calling him in the storm, his name faintly uttered in a slobbering grunt.

"Françoué!"

Farther down on Rue Pleau, which ran perpendicular to the street with the bookstore, two cars facing in opposite directions were blocking both lanes. The streets had been plowed and were lined with tall snowbanks. The cry François had heard came from there, that much was certain. The hunters in the cars had rolled down their windows to talk. One of them pointed a finger at François. Their meeting was adjourned post-haste.

"Boo!" said a dried-out humanoid creature that had just sprung from the corrugated metal entrance of a former employment centre.

François nearly died on the spot. All he saw at first was a glossy tuft of hair on a cheekbone more prominent than the other. He about-faced, holding his hand up to the side of his face like a blinker, and set off through the snow at a jog headed for Montreal.

"Hey!" said Poupette, and grabbed the fugitive by the fur of his coat. "Wow! Your coat's really soft."

"Go away!" François yelled. "It can't be you!"

"Look at me, Françoué!"

Poupette tried to corner his brilliant Gaspésien somewhere between the front of a community clinic and the sea two hundred metres away. The other cheekbone rose up under his skin. The smile he flashed gave the impression an axe had just struck him full in the kisser.

"It's me!"

There was a strange resonance in his elytron-like voice. His rib cage reverberated when he tapped it and repeated, "It's me." François touched his face, which had regained some symmetry. The tuft of hair on Poupette's cheekbone came off in his hand.

"What are you doing here? You…"

"Wait a sec."

In high spirits, Poupette drew a Canada exercise book like those François used out of his mesh camisole. François almost asked him if he had enough clothes on. Poupette flipped through the notebook a few times before finding the right page.

"U-bi-qui-ty," he said proudly, waving his finger. "You're the one who taught me that word. D'you like my bracelet?"

He jingled in what was left of François's face an assortment of shells and mother-of-pearl chips no different from the kind sold at any tourist trap boutique east of Sainte-Flavie.

"And check out my earrings, d'you like 'em?"

Synthetic feathers mixed together with bits of polished glass and a fishing lure to boot. François was somehow relieved and went to embrace his faithful companion, feeling he had better warm him up in his furs. But Poupette, seeing the man he considered his Siamese twin so indifferent to his jewellery, flinched back. A misshapen bump slowly shifted under the mesh of his camisole.

"I'm sorry," François said to make amends, having ended up hugging himself. "Your jewellery is gorgeous. And so very flattering."

Visibly hurt, Poupette motioned to him to be quiet, it was okay. By way of consolation he pulled a small bottle of Yukon out of his snakeskin pants.

"Let's go," he said, after taking a rather laborious gulp. "Let's act as if I'm the one showing you around."

While inventing stories along the way about a social worker and a flying carpet to explain how he'd gotten there, Poupette headed toward a half-deserted warehouse farther up the street. Around them the rumble of engines grew ever closer. François wasn't following his friend. No, he was following the minibar-sized bottle of Yukon. He soon had to plunk himself down on a snow-covered sofa abandoned on the sidewalk. He looked like a bearskin sloppily spread on the back of the couch. Poupette had drained the bottle.

"I get it," Poupette said.

He walked back and plunked himself down too. He took out another bottle of Yukon, which François nearly swallowed whole without even bothering to open it. A Greyhound bus drove by farther up the hill. The sofa cushions seemed to be stuffed with peanut butter. More trash, under piled-up garbage bags, spilled out the sides. Poupette sang the drinking song *Il est des nôtres*. Ten seconds later he was antsy again.

"Right. All rested up, eh. Lean on me. I'll do my level best not to break. Hey, y'know, I'd never been to Gaspésie. Crazy soft, your coat. Gives me a bit of a rush. I don't feel the cold anymore. You? Ha! Drink up, drink up. I've got lots, look. Here, have another. Got an endless supply. Damn, isn't this trippy! C'mon, here we go. That's it. No, no, not that way. We're gonna see some people, we are. Sooo, what about your book? Ya, y'know, I didn't tell 'em a thing, the other guys, Momo and Graton, nothing. Not to Armand or Tibi either. You know how they are."

Back on his feet, sort of, François tried to call to mind the image of his circle of friends. The only picture he could come up with was piles of empty clothes on a sticky floor. All the tension inside him had gone slack over the past minutes. He no longer understood what was happening to him. He walked for the sake of walking.

"And I didn't tell 'em I knew where you were either, because to my mind it's still best no one knows your whereabouts. Sooo play along and, whatever else, don't tell 'em I knew. Got a light? Ah, fresh air. Man, I'd never been out of Montreal. Eh, Françoué, you'll have to put on some cream or something. Me, I don't exist. And the cash you owe me, forget about it. A gift. Wipe the slate clean. Le Roy paid himself back, anyway. One kidney's quite enough for me. I dunno, eh."

Two snowmobiles began to descend the road without a sound, slowly sliding down the gradient in their direction with their engines off. They ruffled the pattern of the snow, which fell even harder. François tensed up, and at that very moment another snowmobile made a U-turn in an opening on the right and positioned itself opposite them. Poupette made François change course in the sudden, almost tangible light that found them quivering. They ran. The trees slipped past on either side in a choppy continuum.

"This way," said Poupette. "We'll take a shortcut."

François did a crawl stroke through the powdered snow and arrived at the thicket where so many people in La Frayère had downed their first beer.

"Here, drink this. Seems like I haven't seen you for ages. You're a writer! I'm gonna put that in my resumé. Feeling sorta droopy all at once? Ta-da, another little bottle of magic potion for my buddy Françoué. We'll have you looking good as new again, don't worry. Me, I'm on holiday, eh. Does a world of good. Go on, bottoms up, you can do it. Yes indeed, that's it. The only fuel still burning inside there, you old crud. Lovely, that's it."

Grasping his arm, Poupette ushered François deeper into the wood, under nocturnal branches reaching out over the indigo snow to stroke their backs.

"I wouldn't mind staying here, y'know. But no problem, champ. I'm gonna take care of you. You could sleep under the staircase at my place sometimes. Here, lemme put up your collar and pull down your hat. I'll introduce you to my sugar daddy, too. Drink your syrup, you poor boy."

The shadows of towering, twisted, dirty clouds glided over the ground and the branches, glooming the night even further. Poupette handed François the last bottle. He knew it would keep him awake, although collapsing would have been the best thing that could happen to him. He sat his friend down on a fallen tree going soft, where the few snow-free patches of bark were ridged with crescent-shaped mushrooms.

"Now then, you stay here," Poupette told him. "You'll be fine. Hold on, I'll wipe the side of your kisser. There. Ha-ha. And now ... Well, we wait!"

Then it was Poupette's turn to sit down on the trunk. He looked haggard, but his bearing was more commendable than usual; he tapped his knee, casting glances left and right.

"What are we waiting for?" François managed to enunciate.

His jaw was too loose. Poupette took pains to put his tongue back into his mouth. Around Poupette's neck, scales appeared like those covering his reptilian trousers. He stood back up when voices began to fill the woods. His eyes like telescope lenses, he stole back into the radiant snow holding a finger to his lips to signal *shush*.

"Poupette, sweetie," François stammered, chin resting on his chest, a spring for a neck. "Don't take this amiss, but I think I've invented you. Poupette? Are you there? This is crucial, crucial. Poupette, are you there?"

But Poupette must have hurried back to the street, because he wasn't there anymore. Or his footprints either. Arabesques of powdered snow swept across the ground between the tree trunks and the legs advancing under the barbed vaults of the thicket. In his acidic reverie François replayed his peregrinations of the past twenty-four hours. His feet crunched against the snow. *My life in a nutshell,* he thought. A backup module turned on in his mind. He felt like a shadow with nobody attached to it. His mouth shaped the sort of pout you put on to congratulate someone ironically. His sole desire, all he would have wished, was to savour recognition and success once again. But he'd somewhat squandered his fifteen minutes of fame that time when he gave a lecture on the Montreal Maroons at Laval University. In any case, he'd have had neither the strength nor the coordination to straighten up on his rustic trunk and speak. Laughter disrupted the excellent silence around him. François was limply applauding himself when the lone ember of a cigarette flared through the tangled branches. His applause was short-lived. A hollow light was already drawing him elsewhere through the hazy trees. One thing was certain: the rare beast wasn't following him as it slipped away in puckish whorls of photons while Monti disappeared into the forests of the great hunt.

EPILOGUE

HENRI MADE LÉON GET UP FROM THE COUCH IN THE slob's house where he was squatting at the time so he could come lend a hand with the furnace at their parents' place. Monti's oil-fired system had seen better days, and with Yannick and François living there now, Henri wasn't about to quibble over safety, not to mention that it gave him a reason to pay his brother under the table and tide him over. Getting his little family to move in with his parents made it easier for him to help out this way. That's how he saw it. There was no lack of space in the house; nobody would be in anyone else's way. As for him, the proximity would allow him to keep the place tidy and to quietly, unhurriedly redo it to suit his taste for when he bought out his siblings' share of the inheritance. Seriously, since he'd taken charge of the homestead, almost nothing remaining there was obsolete, except his parents. Oh, yes, and the barn too. He didn't talk about it, but he was going to demolish it and build a garage cum workshop instead. A temple with two roll-up doors; he'd drawn the blueprint himself.

Monti went down to the basement with his sons and their mind-boggling machine. Hey, an electric furnace! Slumped over his walker, he imparted his instructions, beginning every third sentence with "Well, in my time." It was a big job; already

8 p.m. and they'd been at it all day. Slaving away on either side of the oil furnace, Henri and Léon shared the unspoken hope that the sump pump would start on its own, that the pipe, rousing itself, would snatch their father, suck him in, and spirit the old fellow down the drain while they completed the installation. They'd go down the street later to fish him out through the manhole cover. *I'm going to finish my basement,* Henri promised himself as he lifted the unit. The cross on a Phillips screw on one of the conduits had been stripped by the driver. Monti squawked that it wasn't the right tool for the job. When the bit slipped for the ninth time in a row, Léon blew his top. He pushed his whole weight against the furnace. It fell off the four blocks on which it had been seated.

"Is this your doing again?" Monti scolded, and shuffled toward them with his walker, staring at the blocks on the ground. "Haven't I told you often enough not to fool around with what belongs to me?"

The problem was that half of La Frayère belonged to Monti. He made slow progress as Henri and Léon looked on. They sounded like a bus's air brakes. But, not wanting to insult him, they refrained from helping him. Monti eventually leaned over the lengths of two-by-four that served as blocks and picked up one of them; it turned out to be the library's copy of Homer, lost since the extinction of the dinosaurs. There was the furnace's footprint stamped into the cover. Must be Baptiste put it there, the two brothers quickly agreed. Chewing on the insides of their cheeks, they made up a vague recollection of the event.

Maybe that's what was missing, Monti thought sombrely, by which he meant that the book's reappearance perhaps represented the final coincidence in the vast machinery of chance that had swept him along one poker night in the Klondike and which he'd tried ever since to reproduce over a lifetime without ever truly grasping all the implications. He walked to the staircase, not with the walker but with the book in hand, no longer paying attention to his boys. He repeatedly brushed his thumb over the author's name, Homer, embossed on the cover, delighted to owe the library a fine of four thousand bucks or so. *Where am I?* he thought in surprise, suddenly turning his eyes toward the top of the million steps leading to the ground floor. The kitchen door was poised way up there like the stroke of a pencil on a landing of light.

"Do you need any help, Papa?" Henri ventured.

Meanwhile, he told himself that if his father was still alive when he finished renovating the basement, he'd put in a sort of ramp, a platform, something to let him sometimes disappear downstairs.

"No, can't see how you could ever help me," Monti answered.

He held on to whatever was available, not to keep from falling but from flying away. He set his right foot down on a stair. Then the left foot on the same stair. Then he set his right foot on the next stair. Léon followed behind with the walker. Joséphine was waiting in the doorway for her man to arrive, prostrate but triumphant.

"Sit down in the armchair," she said. "I'll warm up some barley soup for you."

Flourishing her ladle, which was tipped with a tiny yellow-and-red boot, she shouted down to Henri from the head of the staircase something to the effect that he might give his father a hand too. Liette, afraid to dirty herself, was washing the dishes at arm's length in the sink when behind her came the shuffling sound of Monti's extremely white and oversized sneakers. The shuffling was punctuated by the impact of the walker on the linoleum, cushioned by the split tennis balls with which it had been fitted. Monti had the impression of seeing his daughter-in-law always from the back, never full face, and it would have been fun, then and there, to pull the apron strings dangling from the flawless bow draped over the small of her back. A back which the old fellow envied, now that his was acting up. As he saw it, Joséphine was the one who'd insisted on taking in Henri and his brood. With two youngsters underfoot, Liette still had everything to learn about housewifery, and Joséphine had tasked herself with showing her the rudiments. No one doubted that by the time of their golden anniversary she'd elaborated an entire doctrine of married life. On occasion, however, his wife's saintliness exasperated Monti. Not as much as Henri exasperated him, but still.

"Are the kids asleep?" he inquired.

The cushion on his armchair in the living room yielded under his backside. A basin filled with hot water appeared on the floor with a towel beside it. Ruffled by the merest draft, Monti searched all around for the Homer, which he had pinned under his arm.

"Yes," said Joséphine. "Liette put them to bed a while ago."

The break had lasted long enough. Monti made to stand back up.

"I've got to tend to the animals."

The ewe had had a fever this morning, and . . . Joséphine forced him back down with a finger pressed against his breastbone and a poker in the other hand, ready to knock him out if necessary.

"You already fed them today. I'll go presently to see if everything's all right."

Stirred up by the poker, the cinders flamed again in the hearth. The hunting rifle, the same one as before, glimmered over the fireplace. *What an extraordinary woman,* thought Monti, gazing at his wife in disbelief mixed with a touch of suspicion as she brought him his tray. The soup was steaming in the earthen bowl. A few ice cubes jutted out from the surface of the broth. His chunk of bread seemed disturbingly real to him next to the bowl; it came with a nice big slice of the vegetable pâté his wife had forced him to eat for weeks on account of cholesterol. She'd diluted her rascal's Yukon with Coke, feeling it was better to slow down its entertaining effects.

"Thank you, my wife."

"Tomorrow I'll make your cassoulet."

Joséphine gently tucked his bib into his collar with the same movement you use to crimp the dough around the edge of your pie plate. But when she went to switch on the television, Monti gestured to her not to bother. He drummed his fingers on the cover of the Homer he'd just discovered between his thigh and the chair, the second time in over twenty years and on the same evening. Joséphine gaped at him and then returned to the kitchen. Liette was sitting at her usual window, next to a giant spoon and fork hanging on the wall. The young mother looked like a little girl who'd been punished and was watching the other children play outside. One good thing, at least, about Henri's zeal was that he displayed boundless energy even where fatherhood was concerned. The drops of milk on his wrist, the Cheez Whiz on celery slices precisely a decimetre long, blanket-and-pillow castles, he loved it, when he had the time. This was a help for Liette, for whom moving in with her in-laws had entailed severe culture shock, especially as it happened so fast, on the heels of an already rushed wedding. Her youth had been packed into a cardboard box marked with an address in Alaska. But then, sometimes too much help was, well, unhelpful. Henri had trouble delegating. He suffered on account of his excessive perfectionism. One day, in a cloud of baby powder, with his parents there and all, he was so tactless as to criticize his wife because she'd bought a brand of diapers that he'd categorically instructed her not to. The absorbent edge was poorly designed at the crotch, which was naturally where François's virility fit in. Liette thus found herself at the bottom of the family hierarchy, in a black-and-white world, surrounded by outmoded furniture and never-ending conversations about illness. "I'm gonna wither away, Henri," she said when he took her for a drive. But, firstly, they didn't pay any rent. And, secondly, Mother Bouge would soon lack the stamina to endure her husband, whose antics were not on the wane.

Speak of the devil, Monti was steering his spoon around his soup. He chewed his bread as though this was something important he had to do before doing something still more important. Looking up, he tried to figure out, through the ceiling, the precise location of the babies in their cribs upstairs. *Yannick and François,* he mused. He traced their contours in his mind. A crime scene. The ice had melted in his bowl. The molecules seethed a little less frenetically among the beads of barley and the soda biscuits that had been crumbled into the broth to thicken it.

"Ah!" he said.

He took the time, for once, to let himself exist without internally jumping to his feet every three seconds. Nothing in his whole life had brought him as much pride and satisfaction as his journey to the Klondike. A spider suspended in mid-air twirled not very far from his face. He slurped his soup, all the while giggling worse than his first time in the grass behind the salmon smokehouse. The friction of his undershirt, the licks of heat sent out by the fireplace, the nasty ghost fingers, everything tickled him. *I miss Bradley,* he thought, prompted by the ghost fingers. Henri and Léon, having also resurfaced from the centre of the earth, drank and ate and then informed Liette they'd be going down to Rimouski for a missing part.

"Tonight?"

Liette had seen her husband for maybe fifteen minutes that week. They'd be sleeping over at the hotel, Henri explained, so they could get back as early as possible the next day, because he had forty-six thousand items to take care of in the afternoon. The bumper of Léon's car scraped along the ground. They were already heading down the driveway, but Henri, through the rolled-down window, was still promising his sweetie that once the furnace was installed, her life would overflow with happiness and bliss.

"Be careful now!"

Léon had rammed into just about everything in the village except the church steeple. He'd received a warning from the insurance company the last time. His car wasn't covered for collision anymore, just for fire. So Léon tried to convince them the fire had started under the hood and he'd had to extinguish it with a shovel.

Meanwhile, to judge from the howls, one of the infants was being burned alive upstairs, and Liette bounded up there like a cat. *He may be cold,* thought Joséphine as she looked around for a shawl. Monti reached out, almost tipping his armchair over, and placed his tray on the sideboard. He removed his socks, thin socks that he bought in bulk. Between his kneecaps, worn down around the edges, the Homer lay open to page one. No one had ever read it; its pages weren't even cut. Wondering where he'd gotten to in the story, Monti snapped his fingers. A paper knife appeared in his hand. He snapped the fingers of his free hand and, presto, it was holding an already filled pipe. *I do miss Bradley so,* he thought, feeling sorry for himself.

"I'm going to tend to the animals, Honoré," said Joséphine, wearing a light dress and her Kodiak boots. The paper knife whistled. Joséphine tarried in expectation of an answer, pleased, and ever patient, to watch her husband reading like that. He was soaking his feet in the boiling water to relieve his corns. His diamond-shaped chin rested on a hand still capable of a crushing handshake. *What a man he was, that Ulysses,* Monti concurred. Through the window, the moon was on the verge of tumbling down the mountainside all the way to the beach. Monti gnawed at his pipe. It jiggled between his teeth. Crossing the porch, Joséphine stepped out to a garden in full bloom. The splendid vegetation waved on a soft breeze. Her tomato plants waved too, and the tarpaulin over the tractor. Shirts and pants exercised on the clothesline. It was warmer outside than in the house. Willow leaves rained down on the ground, and as she walked, Joséphine blew a lock of hair away from her mouth. The ramshackle barn, on which Henri said no more money should be spent, shrank with every step in its direction. The weather vane tried to find its bearings atop the roof.

"Were you planning to go out riding this evening?" Joséphine asked her husband on returning from her chores.

He had a theory, Monti did. He had several, but this one in particular was based on another one whereby the distance between an arrow and its target is infinitely divisible. Your glass, then, was never quite empty.

"I'm talking to you, Honoré."

Joséphine unfolded her arms, her dress, her tights flecked with various bits of straw. She relieved her husband of the empty little glass that he sucked on insistently while lightly prodding his thigh with the tip of the paper knife. She served him his second evening shot and set the bottle down within easier reach. Shifting shadows leaped from the rifle above the hearth.

"Well, my horseman? Where did you think you were going like that tonight?"

"A humdinger of an adventure, anyway," was all Monti replied.

His feet in the now-tepid basin water were even more shrivelled than usual. His slippers, lovingly knitted, were brought to him. They were whackin' away with their swords down there in Troy, those bare-assed beggars. Monti emptied his pipe with little taps on the armrest, and that's when Joséphine, aware of her propensity for seeing signs everywhere, noticed that his nails had scratched the varnish on the scrolled wooden end of the armrest. And there was nothing left to tickle him, either. On the contrary, Monti sat majestically motionless in a pyramid of moonbeams. The knot in a fire log exploded in a shower of sparks.

"Good night," Joséphine repeated for the third time. "Hello? Good lord, someone is absorbed in his reading."

She didn't know how true that was; she had to take her husband's face in both hands. Because even after so many years, they still kissed each other on the lips at bedtime. Impelled by a premonition, Joséphine lit all the lights in the corridor and on the stairs on the way to her room. She went to look in on Yannick and François. She had her heart in her mouth on seeing the infant's vacant crib, but Liette had fallen asleep with the child in her arms.

In her bedroom, slipping into her nightgown, Joséphine harked back to the days when she would graft in her mind the head of a particular animal onto each patient entering her father's office. No furnace until tomorrow. It was the Far North upstairs, and she huddled beneath her quilt. The bedside lamp spread very slow northern lights over the ceiling. As she did each night in bed, Joséphine read a few poems from an anthology of French classics, which she'd always kept on her nightstand. Tonight it was a Romantic, and her adoring lips moved along with the lines taking shape on the stage inside her skull. The entire verse stood still and trembling at the caesura of a sugary line. The reader's eyelashes fluttered uninhibitedly at the end of the poem. She put out the light and, drifting off to sleep on her side, a pillow between her knees, she wriggled for a few seconds like a freshly caught fish in the bottom of a boat, curled up alone underneath the sheets.

She roused when she heard the porch door closing downstairs. *He must be going out to see the ewe,* she thought, half dreaming, and called the window over to her. One of the tots was mewing in the other room. Joséphine got up and, looking out, saw Monti below. The old fellow gave the swing a push as he passed under the weeping willow. The shadows of the leaves speckled his undershirt and instantly fell away. He'd taken down his gun and was using it as a walking stick. *He's going to kill himself*—the thought stabbed Joséphine in the stomach like a dagger. "One of these days I'm gonna do myself in," Monti had once declared. Her heart pounding, biting her lip till it bled, Joséphine dashed down to the window over the kitchen sink just in time to see a flash light up the grimy windows inside the rectangular barn at the far end of the grounds. Even if she hadn't seen it, she would have heard it. For a few seconds, nothing happened. Then the barn began to list. The nails snapped in the tired wood and the whole frame buckled. It steadied at a precarious angle as though braced at the very last moment.

Morning came. The cuckoo popped out of its clock and cheeped in the hallway. The flap in the fanlight swung open with a squeak and closed again; Joséphine opened the door to a particularly slap-worthy wretch: Rémi Chiasson's son, Gilles, known in his circle as Guilless, as in *Guinness* but with *l*'s. Joséphine hadn't had the pleasure of seeing him at such close quarters since her years as a substitute teacher. She stepped out onto the porch invaded by climbing plants and into a lattice of shade resistant to the bright sunlight. Her silhouette formed a keyhole in the door frame. There were truths to be protected in that house. She held François in her arms, swathed in the chrysalis of his blankie, which really would have to be returned to the neonatology department. The baby was building itself from top to bottom in there.

"Ya," said Chiasson. "Somebody called about some damage? A dead horse, if I ain't mistaken?"

He searched through the sheets clipped to his notepad. His van was still idling in the lane with another employee inside. The company logo URGENCE SINISTRE was emblazoned on the side of the vehicle. Joséphine would have appreciated being sent a grown man.

"Is your mother aware that you're driving around in a van?" she asked.

"Believe it or not," said Chiasson, "my bum has gotten too hairy to be sitting in your schoolroom."

This Chiasson wasn't a child anymore—looks could be deceiving. He patted the company badge on his shirt pocket with one hand, his crotch with the other. *Rude as all get-out,* thought Joséphine. *Makes you wish Dr Maturin were still here.* The animals' friend, Dr Maturin, no more a doctor than this Guilless was Governor General of Canada. But who did you call when you needed someone to stick their arm shoulder deep into the ass of a cow that mooed more sorrowfully than the rest of the herd? You called Dr Maturin. You just had to stay close by in the pasture to keep an eye on him, given his proclivities. Only, that morning, the old kook had a tendency to be fifteen years dead of a stroke.

"Sooo, do me a favour," Chiasson went on. "Spare me your life lessons and your teacherly habits, eh. Your husband here? Or Henri? Us, we've got other things on the agenda besides chit-chat."

"My dear *sir,*" Joséphine said, regaining her composure in the face of such insolence. "If my husband or my son were here, your head would at this very moment be flying somewhere over the bay with the seagulls and the rare gases."

Chiasson snorted back the wad of snot he'd just spat toward

the remnants of bulbs, seedlings, and buttercups in the rockery. The dew was evaporating in front of the porch railing. Too bad the only male Bouge around was the newborn. François blinked his eyes in his grandmother's arms. *It was no doubt because of the Trojan horse,* Joséphine speculated.

"It's in the barn out back," she told Chiasson as his hand brushed over the electrified follicles of the nape of his neck.

In spite of her age and the emotional extremes her people occasionally put her through, Joséphine had remained as upright as ever. For one so slightly built, there was something formidable about her. Her slender limbs were outlined beneath her dress, which the same wind as yesterday moulded to her body, her small breasts, her inconspicuous curves, her prominent collarbones. Her chin formed a plump little ball under her strangely beautiful goatlike features: her scarred lip fringed with white down, drill-bit eyes spaced too wide apart. The green of her irises appeared somehow unfinished but stood out more sharply near the branches of her crow's feet. She'd always kept her hair very long, and now silvery curls peeped out from the headband she was wearing. The kerchief on her neck was folded into a triangle. On the sleeves of her dress lacy cuffs graced her large, still-nimble hands. All his life, Monti had in his own way been head over heels in love with her.

"Hey, whatsit, Pictou!" Chiasson shouted.

The van rocked. Out stepped a mixed-race man sporting a second-hand hat, seriously misshapen but adorned by way of compensation with an ace of spades wedged under the hatband. Chiasson checked the Interview box on his form.

Henri and Léon should be back from Rimouski soon, Joséphine thought hopefully.

The other fellow waved his hand, his fate line illegible under a half inch of callus. A birthmark stretched down his face like an archipelago.

"Go check out the horse in the barn," Chiasson ordered, "and see what's needed."

Étienne-Jean Pictou bent down in the lane edged with painted rocks, pulled out a broad blade of glass from between the paving stones, and proceeded at his own pace alongside the house. A shame Monti wasn't there to meet Billy Joe's son, he'd have swelled with gladness.

Not wearing the peekaboo shorts that Chiasson used to see her in, or the knot she made with the front of her blouse back then to show off her navel, Liette appeared on the porch behind her mother-in-law. Dressed like a granny, she held Yannick, in his underpants, by the hand. Yannick sucked on his pacifier. He sucked on it with a vengeance, his legs covered with scratches and scabs, an unsettling gaze fixed on Chiasson in the cab of his van. No one had ever dared mention to Henri that his son had the same mismatched eyes as the late mailman Bradley. And Liette—who could tell what went through her head? A spade shot out of the van and bounced in the dust. As François was about to burst out crying, Joséphine slipped back inside with him. Holding the baby, she went to look in the Homer to see whether Monti had left a bookmark at the suspected page. *He probably believed his horse was hollow,* Joséphine convinced herself.

In front of the house another shovel landed on the circle of beaten earth, followed by chains, bags, a can of disinfectant. Yannick, attracted by the clunks and the chemicals, babbled something to his mother.

Étienne-Jean rounded the house blowing on the grass blade held taut between his thumbs. He arched his bite-ridden back as he made his way through the willow fronds. The colour-drenched branches parted as he charged in slow motion toward that parallelogram of a barn. The tire swing hanging from a branch was still spinning behind him when Pictou pulled the respirator mask down from his forehead and over his face and wended his way between the bundles of thatch and the broken planks, sundered every which way near the stall where the horse had collapsed.

Poor stallion, its breast was strewn all over the hay. The vet would be sweating buckets to sew it back up. It was a prize animal that Monti had blasted there. He'd acquired it through a contact on a Bible Belt ranch for his grandkids' riding lessons on a nearby farm. For a heck of a long time the stable had been paid rent for nothing because the old fellow would always send one of his clodpolls, usually Henri, to fetch the purebred so he could look after it himself at his place.

With his eyes tearing up, breathing erratically in his mask amid the swarming flies, Pictou knelt down beside the horse and stroked its coat. He'd have liked to have known this creature when it was alive. He'd have wanted to jog one of its legs a bit for the beauty of seeing it roll its shoulder blade. But he knew that rigor mortis had set in, he knew it from the moment he stepped into the buzzing half-light of the barn. The gun Monti had used was still lying in the trampled straw carpeting the ground. Pictou raised his eyes toward the beams bristling with pigeon spikes. He rubbed his palms together, hard, until they tingled. He hummed incantations peppered with Mi'kmaq words. Now, this may sound like hogwash, but when the energy was palpable in that foul atmosphere, he laid his cracked palms on the horse's temples and waited, concentrating so as to be available to its spirit. Nothing happened; he quickly glided his hands over its muzzle. Nothing. He rubbed a bit more, but Chiasson was honking hysterically out front. Étienne-Jean, his communion interrupted, yielded the horse up to death.

Joséphine, holding the volume of Homer, stepped back out onto the porch. She was explaining the situation to a newcomer, one whose father had also once been very afraid of Étienne-Jean's father on the ice rink. Liette sat in a wicker chair with her back turned, smoking and nursing François.

"The first thing we learn," Chiasson muttered to Pictou, "and the last thing we forget."

He pointed to the infant nibbling at his mother's chafed nipple. When Liette turned toward him, he checked the Evaluation box on his form.

The newcomer was Éric Labillois. With his barn-door ears and an apron splattered with organic matter, he'd dashed over from the fish counter at the grocery, where he topped up his monthly income ever since the local demand for piano tuning had fallen off a fair bit.

"I was in bed," Joséphine told him, "when I heard the porch door slam. I thought, he's concerned about the ewe. She was ailing yesterday morning, and I didn't want him to bring her inside the house because of the little ones."

It wasn't like her, but in the troubled hours of the night she felt certain Monti was going to blow himself away in the barn. Yannick was jumping all over the yard, hitting things with a stick. For three seconds he also imitated the Urgence Sinistre employees, and then set off again, smashing every puffball he could find. Chiasson in turn went behind the house and under the willow tree. Pictou followed him unhurriedly, pushing a wheelbarrow loaded with inadequate equipment. *Gonna be a lot of fun getting this outta here,* they both were thinking.

"And then what?" Labillois demanded.

He was dripping with sweat, and not because he had an octopus waiting for him in the ice bin at the grocery.

"At least, I hoped it was that, because I went to the barn last night and…"

Joséphine saw no reason to mention that when she'd gone out in the evening to tend to the animals, the horse was hitched up, harnessed, the works. She'd removed the tack, fearing nothing more than one of her husband's bouts of wanderlust—no reason to panic. Labillois twirled his hands to urge her on.

"So then I got up and went to the window to see what was happening."

Holding the volume of Homer up like a visor, Joséphine was distracted anew by another villager she didn't even know coming up the lane. He was pushing a bicycle and fanning himself.

"And then, ma'am?"

"Excuse me!" the cyclist called out.

"And then, well, through my bedroom window I saw he hadn't taken his walker. He'd taken … I went downstairs as fast as I could. But I wasn't dressed for it."

She didn't know what she was saying but she knew she'd never admit that, in her mind at least, she'd given Monti permission, the green light, go on, my friend, shoot yourself. She was surprised to find herself at peace with that. François let out a catastrophic bleat. Cars were stopping on the grassy shoulder of the road, hard by the fence. *Now, what is going on?* Joséphine wondered all in a fluster.

"You were saying that your husband?"

"I had trouble getting a clear view from the window, despite the moon on the dew. Yes. There was a gunshot in the barn. It made my blood run cold. I was petrified, as you can imagine."

More people were running from the road toward the house. They were *running.* This wasn't how folks usually behaved in those parts, nope. Others were coming through the wheat fields, leaving furrows in their wake. An emu must have escaped from the farm on the outskirts of La Frayère because, well, one of them had caught up with the villagers. *This can't be happening,* thought Joséphine, *it just can't be.* Well, at least Monti's gun had remained in the barn.

"No doubt … I'm sorry. No doubt, under the weight of the horse, the barn began to—"

"But now," one of the newly arrived strangers broke in.

"Yes?"

His face was at once familiar and unfamiliar to Joséphine.

"Your husband, where is he? Right at this moment?"

Waving his stick, Yannick was chasing a chipmunk across the lawn.

"Where is he, where is he," Joséphine said. "That's what I've been bending over backwards to say. I just don't know where he is."

Originally from Carleton-sur-Mer in the Gaspé region of Quebec, CHRISTOPHE BERNARD studied literature in Quebec City, Aix-en-Provence, and Berlin. A prolific literary translator, Bernard was a finalist for the 2016 Governor General's Literary Award for English-to-French Translation. *The Hollow Beast,* a finalist for the 2018 Governor General's Literary Award for Fiction in French, won the Quebec–Ontario Prize, the Quebec Booksellers' Prize, and the Jovette-Bernier Prize. Christophe Bernard lives in Burlington, Vermont.

LAZER LEDERHENDLER is a full-time literary translator specializing in Québécois fiction and non-fiction. His translations have earned awards and distinctions in Canada, the UK, and the US. He has translated the works of noted authors, including Gaétan Soucy, Nicolas Dickner, Edem Awumey, Perrine Leblanc, and Catherine Leroux. He lives in Montreal with the visual artist Pierrette Bouchard.

Biblioasis International Translation Series
General Editor: Stephen Henighan